THE
APOTHECARY
AND THE MAID OF
VALOURESSE

Margot La Fontaine is an author, artist and cartoonist who loves both the Australian bush and medieval fantasy. Her novels are faith based, and she has written and illustrated children's picture books.

Other works by Margot La Fontaine:

The Apothecary and the Unicorn

A High Country Romance

The Apothecary and the Maid of Valouresse
(deluxe full-colour edition)

We Are All Funny Little Creatures, volumes 1 to 4

Coming soon:

We Are All Funny Little Creatures, volumes 5 to 10

MARGOT LA FONTAINE

THE APOTHECARY
AND THE MAID OF
VALOURESSE

A catalogue record for this book is available from the National Library of Australia.

ISBN 978 1 7640 0434 3 (Standard)
ISBN 978 1 7640 0436 7 (Hardback)
ISBN 978 1 7640 0430 5 (Deluxe)

Published in Australia by Margot La Fontaine
margosirr@gmail.com

Thank you to

Clare Steward, Phil Berrie,
Andrew Geraghty, Michael Sirr, Keith La
Fontaine, Maarten van der Kleij, Robyn
Baker and Donna Hume—who made all of
this possible.

Chapter 1

'Why do you believe in unicorns, Nanny?' asked Shelley, her eyes large and searching.

Nanny—dressed in her fluffy, pale blue, chenille dressing gown—was seated on Shelley's bed with the latest draft of her story on her lap. She looked a little trepidatious and fiddled with the book, turning its crumpled pages and shaking her head.

It was time for bed on the first day of the freezing mid-year holidays. Jace and Shelley, her grandson and granddaughter, lay under colourful crocheted rugs and quilts in opposite beds; it was a bitter winter's night in July. Nanny had lit a candle to scent the room knowing the children loved the aroma which was her own favourite—sandalwood.

A plush, pink, unicorn, hobby horse was wedged behind Shelley's bedhead, and it peered over her shoulder as if trying to join in the story that Nanny was about to tell. There was a similar white one looking over the top of Jace's bedhead. Felt ribbons and flowers festooned their bridles like those of medieval palfreys, but the children had long outgrown them and no longer galloped around the house on them. Nanny had already placed her own toys in a wicker basket in the main bedroom to make space for the children. She found it hard to get rid of any toy at all. A mohair lion normally sat on the bed up against the wall.

On the bedside table, as well as the candle, was a lamp with a hand-painted ceramic base. Its frosted glass bowl glowed hazily, giving the walls a soft apricot blush. A wallpaper frieze ran around the entire room at waist height, showing small animals performing anthropomorphic actions, such as a rabbit pushing a pram. On the wall was an oil pastel that Nanny had done of a rainbow-coloured bird with streamer-like tail feathers flying through a verdant, magical landscape. 'Yes, tell us, Nanny,' said Jace, dressed in his flannelette pyjamas, his tousled hair a little damp and squeaky clean. His cheeks were pink after his bath. He plunged his latest superhero toy into the pillow and made jet engine noises.

Shelley nodded vigorously. 'Yes Nanny, why *do* you believe in them? I don't know any grown up who does.' Her long hair fell over one eye and she hastily swept it aside as she leant on one elbow, propped up on her several pillows. She had stopped drawing and held her Nanny in a fixed gaze. The sandalwood aroma wafted around them, alluring and calling mystery into the room.

Somewhat hesitantly, Nanny took a deep breath and then said, 'After I had Uncle James, I got depressed, had a breakdown and had to go into hospital for a while.'

'What's a breakdown Nanny?' asked Jace who was very curious by now.

Nanny's eyes became deep as she looked down and reminisced. Tears welled in her eyes and Shelley took her hand.

'It was a time I did and said very odd and embarrassing things which I wish I could forget. But the worst thing was having to be away from Lillian and James. Lillian was only two and a half and James was only about four months old.'

Shelley nodded, encouraging Nanny to keep talking.

Jace leant over and put his hand on his Nanny's shoulder.

'This story will explain a lot about my life, and yours, and why I believe the things I do. However, first I'll finish telling you about Bethel Hospital.'

Both children's attention was rivetted.

Nanny continued. 'Your mum and your Uncle James were looked after by Nan Polly, your great, great grandmother.'

'She's so *old* now.' interjected Jace. 'How could she look after mum and uncle James? She is too old to do that.'

'She wasn't so old then,' said Nanny, laughing suddenly. 'She did a marvellous job while I was in hospital. She is still such a wonderful, kind lady.'

Nanny's voice went croaky as she ran her hand over and over the rippled texture of the quilt on Shelley's bed.

'I missed your mum and Uncle James so much.' She gripped the quilt hard and swallowed. Shelley squeezed Nanny's hand.

'After I'd been in Bethel Hospital a week or two, a magistrate came to the hospital—he was like a kind of judge—and he decided if I could go home or not.'

'Did you have a jury?' asked Jace with his eyes almost popping out at the thought of his Nanny potentially being a criminal.

'No, no jury,' Nanny replied, 'He seemed to be a nice man behind a desk covered with papers in a fairly dark, musty room, scrutinising me.'

Nanny hesitated for a moment before continuing. 'Scrutinising. By that I mean he was observing me closely, to see if I was safe to be let out of hospital.'

'This may sound a little strange, but I know how you like mysterious things, so I'll tell you everything.'

'Yes Nanny, tell us,' replied Shelley.

'I told the magistrate that I had a vision of myself … in a beautiful forest, sitting on green grass, in a long, pale blue, velvet dress, laced with gold ribbon at the bodice, like the ladies wore in medieval times.'

'Yes,' said Jace nodding. 'I've seen that in books.'

Nanny then said, 'I told the magistrate I could see my unicorn foal in my lap and that I was stroking it, from a time long ago but that I could see it now.'

The children's eyes almost glowed with fascination.

Jace was quiet, absorbing the information, then he suddenly piped up, 'That sounds a bit strange, Nanny. Were you crazy?' he asked with a slight smile and raised eyebrows.

Nanny chuckled, and leant over to stroke his soft, golden-brown face.

'Yes, definitely there were times I was,' agreed Nanny, 'but I don't think that vision of the unicorn was crazy. I think that it was a vision of myself in Heaven, before I was born.'

'Now that really *is* weird, Nanny. But cool,' said Jace. 'What did the magistrate say? Did he let you go home?'

'He probably thought that I was delusional, but harmless,' said Nanny with a giggle. 'I don't remember him saying anything much, but he did let me go home.'

'I have been in hospital quite a few times and I believe the unicorn was my protector. He saved me from seeing things like demons, or vampires—I felt their ominous presence and I've heard of people seeing them in real life, you know, but I never did, because my unicorn kept those things at bay. He is a deep mysterious part of me, and I love him like I love Jesus. To me he is the Holy Spirit.'

'A Unicorn?' said the children together.

'It's something I don't normally talk to others about, but I don't mind telling you two, now that you are grown up enough,' said Nanny.

'So, it's sort of a secret?' asked Shelley, narrowing her eyes slightly.

'Some people wouldn't approve of me seeing the Holy Spirit in the form of a unicorn,' said Nanny with a sigh.

'Why not?' asked Shelley, reaching out for her favourite fluffy toy: a fat, plush, cat unicorn. It was a bit like a pink, powder puff with a silver horn.

'Well, it's … just not done,' said Nanny. 'People probably expect him to look like Jesus, but it doesn't really matter to me what he looks like. He's just the same inside.'

'So, this story,' said Shelley looking with wonder at the book on Nanny's lap, 'explains those things?'

'No, no, *this* story,' she said patting the book, 'is a fantasy novel set in medieval times, and it's called the *Apothecary's Quest*. It's a Christian story with adventure, angels, demons, heroes, heroines, a witch, a unicorn, and even a dragon.' Nanny took a deep breath. 'Writing it has been a good way to find my direction in life and to figure out the bigger picture, such as how your grandfather and I can be friends. It's a brighter vision of things.'

'So that you and granddad will get back together?' asked Jace with shining eyes.

'Not necessarily,' said Nanny, 'But things have been made right. I just feel it.'

'How old were you when you started your book?' asked Jace, who was looking older than his eleven years.

'Well, it was just after I finished high school,' said Nanny. 'I started writing it in the car on a rainy day with fogged up windows and your mum in a bassinet while your granddad played football, skidding around in the mud. I've done two versions of it so far, and the one I'm going to read to you now is still being written.'

'Does it have pictures?' asked Jace, leaning on both elbows.

'Of course, it does, quite a few, painted in colour. I want to leave a beautiful legacy for you.'

'A legacy?' asked Shelley. 'What's that?'

Nanny gazed at her for a moment before speaking. She adored her granddaughter's inquisitive almond-shaped eyes and little peaked nose. 'I think a legacy is something that God gives you to do for the world, as well as for your family,' she replied. 'I'll need you to help me figure it all out though—it's a big job.'

'You mean, we can put things in the book?' asked Shelley.

'You certainly can, darling,' said Nanny.

'Me too?' asked Jace.

'Yes, yes, you too, of *course*. You are *so* smart. I know you will work out the hard parts. You know a lot of facts. Like the time we were driving along, and you said: "That foot bridge, is just like the Golden Gate Bridge but ten times smaller."'

Jace was pleased with himself, and Nanny suddenly jumped up and hugged him. 'You *are* a handsome and funny boy, no doubt about it,' she said, running her hand through his thick, black hair.

'I know,' he said in a matter-of-fact voice with a little smile.

Nanny suddenly noticed the time and quickly asked, 'Are you warm enough, kids?'

'Cosy,' said Shelley in a little voice.

Shelley had turned her head to one side and was stroking her toy with a fixed expression on her face.

Nanny's heart ached.

'Are you alright darling?' she asked, squeezing Shelley's hand.

Shelley swallowed and nodded. Her eyes had become dark and sad.

It was not going so smoothly, starting High School. Some of her friends were in different classes and in some cases, new alliances had to be forged. Nanny looked down at her granddaughter's beloved sketch book lying on the floor next to the bed. It was filled with beautifully crafted drawings of anime characters.

'Do you know what?' she said, picking up the sketch book and stroking it. 'Your passions will make you strong. And this is *my* passion,' said Nanny, indicating the book in her lap. 'My novel. And I'm going to read it to you now.'

'Now?' asked Jace, snuggling under his blankets again and pulling them up around his neck.

Shelley did the same.

'Yep, we're starting now,' said Nanny.

'It's a bit scruffy, Nanny,' said Shelley looking somewhat sceptically at the old handwritten journal Nanny had on her lap.

'Yes, I suppose it is,' said Nanny, patting the book affectionately. '*And* it's up here too,' she added, tapping the side of her head. 'This version is mostly not written yet.'

Then Nanny took a deep breath, opened the book, and plunged into the story.

The land of Valouresse is a mysterious and wonderful place.

To the north are tall, snow-capped mountains which birth the Cyonne river. This babbles and rushes through ravines lined with pine forest, until it reaches the plains, where it wends its way through rich

farmland and forests of oak, birch and ash, until it finally becomes the mighty wide river that runs past the city of La Fonteyn, the capital of the realm.

The city itself is surrounded by a curtain wall made of granite, and a moat. At the highest point is King Lohnn's snow-white, marble castle and from its spires and parapets ripple banners of flashing gold, embellished with the crimson heraldic crest of a lion and unicorn.

The hero of our story—although he wouldn't consider himself to be one—is Gazba Delafoi, which means Guardian of the Faith. He is from an old Gallic family that was not particularly famous, but his father had been known to be a wise, reclusive man. He had spent many days researching plants and making potions to heal the sick—and his son Gazba followed in his footsteps and became famous when he saved his king's life and was appointed Royal Apothecary.

Gazba was in his forties with medium-length brown hair and a beard, grizzled with grey. His eyes were dark and thoughtful, but with a regular twinkle of mirth, for he found many things amusing, even downright ridiculous, but sometimes his humour could be a little caustic. His usual garb was very plain—a woollen tunic, with a leather belt, brown breeches and crimson leather boots.

Every day he would ride high-stepping Helga, his stocky grey mare—of some Andalusian decent—from his unpretentious manor house in the country to his dispensary in the city of La Fonteyn. On the journey, he would pass rich, green countryside and the thatch roofed homes of servants. He relished the odour of the loamy soil and the fresh, green grass, and cheerfully saluted the workers, who lifted their caps and smiled back in reply. Gazba was well liked. His mare would clomp across the drawbridge and, after dismounting, he would take her to the stables.

Gazba's dispensary was in a tower adjacent to the gatehouse and had three levels. Moss clung to the joins between the granite stones and lichen, persistent and aged, covered the walls.

The ground floor was the shop front, a circular room, lined with shelves containing an intriguing—and sometimes a little confronting—array of animals. The vegetable and mineral substances in glass jars were easier on the stomach and eye. Here on the oak bench, he dispensed his medications. Carved oak chairs with cushioning covered with supple leather, lined the walls for the comfort of those waiting.

On the first floor, he consulted with clients in a room arranged with similar leather furniture. A rich, crimson-patterned rug lay on the floor and tapestries depicting herbs and pink hyacinths lined the walls.

He prepared his medications on the second floor, assisted by Joachim—his invaluable older assistant—who lived in La Fonteyn with his family. Joachim was a quiet, meticulous man who spent his days with Gazba collecting herbs and minerals, pulverising them with mortar and pestle, mixing, measuring, and then labelling them with his elegant handwriting. Joachim could also be relied upon to look after the dispensary when Gazba was away.

In the third-floor room, Gazba dried his plants. He also had another drying rack on the battlements, good for sunny days.

All three levels of the dispensary had a view of the city gates and from these windows Gazba could see merchants and others arriving in La Fonteyn, but he was usually too busy to take notice.

From the ground floor, a staircase wound its way up through the three floors to the top of the tower. Looking from the parapet, one could see the marketplace and city square. On a sunny day, King Lohnn's castle had the sheen of a white pearl. However, Gazba most liked the view of the blue and snowy mountains in the distance, on the other side of the battlements best. *That* was the Valouresse he wanted to see one day.

Gazba loved to fossick around in the local forests collecting plants for his potions and powders. Within the dank and musty smelling forest of rotting leaves, he'd discovered an extremely volatile fungi, which exploded if mixed with certain other plants. It was a powerful thing, and it had helped save King Lohnn's life from Kraekhoull the witch, fifteen years earlier.

Gazba had used his plant explosions to expel her and her malignant army from the castle. A smoke screen shrouded the king, and he slipped away to safety. The witch had retreated and not been seen or heard of since then and, as far as King Lohnn was concerned, she was no longer to be feared. These days Gazba did what he loved best which was healing and that included looking after the king as well.

'What about the witch, Nanny,' exclaimed Jace eagerly. 'Why didn't she come back?'

'Despite what I just said, about Gazba's explosives and smoke screen, it was a lion and a unicorn who actually drove the witch away,' said Nanny, putting the book down momentarily.

'You mean that they weren't just pictures on the flags. They were symbols of something real?' exclaimed Shelley with delight, sitting up in bed momentarily and clapping her hands. 'I love the idea of them being real you know.'

'Oh, yes, and they disappeared after the witch was gone,' said Nanny.

'Where did they go?' asked Shelley. She had snuggled back under her blankets, which came up under her chin, but her eyes were wide awake.

'All things will be revealed in good time,' said Nanny sagely and with a twinkle in her eye.

'Oh, why not now?' asked Shelley with disappointment.

'That would spoil it,' said Nanny, turning to the next page.

One day, Gazba glanced out of the window of his dispensary and his heart sank. It was one of his patients, Baron Bardozer, a fearsome display of cantankerousness, plumping along on his big black horse, crossing the drawbridge. He appeared sour and angry even from a distance, and his escort of twenty ferocious-looking men in armour, on equally ferocious-looking black horses, pumping their knees to their chests, fighting the bit, churned his stomach. He would say nothing to warrant the baron's easily stirred bad temper.

The baron soon strode through the door, wearing a cap sporting a gold and black pheasant's feather and also a doublet of the finest green velvet, but his stomach flab hanging over his belt definitely spoiled the regal effect. The baron paused and rolled one tip of his waxed moustache between his forefinger and thumb while glaring at Gazba with bulging goldfish eyes.

'Gazba!' he snapped, with some spit shooting out at the same time. 'That bran is completely ineffective, and it makes me very gassy.'

Gazba spoke as calmly as he could, but it was an effort to accept this barrage of rudeness. 'It takes a few weeks for regularity to return to the bowel, Baron.' said Gazba with a calm demeanour, not being rattled by the baron's fierce countenance.

'Dammit, Gazba!' shouted the baron, banging his fist on the bench then shaking and holding his hurting hand. 'I'm heartily sick of the flatulence. Do you understand?'

Once more he slammed his fist on the dispensary bench causing several bottles to tinkle and gave Gazba another imperious stare. Gazba thought it ridiculous that the Baron should bang his hand again, causing himself more pain, only this time giving a few nasty expletives.

'I'm a busy man,' he said, 'and I don't have weeks to train my bowel. I have suffered enough at your hands.' He tapped his fingers on the dispensary counter showing his impatience with the healing process. 'Come on now, there must be more and better things you can do for me,' he added with a sneer.

'I am giving you my best advice, Baron,' said Gazba, with a disappointment he could not mask.

'Your best is not enough. The stuff tastes like horse chaff,' said the baron in fury.

'It is quite bland in texture and has a nice nutty flavour, Baron,' remonstrated Gazba, thinking, with amusement, *I wonder how he would know it tastes like horse chaff?*

'Give me some paraffin and I will take two tablespoons of it. I must be cleaned out before I meet the widow, Lady Dubblenek, at the Valourenne Ball.'

Gazba's mouth fell open. 'No, Baron, you must not!' exclaimed Gazba in horror. 'I beg you, take only two *teaspoons* and even that is *too* drastic. I only offered it to you before as a last resort, and in the very smallest dose.'

The baron wasn't listening, for his attention had wandered. He had become fascinated by a bottle containing a preserved lamprey that sat on a high and rather dusty shelf. Its multi-toothed, suction-disc mouth was pressed against the glass. The rest of its grey mucous-coated, snaky body was hopelessly knotted.

'Horrid creature,' he muttered absently.

'Yes,' agreed Gazba, but he was not thinking of the lamprey.

'If you insist, here is the paraffin, Baron,' said Gazba, handing the man his medication. 'Now remember, two teaspoons are all you need, believe me.'

'I know how much I need,' said Bardozer, snatching the bottle from Gazba.

As he left the room, his cloak swept around and knocked several bottles off the dispensary table. Gazba was silently furious and gritted his teeth, causing the muscles in his jaws to move.

'A pleasure, sir,' Gazba said with an edge in his voice, relieved that Bardozer was leaving. He felt like slamming his own fist on the bench and giving the baron a few choice words.

'Harrumph!' growled the baron, disappearing through the open doorway. 'Put it on my account,' he snarled in parting.

Gazba frowned and shook his head as he began to clean up the broken bottles, powders and liquids with Joachim's help.

While they worked, Gazba pondered the consequences of the baron's potential paraffin overdose. *No doubt he will have revenge on me even though it would be himself self-administering the dangerous dosage.* But it was his choice, and Gazba felt sure the baron would indeed do as he wished, regardless.

About an hour later, the aforementioned Lady Dubblenek came swishing in through the door in her expensive, magenta, organza skirt.

'Do you like the colour of this skirt, Gazba?' she asked instead of saying 'good morning' first, which struck Gazba as a little rude, but he was used to her lack of manners.

'It is called, "The Marvel of Peru" after the exquisite flowers of that region. I do love the hot pink.'

'It's quite striking, my lady,' acknowledged Gazba, blinking at the gaudy garment. 'Here is your preparation, Lady Dubblenek,' he then said, handing her the little bottle which caused her to shriek with delight.

Lady Dubblenek beamed. 'Oh Gazba, I love it, I simply love the toad skins. They make my skin feel like satin, like the petals of a rose in the springtime.'

'Aloe vera is also very good too, my lady,' said Gazba. 'Not being as smelly or as foul, better than a marshland of toad skins.'

He knew she wouldn't go for the healthy option—he knew her well. She never took advice, much like the baron—indeed they would be a good match.

'Oh no, Gazba,' said Lady Dubblenek, scoffing at his comment. 'Everyone knows that toad skins are the thing, and I must look my best for Baron Bardozer at the Valourenne Ball tonight. Such a prosperous, successful man who could be a real jewel in my crown.'

'You seem made for each other,' said Gazba, giving her a forced smile. He was annoyed at Lady Dubblenek's mercenary, shallow ways. She would never marry for love alone.

'Gazba,' said Lady Dubblenek, as if speaking to a small child. 'It is only right that people of similar class should mingle.' She paused a moment searching his face for some sign of approval or disapproval.

Gazba gave away nothing, so she continued gabbling on.

'So, what do you think we have in common, apart from our elegance and refinement?' she asked with a coquettish laugh.

'Yes, it is as you say,' said Gazba. 'You both have dress style, and what with his impressive eyes and your aristocratic chins ... er.' He coughed. 'Chin.'

He had learnt great sufferance with the nobility, and generally tried to compliment them as honestly as he could but he gave an inward chuckle when Lady Dubblenek missed his sarcasm.

Lady Dubblenek gave him a coy smile, which included batting her big, fake, spider-like lashes. Then, just like the baron, she swept out of the dispensary and also like the baron she said—though not with a snarl, but with a careless, dismissive wave of her hand—'put it on my account.'

Gazba shook his head. The baron and Lady Dubblenek had never learnt basic manners, probably because they were never corrected by anyone. A simple thank you was not part of their vocabulary except when used for those above their station.

'Did she knock over the slimy things in the jar?' asked Jace with interest. 'That would have been pretty gross!'

'No, they were on a top shelf, remember,' replied Nanny.

'I think that the baron and Lady want to marry for money,' said Shelley.

'Yes, that's pretty obvious,' agreed Nanny.

Then Jace commented with disgust, 'Why is he so rude all the time? What's the matter with him?'

'Bardozer just likes to bully people, just like I've seen *you* be a bit short with your mum at times,' said Nanny.

Jace lowered his eyes, and his mouth twitched slightly, but he said nothing.

'You should be kinder to your mother,' said Nanny to Jace.

'I will,' said Jace, looking into his Nanny's eyes.

'Lovely boy,' said Nanny pulling the blanket a bit higher onto his shoulder. 'After all she is due to have your baby brother in only a week or two.'

'Is Gazba married? Does he have any children?' Shelley asked suddenly with interest.

'We'll find out tomorrow,' said Nanny.

'Ohhh, *Nanny*, keep reading,' whined both children.

But Nanny got to her feet and put the book back on the bureau.

Jace was stalling and wanted to hear more. 'Gazba wears strange old clothes' said Jace. 'I've seen the pictures you've been painting.'

'Not so strange for those days,' said Nanny.

'He should wear runners and shorts and a T-shirt like dad does,' said Jace.

'Yes, if he played basketball he might. Funny boy!' she said with amusement.

'Love you, Nanny,' the children both said, almost in unison.

'Love you more,' said Nanny in a whisper.

She turned off the light and left the room.

Chapter 2

The children had a great day at the zoo with Nanny—who had been tempted to leave them there with the monkeys—with their own kind. She chuckled. They adored the tiny moustached marmosets, and she felt that if the children lived in the same cage with them long enough, the monkeys would leap and sit on them, bonding.

They had had a picnic in the zoo grounds and fed the swans for a while, before coming home. After that, it was dinner and time to read the story again.

Jace couldn't wait to tell Nanny where they were up to as she opened the book. 'Baron Bardozer has overdosed on paraffin, and he is going to get sick. Gazba is going to get the blame,' said Jace matter-of-factly.

'You're right as usual. We'll continue then,' said Nanny with a little grin.

Although dozing off, Shelley perked up and her eyes fluttered open.

The baron and Lady Dubblenek had gone. Peace reigned for half an hour while Gazba measured various medications carefully for the clients he cared so much for. A thin stream of light filtered into the room, golden, with sparkling dust particles, very soothing, but not the same as being outside, something which he yearned for. The dispensary was basically a fairly dark room, even with the torches and the light from the window.

Suddenly, his ears were accosted by the shrill, high-pitched laughter of Jasmine, his thirteen-year-old daughter, as she rushed into the room and hugged her father tightly around the waist.

'You look like Christmas decorations in that dress,' he laughed, returning her hug.

'But much prettier,' she giggled.

Then she launched straight into her big news. 'Daddy, the knights have returned. Come and see them from the balcony!'

'You go, Jasmine. I'm just finishing some work here.'

Jasmine dashed away as, Chloe, her mother—an older version of her raven-haired blue-eyed daughter—walked in carrying a beautiful gold encrusted box—but not real gold of course.

'What a pleasant surprise to see you two,' said Gazba smiling and pecking Chloe on the cheek. 'So, you came by carriage?'

'Yes,' said Chloe, 'I thought I might do some shopping today, as well as see the returning knights.'

'Of course,' said Gazba. His expression fell somewhat when he realised that she wasn't just here to see him.

'I suppose I could have come in earlier with you, but nothing is open at that hour, except the fishmonger,' said Chloe putting the box down on the dispensary bench 'And I can't carry much in my saddle bags, especially not *this box*,' she said with delight in her voice as she emphasised the words.

Gazba smiled again at his pretty wife. How she loved to shop! *In fact, what woman doesn't?* he thought with an inward laugh but realised he was being unfair. Men probably spent more on horses and stately chateaus. 'Did you find something nice for the Valourenne Ball?' he asked her.

'Oh, *yes*, and thank you,' she said, removing the lid of the box and revealing the dress, which was a pale, sky-blue satin material with a sea of gleaming sapphire crystals embroidered onto the hem and bodice. 'I won't hold it up so it will be a real surprise for you,' she said.

'You will outshine them all tonight.' He blinked at the crystals glittering in the sunlight.

Chloe replaced the lid of the box containing the dress and gave her husband a winsome smile and sighed. He took her soft hand in his, feeling very blessed to have such a young and beautiful wife.

From up on the balcony, Jasmine cried out, 'They're here! The knights are here! Come and see!'

Suddenly, Chloe's eyes had a wild and joyous gleam. 'I'm going up to see them,' she said. 'Come on, Gazba. This will be exciting.'

'Yes, indeed,' answered Gazba dully as Chloe eagerly pattered up the spiral staircase.

What Chloe saw as she walked out onto the balcony into the sunlight, were the knights trotting in a column of pairs into the city square on their great, muscular horses, immaculately groomed with gleaming coats.

Women leapt up for a kiss from their favourite heroes. Some girls faked a fainting attack, and the big horses leapt aside to avoid them. Not one girl was squashed. After leaving the women admirers behind, the knights—carrying banners displaying the royal standard—trotted around to the far-right end of the courtyard, wheeled around to the left and then assembled in a long line, facing the king.

The knights were mesmerising in their polished armour and their helmets sported peacock feathers with eyes of glowing green and gold that waved gently in the slight breeze.

The crowd's excitement had reached fever pitch at seeing their heroes in the flesh after their months away at tournaments on the coast. Many townsfolk threw their hats high with jubilation and cheered.

Sir Gallant, the jousting champion above all champions, nodded to the women rushing towards him, with garlands of flowers.

Chloe and this leading knight had been childhood friends, and her eyes met his—or rather, met his good eye that wasn't covered by a patch.

She gasped with concern and put her hand to her mouth when she saw this evidence of injury but he smiled up at her and so she relaxed a little and returned his smile.

Gazba, having finished his work downstairs, had climbed up the staircase to the battlements in time to see Chloe gazing at Gallant with what he perceived to be a tender smile. He wondered if she may have feelings for the knight, who had been a squire at her father's castle.

Gazba knew he himself had been her choice for a husband and felt very glad for that, but he also knew that the close childhood relationship between Gallant and Chloe niggled his subconscious and he felt jealousy enter stealthily into the equation.

The gentry looked splendid in velvet and satin. Regal music throbbed from the highest points to the lowest parts of the city square, enchanting the souls of all.

Gazba joined his wife and daughter on the balcony and, after his hard work all morning, found the knights rather like overindulged children, enjoying the adulation of everyone, young and old, rich and poor alike— and maybe not fully deserved, in his opinion.

Chloe giggled with delight at the roar of cheering, 'I love their shine, their gleam,' said Chloe with a heartfelt sigh.

'Their armour,' contributed Gazba, a little cantankerously, sighing as well.

'Yes, their armour, Gazba,' said Chloe, a little irritated by his sarcastic tone. 'Oh, I know you think it's silly, all so silly,' she added, almost hanging over the balcony as she waved to the knights.

'Not at all,' said Gazba cheekily, as he watched her nervously, being ready to grab her if necessary. 'Knocking the stuffing out of others in the name of sport must surely be fun, until it happens to you.'

'That *is* the fun of it Gazba,' exclaimed Chloe, who was still focussed on the knights in the square.

Then he added, 'So, they won the jousting tournament, I presume?'

'Yes, of course they did,' said Chloe, sending her husband a stormy glance and then added, 'Isn't it obvious!'

Gazba turned his head, ignoring her harsh expression.

'Oh, Sir Glum, cheer up.' said Chloe, glancing at him again, but quickly forgetting her irritability as she gazed down.

'Look, Sir Ralph the Regal,' she said, pointing to a swarthy knight in the middle of the front row. 'And there is Sir Gracious the Good,' she said of another. She then closed her eyes in rapture and twirled around in her voluminous skirts. 'I could kiss them all.'

Gazba felt a stab go through his heart. It seemed she preferred the knights to him.

'Yes, Sir Gracious the Good,' said Gazba. 'I remember him well, a brave man. We fought the witch in the throne room, and then Sir Gracious pursued her into the forest. The king was saved.'

Gazba looked deeply reflective.

'Gazba,' Chloe said quietly. 'We are all very grateful to you for saving our king, but it's a long time since that happened.'

Her eyes sympathised but she was insistent.

'The witch is gone but she hasn't been sighted since and, yes, it is largely because of you—but there is no point dwelling on the past. You will lose the joy of the moment, the gaiety, and the wonder,' she said, expressively gesturing towards the action in the city square.

Gazba heard her but was silent. He had never been sure that the witch was gone for good. Given the opportunity she—the witch—would take the joy and peace from the land. The foolish people, even the king, had forgotten how close they had come to defeat and enslavement by an evil, vindictive woman.

Gazba roused from his dark thoughts and started to notice the joy, colour and sounds all around him. He shrugged because Chloe certainly knew how to enjoy the day and maybe he should too. He genuinely loved the people of La Fonteyn and only wanted happiness for these rejoicing peasants and gentry. It was probably *his* problem after all. His gloomy mood could easily seep out of him like spilled ink. The king, on the balcony of his palace, was dressed in a purple robe and wore a glittering crown of gold, encrusted with diamonds and rubies. He raised his hand and then formed a fist and thrust it against the left side of his chest in salute of his knights, and a roar went up from the crowd below. Banners of gold emblazoned with the crimson lion and unicorn fluttered in the breeze from the battlements and twenty trumpeters blasted a fanfare.

'You knights have made La Fonteyn proud,' he said in a loud and regal voice that carried far through the now silent square. 'Your skill is legendary and your courage immense. Your endeavours are now known throughout Valouresse. May our land prosper forever and know the blessings of our God.'

In response, the knights shouted in one loud voice, 'Praise be to King Lohnn. God bless his reign.'

Meanwhile, down below the parapet, someone skulked unseen in the crowd. It was Kraekhoull the witch, and the poison in her heart was brewing. She had come to La Fonteyn to do some shopping, and her trip had just happened to coincide with the return of the knights. She kept her head low, not wanting to be recognised by any knight, or indeed anyone who had lived during the time she had tried to overthrow the king. She hated everything she saw in that city square and rejoiced as she thought: *the gentry will know hunger and pain for the neglect and ill treatment of my family.*

Revenge, yes, revenge when I am queen!

Up at the parapet, there he was, her rival and enemy—Gazba. How well Kraekhoull remembered the searing mixtures he had released, that had driven her and her followers back. She could never forgive nor forget Gazba, who had quashed her bid for power all those years ago. What burned also was her jealousy. He now worked for the king in the position of royal apothecary—his reward for defeating her. She walked past the sign which brought it painfully to her memory - "Royal Apothecary" at the front of his dispensary.

As the crowd was thinning, she moved into the shadow of the tower at the front gates of the city.

She was one of them but nevertheless, she despised the peasants who seemed to her to be gullibly engrossed in the pomp and ceremony designed for the class that oppressed them—at least, this was as she saw it.

Kraekhoull noticed a man of the gentry—she could tell that from the symbol emblazoned on his jerkin—chatting animatedly with a peasant. Surely, he was patronising the lesser man otherwise why would he be talking to him. It made her sick and it struck her as strange that the peasant was chatting animatedly back to the baron with no sign of nervousness. She thought that there seemed to be no condescension on the part of the baron, and no obsequiousness on the part of the peasant. The witch assumed that the peasant must be putting on a particularly good act to disguise fear and detestation of this man of great rank. Kraekhoull's stomach gave a hateful squeeze.

She turned and pulled the cloak around her even more tightly. *I mustn't be seen by any of those hated nobility or knights.* Her eyes burned like twin coals under her cloak's hood. She left the noble and the peasant talking and began muttering under her breath.

'Such a farce will end with my reign. I can't wait to bring down the detestable, privileged few.'

She continued striding towards the drawbridge and soon she would be in her lair in the cleft of a mountain near La Fonteyn. It was close, but invisible to all. The forest canopy and its shawl of trees, with the addition of a few spells, meant it was unremarkable to any passer-by. She sneered as she went on her way.

'Why does she hate the gentry so much?' asked Shelley.

'It's because they were always mean to the poor people. That's why Nanny, isn't it?' interjected Jace.

'Well,' said Nanny, 'not *always* at all. Many of the gentry were in fact honourable and cared for their servants with consideration and equanimity, wishing them to prosper and be in good health. However, there definitely were times when the gentry oppressed the peasants and Kraekhoull had had that experience. Shall we continue?'

'Sure,' said Jace.

'Yes, carry on Nanny,' said Shelley imperiously and with a little snigger, looked up from her computer on which she was drawing yet again—her great love.

'Thank you, madam,' acknowledged Nanny, with an amused glint in her eye.

The witch had no idea that the discussion—which continued between the two men—was about the running of Baron Jardine's estate.

Baron Jardine's hair, and that of his servant overseer Arlon's, was flecked with grey—both were handsome men.

'The market on the coast for this batch of wool will be competitive,' said the Baron.

'Indeed, so, but our wool is both fine and strong, just right for durable garments,' replied Arlon, who turned to see Lady Jardine jiggling his little son on her knee, talking fond nonsense to him.

'She loves the little ones,' said the baron smiling.

Then he continued the discussion with his servant.

'With the profits, we will mend the thatch on the houses and build an extension onto the sanitorium.'

'Wonderful, Sir,' said the overseer enthusiastically.

They chatted for a while longer and then the overseer said to the baron, 'We must be on our way now, my lord. The little one is tired.'

'As *we* all are when babies are around,' said Lady Jardine smiling knowingly as she passed the little boy to him. As Arlon walked away, the little boy was twisting around and still watching Lady Jardine laughing and cooing. She blew him kisses back.

'So, you see,' said Nanny, 'the witch got it all wrong on this occasion.'

'Baron Jardine respected his overseer and treated him like a friend,' said Shelley.

'That's all for now, kids. It's the end of the chapter,' said Nanny closing her book.

'Can we hear more tomorrow?' asked Jace.

'Sure,' said Nanny. 'The story is going to get pretty exciting soon, and mysterious.'

'Will they stop her?' asked Shelley with a worried look on her face.

'The witch?' asked Nanny.

Shelley withdrew into herself. She was silent and her eyes stared down at her toy unicorn cat.

Nanny didn't know what to say to her granddaughter, but it was clear that it wasn't just the witch in the story that was upsetting her.

Suddenly Shelley said mournfully, 'Things just go bad, don't they?'

'Well, sometimes yes but—'

'Will there be magic that can fix it, Nanny?' piped up Jace.

'Oh yes,' said Nanny. 'As a matter of fact, magic exists in the real world too, you know.'

'Like how?' exclaimed Jace, suddenly pulling down his blankets and sitting up. He wasn't stalling now. He was intrigued.

'I'll tell you and I trust it will give you hope,' she added, gently tilting her granddaughter's chin up so that their eyes met.

'When I was only five years old,' Nanny began, 'I was dragged into a classroom corner by the teacher on the first day of school, for talking - I was only five and so felt utterly shamed. It was one of the worst days of my life.'

'Nanny, that is so sad,' said Shelley with big sympathetic eyes.

'No, actually, I take that back,' said Nanny suddenly, surprised by her own sudden epiphany. 'It was one of the *best* days of my life.'

Shelley looked up through her long black hair with interest. 'Why, Nanny?' she asked, curiously.

'On that day, as I sat in the corner, I had a vision in my mind—almost like a television screen—of my unborn children: your mother, Lillian, and your uncle, James. In my vision, your mum was about three and a half and Uncle James was one and a half.'

'Wow, Nanny, that is *so* strange,' exclaimed Shelley. 'How could you know it was them if you were only five?'

'I just did,' said Nanny shaking her head at the wonder of it all and with a rapturous look in her eyes, as if seeing a long way off to a land beyond the world she inhabited now. 'I didn't even know their names yet, but I *knew* they were my children. They were so precious and sweet. They still are—like Christmas presents on Christmas morning—my treasures who have special gifts themselves.'

'Yeh,' said Jace, 'Mum plays music and sings really well.'

'And I like the way she saved the horses from the pet food factory,' added Shelley.

'And Uncle James plays AFL really well, and cricket, and he runs marathons,' said Jace enthusiastically.

'There are other things I would love to tell you about your uncle and mother, wondrous things—magical things, but I can't right now. As we go further into the story about Gazba they'll be explained.'

'I want to know now, Nanny,' said Shelley. Her inquisitive face begged information.

'No, Shelley,' said Nanny gently. 'Just be patient.'

'There is another magic that I *can* tell you about now, like the miracle that you were even born at all, considering your mum had had cancer.

There was a high chance that she wouldn't have been able to have children after that,' said Nanny.

'Oh,' said Shelley slowly at the revelation. Her eyes pooled up and a few tears spilt out onto her cheeks.

'Why didn't she tell us?' asked Jace frowning.

'She probably didn't want to worry you,' said Nanny. 'My point is that you are *meant* to be here and are ordained for God's greatness.'

'How *can* you be sure?' asked Shelley, with a glimmer of hope in her shimmering eyes.

'If God could show me what my future children looked like when I was only a child myself, then I'm sure he will have amazing plans for you, because you are my special children. That's a mystery in itself, don't you think?'

Jace piped up again, leaning on his pillow with his elbow, 'That's sort of weird, but I like it. Does it mean we will win in the end?'

'Always,' agreed Nanny, smiling at Jace, and reaching over to stroke his cheek.

'And your stories will join up with ours?' asked Shelley.

'I believe we are connected and yes, our stories will be filled with wonder and mystery. I promise the story will all unfold as we go along, but I will need your help.'

'We'll help,' said Jace happily.

'Thanks kids, I'll look forward to all of your ideas,' said Nanny.

'But now it's time for sleep. Do you want to pray, Jace?'

'Okay,' said Jace quietly and somewhat shyly, before bringing his hands up to his face. 'God bless everyone and Nanny and Granddad and Nan and Pop and Mum and Dad.'

'And Yao Ming and Snowflake and Tikki,' Shelley added cheerfully.

'And Sparkle. You can't leave her out,' added Jace.

'Yep,' said Nanny, 'She is the best rabbit we've ever had and Tikki is a good little budgie—so tame and cute the way he sits on your toe. As for Snowflake, she is a bit of a crazy Pomeranian, I'm afraid—a barker.'

'No, she's not,' said Shelley, with mock reproach in her eyes.

'Let's just say she's a very, *very* friendly dog and a jumper, but she also barks too much at strangers,' said Nanny.

'That's true,' acknowledged Shelley.

Nanny smiled and leant over each bed in turn and kissed them goodnight. Then came the obligatory back scratches, and head massages before the lights finally went out.

Chapter 3

The next evening, the children were perched up in their beds waiting for the story to resume.

'All the rituals have been observed,' said Nanny with a laugh.

'What do you mean, Nanny?' asked Shelley.

'I mean the teeth, the back scratches, the prayers, the things we always do,' she replied.

'Can we have the story now?' asked Shelley. Her little eyes sparkled, as she brushed her long black locks.

'You must have used half a bottle of conditioner tonight, darling,' said Nanny with a little smirk. 'It'll make your hair greasy, won't it?'

'Nuh,' said Shelley, shaking her head. 'Very shiny.'

'I want to hear more about the witch,' Jace said with a ghoulish grin, clearly hoping it would soon get creepy.

'Actually, by complete coincidence, we *are* going to hear more about her right now,' said Nanny with a grin. 'So here we go then.'

The witch wove her way through the crowd, very secretively, back to the city gates. She kept her head down as she passed a young knight on his prancing, sweating steed.

'Hey woman, don't rush by,' he called. 'Have you no time for a knight of the realm?' The knight was a bit full of himself and full of mead.

Kraekhoull just turned and hissed at him.

'Quite a rebuff, you old hag,' he shouted after her as she hurried away.

She didn't look back, and the knight, who had been surrounded by some pretty flirtatious young women, flushed in embarrassment, not used to being snarled at.

Kraekhoull crossed the drawbridge and held her black skirts as she strode along the path that led from La Fonteyn. After a short while, she turned off the road into a copse of poplar trees and, after looking around to check she wasn't being observed, took a small, intricately decorated box with the symbol of a golden snake, from a pocket in her robe and opened it.

Suddenly, there was a whoosh of sparks and some purple smoke, then she was back in her haven with her bag on her arm, which held the items she had bought in La Fonteyn. She was her regal and beautiful self again as she threw off the hag-shawl. Her hair was jet black and she laughed to herself and said, 'If that impudent knight could see me now, he would not see a thread of grey nor a single wrinkle and I would reject him even more so.'

Her cackle echoed in the antechamber.

'I have so much to do,' she whispered to herself as she put away the groceries and ingredients for her potions in boxes, bottles and onto shelves.

Her inner sanctum was a room eerily lit by the green light of many caged fireflies, as well as by magical torches.

All around were signs of the witch's extravagant taste. Silk curtains draped luxuriously all around the walls and the furnishings were of the finest velvet or leather. Carpets of purple and peacock blue lay on the floor and in the centre of the room was her most-prized possession—her crystal ball. It sat on a pedestal of dark grey marble and was covered with a black velvet cloth.

Kraekhoull whipped the cover off the crystal ball and gazed, mesmerised, into its depths. She wanted to see them, her arch enemies—King Lohnn, Gazba and Sir Gracious the Good—the ones she hated for taking her prize, the land of Valouresse.

Initially, the ball was cloudy, black, and grey, but then came the streaks of coiling fire which gradually cleared, and what she saw was the city square and all unfolding within it. Her eyes narrowed and her mouth became a thin line of grey hatred. She was still very beautiful, but in a hard, cruel way.

She saw the king gesturing towards the knights obviously and animatedly discussing tournaments. It would be *her* kingdom soon and this life of ease would end. *In Valouresse, there will be no more jousting. Such a waste of time.*

Now on the snowy, marble parapet of King Lohnn's castle, Gazba, his wife and child—who were exquisitely garbed in pale silk with laced bodices—still watched the knights. The witch gave a nasty smile. To take his family from him would make revenge sweet.

Bitterness churned her stomach, when she saw her enemies, the Pleasures, the lord and lady, who had oppressed her family. They embraced Gazba's pretty wife and then the witch, after studying her face, realised that this was surely little Chloe, their daughter all grown up and now a silly woman thrilled by these thick necked knights and probably dressed to impress them as well. Fury filled her and she especially felt a huge enmity towards Chloe, who looked so elegant, dressed like a lord's daughter.

She watched Chloe leap, shriek and clap her hands with excitement as the knights, having finished conversing with the king, were now trotting back towards the royal stables.

Kraekhoull gritted her teeth with hatred. *Look at her, dressed like a gaudy Midwinter decoration, admiring those thick-necked knights. What a disgrace when others dress so plainly. Your father, Chloe, the great Lord Pleasure, caused my family suffering from his neglect. Spending his money on your dresses and expensive racehorses while we starved.*

The witch then looked carefully at the smiling dark-haired girl frolicking on the parapet next to Chloe.

That must be her daughter, so much like her mother ... there is something about that child, thought the witch.

A girl.

The prophecy of the Maid of Valouresse flitted through her mind: a girl who would arise to rescue the land in its hour of greatest need. Momentarily her heart missed a beat as it squeezed in her chest but then she relaxed as she dismissed the thought. Such predictions were often so much fantasy.

No one knows who the maid might be and surely it wouldn't be such a ridiculous young girl, who leaps around like a small goat.

Her thoughts returned to Gazba and his beautifully attired wife. Her hair was coiffed in a sleek elegant bun as was her daughter's, both decorated with a string of pearls across their foreheads.

Yes, we starved while you, Lady Chloe played—you, like all of the other idle, wealthy girls. Their glittering ballgowns must have looked so beautiful as they danced so elegantly in sumptuous ball rooms, while we scraped and ploughed and harvested, working till our hands bled. I will make you all pay when I am queen.

Her face was set in a narrow sneer, and her eyes were slits of blackness which made her expression ugly. She turned away from the scene in the crystal ball and growled in disgust but then, when she looked again, it was Sir Gracious the Good she saw joining them on King Lohnn's parapet. He bowed to Lord Pleasure and kissed Lady Pleasure's hand.

Kraekhoull shuddered at the sight of him, remembering her narrow escape years ago. She had had no magic box at the time the knight's cold, sharp steel had come so close.

'I have plans for you, sir knight,' she said and then chuckled ghoulishly.

The knight had been both champion of the tournaments and protector of the king at the time.

Now she spoke out loud. 'Dark Prince, send me two from your kingdom, an insightful woman a prophetess and a seer—a wise old man because now is the time,' said the witch as she started her incantation.

Kraekhoull waved and wove her hands around and over the crystal ball, shaping signs with years of long practice. Her eyes were wild, and froth gathered at the corners of her mouth. 'Send me the two you promised, my lord!' she screamed.

The chamber began to grow cold, and colour faded from the centre of the floor. The witch continued spewing arcane, accursed words, and gradually something took shape in the room. They seemed to her beautiful and wise entities but hidden beneath their pleasant façades was the stagnant rot of hell-sent demons.

First to manifest was the seer. An elderly man with a flowing grey beard, dressed in a long grey robe and carrying a staff of ivory with a handle in the shape of a small skull. His real form was that of the demon, Fear, a tall, thin but powerful creature with long canine teeth and eyes that were pits of darkness.

After this, a beautiful prophetess materialised. She had long, golden hair and a serene face—which could have been interpreted as expressionless. She was dressed in a black velvet gown and her eyes were an unsettlingly very pale blue. She was actually the demon, Bitterness, whose real appearance was that of a putrid, diseased being, with a sliver of wobbling slimy flesh for a mouth containing broken, rotted teeth and eyes like sunken, dry, raisins, which strangely seemed to glitter with malice.

'Greetings from the prince,' said the seer, resting both hands on the top of his ornate walking stick and nodding in a dignified fashion. 'My name is Fear.'

The prophetess gathered in her black skirts and gave a slow curtsy. 'And my name is Bitterness,' she said in a milky smooth voice.

Both looked around the witch's lair, noting the witch's love of the opulent. Strings of rare jewels winked and revolved in the light of the cave and draped from the roof to almost head height.

'As you probably already know,' the witch began, 'the dark prince has promised me the Kingdom of Valouresse, but there are some hinderances to this.'

'And what would these problems be, my lady?' asked the old man, gently pulling at his beard in what seemed an expression of deep empathetic concern. 'How can we help?'

'I need you to advise me on how to get rid of Sir Gracious the Good. He is one of my sworn enemies, a veritable thorn in my side. He must be killed,' she blathered eagerly.

The seer was silent and looked deep in thought for a few moments before he began to speak. 'Sir Gracious loves fiery horses, does he not and is also quite proud of his daring riding?' he asked slyly.

'That is true,' said Kraekhoull. 'As a matter of fact, his latest horse is a highly strung, young stallion. In my crystal ball I saw him in the city square, having quite a tussle trying to keep it still in line while the king inspected the knights.'

'Yes,' said the seer, as he sat down nearby on a purple-upholstered armchair.

He rested one hand on the armrest of the armchair and with the other hand he caressed the crannies and undulations of the skull on the top of his stick. 'The knight *does* love the spirited ones,' he began. 'Now he will be riding to his estate alone. It could shy at the slightest thing.'

He then gave the witch a knowing smile.

'Yes, it could,' said Kraekhoull, with a snigger, realising what the seer was alluding to. 'It could be most unreliable, even dangerous. Do it Fear; startle that horse.'

'It will be my pleasure,' said the demon, giving the witch a devious smirk. A nod of the head and he was on his way.

Sir Gracious trotted along the road out of La Fonteyn, with his horse tossing its head and frothing at the mouth. After a while, the horse calmed down and came back to a walk. The knight relaxed a little.

Fear waited patiently until the young stallion rounded the bend. A flock of crows were feeding close to the side of the road but were hidden from the vision of the knight by a large hawthorn bush. The demon was unseen by the knight or the horse, but the birds could feel its evil presence.

Fear charged towards the birds and a chill terror possessed them.

Meanwhile, the witch threw her head back in a frenzy of bloodlust and laughed as she watched from her lair. It felt good to vent her hatred, and her presence also now filled the birds.

The black, flapping, cawing wall of crows struck the young, inexperienced horse which shied violently and the knight, taken by surprise, was thrown headlong into a ditch.

Sir Gracious' servant was expecting his master to be back in time to get ready for the Valourenne Ball. However, when the knight's riderless charger came careering across the drawbridge of Sir Gracious' castle, foaming, and blowing hard, Sir Gracious' valet feared the worst.

He and several other servants immediately set out on horseback to look for their master.

They pounded along the road back towards La Fonteyn. About half a league along, they saw, to their horror, a large group of crows pecking and harassing the dying knight, who was lying in a ditch on the side of the road.

The valet rushed to his master's side and gently raised the man's head onto his lap. A thin trickle of blood came from the corner of Sir Gracious' mouth, and he looked up with pain-filled eyes into the eyes of his servant.

'Don't worry, Sir,' said the valet whose anguish for his master told in his quavering voice and tear-filled eyes. 'We will get you home and I will send for the apothecary at once.'

One of the other servants volunteered. 'I will bring the apothecary,' and then he galloped off.

The servants and the valet took Sir Gracious back to his estate and made him as comfortable as they could on a soft bed with a light warm quilt.

The witch, who had been watching in her crystal ball, exhaled with relief and joy to see the knight mortally wounded. She covered the crystal ball with the black velvet cloth and sat down on an armchair savouring her victory with a small glass of spirits.

Fear appeared in the room, like a wraith at first, and then suddenly became a solid figure. He wore a satisfied smile on his face.

Kraekhoull started and almost dropped her drink.

'He has been taken down, good witch, and will no longer cause you grief,' said Fear.

The elderly seer then sat down in a chair and rested one hand on the carved ivory skull on the top of his walking stick.

'Oh yes,' agreed Kraekhoull with a huge grin. 'You have done magnificently.'

Nanny put the book down and looked up to see the concern on the children's faces.

'Don't worry kids, the witch won't win,' said Nanny.

'But she already has,' said Shelley sorrowfully.

'There is more to this than you know,' said Nanny.

'But Nanny, the knight is going to die, and he's done nothing wrong!' exclaimed Jace with a combination of sorrow and indignation, while sitting upright in bed.

'Is death the end for him?' asked Nanny.

'I know there is a Heaven, Nanny, but where is it? It's so far away,' replied Jace.

'We'll see about that,' said Nanny. 'Just be patient and see what can happen.'

'Okay, Nanny,' said Jace, a little sceptically.

'Sweet dreams and we will hear more tomorrow,' said Nanny, placing the book up on the writing bureau and then going across the room and switching off the lights.

Chapter 4

The next night the children were eagerly awaiting to hear more of the story. Nanny opened the book to read but Jace had a question.

'What happens to Sir Gracious?' he asked with concern.

'I am sure that Gazba will make him as comfortable as possible,' replied Nanny.

'I don't want him to die,' said Shelley.

'Do you remember Tikki, your budgie? He died, but he is only gone from this world but in Heaven, he is alive, and I bet she has met Peachy,' said Nanny.

'Who was Peachy?' asked Jace, leaning on his elbow with an inquisitive expression on his face.

'Peachy was your mum's peach parrot that I accidentally slammed in the laundry door when he was sitting on it.'

'Nanny! That's terrible,' exclaimed Shelley with genuine horror.

'Yes, it sure was. I screamed in the car all the way to the kindergarten that I was picking Lillian up from, and I even put two different shoes on Uncle James feet. The kindergarten teacher was shocked.'

'Oh Nanny, that's so sad,' said Shelley. 'But what has Peachy got to do with Heaven?'

'Well, this happened the same week my friend's little girl, Lisa, was run over. And, also about the same time, your mum's little six-year-old school friend died of cancer—and her name was Lisa too. And my sister's little baby girl died at birth, and her name was Lisa as well,' said Nanny.

'Wow, that's a lot of Lisas, Nanny. Is that actually true?' asked Jace.

'Yes, it is,' replied Nanny.

'So, what you're saying is that all the Lisas died around the same time and were all in Heaven at the same time, as well as Peachy?' said Jace.

'Yes, that's right,' answered Nanny. 'And that's not all. Your mum's little friend Lisa had a golden retriever that died of old age around the same time.'

'I can see them in my imagination, all in Heaven, playing, even Peachy, flying around and landing on their heads and the dog's head too,' said Shelley with bright excited eyes.

'Oh yes, so can I. And I remember your mum's first day of school, I was so worried about her,' said Nanny.

'Because of what happened to you on your first day of school, Nanny?' said Shelley.

'Probably. Your mum and Lisa—the little six-year-old who later died—just held hands and skipped into school and I was so happy and relieved because I thought she might get bullied by the teacher or the other kids.'

'So, in a way, even though it was sad they all died, it was sort of happy too that they were all together in Heaven?' said Jace.

'Yes, I agree,' replied Nanny thoughtfully, before brightening and adding, 'That's enough talk about death and dying. Shall I go on with the story?'

'Yes,' said the children in unison.

The evening after the knights Valourenne victory ceremony, was the Valourenne Ball—the most thrilling time of feasting and dancing in the great hall of King Lohnn's castle. This year, it was even more exciting since the knights had won the tournament.

Chloe was getting dressed for the ball and was being helped by her maid, Misk. Misk was a dark-haired, slightly built girl with eloquent oriental eyes from the far east. She had an uncanny knack for knowing what Chloe needed, even before she knew herself.

Chloe chose to wear the dress she had purchased in La Fonteyn earlier that day. It was a complete ensemble of dress, shoes, jewellery, and a purse. She looked forward to seeing her handsome husband in his outfit. He was the royal apothecary and after all he should look impressive. She had chosen his trousers of peacock blue satin, and his puff sleeve shirt with bell-shaped wrist, was made of pale blue silk. Her dress was like a shimmering sea of diamonds with light dancing off its surface. Chloe gasped at its beauty. She and Gazba's colours would blend beautifully. Together they would make a magnificent entrance.

Soon they would leave for La Fonteyn. The carriage was at the ready, and in the courtyard the fine black Friesian horses stamped impatiently. Where was Gazba?

Chloe met him in the corridor, striding along carrying his apothecary bag. Not only was he not dressed for the ball, but he looked very worried.

'I am sorry Chloe, but I must go to Sir Gracious the Good. He has just had a riding accident on the way home from the ceremony. Can you please give my apologies to King Lohnn?'

'The poor man!' exclaimed Chloe. 'Of course, I will.'

Gazba shook his head and pursed his lips as he felt her disappointment. He was going to miss another Valourenne Ball.

Quietly she said, 'I do understand.' She reached for and held his hand, giving it a little squeeze.

He smiled and then turned to go on his way but stopped and gave her a half smile. 'Please enjoy yourself.'

She lowered her eyes, and her lip trembled a little.

'Very well,' she murmured 'It is as it is. I know this is a part of our life—you having to visit sick patients and missing events. It's alright. Gallant will be there. He can be my escort for the night, although you know I really wanted you.' Tears brimmed in her dark, doe-like eyes.

'I must go now,' said Gazba, placing one hand on her shoulder. Then, with the other hand, he gently tilted up her chin, so she met his gaze. '*Do* have fun, and by the way you are a vision of loveliness in that dress.'

'Thank you,' said Chloe, giving him a light kiss on the cheek.

A small tear glistened in the corner of her eye, and she hastily brushed it off.

'I will pray for Sir Gracious,' she said. 'Not having you accompany me to the Valourenne Ball is a trivial inconvenience and not as important as being with your friend at this time.'

Gazba gave her a sad smile, then turned and went on his way down the hallway toward the courtyard, while Chloe returned to her bedchamber to make a final check of her appearance. She did look beautiful, and she *would* have a nice time. She would make sure of that. She lifted her chin as she gazed at herself in the mirror. After all, this was the Valourenne Ball!

Once mounted, Gazba cantered out of the courtyard and along the road to Sir Gracious' estate. It was dark but he knew the way well. He and the knight were good friends and had shared many happy times eating and drinking. Once in Sir Gracious' courtyard, he leapt off his horse and sprinted to Sir Gracious' chamber carrying his apothecary bag. His old friend smiled wanly when he saw him and Gazba smiled back, but his heart sank.

The knights' breath was coming in laboured rasps and his skin was cold and clammy.

'I will not leave you old friend,' said Gazba when they both realised that there was nothing that could be done.

'Thank you, Gazba,' murmured the knight, weakly squeezing the apothecary's hand.

As he lay there on his deathbed, Sir Gracious continued to speak, haltingly.

'I felt something evil out there, not just the birds. It was the sound they made, almost a cackle, and within their blackness, I thought I saw a face. Beware, Gazba, for I fear the witch may be on the move again.'

'Rest, Jasper,' said Gazba, with tears spilling from his eyes.

'Do not despair. She does not scare me. And if she is behind this, I will bring her to justice.'

In the carriage on the way into La Fonteyn, Chloe had a worn and weary expression. Her dark cloak covered her sparkling dress.

Misk suddenly spoke into the silence that had sat between them as they travelled the several leagues towards La Fonteyn.

'I am sure the master would have gone to the ball if he could. Maybe next time he will.'

'Yes,' said Chloe dully. 'Next time. But I would never deny him being with his desperately ill friend.'

'Of course,' answered Misk, lowering her expressive eyes, and giving a little sigh, unable to lighten the mood.

The carriage bounced and jolted on the ruts that were always being fixed but always kept reforming with every downpour of rain. Moonlight shone through the windows. Chloe stared out and saw silvered images of cattle and trees and servant's dwellings as the carriage passed by them.

Before long, the carriage pulled into the entrance of the king's palace. Chloe and Misk alighted, helped by the footman. Immediately, they could smell the heady aroma of scented candles, frankincense in particular. Torches lit the way as they as they walked through the ornately decorated entrance of the palace. They then walked up the steps towards the passage that led to the great hall. Misk said goodbye to Chloe and went to join her fellow servants in the kitchen and surrounding rooms.

'Enjoy yourself, Misk,' said Chloe. 'I believe some very good violinists will be playing.'

'Thank you, my mistress. I will dance my legs off, and I think you should too,' she giggled.

Chloe gave her a wry smile before continuing on.

She met her parents and Sir Gallant at the great hall entrance, and all were ushered in by pages garbed in pink and green pastel coloured satin.

'How is your eye?' Chloe asked Gallant as she took his arm.

'Oh, it's nothing too serious,' replied Gallant with a smile. 'A wee bit of gravel flew up when an opponent galloped by.'

'Thank goodness,' said Chloe with a sigh of relief.

Chloe, her parents, and Gallant assembled to be presented to the court and the king.

'Lord and Lady Pleasure,' said the page and there was polite applause as the Marquis and Marquisa nodded and smiled.

Then he announced: 'Sir Gallant'.

Gallant stepped forward. Suddenly there were cheers and clapping as the guests rose from their seats. Gallant—having performed brilliantly in the jousting contest—was the king's champion and theirs. Chloe felt a flutter in her heart as the knight was enthusiastically praised and felt proud to be with him, even as an escort.

'Madame Delafoi,' announced the page as Chloe slowly glided to the entrance in her voluminous, swishing gown. Many sighed with admiration at her glorious appearance. She had both a thrill—which caused her stomach to squeeze and her heart to miss a beat—as she sensed she was being noticed—and an ache that she was not with her husband.

Gallant and Lord Pleasure bowed low, and Chloe and her mother curtsied to the king who smiled and nodded in response.

Chloe was wide eyed, as she briefly glanced up at the high, vaulted ceiling, painted with murals of floating cherubs amid glorious light filled clouds from a heavenly realm. She was careful to watch where she walked.

How embarrassing if I fell over! I can admire the Great Hall later.

The flames from golden candlesticks flickered and highlighted the colours of the scarlet roses, and the exotic tangerine and pink lilies. Heady, delicious scent filled the air.

Chloe passed rosewood-panelled walls and the floor—on which she trod so carefully—was white charcoal veined Florentine marble.

She walked by—the wife of the Royal Apothecary—the hero of Valouresse—she too, was highly esteemed by King Lohnn. Sighs and murmurs followed her, as she was escorted on Gallant's arm to the king's table and a dignified page in his pastel pants, waistcoat and jacket started to pull out her chair.

However, Chloe shook her head and gently raised her hand to the page and instead made her way towards the king.

The many shades of glittering blue crystals from the palest sky to the deepest peacock blue reflected the light and danced on the walls. She wore a bun in her sleek, ebony hair and a sparkling tiara of deep blue sapphires. Her large, dark eyes were lowered as she approached the king, who was already seated at his sumptuously laid table.

She curtsied and spoke, 'Sire, my husband is attending Sir Gracious the Good who is gravely ill. He will not be attending the ball and sends his apologies.'

'His apology is accepted of course, Madame Delafoi, but when and how did this happen?' he asked, leaning forward and frowning.

'It was a riding accident on his way back from the celebration today,' said Chloe gravely.

'Madame Delafoi, it is good your husband is at his side. He is full of compassion and knowledge—no one could be better.'

After Chloe went back to her seat, the king was thoughtful and quiet for some time then he noticed Gallant's eye patch and beckoned him over.

'How is your eye?' asked the king.

'No permanent damage, Sire,' replied Gallant cheerily.

The king then placed his arm on Gallant's shoulder and said loudly. 'Here is your champion. Then he turned to Gallant and said, Congratulations Gallant, very well done!'

'Thank you, Sire,' said Gallant. 'It is always a pleasure to serve my king and country.'

He bowed low and the applause was deafening, and some women threw their head dresses into the air.

Chloe's lips were like blood-red, velvety rose petals—and they pouted as she anticipated her father's comment. Jumping in, she said, 'Gazba has a sick patient he has to attend to.'

'He makes a habit of missing important events, it seems,' said the Marquis gruffly, looking bigger than his real size in his huge, puffed doublet detailed with ermine.

Chloe did not register anger or disappointment at her father's comments but wore a serene expression, not wanting to get into a conflict. Gallant the grand knight would be a buffer between her and her intimidating father.

'Gazba is attending Sir Gracious the Good,' said the knight, interceding for Chloe. 'He was in a riding accident and is seriously injured.'

'Oh,' said the Marquis softly, and looking a little shamefaced.

Gallant then changed the subject and said, 'You look absolutely beautiful, Chloe.'

'Why thank you, Gallant, I was afraid of looking sullen and spoilt as you know I can be,' she said with dismal sarcasm.

Gallant laughed at her attempt at levity and answered with more levity, 'No, not *you* Chloe.'

Chloe gave a wry smile and warmed up a little.

On the banquet table the cooked white swan, was dressed in its own feathers and had a golden crown on its head and would soon be served with crisp, golden-baked vegetables. Close by, on beautiful porcelain dishes, were exotic fruits, such as were not often seen in the realm.

Suddenly, there was a loud fanfare of trumpets. Every head turned and there was silence.

Entering the great hall was Brother Lucas, dressed—as always—in a ragged, sackcloth cassock and accompanied by a pet deer and a black sheep, which nervously pressed in close behind him.

One of the king's deerhounds at the entrance to the great hall barked and wagged its tail, pulling on its lead to reach the visitors but a grey and grizzled wolfhound, a large and powerful animal, was not so friendly. It lunged and growled, showing its gums and teeth as it repeatedly snapped at the brother's terrified animals. The dogs were beloved by the king and accompanied him everywhere, even to the Valourenne Ball.

'Peace, brother,' said the Brother, holding his hand out in a calming gesture. The massive wolfhound immediately settled on its haunches, bowed its head, and gave a little whine.

As the Brother approached the dog, it held its paw out, which the Brother took and held.

A sigh of awe came up from the crowd. The holy man was here and how they loved and revered him.

'Blessings, friends, do not get up,' he said to the assembly. 'Knights, enjoy your celebration. King Lohnn, bless you and this land and may joy always come in the morning.'

The Brother then gave both dogs a rub on the head and walked over to where the musicians were stationed. The deer and sheep trotted closely beside him. The formerly ferocious wolf hound now lay quietly next to King Lohnn's throne, with its head resting on its paws and had no more desire to attack the Brother's timid animals.

'Come,' said Brother Lucas, raising his voice so all could hear. 'As the glorious scriptures say, "the joy of the Lord is our strength", so people enjoy the merriment, enter the realm of Heaven.'

The musicians performed lilting, melodies with harps, strings, and woodwind instruments. The beautiful sound welled and pulsated in the hall and in Chloe's heart.

The king stood from his throne, raised his glass, and said loudly:

'We will have a feast and a lot of dancing to do but first a toast. To Brother Lucas and the knights!'

'To Brother Lucas and to the knights!' responded the crowd.

'You choose the dance, Brother Lucas for we all must work up an appetite!' said the king with a laugh.

The Brother smiled a gentle apologetic smile and said to the king, 'Forgive me for not dancing my king, but my animals will not under-stand—I will enjoy watching all of you having fun.'

The king clinked glasses Brother Lucus who then beamed as he faced the musicians, raised his glass, and shouted, 'Let it be the Gavotte!'

'No, not the gavotte,' moaned Lord Pleasure, shaking his head as his wife dragged on his hand trying to get him up to dance. 'It is for the young ones.'

'Lord Pleasure,' said the king laughing—for he had heard him complain. 'It is for the young at heart.'

From his throne the king walked down to the dance floor, bowed to a young lady who curtseyed back. He took her by both hands, and they energetically dipped and led headlong into the dance, skipping, and hopping to the merry yet regal music. Everyone joined in including Gallant and Chloe, who had cheered up considerably. She laughed as she swirled around, holding hands with her partner Gallant, among the other couples in brilliant finery of satin, feathers, and sparkling jewellery.

While Chloe, with flushed face, was catching her breath after the dance she said, 'One moment, Gallant, I must speak to Brother Lucas.'

'Of course, go at once,' said Gallant, releasing her hands and watching her as she walked gracefully over to the Brother.

'Brother Lucas,' said Chloe, as she gently stroked the forehead of the spotted deer, which was not afraid of her in the slightest.

'Chloe,' answered the Brother in a familiar and kindly voice.

Then, after a pause, he asked, 'Has Gazba left already to go on his quest?'

'Why no,' answered Chloe, surprised. 'What quest? I have heard of no quest!'

She was intrigued and a little shocked.

'Ah, good, good, good,' said Brother Lucas with a relieved sigh. 'We have a mutual friend from the realm of mysteries—it is he who told me that it is to be.'

'Who is that? Please tell me,' asked Chloe with a gasp.

'It is Chraston the unicorn. Do not fear Chloe, for everything works together for good for those who love the Lord—and I know you do—love the Lord.'

'I do, but I have my fears,' said Chloe, quietly mesmerised by this news and with eyes that stared into the crowd, but not noticing anything.

The Brother took her hand. 'I am relieved he hasn't left yet. I have some special words for Gazba.'

'Oh, yes please, tell me what they are!' exclaimed Chloe trembling like a butterfly alighting on a flower.

'They are,' said the Brother, '"In the name of Jesus Christ of Nazareth"—these words—and he will know when to use them.'

Chloe was mesmerised and watched the Brother form the words with his mouth and became deep in thought. She repeated the words slowly and quietly: 'In the name of Jesus Christ of Nazareth.'

'Isn't Nazareth in our world?' asked Jace with surprise.

'Our world and Heaven are closer than you think and can sometimes coincide,' said Nanny, putting the book down on her lap for a moment.

'Oh, do you mean?' Jace excitedly—as he grasped a revelation—that when Jesus said to God "Let your kingdom come and your will be done on earth as it is in Heaven," 'He wants God's Kingdom to come on earth?'

'That's right,' said Nanny. 'And I think we can bring a bit of Heaven to earth every day because the Kingdom of God is inside us and we actually live in Heaven and earth at the same time,' said Nanny.

'How do you mean, Nanny?' asked Shelley who was quite intrigued by this time.

She leant on her elbows and gazed up at her Nanny.

'We live here on earth, but the Bible says that we are also seated in Heavenly places, which means we live there too. We can draw on its power and glory of Heaven to bring joy and peace to the world here.'

'On earth as it is in Heaven,' murmured Shelley with luminous eyes, 'I like that,' Shelley piped up. 'So really, we are partly like Heavenly beings. Maybe unicorns can come into our world.'

'I agree,' said Nanny, 'or fauns and centaurs and dancing forest nymphs. Sometimes we see things in the spirit—things found in Heaven. The scriptures say in Two Corinthians Chapter Four verse eighteen: "We don't focus on the things that can be seen but on the things that can't be seen."'

'What is that like, Nanny?' asked Shelley, not completely understanding.

'To me,' said Nanny slowly, 'it's like seeing through a fine veil—but still very real. I will tell you more about that later, but for now we should get on with the story.'

'Okay,' said Jace, who then added, 'The Brother was telling Chloe some important stuff wasn't he?'

'Thanks, Jace,' said Nanny who began reading again.

'Go and enjoy the night, and take this,' said the Brother with a smile, placing a small brass cross into her hand.

Chloe looked up and her eyes met the wise old man's an intense gaze. 'Thank you, Brother Lucas. I will pass these words, and this cross, on to my husband.'

The Brother gently squeezed Chloe's hand closing the brass cross within it and studied her face. 'Do not worry my dear,' he said. 'God's plans will not be thwarted.' Then he changed the tone immediately, released her hand saying, 'Go and dance, join the fun.'

All at once the mystical quiet time with the Brother was gone as she made her way back to the dance floor. Her senses were filled with the sights and sounds of hundreds of swirling, colourful, laughing, dancing people. She saw the Brother in a corner of the huge ornate room, sitting with his animals, and stroking them; they seemed calm. He smiled sweetly at her and was nodding his head in time to the music. She smiled back.

Gallant took her hand, and they joined the other dancers, whirling and dipping.

'Are you alright, Chloe?' asked Gallant as they danced. 'You seem a little preoccupied.'

'Oh, I'm fine,' she replied, looking quickly into his eye—the one without the patch—engaging him with a gay expression, snapping out of her reverie.

Chloe's arm rested on Gallant's, and he winced.

'So sorry Gallant. I forgot you were injured!' she said, gazing at him with soft sympathetic eyes.

'Not to worry Chloe,' replied Gallant. 'I'm made of strong stuff.'

'Nevertheless, I shall be more careful.' With that Chloe gingerly now rearranged her arm on his to relieve him of as much weight as possible.

The knights wore dazzling clothing similar to that which that Gazba would have worn, had he been there. They twirled and pivoted expertly, with the graceful daughters of the nobles.

The knights nodded to Chloe—clearly transfixed by her beauty—and to Gallant, as a mark of respect—as the two passed by. Chloe politely nodded in return but was oblivious to the wide-eyed stares. She had her attention fixed on Gallant, her escort.

Meanwhile Gazba attended Sir Gracious, who had become deathly grey and seemed distant.

'I am not sad,' said the knight. 'I am going to my beautiful wife and child.'

Gazba swallowed and he felt tears welling. He knew the knight had been on his own for many years since his wife and baby had died during childbirth. Sir Gracious sighed.

'I see them both by a blossoming cherry tree and there is someone else with them. I think it is the Lord Jesus.'

With that he closed his eyes and a smile settled sweetly on his face.

Gazba lay his head on his friend's chest and sobbed.

After dancing for a while, Chloe whispered into Gallant's ear, 'Look. Lady Dubblenek is tugging at that baron's hand, and he is not getting up to dance. It is the saraband, a slow and easy dance too. I wonder why he is refusing her?'

The baron still shook his head and was waving away Lady Dubblenek.

'She looks quite upset,' said Chloe.

'I think he is safe. The music will stop soon,' said Gallant with a wry smile.

After a few minutes the refrain slowed and stopped, and the musicians took a break.

'The baron is a bad colour,' said Gallant. 'And holding his belly. He's unwell.'

Chloe saw a group of nobles muttering and shooting acrimonious looks, like darts, towards the baron.

Walking back to her seat with Gallant, Chloe overheard some of their comments.

One thick-haired, ruddily handsome noble commented angrily, 'How dare that Baron Bardozer refuse to dance with Lady Dubblenek. She is related to the king.'

'Distantly,' remarked another noble, who wore a rather mournful expression on his sallow face.

'He is so different from his father,' said the sad-looking noble. 'It is the wine from his estate that supplied this ball.'

The first noble shook his black locks and said, 'A worse buffoon of a man you will never find.'

At that moment, Bardozer was passing by and heard the comment. He shot the men a murderous scowl and with face blotched red and white, hurried out of the entrance of the Great Hall.

He was gone for some time and emerged looking somewhat dishevelled. The music swelled and Lady Dubblenek grasped his hand, swirling him again onto the dance floor.

While he was tripping and hopping to the gavotte he suddenly stopped, and a look of abject horror came over his face.

His eyes bulged like a frog as he lurched forward groaning and holding his stomach.

The dancers jostled each other as they made way for the barging Bardozer, who emitted loud windy noises as he ran to the garderobe.

Most of the guests heard the noise and stifled laughter.

Lady Dubblenek was red-faced with embarrassment and humiliation.

The baron relieved himself in the garderobe and then decided to abandon the ball, post haste. He had suffered enough shame for one night and probably for the whole of his life. He hurried down the corridor from the great hall and back to the entrance, where he found his carriage waiting.

'Madame Dubblenek can find her own way home. I need a change of pants,' he muttered to himself as he climbed into his carriage, helped in by the footman who closed the door behind him with an ill-concealed look of distaste on his face.

'Home, and hurry!' he roared to his driver. His chin was set, and his eyes glittered with malice.

As the carriage pulled away the baron hissed through clenched teeth, 'Those nobles and that damned apothecary Gazba, they'll wish they'd never been born.'

The noisy, tumultuous dance floor was once more filled with hundreds of swirling, swaying people after the interesting exit of the baron.

Standing on her own, Lady Dubblenek was surrounded by many dancers.

'I want to go home,' she sobbed.

Lord Pleasure came to her aid and said kindly, 'Lady Dubblenek, we can take you home in our carriage, but surely you will stay for the royal banquet.'

'Why of course I will stay,' said Lady Dubblenek, batting her eyelids at the Marquis and wiping a tear from her eye. 'How kind of you to offer to take me home.'

The Marquisa arched her eyebrows. 'Certainly, you may come with us. You can sit beside *me,* and we can chat all the way there.'

Lady Dubblenek looked the tiniest bit crestfallen and certainly not flirtatious anymore and said with forced enthusiasm, 'Oh yes, Marquisa, we will have so much to talk about.'

She would have loved to spend the carriage ride home flirting with the Marquis, but now she would be under the scrutiny of his wife.

Chloe made the most of the night despite missing her husband. After the dancing, they enjoyed the sumptuous banquet.

Baron Jardine and his wife sat near her, and the baron was keen to tell her about the new hospital for his servants.

'I admire your husband, Gazba,' said the baron. 'He helps everyone— rich and poor alike—a true gentleman.'

'Yes, he is dedicated,' said Chloe, sighing and agreeing with the baron. But her face was sad.

Baron Jardine's wife spoke to her husband, saying, 'You are making Chloe unhappy, it is obvious she would have loved to have her husband by her side at the ball.'

'What a clumsy oaf I am,' said the baron sheepishly.

'Not at all,' said Chloe with a reassuring smile.

The baron smiled and got up saying, 'Please, take my seat, so you two can chatter.'

'Why, how kind of you, Sir,' said Chloe, moving over.

'Thank you, my dear,' said Baroness Jardine.

'I will leave you ladies to it,' said the baron, as he tucked into his steaming plate of swan meat and vegetables.

'We haven't had a good chat for a long time,' said Baroness Jardine, giving Chloe a warm smile and taking her hand.

'Yes, Charlotte,' agreed Chloe speaking softly. 'It is long overdue, and I miss having someone to confide in actually.'

'Some things can only be talked over with another woman,' said Charlotte.

Chloe glanced at Sir Gallant, who was engaged in talking to another knight across the table.

'It is a shame Gazba is not here with you, Chloe,' remarked the baroness. 'This is the second Valourenne Ball he has missed. Is there no-one who could step in for him to leave him free for this night of nights?'

'His patient is Sir Gracious the Good, an old and beloved friend, so I understand him being loath to abandon such a one,' said Chloe, feeling protective towards her husband.

'Yes, Chloe,' agreed Charlotte. 'Of course, you are right, and I am being horrid to say such a thing. Please forgive me.'

'Of *course*, I do,' said Chloe, smiling before continuing. 'All of these knights are skilled, and no doubt very brave, especially Sir Gallant ...'

'But Gazba is the true champion of Valouresse, and its saviour,' said the baroness, finishing Chloe's statement.

'That's right,' agreed Chloe. 'He is not a champion jousting knight, but someone much more important in my eyes—he is my soulmate but things are not right between us at the moment. It seems he doesn't even know that I exist most of the time.'

'But you really were besotted with Gazba, weren't you?' asked Charlotte. 'Pray tell me, what could have cooled that ardour? Could it be his work? He really takes it seriously and spends a lot of time with colleagues.'

Chloe then lowered her voice even more. 'Gazba was older than me and I was in awe of him. So, when he asked for my hand in marriage, I gladly accepted.'

'I know, my love,' said Charlotte squeezing Chloe's hand again. 'But it is nice to have the attention of someone like Gallant, so you don't miss out on the Valourenne.'

Chloe shrugged and then changed the subject. 'Anyway Charlotte, let us eat,' she said enthusiastically. 'Good conversation always helps awaken an appetite.'

'I agree, enough talk,' said Charlotte with a laugh.

As she was quietly eating, Chloe's attention turned to Gallant, and, as she watched him talking with the other knight, she thought what a handsome man he was.

Gazba, however, was someone she both admired and loved. But was that enough in the scheme of things? Did they in fact share anything, apart from their daughter, Jasmine?

Maybe I should have married Gallant. We have a lot in common and have known each other most of our lives.

Gallant turned to see her staring at him.

'What is it, Lady Chloe?' he asked quizzically.

'Oh nothing, nothing at all,' she replied with a smile and began eating.

Lord Pleasure spoke to his wife quietly. 'Chloe never should have married the apothecary,' he said.

'He was the saviour of Valouresse—if you don't remember my dear,' answered the Marquisa. 'The greatest hero of our times.'

'Yes, yes, but with no noble lineage to mention and no useful contacts,' said the Marquis between mouthfuls of the irresistible food.

'He is the king's Apothecary!' retorted Lady Pleasure.

'Yes, true,' acknowledged Lord Pleasure, taking a mouthful of his meal.

The stuffed swan meat was swimming in a steaming gravy and a creamy, white sauce accompanied the poached quail eggs, scalloped potatoes, broccoli, as well as the baked carrots and onions. It was almost too much to bear in its deliciousness. Chloe forgot her inner misery and tucked in like everyone else.

Chloe didn't hear her parent's conversation. She had grown curious about Baron Bardozer's hasty retreat and remembered Gazba saying that the baron would never take the correct dosage of his medication. She deduced that this was probably the cause of his distress.

Later, after even more dancing, dessert was served. There were several kinds of highly decorated cakes and plenty of conserved fruit, such as plums and cherries, with custard and cream.

Now there was slower dancing because everyone was replete with food and wine. Many sat and drank wine, ale or fruit punch and socialised. Lady Dubblenek infiltrated some noblemen conversations and flirted unashamedly with them. Just after midnight, Chloe decided it was time to go home. She kissed her parents goodbye, as they were leaving too.

'Goodnight, Chloe,' said Gallant, who bowed and then kissed her hand.

'Goodnight, Gallant. Thank you for cheering me up,' Chloe replied warmly.

'The pleasure is mine,' said the knight gazing into her eyes with great kindness and maybe a touch of something more, which Chloe chose to ignore.

The Pleasures and Sir Gallant travelled home, taking Lady Dubblenek with them to her own chateau, having to put up with her inanities regarding toad skins and the like. Meanwhile, Chloe and Misk went home in their separate carriage.

'It really was fun,' said Chloe as they jolted along under the moonlit sky to the sound of steady hoofbeats and jingling traces.

'The servant's party was wonderful too,' said Misk dreamily.

'Oh, I am glad,' said Chloe with a little yawn. 'So sorry,' she added, 'I'm not bored, just weary, probably from all the dancing and I always get sleepy after a big meal.'

'I do too,' said Misk, doing a copycat yawn, caught from her mistress.

Once back home, Chloe was helped out of her elaborate dress and into her nightgown by Misk and then she checked on Jasmine. She found her sleeping soundly. Briefly Chloe thought of her husband, who would probably be riding home now as he had done many times before. Normally she would not worry but she still slipped in a little prayer for his safety on this night. Then she went back to her bedchamber and settled herself comfortably under the downy quilt and dozed off.

Gazba came in very late.

'How is Sir Gracious?' asked Chloe sleepily, leaning on one elbow and pushing her long, black hair away from her face.

Gazba lay down next to her and breathed a big sigh. 'Very sadly, he has died.'

He was silent for some time and Chloe saw tears rolling from his eyes and down his cheeks.

'I am so sorry,' said Chloe gently pressing her cheek against his. Then she put her arm around him and just held him close.

'I always thought we would be friends forever,' said Gazba of Sir Gracious.

'You *are* friends forever. He's just in a different place now,' said Chloe.

'Yes, you are right. A place where there are no more tears and where we will meet once again.'

'He shall be with his wife and child,' said Chloe.

'Of course, that is a thing of joy. But to have him gone is a hole in my life,' acknowledged Gazba, sadly.

'I am here my love,' said Chloe, now gently stroking his forehead.

'You are,' replied Gazba looking deeply into her eyes and smiling a gentle sad smile.

There was a long time of silence and then Chloe spoke again.

'I don't think Baron Bardozer took your advice.'

She told Gazba about the ball and the bloated, bamboozled baron.

Both gave a heartfelt laugh.

'He will blame me of course,' said Gazba. 'He is sure to have taken too much paraffin.'

'Nothing can be done now. He will just have to wait it out,' said Chloe. 'Though I suspect there will be little waiting and a lot of outing!' Both had a giggle again which temporarily assuaged Gazba's grief.

'I can sleep on it,' said Gazba wearily, giving Chloe a tender little peck on the lips. He lay back with eyes wide open, looking intensely into the darkness.

'I cannot sleep,' said Chloe, brushing the hair out of her face. 'I know it's a sad time—but I saw Brother Lucas, and he said you are going on a quest?'

'How did he know?' exclaimed Gazba, sitting up.

'I don't know, but he gave me a message of eight words to give to you, which are: "In the name of Jesus Christ of Nazareth"—and he also gave me this,' added Chloe, reaching into the top drawer of her bedside table, and handing him the brass cross.

Gazba handled the cross and murmured the words, 'In the name of Jesus Christ of Nazareth.'

'Brother Lucas said you will know when to use those words,' said Chloe, as she grasped Gazba's hand and said impatiently, '*Please* tell me more, I must know.'

'Of course, my love, I was going to tell you in the morning, but now is the right time,' he replied, placing the cross on the bedside table and putting his arm around her.

'Yes. And?' said Chloe.

'Tonight, as I was riding back from Sir Gracious' home, I met the unicorn Chraston—right in the middle of the road.'

'The unicorn?' said Chloe.

'Yes, he was as beautiful as I remember him, with a wavy, lustrous mane and feet like alabaster. A bluish haze surrounded him ...'

'His horn, what was *that* like?' asked the fascinated Chloe.

'It was golden and gave off a glow, a bit like lightning, but then everything seemed to fade away—the road, the trees, everything. I fell into the depths of his dark liquid eyes.'

'What did you see there?' asked Chloe.

In a lowered voice, scarcely able to meet her horrified gaze he replied. 'I saw Jasmine, running for her life,'

'No!' said Chloe gasping and covering her mouth., 'Running from what?'

'I don't know,' answered Gazba with a helpless shrug.

'Will she be saved? asked Chloe, trembling.

'The unicorn told me: "Trust the Great King and your daughter will be safe. I am here to help you on your quest." Evil is afoot.'

'What else is there?' urged Chloe.

Gazba looked intently into her eyes. 'I asked him if I was up to the task and he answered: "*You* are not perfect, but the quest is, and all things work together for good for those who love the Lord.'"

'Does he mean our lord, King Lohnn?' asked Chloe.

'No', said Gazba, 'he means God, the King of Kings and Lord of Lords—Jesus Christ of Nazareth—the one I will follow.'

'God will protect her?' asked Chloe, saying the words in little pants.

'Yes,' answered Gazba, grasping her hand in his.

Gazba lowered his voice. 'The unicorn then said: "Your pleas, wishes and dreams are known to The Lord—and Valouresse needs a champion— but you will not be alone. The armies of Heaven are gathering."'

'What else is there?' asked Chloe. Her face was flushed.

Gazba took a deep breath then spoke. 'He then said something that perplexes me. He said that I am to protect the Maid of Valouresse.'

'The one spoken of in the legends?' asked Chloe.

'Yes, but I don't know her or why she would need my protection,' he replied. 'But first of all, you and Jasmine must go to a safe haven—your father's home.'

'I do love you,' she whispered. 'And I am so sorry for my harsh words earlier today at the knight's ceremony.'

'And I, my dearest, am sorry for neglecting your needs,' replied Gazba.

'Together we can make things right,' said Chloe, looking deeply into his eyes. 'But I'll be thinking about this all night.' Chloe then leaned over and kissed her husband softly on the lips.

'I will be too,' said Gazba as he caressed her cheek.

He then snuffed out the candle and they both lay still holding hands and silent in bed, staring out at the stars through the window.

'Why did Gazba like the cross? Was it magical?' asked Jace, as Nanny closed the book for the night.

'It's a sign of things to come, special things,' replied Nanny, giving him a mysterious smile.

'How will it help him?' asked Shelley struggling with a tangle in her hair.

Nanny helped her get the knot out as painlessly as she could with a few little squeals from Shelley, then lovingly swept it back from her face and said, 'I will try to explain it, although I can't do it as well as I would like.'

'Just tell it your way, Nanny,' said Shelley. 'We will understand.'

'My doctor once told me something that changed my life forever. It didn't mean much to me at the time, but it does now.'

'What did he say, Nanny?' asked Shelley.

'Well, as I was leaving his office and walking down the stairs, he came out to the landing and yelled out—but not angrily—"Handel wrote the Messiah after he had a vision of Christ seated on the throne in Heaven." I thought it was really odd at the time, that a doctor would believe such a thing, a thing that most people wouldn't believe.'

'What is that—the Messiah?' asked Jace, looking at Nanny with his bright eyes.

'I think it's one of the most beautiful pieces of music ever written, and only in a matter of weeks, simply glorious, and it's about Jesus and his kingdom,' said Nanny.

'I've heard it on Christmas Eve on television,' said Shelley. 'I really love it.'

'Yes, that's the Hallelujah chorus and it's very beautiful. My doctor believed in the mystery and wonder of God.'

'What do you mean?' asked Jace.

'He knew that the Lord can inspire you to do great exploits by giving you visions, or other supernatural help—which are just normal things for God—like He did for Handel,' said Nanny with a rapt dreamy smile.

'Exploits means brilliant feats,' said Jace. 'I had to look that word up for school.'

'Well done, Jace,' said Nanny, who was proud of this clever child.

'So, he yelled that from the balcony and now you can get inspired by it years later,' said Shelley, wisely stroking her cat unicorn toy with the many colours.

'Yes,' said Nanny. 'It helps me to tell the story of our *mystical union* with God, who loves us, and gives us knowledge directly from him that is not intellectually possible.'

'That's pretty complex, Nanny,' said Jace.

'Well, I *have* looked it up in the *Oxford English Dictionary* and I'm trying to explain mystical to you,' replied Nanny.

'Just say it your way, Nanny,' said Shelley.

'I'll try,' answered Nanny. 'Mystical means, for me, just knowing what God is telling you—sometimes in a symbolic way, even if it makes no logical sense—like the brass cross is for Gazba—he will understand the meaning at the right time, just like the vision that Handel had, inspired him to write the Messiah in the seventeenth century.'

'That's interesting, Nanny,' said Jace, giving a little yawn. 'Maybe I'll have a vision tonight when I'm asleep.'

'Or maybe when you're awake,' said Nanny. Then she added, 'Sleep tight kids and we can read more tomorrow. The holidays go for a couple of weeks, so we have plenty of time for this.'

'Love you, Nanny,' said Jace sleepily.

'Me too,' said Shelley.

'Goodnight my darlings,' replied Nanny, as she got up and kissed them both.

Then she put the book on the top of the writing bureau, went to the door and switched off the light.

Later, she lay in bed for some time, looking up at the stars from her window, thinking about God's wonder.

With that, she happily settled down to sleep.

Chapter 5

The next day Shelley spent her time drawing emojis and Jace played his computer games. Both went for a walk to the pine forest with their tiny Snowflake the Pomeranian, who wanted to take on any big dog for a fight.

The next night Nanny opened the book and said to the sleepy children, 'Now, shall we get on with the story?'

'Yes please,' said the children enthusiastically.

With Sir Gracious gone, one enemy had been disposed of and Kraekhoull was now one step closer to gaining the throne.

She was in no way remorseful. She wanted the crown and wanted to oppress those who had oppressed her. It was pure revenge.

The witch swept the black, velvet cloth from the crystal ball and then peered into its glassy depths.

'Now to deal with the apothecary and King Lohnn,' the witch muttered as she moved her attention to Gazba, who was having breakfast with Chloe in the dining room of their home.

They were looking into each other's eyes as they ate but weren't talking. Gazba reached out and placed his hand on Chloe's. She smiled a little sadly, put down her fork and with her other hand covered his.

Good, thought the witch. *The death of Sir Gracious is a blow that they will take a while to get over.*

Kraekhoull turned to the prophetess, Bitterness, who was suddenly and unsettlingly close, gazing into the crystal ball over her shoulder.

The demon watched the witch closely. His ugly self within the prophetess' body could sense Kraekhoull's jealousy and hatred for the apothecary and his wife.

'How can Bitterness be both male and female?' asked Shelley, interrupting Nanny as she was reading.

'That's just the way I wrote it. Sort of like weird fancy dress!' exclaimed Nanny with a laugh.

The prophetess turned and looked impassively into the witch's eyes and said, 'I can drive a wedge between them, gradual and filled with pain and distrust—everything to ruin his perfect family—if that is what you want.'

'Oh yes,' said the witch with a gleeful sigh. 'I do want that. I want his whole family to turn against him.'

'It will be my pleasure,' answered the demon who was in the form of the beautiful prophetess. With a beguiling but crooked smile, she disappeared in a puff of acrid smoke.

With that, Nanny closed the book, got up and put it on top of the old writing desk.

'Oh,' said Jace, 'we didn't get much story tonight.'

'I know, sorry,' said Nanny. 'I'm tired'.

'The witch is very bad?' said Shelley, disgruntled.

'Yes, I guess she is bad, but don't despair,' said Nanny, 'It's always the way with a story like this. There are baddies and goodies and others caught somewhere in-between.'

'I thought you said that God works things out for good,' said Shelley, sounding disappointed. 'The witch is definitely a baddie.'

'He does work things out, but it is still early days, and he doesn't always work things out the way we think He should. He can give you a sign to give you courage for the hard times ahead.'

'Such as, Nanny?' asked Shelley.

Nanny sighed and began. 'When your uncle and mum were only little, I got very depressed, and that went on for a long time. Then, one night, I had a dream, and I saw some writing that said, "One Corinthians, Chapter Four, Verses one and two", which I didn't know at all.'

'At Sunday school they told us that that's a scripture, right?' asked Jace.

'Correct,' said Nanny. 'In my dream, I saw that scripture, then I got up and got a drink of water and went to the toilet and went back to bed—and dreamt the same scripture again!'

'How weird,' said Jace. 'That's never happened to me.'

'In the morning, even though I was feeling pretty terrible, I thought I might as well look up the scripture because it might be important, but I didn't think it would. I got out my Bible and turned to One Corinthians Chapter Four Verses One and Two.'

'And?' asked Shelley.

'It said: *"Therefore, we are to be considered stewards of the deep mysteries of God. What is expected of such a one is obedience."'*

'What does all that mean, Nanny?' asked Shelley.

'At that time, it meant nothing to me—but now!' exclaimed Nanny, with excitement in her voice and radiance in her face, 'it has become like an anchor for my faith. It means to me that we are God's trusted servants, who interpret the deep mysteries of God and share them with the world, to bring Heaven to Earth.'

'To dream the same thing twice in the one night, *is* a bit strange but dreams *can* be strange,' acknowledged Shelley.

'*And* they can make a lot of sense,' said Nanny, 'don't be *too* surprised, if they happen to you. As far as I can remember, it says in the Bible: "Eye has not seen, ear has not heard, nor can the mind of man comprehend the things that God has prepared, for those who love Him and walk according to His ways."'

'In ordinary language, Nanny, *please*,' said Jace.

Nanny replied, with a little giggle at Jace's impertinence, 'Knowing what it's like in Heaven is not really possible, because it's even better than the best things you can imagine.'

'Okay,' said Jace, looking at Nanny with wonderment in his eyes. 'So, Superman could teach me to fly in Heaven, right?'

'I don't see why not,' said Nanny with a laugh.

Both kids were now very excited at the thought of flying and Shelley blurted out, 'I think I'll just ride a flying horse. Just like the one in your painting in the living room.'

'Why not indeed,' said Nanny. 'The Bible also says that in the last days—meaning the time since Jesus rose from the dead—young men will see visions and old men will dream dreams. That could be you kids.'

Nanny noticed that Jace was gazing at a painting on the bedroom wall that she had done as a young girl. 'Do you like that, Jace?' she asked.

'I love it,' said Jace. 'Especially the bird with the colourful tail.'

'You can have that painting,' said Nanny happily. 'That is the bird of Valouresse. It will appear when all things are made right in the story.'

'I can't wait for that to happen,' said Jace, before hugging Nanny and adding, 'thanks for the painting.'

'Sleep tight and don't let the bedbugs bite,' said Nanny, giving the kids one final hug and kiss.

'Night, Nanny,' they said almost together.

'Night sweethearts,' said Nanny fondly, and switched off the light.

Nanny closed the door behind her. She seemed to have accumulated a million dirty dishes, so she turned on the radio to give her energy, but only very quietly. She listened to a lot of awesome, beautiful music, switching stations to suit her mood—sometimes classical, sometimes hip hop, rap, techno, country, and even heavy rock—so much diversity and she could hear God's voice in it all. She was soaking up God's Kingdom, even as her hands soaked in the bubbly, detergent water of the kitchen sink.

Chapter 6

The next night the children were eager to hear more of the story. Jace even put his electronic gaming device under the bed.

'Keep reading Nanny,' said Jace eagerly. 'I want to find out more about the demon. I bet he has wings like a big bat.'

Nanny was always keen to hear what the children may have to add to the story—it was a bit of an adventure really, just seeing what would happen next. The bat wings were a good idea, and she would add it to the story.

'Very well, here we go,' said Nanny.

Gazba and Chloe continued to eat breakfast as the demon Bitterness invisibly arrived and folded his dark greasy bat-like wings to his body. He smiled as he felt the conversation become vitriolic with his mere presence.

'I will be travelling to La Fonteyn today,' said Gazba offhandedly as he picked up his mug and then put it down quickly, adding, 'It's gone cold.'

'Oh, I thought we were going to my parent's home,' Chloe said with an edge of anger in her voice. 'And' she added, 'you should have drunk it sooner.'

Bitterness saw his chance to begin driving the wedge between them and placed a picture in Chloe's mind of her husband in La Fonteyn watching the knights return with barely concealed disdain.

'You always seem to be in La Fonteyn, but you don't really like celebrations. Dare I say the knight's return, which you seemed to only just endure,' said Chloe, giving voice to her sudden bitter thoughts about her husband's lack of interest in the things she loved.

Gazba's thoughts were being poisoned by the demon as well.

Chloe is like a nagging harpy, with grappling hooks for feet, determined to bring me down. This is no way for love to be—and it's just not like her.

The demon smirked.

'I shall keep my sleeves rolled down,' said Gazba under his breath. 'Otherwise, you'll have a bite of my arm.'

The demon sneered and continued to hiss his evil insinuations into Gazba's mind.

'Pardon?' asked Chloe suspiciously.

'Is this constant jousting necessary?' retorted Gazba, who was now inexplicably irate and exasperated.

'Do you mean *us* fighting like knights jousting, constantly trying to unhorse each other?' asked Chloe, with eyes darkening.

'No, Chloe, it's not *just* us. The king wants to unhorse me as well—wants to knock me off my role as healer and make me an inventor of weapons. For Heaven's sake, I am an apothecary. I'm meant to help people, not hurt them.'

The demon smiled cunningly as he stored away this knowledge. Maybe he could turn both king and apothecary *against* each other, Kraekhoull would like that.

The demon was sewing a bitter seed between husband and wife, but the ground was not as ready for planting as he thought it was.

'There are things I would love to talk with you about, but you are seldom available. And, since the death of your beloved friend, it is probably not a good time to rake up old hurts,' said Chloe a little nervously.

'I have been occupied with my own problems, to your detriment, I'm afraid,' said Gazba placing his hand on hers.

'That is true,' said Chloe sadly.

'Please, tell me what I have done to hurt you,' replied Gazba.

Bitterness could feel Chloe's bottled anger, but he also sensed that she was trying to control it so as not to hurt her husband. Thus, he fuelled her with his poison, hoping she would lash out in fury.

She sniffed contemptuously, turning her face from his and then said, 'I only ever wanted to make you and Jasmine a happy, beautiful home, but all you seem to want to do is spend time with your apothecary colleagues—full of mead. You don't know what I need.'

'Very clever, Chloe,' said Gazba, trying to diffuse the situation. 'That rhymes.'

The demon growled. He was finding his task more difficult than he thought.

'Yes, mead and need, it does rhyme, like a bitter little poem.' Chloe gave a sad laugh and pulled her hand away. 'Did you know that when Jasmine was a baby and I told you of her success on her tiny commode, you weren't interested at all?'

'I'm sorry for that Chloe,' said Gazba, a little confused and lowering his eyes.

'Also,' said Chloe, 'did you ever consider my feelings of abandonment when I sat up waiting, dressed in my best clothing, hoping that you would join me for dinner? But by the time you *did* arrive home—so late—I had changed into my nightgown and was in bed. You often left so early in the morning, that you assumed I was never got dressed ever.'

The demon smiled and turned his attention to the husband.

Gazba felt his anger rising. 'That's ridiculous—'

'Look at Puppy,' said Jasmine running into the room holding her dog.

Bitterness's face suddenly contorted as the dog yapped. He gagged, recoiled, and fled, no longer able to do his wicked, twisted work. His black wings unfurled, and he flapped away as quickly as he could.

Jasmine held up Puppy. 'Look, isn't he cute,' she exclaimed as her small dog wriggled in her hands.

'Why was the demon afraid of the dog?' asked Shelley.

'It wasn't,' replied Nanny, in a mysterious voice.

'So, what was it afraid of?' asked Shelley.

Nanny just smiled at her and then Jace said, 'I know what you're going to say. You're going to say you'll tell us the reason later in the story.'

'That's right,' said Nanny with a laugh, as she patted him on the head.

'Could we get a puppy, Nanny?' pleaded Shelley.

'Oh, no,' said Nanny firmly. 'You already have Snowflake and that's enough animals I think.' Then to change the subject she said, 'We have to finish this story some time, so unless you want to talk about ways of improving it, we had better keep going.'

'Okay,' chimed the children in unison.

Now that the demon had fled, Gazba became mortified that Chloe had been so unhappy, but he said no more because of Jasmine's presence.

Both smiled at their daughter and then Jasmine passed Puppy to Chloe who stroked him absently, still thinking of the conversation with her husband.

'You're a funny little one,' she said as her mind was now focussed on the dog.

Gazba's exasperation and anger dissipated as he watched Chloe with the small animal.

Jasmine piped up, 'Yes, he's *so* cute.'

'Cute but not very pretty,' acknowledged Chloe, as she gave Puppy back to her daughter who then rubbed his soft little face against her own.

A bright shaft of light came through the window and lit up the break-fast table. Gazba reached for Chloe's hand and searched her face trying to meet her gaze. She allowed him to hold her hand and reticently looked up, relaxed, and smiled.

'Story's over for the night, kids,' said Nanny, closing the book.

'Oh Nanny, it would be great to have a new puppy,' said Jace. 'Better than a unicorn. You can't see them.'

'I *do* like puppies very much,' said Nanny, 'but your Mum could not cope with any more pets. And, by the way, I have seen my unicorn—in the spirit.'

'What do you mean by you've seen your unicorn in the spirit?' asked Jace.

'He is my friend who came to protect me when I was very frightened,' replied Nanny.

'Is he like this one?' asked Shelley, reaching up to touch the toy on the bedhead that had looked over her for many nights.

'Well, no,' said Nanny, shaking her head. 'He was actually a big, powerful horse with a horn.'

'Was he actually there?' asked Jace. 'You said you saw him in the spirit?'

'Well, it's like seeing something through a thin veil of fabric—a bit like that, like a picture in your mind. The Bible describes it by saying that you should not believe in things you can see, but in things you can't see.'

'So, what you're saying is that those visions are more real to you than things you can see with your real eyes?' asked Jace.

'Yes,' replied Nanny.

'Heaven and unicorns and Superman can be more real, even though we can't see them properly,' said Jace with a revelatory light shining in his eyes.

'Can't see them properly *yet*,' added Nanny with a dreamy smile.

'Like we can't see angels yet?' asked Shelley. 'You told us that sometimes people *do* see them and even talk to them, but they say in church that we shouldn't do that.'

'There are many beautiful, good angels here to help us, and as long as you're sure they come from the Lord, there is nothing wrong with talking to them. I have seen them in the spirit.'

'But how do you know if they come from Jesus?' asked Jace.

'I think you will just know and you will feel the love of God all around you,' continued Nanny.

'But what do angels have to do with unicorns?' asked Jace.

'There are other creatures in the Bible, like unicorns, that look very strange by our normal standards—but they are good,' said Nanny. 'And I want people to know about them, and that they are on our side. That's why I've included some of them in the book and why I have done paintings of them as well. Some of them fly around the throne of God.'

'They're not bad? asked Shelley.

'Not the ones I'm thinking of,' answered Nanny. 'They are the heroes in my story.'

'What are they?' asked Jace, with sudden interest.

'I won't spoil it, you'll find out all in good time,' said Nanny with a laugh. 'Night kids.'

'Oh Nanny, tell us now,' whined Jace.

'Nope,' said Nanny with a smile and then gave both kids a goodnight kiss.

Jace settled his head comfortably on the pillow.

'Do you think I could go to Heaven and see angels?' asked Jace, with wonder in his voice.

'Of course,' said Nanny.

'I want to see one tonight,' said Shelley impatiently.

'All in good time. You need to relax and trust the Lord for this to happen,' replied Nanny.

Nanny turned on the night light.

'I don't need that anymore. I have good night vision,' said Jace confidently.

'Okay,' said Nanny, flicking off the switch. 'I'll leave the toilet light on then, with the door open a little bit. Is that alright?'

'Yes. Thanks Nanny,' said Shelley settling down into her snuggly bedclothes.

Nanny loved having the children stay, but now that they were in bed, she could get on with one of her passions.

She walked down the hall to the family room where she got out her sewing basket and picked up a toy lion that she had found at the recycling centre.

'I think I will call you Judah,' said Nanny thoughtfully, examining the tatty toy.

'You must have had an interesting history,' she remarked as the toy gazed back at her with soulful glass eyes.

'Can never have enough toys,' she said to herself with a chuckle and started mending the lion.

Chapter 7

The next day the children walked their dog along a bush track accompanied by their mother, who led her handsome, bay gelding, Gwilliam. It had been a warm, ripe, and hazy day with the deciduous trees glowing russet red and gold. "A day made in Heaven", as Nanny Polly, the children's great grandmother, would probably say, and she was still alive now, despite being in her nineties.

They wound their way through the forest of English trees. Gwilliam enjoyed being with his humans and was not afraid to be out without the company of other horses and didn't even start when a rabbit dashed across his path.

Snowflake, the Pomeranian, happily tripped and trotted hurriedly with tail curled up behind her, filled with the joy of being with her people also. The walk lasted an hour, and it was a round trip back to the yards where Lillian unbridled and released Gwilliam back into his paddock.

He hung around for an apple and a rub behind his ears. In fact, he loved Lillian so much that he didn't want to leave to join the other horses but finally, when he did, he took off at a gallop, up and over the hill.

That night the children were pleasantly tired and snuggled up in bed with only their faces showing from under the colourful quilts and crocheted blankets piled high on their beds.

'Do you think Mummy loves Gwilliam more than us?' asked Shelley a little wistfully.

'Definitely not!' exclaimed Nanny putting her arm on her granddaughter's shoulder. 'She took today off work to be with you.'

'And to see Gwilliam,' said Shelley a little disapprovingly. 'She can't ride now that she is having the baby so soon. Mummy says that Gwilliam is more relaxed when he is next to us and Snowflake.'

'Horses like company, even a squeaking little Pomeranian,' acknowledged Nanny with a laugh. 'Strangely, it must be a calming noise for him.'

'Nanny!' said Shelley with a slightly reproachful glare but with the hint of a giggle.

It was cold, and Nanny pulled her dressing gown more tightly around herself and then opened her manuscript.

'On with the story, kids?' asked Nanny.

'We are up to the part where Gazba is going to take Jasmine to her grandparent's home to keep her safe,' said Jace somewhat smugly—because he knew he was usually right.

'Will it, Nanny—keep Jasmine safe?' asked Shelley.

'That's still to come,' said Nanny. 'We can't get ahead of ourselves.' And then she added rather slyly, 'But first we have to see what the villains are up to.'

Bitterness was now before the witch reporting on his activity in the Delafoi household.

'I cannot go back now,' said Bitterness, again in the guise of a woman.

'Why, what is it, my prophetess?' asked the witch, perplexed, and irritated.

Bitterness pulled back the hood of his cloak, brushed the golden hair back from his lovely face and glanced at Fear, who was still masquerading as the old man.

Fear read the look of trepidation on his fellow demon's face and said to Kraekhoull, 'There will be a better time to bring Gazba and his family down and I will help make sure of it.'

Kraekhoull was livid and said spluttering, '*What* is the problem? I want them destroyed. *Now*.'

Bitterness folded his hands and sat quietly, disconsolately. Then, after a while, he spoke again in the sweet voice of the prophetess. 'I had no power when she was near. I could do nothing. It will not be as easy as you think to put an end to that one.'

'What do you mean—that one?' the witch shrieked.

'The child, she is the Maid—the Maid of Valouresse,' said Bitterness quietly.

'What—that gidcy little goat of a girl I saw on the parapet of Lohnn's Castle? The Maid? I think not,' exclaimed the witch with scepticism.

Then, after a moment or two of silence, she spoke again, and her eyes became dark and thoughtful.

'If this Jasmine—Gazba's child—*is* the Maid of Valouresse,' began Kraekhoull, 'I must defeat her. How hard could it be? I cannot let a child stand in the way of my becoming queen of Valouresse.'

'So Kraekhoull, you have the incentive, but do you have the will to kill a child?' asked Bitterness, with his ugly mouth quivering with relish in his true demon form, which she couldn't see.

'I will need to think on it, my prophetess,' said the witch, distractedly contemplating the enormity of her future actions.

I have nothing against the child personally, she thought. *Should I kill an innocent to avenge my family? … I should … but …*

Kraekhoull's face wore a haunted expression. 'Can there be another way, without having to kill the child?' she asked the two demons with a tremble in her voice.

Then Fear—who was an expert in *that* emotion—saw it gripping the witch and moved towards his fellow demon and whispered in his ear. 'The witch is wavering. She is part of our plans and is needed by the Dark Prince. She must follow through.'

Fear spoke up. 'You will never be queen of Valouresse, never settle old scores, unless you do this.'

The witch's face was always white, but now it took on a greenish tinge and she looked mesmerised.

'I will do it then, for I must be queen!' she exclaimed as she emerged from her world of doubt. 'With your help my friends,' she added with resolve, addressing the old man and the young woman who now stood before her. 'I *will* be queen and *will* pay back a hundredfold those who did evil by me.'

Kraekhoull then turned away, absorbed in her thoughts. She didn't see the true forms of the two black demons sharing a conspiratorial glance.

This witch thought they answered to her, but they knew better. She may become a queen for a season—and her hatred spurred her to become this—but their Prince of Darkness would ultimately rule everything. Kraekhoull was nothing but a glorified pawn in his game.

Breakfast had started out pleasantly for Chloe and Gazba, but Bitterness had brought heavy clouds of acrimony between them. When the demon departed it was just like the sun coming out after a rainstorm and the couple were happy to be with each other once more.

Gazba rose and left the table to prepare for his trip into La Fonteyn to seek permission from King Lohnn for a leave of absence.

'Did you like seeing the knights at the celebration yesterday?' Chloe asked Jasmine.

'It was quite good,' answered Jasmine, 'and it *was* nice to see Velenia again.' Then she added with a sneer and a giggle, 'She's in love with Sir Vallio.'

Chloe gave a little smile as she knew her daughter's friend had had a number of crushes on several of the mighty armoured men. Then her own guilty conscience jolted her. *I made such a spectacle of myself. Gazba must have been hurt by my overt applause.*

'Can I take Puppy to Grandmother and Grandfather Pleasure's house?' asked Jasmine, unaware of her mother's shame-faced reflection. 'They don't like him much, but I do *so* want to take him.'

'I'm sure you can,' said Chloe, distractedly giving Puppy a scratch under the chin.

'Oh goody,' said Jasmine as she thought of the fun it would be to have her dog with her.

Later that day, Gazba visited King Lohnn in his snow-coloured marble castle. It was tall and linear, with a high-pointed arched entrance, flanked by ten fully armed soldiers on each side.

He passed the reins of his horse to one of the footmen, who led it away to the stables, then trotted up a dozen steps, nodding in recognition to the soldiers, who returned him a slight bow. He entered the huge, arched entrance and walked briskly along the rich plushness of the crimson carpet in the hallway.

As he passed courtiers and soldiers—who were stationed at intervals along the length of the hall—he noticed gilded bronze sculptures of jousting knights and other heroes. Adorning the walls were some rather overpowering painted scenes of battles and hunts, and the cornices of the room gleamed with leafy designs.

Gazba shook his head sadly at the king's overt love of luxury as he continued down the hall.

Finally, he reached the king's throne room in all its sumptuousness. The marble floor was now, after the ball, covered in thick rugs made of silk fibre with exotic design woven into them. The roof was high, and torches flickered on the walls in an almost mystical way, even in the daytime, when light streamed in through the large stained-glass windows.

'The King's Apothecary!' exclaimed the page.

Eyes of knights and ladies in waiting focussed on Gazba as he approached his king's throne, which was wreathed in scrolling gold ornamentation. He felt very self-conscious in his ordinary robes.

A huge gold, satin banner with a crimson image of a lion and unicorn on a gold background was spread out on the wall behind the king.

'Your Highness,' said Gazba, giving a courteous bow.

Jace suddenly piped up. 'Where is the queen?'

'I don't know, Jace, I hadn't thought about that,' replied Nanny. 'But now that you mention it, he does need an heir, so he needs a queen. I'll just make up a bit of stuff now, and thanks for being on the alert and making me put in more detail—it makes the story come alive.'

Nanny scribbled some notes down before speaking again.

'How about this, Jace,' began Nanny. 'King Lohnn's father died when Lohnn was fifteen. His father had a jousting accident and died. The queen regent pined to death shortly thereafter. Kraekhoull attacked the kingdom a little while later because she thought, as he was only quite young, that he would be a weak king. Defeat had been a shock to the witch, while it catapulted Lohnn's star into the ascendant. Now, he is in his thirties and his advisors are pressuring him to take a wife. Gazba may not understand this, but there are good reasons for King Lohnn to take such an interest in jousting tournaments, because it allows him to go out into the world to seek out a suitable queen.'

When she had finished speaking, Nanny asked, 'Is that enough background detail for you, darling?'

'Yes, that's good now,' said Jace sagely nodding his head.

'It's really hard being a writer, Nanny, isn't it?' said Shelley. 'There is so much extra detail that needs to go in.'

'So true,' replied Nanny, a little wearily. 'Probably too much. Anyway, back to the story.'

'Gazba,' said the king with a perfunctory nod. 'I have just heard the news of Sir Gracious.'

'We shall not see the like of him again,' said Gazba, wiping a tear from the corner of his eye. 'Sir Gracious the Good was a brave and beloved friend.'

'Gallant and he were the champions,' replied the king, 'but now that Gallant is injured, I shall have to step into the breech and do more jousting,' He sounded slightly irritated.

The young King Lohnn was dressed in great finery. Peacock feathers crossed his rich, burgundy-coloured doublet. The green eyes of the feathers arched over each of his shoulders. A gold chain circled his waist, and his leggings were the finest purple velvet.

Seated on the throne he started tapping his foot, which made Gazba notice his soft red leather-pointed boots.

'I will attend Sir Gracious' funeral of course,' said the king.

'As will I,' replied Gazba with voice lowered.

'Your Majesty, I have actually come to ask for release from my duties as Royal Apothecary, to go on a mission to identify possible threats to your kingdom. I fear an evil force will try to destroy your lands.'

'Ah, not another one,' sighed King Lohnn. 'There are always threats to a country or city. Where did you hear this rumour?'

Gazba told the king about his meeting with Chraston.

'You must also be on guard, Sire,' said Gazba. 'And I question whether you should be going to a tournament at a time like this.'

'Gazba,' began King Lohnn, 'life cannot stop because of a threat which may or may not eventuate. And in any case, I have a strong, well-trained army that can protect the city,' added the king, rather petulantly.

Gazba continued. 'I will be taking my wife and daughter to Lord Pleasure's estate for their protection and my attempts at alchemy will have to wait—if that is acceptable to you, my king.'

King Lohnn's expression now seemed graver as he took the threat more seriously.

'Yes, you may go, and I will send an escort for your family, of course. Do you need men for this quest of yours?'

'Thank you, Sire,' said Gazba, lowering his voice. 'But I wish to travel alone after I deliver my family to safety. I must go secretly to discover the nature of this threat and I will send a pigeon if I need reinforcements.'

'That is good,' replied the king in little more than a whisper. 'Feel free to get reinforcements. I myself will only be gone for a short while.'

'So, you are going to the tournament?' asked Gazba, somewhat dismayed. 'Chraston the unicorn saved you and your throne just fifteen years ago, surely you should take notice of his warning. Chraston says the threat to Valouresse is imminent. Please, Sire, forget the competition this once and attend to the safety of this land and its people.'

'Despite you continually bringing her up, the witch is no longer a threat—she and her army were vanquished years ago,' said King Lohnn deprecatingly.

'I did not mention the witch, my lord. So why do you think she is not a problem?' said Gazba, curious.

The king glared at Gazba and went into somewhat of a tirade.

'You always seem to be talking about Kraekhoull. And yes, her body was never found, but it has been fifteen years without any sign of her.'

The king then settled down again and went on to say, 'This is a crucial competition that I must attend. I am meeting a princess that I wish to marry, and I must prove myself worthy of her hand. My new champion, Sir Otto the Overcomer, and myself will perform with excellence to show her parents that we of Valouresse are a mighty people—warriors at heart.'

'As you wish, my king,' said Gazba, trying to disguise his disappointment. 'I will take my leave now and I wish you well.'

'Godspeed, Gazba,' said the king. He then inspected the new, silky heraldic pennant that had just been presented to him by one of his courtiers for his approval.

Gazba had already turned and as he walked down the hall, he punched his arm down in frustration. Angry with his recalcitrant king, he left the castle feeling that his king was more interested in the up-and-coming tournament and had not realised the gravity of the situation.

'That king is stupid,' said Jace. 'He's just like a boy I know at school, who only cares about getting the cool kids to be on his team when we play handball.'

'So, you think the king is selfish for going jousting?' asked Nanny.

'Yes, he should look after his people,' replied Jace, a little heatedly, 'and not be so recalcitrant!' he exclaimed with a laugh.

'You're the opposite of that Jace, and that's a good thing,' said Nanny. 'I remember you last year at the swimming carnival with your friend—the skinny little boy with pale skin and freckles.'

'Nanny, do we have to talk about that again?' said Jace with slight annoyance.

'I like to,' said Nanny. 'That little boy had to get his rash top off but didn't have the strength to get it off and the bus was going in a few minutes.'

'Yeah, and I came second in one of the races, the width of the pool,' said Jace trying to change the subject.

'That's right, that was a fantastic effort,' agreed Nanny. 'But do you remember the boy looked at you so helplessly and *you* knew just what to do.'

'Oh Nanny, you always talk about this. It's so embarrassing,' said Jace.

But Nanny continued, saying, 'He put up his arms and you peeled off his rash top for him. It was so beautiful that it made me cry. I don't know why, but it just did. It still does when I think about it.'

'Why would you cry about somebody taking a rash top off someone, Nanny?' asked Jace, perplexed at what was, to him, Nanny's silly sentimentality.

'I don't know,' answered Nanny. 'Maybe it's because you took the time to help someone who couldn't help himself. You came to his rescue. He just didn't have the strength. You are just a kind boy which is more important than all the fame and fortune in the world. Maybe King Lohnn could take a leaf from your book.'

'My book?' asked Jace confused.

'It's a saying. It means for someone to copy something good from *your* life.'

'Oh,' said Jace, snuggling his head in his pillow with a proud little smile on his face.

'I think Gazba is silly to go on the quest alone,' interjected Shelley. 'Even if it is to find things out in secret.'

'Don't worry,' replied Nanny. 'He *will* get help—he won't be on his own the whole time.'

'That's good,' said Shelley, approvingly.

'Shall we get back to the story then?' asked Nanny.

Once outside the castle, Gazba was presented with his mare by the footman. He mounted her and trotted off to his dispensary where he tied Helga to a hitching post and carried in the saddlebags, which he had brought from home.

His assistant, Joachim, was in the dispensary when Gazba told him of the death of Sir Gracious and the encounter with Chraston.

'So, you think the witch is behind this?' Joachim was gravely attentive.

'I think it is likely,' replied Gazba. 'And I need to find Epiron Rock,' he added.

'Oh yes, it is somewhere in the mountains to the northwest of La Fonteyn. I remember seeing it on a map in the library. I'll go and look for it now,' he said.

While Joachim was away, Gazba placed the saddlebags on the bench and started to gather together some of the things he would need. Joachim came back some time later waving a scroll canister excitedly, saying, 'I've found it.'

He removed a map from the canister, placed it on the table and unrolled it carefully.

'There it is,' he said pointing. 'Epiron Rock. It's above a deep mountain valley off the road, but hidden by different, severe land formations.'

'Marvellous!' said Gazba studying the map. He then rolled it back up and put it in its canister. 'I trust you to manage everything while I'm away.'

'So, you are going to Epiron Rock?' asked Joachim.

'Yes, I have just spoken with the king, and he has given me leave to go on this quest. I believe all of Valouresse is in danger, and I am to meet Chraston at Epiron Rock as part of a prophecy,' replied Gazba.

'Never fear, sir,' said Joachim. 'I shall be here to deal with all eventualities: patients, mixing, dispensing, and all the rest. Don't you worry about a thing.'

'Good man. I knew I could rely on you,' said Gazba, patting his assistant on the shoulder. 'Now, I will need to take some of my most powerful alchemical supplies to fight off any enemies and I will have to take medicine as well. Can you and I prepare them now, as I want to leave as soon possible?'

'Of course,' said Joachim, nodding and peering attentively at Gazba through his glasses.

'You know all about my patients,' said Gazba as they began gathering the supplies.

'Oh yes, I do, the Dubbleneks and Bardozers of the world are irritating—the rest are easy,' said Joachim with a chuckle.

Some of the mixtures could be combustible, so Gazba packed them meticulously into his saddlebags. He would use them should he need to defend himself. He also added ointments for injuries to horse or man and a sewing kit for tents and clothing, knowing full well that it could also be used on torn flesh as well.

It was now the afternoon and Gazba attended the funeral of his friend Sir Gracious, as did many others who had loved the knight well. King Lohnn stood at the graveside looking pensive. Sir Gracious had given his chateau and lands to his servants and peasants—something unheard of in those times. It showed what a humble and altruistic kind man he was.

Gazba returned to the dispensary. Once his precious cargo was in the saddlebags on the mare, Joachim held the bit while Gazba gathered the reins and swung up easily onto the horse.

'Farewell and Godspeed, Gazba,' said Joachim.

'Thank you and good luck with Baron Bardozer,' said Gazba, winking at Joachim before urging his horse into a brisk walk.

Joachim went back into the dispensary and continued working. There would be clients coming soon, they always did!

Gazba trotted into the courtyard of his estate house and saw his wife and daughter talking with Juniper, the young overseer. He was a good-looking northerner with blonde hair and an air of quiet authority mixed with gentleness. He had wisdom and skills well beyond his seventeen years.

Gazba dismounted, removed the saddlebags, and passed his horse over to the ostler—a sturdy, elderly gentleman known as Beacon—who led her away to the stables.

'Can I take that for you sir?' asked a manservant stepping forward.

'Yes, thank you. Be very careful. It contains volatile chemicals. Take them to my workroom please.'

'Certainly, sir,' answered the man, looking at the saddlebags as if they might explode at a mere touch.

Smiling at the man's trepidation, Gazba walked over to Chloe and Jasmine who had been back for a while after a ramble through the fields. Jasmine's attention was completely absorbed by something she held in her hand.

'You are back, sir,' said Juniper.

'That I am,' said Gazba, acknowledging him and then, intrigued, turned to Jasmine, and asked, 'What have we here?'

Jasmine opened an egg covered in gold decoration, revealing a small blue bird which began making a twittering noise and flapped its wings.

'Ah, an automaton,' remarked Gazba with fascination.

'Amazing things,' said Juniper who had seen it do its little routine several times already.

The bird finished its performance and Jasmine closed the egg and smiled winsomely at Juniper.

'It has provided her with many moments of entertainment, and you know how quickly she becomes bored,' said Chloe laughingly, glancing both to Juniper and then to Gazba.

'Oh Mummy,' said Jasmine with a little frown. 'You make me sound like a child.'

Chloe smiled at her daughter and then said, 'If you gentlemen would excuse us, I think we ladies should freshen up before dinner and certainly change our shoes.' she said with a laugh as she turned her foot to show the muddied sole of her shoe. She then gave her leave and walked towards the house with her arm around her daughter's shoulder.

Jasmine gave Juniper a cheeky backward glance—which did not go unnoticed by her father.

Juniper smiled back and shook his head ruefully. However, before he could say anything, he was interrupted by the loud, hoarse voice of his ostler shouting from the stables. 'I'll give Helga a warm bran mash tonight, but I've just got to do something for my missus at the moment.'

'Thank you, Beacon,' replied Juniper.

Gazba put his hand on Juniper's shoulder and asked, 'Can we talk? Let's go into the stables where it's private.'

'Yes, of course, my lord,' replied Juniper. 'I actually wanted to talk to you about the small wood at the top corner of the estate.'

'What about it?' asked Gazba.

'One of my workers saw a wolf there today,' replied Juniper.

'A wolf? That's strange,' said Gazba. 'They normally don't come this close to the farm until winter.'

'The white dogs should keep them at bay,' said Juniper. 'But I am wondering if we should remove that copse of trees.'

'I am loth to tear down the trees because they are such a good wind-break,' said Gazba. 'But a shepherd could stay in the field from now on, as you see fit.'

The young overseer nodded in agreement.

Both men entered the stables and Gazba lowered his voice and looked around to make sure they could not be overheard. Even though he believed his servants to be trustworthy, the information he was about to give Juniper was too great a secret for everyone's ears.

'I haven't had the chance to tell you until now,' said Gazba. 'But on my way back from Sir Gracious' home—after the poor man died—I saw Chraston.'

'My lord!' exclaimed Juniper. 'You met the great unicorn again?' Then he spoke more quietly, after seeing Gazba raise his forefinger to his lips. 'I've only ever seen the lion and the unicorn on banners and flags, but you actually saw him in the flesh?' he added in awe.

'Yes, it was him. One and the same,' answered Gazba. 'He showed me a vision *and* has given me a task. The vision was one of a darkness that stalks my daughter, and my task is once more to protect Valouresse.'

Juniper shook his head. 'Will Jasmine be safe?' he asked quickly.

'I believe so. Jesus, the Great King, will protect her,' replied Gazba.

'Have you seen *Him*?' asked Juniper.

'No, I haven't, but I trust the messenger,' replied Gazba.

'And what of the task, my lord?' asked Juniper.

'I am to protect the Maid of Valouresse—whoever she may be—and must meet the unicorn at a place called Epiron Rock,' said Gazba. 'I have spoken to King Lohnn, and he has given me a release from my duties to go on this …'

'Quest, my lord? To vanquish evil?' asked Juniper eagerly.

'It appears so,' replied Gazba, somewhat reticently.

Juniper's face shone with excitement, and he asked, 'How can I help?'

'I will need you to manage my estate and defend it,' said Gazba.

'Yes, I know battle technique and strategy learnt from my father,' said Juniper. 'I have trained mainly with a wooden sword, but the enemy won't get a splinter for his trouble,' said Juniper with a laugh, adding, 'I *did* graduate to cold, hard steel.'

'Yes, that I know full well, jester Juniper,' said Gazba, giving him a wry smile.

Juniper shrugged and grinned, saying, 'I'm not much of a jester—but just watch my moves. Father taught me well. I may be an overseer, but I am an overseer who can fight.' He then pretended to parry and thrust with an imaginary sword.

'I'm sure you could outfight me anytime,' replied Gazba.

Then, becoming serious once more, Gazba said, 'My family and I will travel to Lord Pleasure's castle tomorrow. Jasmine will be safe there. You can start to prepare for their departure, and for myself—a full camping kit—winter's at the door.'

'Of course, my lord' said Juniper and then asked, 'which horses will you take?'

'Helga, of course and Bella as a pack horse,' answered Gazba.

'A good choice—sure footed and sensible horses,' said Juniper.

'Anyway,' said Gazba, 'we can talk more tomorrow, but now I look forward to the evening meal—beef burgundy tonight.'

'Oh yes,' replied Juniper eagerly.

Both men then left the stables and Gazba headed into the house towards the dining room while Juniper headed to the kitchen, where the servants ate.

Neither realised that their secret discussion had been overheard.

Inside one of the stable stalls, close enough to where Juniper and Gazba had been speaking, was Jerkel, Juniper's cousin. He was lying up against one of the walls and had woken from a nap and had heard some of the whispered conversation. He sneered and thought, *this could be useful to bring down my privileged cousin who hobnobs it with the master.*

Jerkel smiled slyly and then stood, stretched his back, and went off to dinner.

In her room, before the evening meal, Chloe had been preparing for the stay at her parent's home.

'Will you take this dress, marm?' asked Misk. She was holding up a sparkling, shell-pink creation. 'It is ever so pretty, and it would be good to wear to a ball while you are away.'

'I'm not planning to go to any balls, but you may be right. Pack it please,' said Chloe in a dull, disinterested tone as she sat on the bed and stared into space.

'Don't you think it would be fun?' asked Misk.

'Misk,' said Chloe, 'I haven't told anyone this, but my husband is going on a journey and a dangerous one, for an unknown time, and I don't even know if he *will* return. I am certainly not interested in socialising at the king's court.'

Misk stopped folding the clothes and said, 'Oh, of course you wouldn't be.'

'I may have spoken out of turn, but it is a relief to tell someone, 'replied Chloe in a tired voice and then she added, 'I'm glad you will be coming with me—and, by the way, could you pack my riding habit in case I get the chance to ride, although I probably won't.'

Chloe started to cry, and Misk sat beside her on the bed and held her hand.

'I am sure things will work out for the best,' said Misk.

Chloe stared blankly at the pattern of the quilt on the bed then added, with forced brightness, 'I must go to dinner now—that's something I always look forward to. Mrs Beacon can bring one back to life with her delightful food.' She then laughed and wiped her eyes.

Misk tilted her lovely head and gazed at Chloe with her fine, oriental eyes and added softly, 'Your secret is safe with me, my lady.'

'Thank you, my Misk,' said Chloe, giving her servant a hug.

Lining the dining room walls were chiffoniers of rich, mahogany-red, with swirling carved designs on the headboards. Upon them were silver and bronze statues of deer and other animals, as well as pottery vases covered in ornate flower patterns. Chloe walked into the dining room as a shaft of evening light from the windows lit the table.

Gazba sat at the head and Jasmine, halfway along the length of the table, looked quite small. The white linen cloth was covered with an array of silver goblets, wine and water carafes, a breadbasket, cutlery, and an arrangement of pink roses in a vase.

One of the male servants helped seat Chloe, at the opposite end of the table from Gazba.

Another of the servants, Gillia, poured water for them. She was tall and slim, with a dusky complexion and was dressed in a blue skirt and shirred white blouse. She then served them bread and, later, delicious beef burgundy on warmed plates.

When all was ready for their meal, Gazba bowed his head and said grace: 'Lord God, bless us all and this food. May our lives be filled with Your goodness in the coming days.'

Gazba picked up his utensils and said to Chloe, 'This may be the last dinner we eat together for a while, darling. King Lohnn has given me release from my duties here in La Fonteyn, so that I may go on an important journey.'

He then spooned in a mouthful of the delicious stew, while watching Chloe's face for any sign of approval or disapproval at what he had just said.

Chloe just nodded and lowered her eyes.

'Where are you going, Daddy?' asked Jasmine with wanderlust in her eyes and a forkful of food raised but suddenly forgotten. 'Into the wilds?'

'I am going on a mission for Valouresse, and yes, into the wild country.'

'Can I come, please?' pleaded Jasmine.

'No, Jasmine,' answered Gazba firmly. 'It is not the place for a little girl.'

'But Daddy,' said Jasmine, 'How can you call me a little girl when I can hunt and ride and I'm good at archery. Don't you remember, we used to all go, Mummy too.'

'That is not the point, my darling. I could never risk your safety.' Gazba stood firm and exchanged glances with Chloe who nodded in agreement.

'Dearest,' said Chloe to Jasmine, 'you must come with me and stay with Nan and Pop Pleasure. I would be very lonely there without you.'

'But you have Misk, Mummy—and Daddy *needs* me,' whined Jasmine.

'I'm sure Daddy will have someone to go with him,' said Chloe.

Gazba exchanged a barely perceptible frown with Chloe, and she said no more. Gazba would be going on his own, but this knowledge was not for Jasmine, as he knew this would fuel her desire to keep him company on the journey.

Chloe then quickly changed the subject. 'Misk is packing all we will need for our stay.'

'Good,' said Gazba, 'We shall be away just after midday tomorrow.'

'Oh, please Daddy, can I go with you?' Jasmine pleaded again.

'No Jasmine,' replied Gazba firmly. 'I have said "no", and we will talk no more about it.'

Jasmine's eyes lowered and she slowly began eating her dinner.

In the silence that followed, Chloe's eyes roamed the large hall, savouring every beautiful ornament, rich embroidery, and rug which she had lovingly chosen for her home. She was going to hate leaving it and would especially miss the stained-glass windows she liked looking through, to the partially paved and grassed courtyard, where a fountain played night and day. It had been her private nook and comfort, and although her parents had a similar one, she did not find it as pretty or well planted as her own.

Jasmine went off to bed shortly after dinner and Gazba followed her, as he knew she was upset.

'It will be fun at Nan and Pop Pleasure's,' he said, holding his daughter's hand as she lay in her bed.

'But I want an adventure,' said Jasmine unhappily.

'Remember that you will have Puppy with you,' said Chloe, who was also with them.

'I suppose *that* will be fun,' acknowledged Jasmine reticently.

'Anyway, it will be a big day tomorrow so it's time to sleep now,' said Gazba, giving his daughter a goodnight kiss. Chloe gave her a kiss as well. Then both parents went to the drawing room, where they sat by the fire discussing the incredible events of the past few days.

Nanny looked up from reading to see Jace and Shelley sleeping soundly. They had had a long day, so it was hardly surprising. She smiled and wondered how much they had missed but decided that they probably hadn't lost track of the main story and what she had just read may not have interested them anyway.

With a quiet yawn of her own, Nanny got to her feet, put the manuscript away and went to her cosy bed.

Chapter 8

The next morning, Nanny woke the children early and said excitedly, 'Come and see this.'

Bleary-eyed, the children followed Nanny into the laundry where they saw the budgie, Opal, and Rosy, the new Bourke's parrot, perched side by side in the cage.

'Your prayers have helped I'm sure,' said Nanny who was much relieved. 'They are having an interspecies friendship.'

'Thank goodness,' said Shelley, 'I'm so glad they aren't fighting. They're so cute together.'

'Hey Nanny,' said Jace. 'Where are we up to in the story? I fell asleep.'

Nanny looked out the laundry window and saw it was a cold, bleak day and ominously grey clouds were speeding in from the west. 'Hey kids, do you want breakfast in bed?' she suggested, 'I'll read some more story, if you like?'

Once the children were tucked up in bed and eating their breakfast of eggs and bacon on sourdough toast, Nanny opened the book.

'You didn't miss much,' Nanny said, flicking through the last couple of pages, 'and it was pretty boring anyway, so I'll just go on with the next bit.'

'But first, do you remember when you were little, and you messed up all of the clothes I had folded and put on the spare bed at your mum's house?'

'Yes, I remember,' said Shelley with a giggle. 'You put us in the room for time out.'

'And as I walked past the room, I heard you say, 'Let's kill Nanny.'

All three laughed uproariously. It was such a funny thing.

Then Nanny continued reading.

Early the next afternoon the courtyard was a hive of activity as trunks full of items for the stay at Lord and Lady Pleasure's castle were secured onto the carriage. While all this was going on, Juniper, Beacon and Gazba were once more in the stables.

'Bella is a steady sort, and a shifting load won't worry her as it would some other horses,' commented Beacon, indicating the brown mare who was having the saddlebags carefully attached to her saddlery by the same nervous servant who had stored them for Gazba the day before.

'That's good to know,' replied Gazba, still watching the servant intently. 'It's good to have you here Beacon—you know your stuff.'

'Thank you, my lord,' replied Beacon with a proud smile, as he stroked the horse's neck and gave her a handful of hay.

The bay mare's black nose quivered as her lips swivelled around and grasped a long stem and began moving it steadily into her mouth.

Gazba double-checked the saddlebags and then, turning to Juniper, placed his hand on the young man's shoulder and said, 'I entrust this estate to you, lad. I have been impressed by the way you've handled yourself and I can think of no better person to care for my livestock, or my servants.'

Suddenly there was a shriek and Gazba turned to see the stable hand who had been cleaning Bella's stall, flat on his back in the soiled straw.

The man shot a murderous scowl at the other stable hands who had roared with laughter.

Beacon commented to Gazba, 'that Jerkel is probably hung over again.'

Juniper leapt forward and grasped Jerkel's filthy hand and pulled him to his feet.

'Bad luck, cousin,' said Juniper.

'Hmphh,' replied Jerkel, recoiling from him and resuming his work after first dusting off some straw.

'I didn't know you two were cousins,' said Gazba.

'Yes, well, we are,' said Juniper cheerily.

'Interesting,' said Gazba, noticing Jerkel's sullen expression, which was so different to Juniper's sunny countenance.

Meanwhile, in the busy courtyard, Jasmine was talking to her friend, Ellis, a young servant girl of her own age. Ellis was thin and pale with mousy brown hair and freckles. She was dressed in a suitably neat but plain outfit, as befitted her station as a servant.

'My mother said I don't have to do school if I don't want to, Ellis, which means I can do whatever I like. This will be so exciting,' said Jasmine, who was holding and stroking her hairless puppy.

'Oh, you're so lucky,' said Ellis a little sceptically.

'I think so,' said Jasmine and then in a whisper, she asked, 'Have you packed my things?'

'Yes,' said Ellis. 'It's there,' she said pointing to a haversack amongst the other items in the back of the carriage storage area. 'I put a lamp in as well, and some flints, and some of my old clothes that you may need for a disguise,' she added secretively.

'Good thinking Ellis,' said Jasmine and then she asked, 'Did you pack a riding pad and bridle?'

'Yes,' Ellis replied. 'Beacon said I could have both in case I want to ride a pony to market.'

'Ideal!' exclaimed Jasmine. 'They are so small and easy to carry. But will you get into trouble if he discovers it is gone?'

'I don't think so, there are others of them in the stables and I don't think he will notice,' answered Ellis.

'If I can catch my pony and saddle her up, I can ride with father into the wilds,' said Jasmine.

'Will he let you?' asked Ellis. Her eyes showed some doubt, but she believed practically anything that her intrepid friend told her.

'I hope so, but I just think he will need me,' answered Jasmine, speaking softly and seriously. Suddenly she added, 'Look, here comes Juniper. Keep talking and look natural.'

The girls chatted on with even more animation as Juniper approached. He was dressed in fawn breeches with black boots, a woollen overshirt tied at the waist with a leather belt, with a jerkin over the top of this.

Jasmine launched into conversation with Juniper. 'Will you look after my rabbits and give them carrots?' she asked.

'Of course, I will. Don't you worry about them,' Juniper replied amused. 'And I'll make sure they don't get into Mrs Beacon's garden like they did last week.'

Abruptly changing the subject, Jasmine asked, 'Do you want to say goodbye to Puppy?'

She held the dog's snout up close to Juniper's face, who observed its small, pointed muzzle at close range. It was about the size of a large rabbit and practically hairless, with dark patches on its pink skin.

'A fine dog,' said Juniper, with a slight grimace that Jasmine interpreted as a smile of admiration. 'I must get on with my work now. Have an enjoyable stay at your grandparent's home and I will see you back here in due course.'

'Thank you, Juniper, I will see you soon I hope,' she said quickly squeezing his hand.

He smiled back at her, and a flush of colour came to his cheeks. Embarrassed, he turned to leave and saw Ellis looking at him.

'Ellis,' he said, acknowledging the servant girl's presence.

Ellis curtsied back and gave him a knowing smile. She could see a definite attraction between the young overseer and her mistress.

With that, he turned and hurried off to the stables to get some more rope for securing the luggage.

'I must go and help with the laundry now,' Ellis said reluctantly. 'I will miss you, dear Jasmine.'

'As I will you, my Ellis,' replied Jasmine, giving her a little kiss on the cheek.

Jasmine sadly watched her friend leave and wished she could take her with her.

Beacon noticed Juniper standing with the extra rope for the carriage looped in his hands staring rather soulfully in Jasmine's direction.

'Come on lad, she has to go,' he said. Then, with a bit of a tease in his voice, he added, 'You look like a devoted puppy, and I know you're going to miss her.'

'That I will,' acknowledged Juniper.

Then, in a kinder tone, Beacon said, 'you would probably give your life to protect her, wouldn't you?'

'That I would indeed,' answered Juniper quietly.

Leaving the stable he then headed back towards the carriage.

'That may be enough for now', said Nanny. 'You can stay in bed and read or draw on your little computer, Shelley. And Jace, you can play games. Get up when you feel like it. It's a cold old day outside.'

Shelley wanted to talk about the story.

'I really like the way Ellis is Jasmine's special friend, like my friend Estée at school.'

'You two do a lot together, don't you?' said Nanny. 'Like the anime characters you both draw.'

'We're going to have an animation company when we grow up,' said Shelley.

'A lot of your anime stories are about boy and girl relationships and romance, aren't they?' asked Nanny.

'I guess so,' said Shelley shyly.

'Well, I think they are just so lovely and sweet, and they remind me of Jasmine and Juniper,' said Nanny.

'In a way … but my animes are set in modern times,' acknowledged Shelley thoughtfully.

'That doesn't matter. It is still about a boy and a girl,' said Nanny.

'Why would a seventeen-year-old have romantic feelings for Jasmine? She's only thirteen,' said Shelley, with a frown.

'In those days, a man was considered an adult at seventeen and that's Juniper's age. And girls used to often get married at thirteen. It's all a bit different now-a-days,' said Nanny.

'Oh, my gosh, that's *my* age.' said Shelley, looking shocked.

'There's a boy at school who really likes Shelley, maybe they should get married,' interjected Jace with a giggle.

Shelley scowled at Jace.

'Is there?' asked Nanny, raising her eyebrows and smiling.

Shelley hesitated and then said shyly, 'Yep, he really likes me. He asked me out, but I told him I just wanted to be friends.'

'That's probably a wise decision, darling,' said Nanny, smiling fondly at her granddaughter.

'I told him I'm not ready to go out,' replied Shelley.

'Well, that shows foresight,' said Nanny.

'For-what?' asked Shelley.

'Foresight. It means you have wisdom well beyond your years,' said Nanny.

'What do you mean, Nanny?' asked Shelley, once again.

'Just be proud you aren't rushing into anything yet. You still have to find—the one,' said Nanny mysteriously.

'Who is the one?' asked Shelley.

'The one who is meant for you and you for them,' answered Nanny.

'Oh,' said Shelley. 'And how will that happen?'

'I don't know,' answered Nanny. 'But these things have a way of happening. Shall I read some more to you now on this cold, wintry day?'

'I think I'll just draw,' said Shelley.

'And I'll do some gaming,' said Jace.

'Have fun kids,' said Nanny, turning to walk out of the room to go about her "house-wifely duties".

'While I think of it, Jace, do you need your uniform washed before you go back to school?' asked Nanny.

'Yes, thanks Nanny,' replied Jace.

'Your last basketball game was great to watch—your five goals and your team winning forty to nine.'

'It was a flogging,' said Jace, chuckling.

'You heard that from my mum, Nanny Dora, didn't you?' said Nanny.

'Yep,' answered Jace with a big smile. 'And she asked me three times how many goals I got.'

'She *is* eighty-seven. Her memory isn't too good,' said Nanny with a giggle.

'Will you be like that at eighty-seven?' asked Jace.

'That remains to be seen,' said Nanny, as she tousled his hair.

Chapter 9

The next day was full of excitement. Lilian rang the children in the morning to tell them that her baby was due in about a week or two. She came and took the children out to lunch to celebrate with take away food—hamburgers, chips, and milkshakes. She knew it was important to cheer Shelley up, who still felt a little nervous about the prospect of a new sibling.

That evening, when Nanny settled down to tell the story once more, Shelley seemed very subdued and Nanny asked her, 'why so quiet, darling?'

'Oh, it's nothing,' she replied.

'Are you sure?' asked Nanny.

'I'm not so happy at school and none of my friends' mothers are having babies,' she added with a little sob.

Nanny held Shelley close and stroked her forehead.

'Do you want to hear some story? The mother and daughter in the story are going through a hard time too.'

'Yes,' replied Shelley, with a sniff. 'I want to hear that.'

Jace suddenly appeared in the bedroom after having to clean his teeth again because he'd had a glass of milk and a snack.

'Let's read the story, Nanny,' he said enthusiastically as he leapt into bed and pulled the covers up to his neck, snuggling in.

Juniper looped the last rope through itself, securing the luggage on the carriage. All was ready for the journey to the Pleasure's castle.

Gazba and Chloe said their goodbyes to the servants, including Ellis, who all stood in a row in the courtyard.

'Keep that Beacon in line,' Gazba said to Juniper with a laugh.

'More likely I'll keep the youngster in line,' said Beacon with a guffaw.

After the men had had their joke, Chloe took his hand and asked Gazba, 'can we speak in the garden for a moment?'

Gazba nodded and indicated the way to a nearby walled garden.

Once away from the view of others, she said, 'I long for your companionship. I want to go with you.'

Gazba gazed back sympathetically and said gently, 'You cannot come with me. There will be time enough for us when I get back from my mission.'

'Don't say something you don't mean,' said Chloe, pulling away. 'Do you think all I want is the life of a noblewoman—just luxury and frippery? I know you probably think me selfish and stupid—and I am desperately worried about Jasmine—but there is something else that worries me.'

'Yes Chloe, what is that?' he asked patiently and tenderly.

Chloe spoke hesitantly and sadly. 'I have seen a painting which foretells the prophecy of the Maid of Valouresse.'

'Yes, go on,' encouraged Gazba.

'She is so brave, the Maid, riding a charger and with a sword in her hand. She is bold and strong, everything I no longer am.'

Gazba took her face in his hands and said, 'I remember your skills and your courage, and I am relying on them to protect Jasmine.'

Chloe shook her head and said, 'It's not that. When you meet the Maid, I fear that you may fall in love with her, Gazba. You and I have been having arguments for a while and I *fear* you may find someone else to love.'

Her eyes were like dark pools of water shimmering with tears.

'I'm not going to fall in love, nor lose my love for you,' he said, shaking his head, giving a little laugh, and smiling at his wife. 'I'm going off to save the land.'

Chloe's mind was instantly set at ease, and she gave a faint smile at the thought of his great mission and the relative silliness of her own insecurity.

He stroked her hair and gazed towards the mountains. The blue hills beckoned, and he remembered a line from a favourite scripture. Pulling her close, he said, '"I look to the hills from whence comes my salvation." and then he added after a moment, 'All will be well my dear.'

'I remember that line and I will read that scripture to comfort me while you are away,' said Chloe.

Together they walked hand in hand from the garden back to the courtyard and Gazba helped Chloe to climb into the carriage. She gave him a wistful smile as she settled onto her seat opposite Misk, whose back was to the driver.

The door was still open for Jasmine, who stopped outside the carriage and spoke to her father.

'Daddy, I want to go with you. I can cook and ride and start a fire. I can cook flour cakes,' she said plaintively.

'All good things, Jasmine,' Gazba told her. 'But I've told you that it is too dangerous for you to come. Stay with your mother. I am sure she would like your company.'

'But you are going on an adventure and Mummy could come too!' exclaimed Jasmine excitedly.

'Mummy used to come out into the wilds,' said Gazba. 'But now she is going to look after you and keep you safe.'

'That's right darling,' said Chloe from the carriage.

'There could be dragons out there, you know,' said Gazba.

'That would be exciting, Daddy. Please may I come?' begged Jasmine.

'Sorry, but no.' said Gazba lifting his daughter into the carriage.

Chloe was shaking and held a hanky to her face, trying to hide her grief at parting.

Jasmine's eyes were brimming with tears as she sat down and slid her hand into her mother's.

Chloe gave her daughter a little smile and said, 'This is for the best, darling.'

Gazba smiled at his wife and daughter, and then turned to the stable hand who would be riding Helga and leading Bella during the journey and said, 'Be careful with the saddlebags.'

'I certainly will, my Lord,' said the nervous man, looking white and clammy.

Gazba was about to climb up next to the driver, when a horse and rider came galloping through the entrance to the courtyard and skidded to a halt in front of the carriage.

'Bon!' Juniper shouted in welcome to the new arrival.

'My friend!' exclaimed the man, dismounting from his horse.

'And who would you be?' asked Gazba, striding towards the rider, while Juniper had already run up and was shaking the man's hand.

'My name is Bon and I have just come from Baron Bardozer's estate.'

The man was still puffing, clearly his ride had been exhausting and so, to avoid frightening his family, Gazba took the man aside and asked, 'What is the problem?'

Bon spoke quickly. 'I have just left Baron Bardozer's estate. He has been confined to the commode for days, and I heard him say, "Gazba must die tonight". It was then I realised how dangerous the man really is, and I came here as fast as I could to warn you. He is on a rampage.'

'I feared as much,' said Gazba, 'He has taken too much paraffin and now blames me.'

'I would say, avoid the baron at all costs,' said Bon emphatically.

'Juniper, make sure Bon is given food and sanctuary while I am away, for I fear the *good baron* will be after him as well now,' said Gazba with a note of scorn in his voice.

'I certainly will,' said Juniper and added, 'Bon can help me protect the estate. We both practiced the sword together with my father, before I became overseer.'

'Thank you,' said Gazba putting a hand on each man's shoulder. 'We shall go now, to draw the baron's attention away from the estate.'

After this he turned and climbed up next to the driver, who clicked his tongue and the horses sprang forward, pulling their load with ease. As the carriage swept out of the courtyard Gazba nodded to both men who acknowledged him and nodded back. Juniper then gave Jasmine a little wave as she waved back at him with exuberance.

The journey to her grandparent's home having begun, Jasmine became interested in everything that they passed.

'Look!' she exclaimed, pointing out the window. 'Shouldn't the farmer stop the deer eating the young poplar trees?'

'If they didn't eat them, we would have too many trees to ever walk through,' said Chloe in a sad tone as she looked out of the carriage window.

'I can see a fawn, Mummy, with spots,' added the excited Jasmine.

The fawn darted away with its mother and a big stag stood by until its family was safely hidden in the forest.

Chloe thought it strange that a young fawn would be born at this time of year. How would it survive a winter? Her thoughts then turned to her own child's predicament. Like the stag, her own mate was trying to protect his family.

Gazba's idea is for the best, she conceded to herself. *Jasmine will be safe with my parents.*

Chloe settled back and tried to enjoy the bumpy ride as the fine bright light of afternoon became veiled with grey as the day passed towards evening.

The last glimmer of the sunset and smoky streaks of cloud were on the horizon, as they approached the huge and awe-inspiring chateau of her grandparents. Jasmine leaned out of the window and spoke to her father.

'Please,' she begged. 'Can I run across the drawbridge and be the first one there?'

'Driver, will you please stop?' asked Gazba.

'Certainly sir,' said the driver with a knowing smile as he reined in the horses to a stop. This was a routine that played itself out many times with Jasmine.

A sentry on the parapet had seen them coming and the drawbridge had already been lowered and, standing in the gateway, were the Marquis and Marquisa Pleasure—Jasmine's grandfather and grandmother—and Sir Gallant, the knight champion. They knew of Jasmine's need to be the first to arrive—they waited for her to come running over the drawbridge, as she usually did.

'Go on then Jasmine,' conceded Gazba, knowing that this was her little delight.

Jasmine dropped to the ground from the carriage step and, with her dog wrapped in a blanket clutched in her arms, started to skip across the drawbridge.

'Grandmother! Grandfather!' she shouted, waving.

She tripped on a slightly uneven wooden plank and the excited Puppy and the blanket, slipped from her arms and fell with a splash into the murky water of the moat. The dog, still tangled in the blanket, began spluttering and struggling to keep his head above water.

'Puppy!' wailed Jasmine like a wounded animal.

'What is it child?' shrieked the Marquisa, whose eyesight was not great. Gathering her skirts, she ran across the drawbridge to her granddaughter.

The Marquis also ran forward, followed by a quick-thinking Gallant who had grabbed a landing net that he used for catching carp in the moat during quiet times on duty.

'It's my puppy, down there!' she cried, pointing down into the moat. Puppy was gone for a few seconds but then appeared on the surface gasping for air.

The Marquis shook his head saying, 'Silly girl. That could have been you, Jasmine.' But then straight away he got down on his knees and tried to grasp the dog.

Gazba had also leapt down from the carriage and rushed onto the drawbridge.

'I can't see properly with this eye patch,' said Gallant and handed the net to Gazba, who began sweeping it through the water trying to catch the dog.

It was quite dark now and it was very hard to see Puppy in the murky water of the moat as he bobbed up a few times, still gasping for air.

'Hurry Gazba, he's drowning!' exclaimed Chloe, who was now on the drawbridge as well.

Gazba scooped up Puppy, who was now free of the blanket, and dragged him towards Chloe who grabbed the dog by the back of the neck and pulled him up and out of the net. He was limp and not breathing.

Jasmine was crying loudly and shaking. The Marquisa, who had her arm around her, said, 'Do not worry, your daddy will fix him, he's an apothecary.'

'Puppy's dying!' exclaimed Jasmine.

Gazba gave Puppy a couple of good strong pats on the back. In response, the dog shuddered and coughed up water.

'Here, sir, take my coat,' offered Gallant, removing the item.

'Thank you,' said Gazba, wrapping the dog up tightly.

Gallant nodded and moved to one side as Gazba walked with Puppy through the great hall and down to the kitchens at the back of the castle.

Jasmine, tearfully following her father, asked, 'will he die from pneumonia?'

'Not if I can help it,' replied Gazba.

Once in the kitchen, Chloe rubbed the limp Puppy with a dry cloth and said, 'When he can take it, give him some butter with honey and rum.'

'You know your stuff,' said Gazba approvingly.

'It's common knowledge,' replied Chloe, concentrating on reviving the dog.

'May I?' asked Gallant, reaching down to pick up his discarded coat.

'Thank you. That was kind of you,' said Chloe, placing her hand on his arm.

'Ouch careful! 'he exclaimed. 'It's still a bit sore.'

'Put him near the stove, Daddy, like we did with the kittens when they were cold,' implored Jasmine.

'That's what I have in mind,' said Gazba, wrapping the dog in a blanket and placing it in front of the oven.

Meanwhile, the Marquis was looking on with disgust from the hallway. He would not set foot in a kitchen at the best of times, but now he definitely wouldn't.

'A dog—in the kitchen where my food is cooked,' he complained to his wife, shaking his head.

'It is Jasmine's beloved dog. Have a heart,' said the Marquisa, frowning at him.

'Chloe should never have married that man,' retorted the Marquis grumpily. 'This sort of thing would never happen in a proper family.'

'She loves him, and he was the one who saved La Fonteyn from that witch,' said the Marquisa.

'He may be a hero, but he's not one of us,' said the Marquis.

'You said it yourself, my lord, he's a hero,' said his wife.

The Marquisa dug her husband in the ribs, as he was about to say something caustic while a servant was passing by. The Marquis got the hint and shut his mouth.

'Does he have a chance?' asked Chloe as her brows furrowed anxiously.

'Yes, he does, and keeping his temperature up will help a lot,' replied Gazba. Then to the cook he said, 'Just make sure he doesn't get too hot.'

The cook gave the slightest grimace at the thought of a dog being in her kitchen but nodded compliantly. She was good at moderating the temperature of a lamb roast, but a tiny sick dog was another matter.

'That's pretty exciting, kids, isn't it?' said Nanny closing her book. 'But we might finish here for the night.

Jace yawned, scratched his head, and said, 'Okay.'

'How are you feeling now, darling?' she asked Shelley, taking her granddaughter's hand and stroking it gently.

'Oh,' said Shelley, 'I think I'm alright, but I still feel sad.'

Jace was now happily playing his game on his computer and didn't seem at all interested in Shelley's woes.

'Did you know that God can give you a sign that He is here with you all the time,' said Nanny. 'And that He really cares for you.'

'How?' asked Shelley.

'By giving you synchronicities.'

'What is *that*?' asked Jace suddenly looking up from his computer.

'Well,' said Nanny, 'God works in signs and wonders, and when you see something on television or hear it mentioned on radio just as you think of it, that is a sign from God that He controls the universe and that He is close by, caring for you. You may be working on your computer and hear a word in a song just as you type it—that kind of thing'.

'God often shows us his great sense of humour with these synchronicities too.'

The children were wide-eyed that such things were possible.

'I'll give you an example,' began Nanny, 'I had been out with Uncle James' little Anna—your cousin—and when we came home, we watched a children's program from the couch.'

'What was it about?' asked Shelley, who was mildly interested.

'It was a girl, pretending to fly around like an aeroplane and singing, "Whirl, whirl, whirl".'

'She dipped and swooped but I wasn't terribly interested in the show, so I picked up where I left off reading *War and Peace*.'

'And then what happened?' asked Shelley.

'I opened up the book and the first word I read was "whirl"!' said Nanny, who was still excited by what had happened.

'That's a weird coincidence,' said Shelley.

'Would you believe it? "Whirl",' repeated Nanny. 'One of the main characters in the novel was watching the people "whirl" across the dance floor.'

'How many words are there in *War and Peace*?' asked Shelley.

'Almost six hundred thousand according to one search engine,' said Nanny. 'And it's probably a million to one chance that the two "whirls" would coincide like that.'

'So, what did that mean?' asked Shelley.

'Well,' began Nanny, 'I thought: how on earth could that happen? It was impossible unless God had made the words on the television, and the word I read in the book, synchronise. I was awestruck. Then I heard Him say directly into my mind, "You think that's amazing? I have so much more up my sleeve for you."'

'That's amazing, Nanny. God really speaks to you?' said Shelley.

'Yes,' replied Nanny. 'I hear Him clearly sometimes and other times not so much, but that time I believe God wanted to get my attention and show just how close He really is.'

'Does "whirl" have some sort of a special meaning and why did He want you to see it?' asked Shelley.

'Yes, I wondered that too,' replied Nanny. 'I looked it up in a book that explains the symbolic biblical meaning of words, and the closest I could find to "whirl" was "whirlwind", and that can mean a few things. One meaning is: "Open heaven bringing rapture" and, as far as I understand, "rapture" means taking a person into Heaven and into the Kingdom of God, with its joy and wonder and also intense joy.'

'Really?' asked Shelley, who was now keenly interested.

'Yes,' replied Nanny. 'That book also explained that another meaning for "whirlwind" is "revelation", which for me, means the revealing of previously not understood mysteries of God.'

Nanny noticed that Jace had now lifted his head up from his game and was listening.

'And the third meaning is "resurrection",' continued Nanny brightly. 'Meaning coming back to life when there seems to be no hope—God brings a new adventure. The Holy Spirit is likened to wind.'

'Adventure?' queried Jace. 'Like on the television. Something exciting?'

'Yes,' said Nanny. 'Or even just in everyday life. When there seems to be no hope, God brings a new beginning.' Nanny stroked her granddaughter's hair and added, 'And a little baby in the house will be a new beginning for all of you.'

'Oh,' said Shelley. She smiled and light came into her eyes.

'So, do you think that strange things like the "whirl" coincidence can happen to me?' queried Jace.

'Yes, and why not?' said Nanny, looking at her watch. 'You might even have an amazing dream. And, seeing as it is now time for sleeping, why not ask God to show you Heaven while you sleep?'

'Can that happen?' asked Shelley.

'It happened to me,' said Nanny. 'I had a dream where I was among some old people dressed in black and it was kind of depressing—a bit like it is now, that my mum and dad are old. Then I saw my guardian angel.'

'Cool,' said Shelley while rhythmically brushing her long locks, asked, 'What did it look like?'

'It was a she and she was coloured like fiery opal with red and orange, green and blue. Her eyes were calm, strong, and filled with love. The moment I saw her I knew she was my guardian angel,' said Nanny with a sigh. 'When I think back to that dream, I am comforted to know that my parents have guardian angels too, and that everything will be alright in the end.'

'You'll have the shiniest hair in class, Shelley, after using half a bottle of conditioner again,' said Nanny with a laugh.

Shelley giggled, put her brush down on the dressing table, and snuggled down into the blankets and said, 'I hope I see my guardian angel in a dream'.

'Me too,' said Jace sleepily.

'Night-night, kids. Sweet dreams,' said Nanny.

'Night-night, Nanny. Love you,' the children replied sleepily, as Nanny put her manuscript away and turned out the lights in the bedroom.

Nanny then did a quick whip-around to tidy up the house and then the lights went out, and before long all were asleep, including Nanny.

Chapter 10

The next day started with a terrible phone call. Ming Po, the older other family dog, had to be put to sleep; it was a sad event for the holidays. Lilian had taken the day off work to be with the children to help them with their grief. She had done her best to comfort them but now, once more at Nanny's, both children lay in their beds still sniffing a little.

'I miss him,' said Shelley with a sob, as she hugged Nanny.

'So do I,' said Jace, now also leaning against Nanny. 'When I gave him a last pat, he looked up at me with his big round eyes.' Jace then broke down and shook with sobs.

'We'll all miss him,' said Nanny, putting her arms around both the children before adding. 'He was old, and had had a good life, but he was suffering.'

'He couldn't see,' said Shelley soulfully, looking up and wiping her nose.

'His eyes were all blue,' said Jace, still tearful, 'and now he is going to be cremated.'

'I'm sad he's gone but he's not the first pet we've lost. We lost Tikki the budgie too. It's a sad part of life,' said Nanny.

'But Ming Po is gone now, and we won't see him again,' said Shelley.

'Are you so sure you won't?' asked Nanny gently. 'I have something I can tell you later that might make you think differently, but let's read some story now.'

'Okay, Nanny,' said Shelley, a little uncertain.

The children snuggled down into their blankets as Nanny opened her book and began to flick through the pages.

'We are at the part where the dog is being warmed up near the oven,' said Jace. 'Roast dog!' he said, laughing.

'Hmmm,' Nanny smiled and then said. 'Let's start,' she found the right page. 'And this is what happens next.'

Jasmine sat in the kitchen with her father, stroking Puppy and watching his chest rise and fall. Watching and hoping he would soon come to consciousness. Her face was red and blotchy from crying.

'Come, Jasmine,' said Chloe, gently.

'No, Mummy, I can't leave him!' exclaimed Jasmine.

The Marquisa, who was standing nearby, said, 'Jasmine dear, he is sleeping now, and your father says he's over the worst.'

'I don't want to leave him alone,' said Jasmine, as she kneeled, caressing the sleeping form of her little dog.

'Don't worry darling,' said Gazba. 'I will not leave him.'

'Alright,' said Jasmine tearfully, taking a last look.

'Darling,' said the Marquisa, 'Papa Pleasure has a surprise for you.'

Jasmine's eyes lit up. 'Is it the rocking horse? Is it finished?' she asked, springing to her feet.

'Go and see,' said the Marquisa smiling.

As Jasmine left the kitchen, she ran past the long dining room table with its embroidered chairs and, despite her excitement, her attention was captured by a tapestry on the wall. It depicted the unicorn of Valouresse, and the creature seemed to be almost alive in the illumination from the torches.

You've been in my dreams, thought Jasmine, *but I want to see you in real life. In my dreams I ride you and you save me.*

But the thought of the rocking horse was too tantalising, and she quickly forgot about the unicorn as she scampered up the stairs.

The Marquisa and Chloe followed behind her at a more leisurely pace, and the Marquis was already at the door of Jasmine's room and keen to see the reaction of his granddaughter to his handiwork.

Jasmine ran along the upper corridor to her room.

'Wait Jasmine. Don't go in yet,' said the Marquis, who stood waiting with his hand on the doorknob until his wife and daughter arrived. He then asked, 'Are you ready for a surprise Jasmine?'

'Oh yes,' exclaimed Jasmine.

'Here we are,' he said as he opened the door with a flourish.

Jasmine walked through the door, gasped, and stared in rapture.

'It's so beautiful—the same colour as Grunjion, brown with a golden mane and tail.'

'But easier to ride,' said the Marquis with a hearty laugh as his granddaughter ran over, jumped on the wooden horse, and started rocking.

'It took him months to finish, and he's been waiting eagerly for this day,' said the Marquisa to Chloe. She then smiled fondly at the delight on her husband's face.

Chloe smiled wistfully as she watched her proud father and his happy granddaughter.

'He never seemed as pleased with me,' she said to her mother.

'Oh,' said the Marquisa with a sigh, taking her daughter's hand. 'He has grown kinder my dear, and he *does* love you very much, he just never knew how to show it.'

The Marquis, Marquisa and Chloe watched Jasmine ride the rocking horse for a while and then left her and went back down to the great hall where a fire and pre-dinner refreshments awaited them. While they talked, Jasmine rode for at least an hour, forgetting to be unhappy about her dog.

In the kitchen, Puppy finally started to rouse. He gave a sneeze and Gazba, who despite himself had been a little concerned, sighed with relief. He gathered the dog up in a blanket and took him up to Jasmine. When she saw her beloved Puppy with his tongue hanging out and eager to be with her, she jumped off the rocking horse and ran to him.

Once in Jasmine's arms, the dog went wild, licking her face and wriggling like a freshly caught trout.

'He's happy to see you,' said Gazba with a grin.

'Thank you, Daddy, for saving him,' said Jasmine, hugging her dog close. 'I'd like him to sleep with me tonight. Can we put his toilet tray in here so he can stay with me?'

'Very well,' said Gazba, putting his arm around his daughter. 'Just this once. I'll have it sent up, but don't tell your grandfather.'

After dinner, Gazba and Chloe, and the Lord and Lady Pleasure, had a private conversation in the drawing room. They sat on red velvet chairs near a flickering fire and Gazba explained the situation and then told them he would have to leave that very night to get through the baron's lands.

The Marquis was somewhat sceptical.

'So, you would go on some sort of a mystical quest—which is what this seems to be—just because you saw a vision?' he asked.

'Yes, my lord,' replied Gazba. 'But it was a vision as real as you or me here now, and it spurs me to action, especially because my daughter's safety, and the safety of the whole country, is concerned.'

'Well, so be it,' said the Marquis, thumping the table. 'We *will* protect Jasmine, of course, and the baron will get more than he bargained for should he come calling. I'll double the guards, and I will definitely talk to the king about that upstart baron. He needs to remember his place.'

'The king is going to another jousting tournament,' said Gazba. 'You will have to speak to his generals about the baron.'

'But Gallant was injured at the last tournament, surely he cannot go,' said Chloe, now entering the conversation.

'Well, I believe the king will be competing this time as he is trying to woo a princess,' said Gazba, with a tinge of resentment in his voice.

'Ah, now I understand why the king is going, but I will still send a message to the generals about the baron,' said the Marquis.

'Daddy, I am a fighter, please can *I* help save Valouresse?' said Jasmine from the door where she had been secretly listening. As she spoke, she inadvertently squeezed her dog a little too hard and he gave a sharp yelp.

Gazba shot her a stern glance and said, 'There will be no need for *you* to fight my darling—and be careful with Puppy, he's still quite delicate at the moment.'

Jasmine sighed with disappointment and then looked down at her dog and said, 'Sorry Puppy, I didn't mean to hurt you.' The dog grinned back and then licked her on the chin.

'Go play with him in your room darling,' said Chloe curtly. 'Mummy and daddy will come up to you shortly.'

Jasmine's lip quivered and a tear rolled down her face. Wordlessly she turned and dashed off.

In the wake of Jasmine's departure, there was silence in the room for a moment and then Gazba got to his feet.

'Chloe and I will take our leave now to discuss a few things before I depart,' he said.

Chloe rose to her feet and then she and her husband left her parents staring silently at each other.

Taking her hand, Gazba walked with Chloe up the stairs and around the curve of the wall to their room in the solar.

Once in the room, Chloe came close to her husband and said in a small voice, 'I know you love adventure and must leave but I envy you in a way.'

'Don't,' said Gazba, stroking her cheek.

'I wish you would stay. Please stay, or at least let me come with you,' begged Chloe.

'I would love you to come, of course, but I fear it is far too dangerous,' said Gazba. 'And, unfortunately, I must leave now to get through the baron's lands unhindered this night.'

'Of course, but please, promise me that you will come back to Jasmine and me,' Chloe pleaded with wide, fearful eyes.

'All hell could not stop me,' declared Gazba, as he ran his hands over her shiny, smooth hair and then gently tilted her chin upwards. They leant silently for a moment, forehead to forehead, and then Gazba broke away to prepare to leave.

Once he was ready, they called Jasmine from her room, and she walked between them, holding their hands as the three of them passed along the corridor of the solar and down the stairs with Puppy following behind. Then they went through the sumptuous great hall and along the corridor to the entrance of the castle where a servant had Gazba's horses waiting.

As Gazba checked he had everything he would need for his journey, the Marquis and the Marquisa joined Chloe and Jasmine in the courtyard to farewell him.

Jasmine picked up her dog and held him up to Gazba and said, 'Puppy wants to say goodbye too,' and then she added, 'I love you, Daddy. Come back soon because I miss you already.'

'I love you too, darling,' said Gazba and then he kissed Jasmine on the forehead. He then patted the dog. 'Take care of Puppy. That is your important job.'

'I will guard him with my life,' said Jasmine, hugging Puppy so hard that he gave another yap.

Chloe moved over to her daughter and placed her arm around her.

Gazba then mounted Helga and, holding her and Bella's reins in one hand, blew Chloe a kiss with his free hand.

The Marquis nodded sternly in farewell while the Marquisa waved, and said, 'Godspeed Gazba.'

Gazba acknowledged them both saying, 'Marquisa, Marquis.'

He then turned Helga and, leading Bella, went on his way. He trotted across the drawbridge and onto the road leading from the Pleasure's castle, and then began pushing his horses hard, knowing that he would have to travel quickly to get through the baron's lands before the night was over.

He trotted on for leagues, passing sleeping cattle who were just perceptible in the moonlight, which was bright enough that he didn't need any other light to travel by. The night wore on and finally he recognised an important landmark: a huge rocky outcrop with a stream running by it; a stream that indicated safety.

'At last, I'm through the baron's lands,' he said with relief and then he yawned.

He had had a busy day, so soon afterwards he set up camp in the forest a safe distance down from the road and near a stream that meandered by. He secured his horses and soon had a fire crackling away, which he started with his magnesium flint and the blade of his knife.

Later, while he lay in his bedroll admiring the stars through a gap in the canopy, he imagined they were the light from another world, shining through holes in the blackness of the night. He wished he knew how the holes got there or even who had made them. Then he saw a meteor streak across the sky.

It almost seems like a fiery angel has burst from Heaven as a sign, he thought, *made by You, God of the firmament. I trust you will watch over my daughter and wife, while I follow the quest of the Holy Spirit in its form of the Unicorn.*

'Do you think that they are watching us?' asked Jace with his elbows on the pillow and his chin resting on the palms of his hands.

'The stars? Maybe,' replied Nanny, adding '"There are more things in Heaven and Earth than in your philosophy, Horatio."'

'Why did you say that, Nanny?' asked Jace looking at her curiously.

'A character called Hamlet says it in a play that Shakespeare wrote about four hundred years ago. In those times, there were a lot of phenomena that couldn't be explained and even now we don't know everything. Perhaps some of the stars *are* actual beings that *do* look down on us from Heaven—certainly God is always watching.'

'It's alright for Jasmine,' said Shelley mournfully interjecting. 'Puppy is alive, but we've lost two pets, more counting the fish.'

'They are gone but not forgotten, and never forgotten by God,' said Nanny. 'Speaking of gone but not forgotten, do you want me to tell you about that thing I mentioned earlier: it is a story about my uncle?'

'Isn't he dead?' asked Jace, now lying on his back with his hands behind his head.

'Yes, but he's alive in Heaven,' replied Nanny putting her manuscript on the top of the writing bureau. She then sat down on Shelley's bed and caressed her granddaughter's blanketed shoulders.

'How do you know?' asked Shelley.

'Oh, I *know*, and I'll tell how I know,' said Nanny, almost bursting with anticipation. 'A few years ago, my uncle went to hospital because he was very sick. He was dying and even though your mum and I had tried to tell him about Jesus, he had been in the war and—'

'Which war?' said Jace with sudden interest.

'The Second World War, in New Guinea, against the invading Japanese forces.'

Jace nodded, satisfied with the information.

'Terrible things happened there, and we think that stopped him from believing in a loving God.'

'Things like what?' asked Jace with great interest.

'Things that I will tell you when you are older, darling,' said Nanny. 'Anyway, your mother and I were worried that he would be going into eternity without God, and so we wrote him a letter.'

'What did it say?' asked Shelley, now on her elbows and looking at Nanny from behind a lock of black hair.

'It said something like: "Jesus really loves you, and He died so you can go to live in Heaven forever. Just lean on Him and He will look after you".'

'So, he read that letter? What did he think of it?' asked Shelley.

'He never read the letter … he didn't have to,' said Nanny mysteriously.

'Why?' asked Jace.

'Because of something that happened to him,' replied Nanny.

'What was that Nanny?' asked Jace, his face animated with excitement.

'My cousins—his daughters—who were with him to the end, told me that he had been suffering a terrible headache in the hospital one night, and that Jesus visited him and took the pain away.'

'What do you mean, Nanny? In a dream or something?' asked Jace.

'No, Jace,' replied Nanny. 'I mean Jesus came in real life—with a crown of thorns on his head, as if He knew the suffering my uncle was going through. He reached out and touched my uncle on *his* forehead.'

'Then the pain left?' asked Shelley.

'That's right, and his last remaining days were *really* happy.'

'He was happy to die?' asked Jace.

'He was happy to be going to Heaven,' said Nanny 'He would smile and point up, saying, "the captain's coming for me soon."'

'Like a captain in an army?' asked Jace.

'Yes, sort of like that,' replied Nanny. 'My uncle now felt love and respect for Jesus, as his ultimate superior officer and he couldn't wait to go and be with Him.'

'Why would that be fun?' asked Jace.

'My uncle loved fishing and he was beaming with joy as he told his daughters: "I'm going up the Murray, fishing for cod with Jesus."'

'But isn't the Murray River in Australia?' asked Jace.

'Well, yes,' replied Nanny, 'There *is* a Murray River here in the earthly realm, but I think it's like a mirror image of the real one in Heaven. So, you see, my uncle is having a fantastic time there, even as we speak.'

'Fishing you mean?' asked Jace, a little dubiously.

'Yes,' replied Nanny, 'and having a yarn around the campfire with his friend, the one he loves the most—his captain and saviour, Jesus.'

'Will they cook marshmallows?' asked Jace.

'Yes, and better than that,' said Nanny with a big grin and a happy dreamy look on her face. 'One day we'll get to join them; I can't wait.'

'So, what you're saying is that death is not the end of life?' said Jace.

'No, that's right,' answered Nanny. 'It's just the beginning of the rest of your wonderful life in Heaven.'

'So, I'll get to see Tikki and Ming Po again?' asked Shelley.

'Oh yes, I believe so,' replied Nanny. 'The Bible says you get a new healthy body, so Tikki and Ming Po will too. It also says that God knows even when a sparrow dies.'

'That makes me feel a lot better, Nanny, that he cares about our pets,' said Shelley.

'It's kind of cool,' agreed Jace.

'We'll hear more of *The Apothecary's Quest* tomorrow night, if you like,' said Nanny. 'Goodnight now, sweethearts.'

'Night-night, Nanny. Love you,' said both children.

'Love you too, kids. Sweet dreams.'

Nanny smiled and got up off Shelley's bed and walked to the door and, closing the door quietly behind her, she went about getting ready for bed herself.

Chapter 11

The next morning was crisp, cold, and frosty. Nanny put the heater on and cooked the children scrambled eggs just the way Lillian did for them. When they were ready, Nanny took the kids to the mall.

That evening, after a day of fun and shopping, the children got snuggled into their beds, ready to hear more of the *Apothecary's Quest*.

Shelley had become withdrawn again, and Nanny thought about the sign she had noticed on the door of Shelley's room the last time she had visited her daughter's house; a sign which read: "Keep out".

'Are you alright, Shelley?' Nanny asked.

'No,' replied Shelley.

'Why does Mummy have to have another baby?' she asked, her voice breaking with anguish. 'My friends will think she is weird for having a baby when she is so old.'

'I thought you were all okay with that, darling,' replied Nanny, 'Your mother always wanted more children, and she's not old.'

'But how can she care for me *and* a baby?' asked Shelley sadly.

'She can, and believe me, there is always enough love to go around, God has made sure of that,' replied Nanny, putting her arm around her granddaughter. 'Your mother will never forget how cute you were as a baby and will always love you.'

'Can we look at pictures and videos of me—when I was a baby—tomorrow, Nanny?'

'Sure, darling, I would love to do that,' said Nanny enthusiastically.

'Let's do the story now,' said Shelley, looking a little more animated.

Nanny started reading.

As Gazba slept, Kraekhoull plotted revenge in her mountain lair, the place where she always returned to churn her magic into a storm. Deep inside the mountain cave was a flickering, eerie glow made by many entrapped fireflies within lanterns. The plushness of the décor with crimson carpet and wall hangings seemed almost decadent and out of place, when compared to the starkness of the rough stone walls of the room. Sparkling green crystal wind chimes swayed as the power of Kraekhoull's fierce energy filled the air.

'I need a man who is embittered with the king and the nobles as I am,' said Kraekhoull, almost spitting out the words. 'Someone with an army or who can get an army.'

The seer and the prophetess—demons in disguise—sidled up to the witch as she now waved her thin white hands with pointed nails, in cryptic gestures over the crystal ball.

Kraekhoull gave them both a piercing glance and said in a low menacing voice, 'Find him, find me that man.' She then turned her attention back to the orb.

'As you wish, my lady,' said both demons, starting to do a weaving dance around the crystal ball.

The witch joined in, singing in an eerie, archaic language. She danced with the others, becoming more and more frenzied, until all were almost writhing like snakes.

The thick grey smoke within the ball cleared, and Kraekhoull now saw in its depths a dark and imposing castle, a castle which she did not recognise.

Kraekhoull ceased dancing and demanded, 'Where is this? Why have you shown me this?'

'As you will see, my mistress,' said the seer with a demonic leer. 'Here is a man of power. A man with similar desires to your own.'

The scene in the crystal ball moved to a great hall where she could see the master of the castle seated on a carved oak chair, alone at the head of a huge dining table, in his purple velvet and brocade dressing gown. She could see several elaborately dressed servants were positioned around the resplendent room but only one older man in particular seemed to be doing any work.

'Fletcher, hurry up with my supper before I starve!' the master of the house roared at his quaking servant, who was carrying a bowl of steaming beef stew. 'You know I need sustenance before I sleep.'

'Certainly, Baron, immediately,' said the harried looking but well dressed, head butler as he placed the bowl on the table.

'I told you to refer to me as *sire* when we are here in private,' said the baron haughtily. The dark-haired, moustachioed man—who was quite overweight—then grabbed the bowl and greedily began stuffing spoonfuls of food into his mouth as if he hadn't eaten for days.

He muttered to himself as he ate—spilling food in the process—and then he began complaining to his servant.

'I will never get any respect after that humiliating accident,' the man said, slamming his fist down on the table and upsetting a silver goblet that spilled red wine onto the white linen tablecloth. In the flickering light of the torches, it looked like a splash of blood to the watching Kraekhoull.

The man continued to rant. 'My esteemed moustache will never compensate for the loss of my bodily function at the banquet.'

'Sire. It is not a crime you have committed,' said Fletcher, gesturing to one of the other servants for a cleaning cloth. 'People will forget.'

'It will be forever etched into the minds of the nobility. They are probably still sneering and laughing about it,' complained the baron.

As the baron continued to bemoan his woes, a servant stepped forward, passed Fletcher a napkin and then retreated back to his station.

'Get the cheese, Fletcher, and leave the cleaning to someone else,' demanded the baron as he dropped his spoon into the now empty bowl.

'As you wish, sire,' said Fletcher, passing the napkin to another servant and then going to a sideboard where he picked up a large platter of cheese. He placed it in front of his master.

'The cheese, at last!' barked the baron. He then grabbed a whole huge piece and started gorging on it.

Meanwhile, Fletcher picked up the overturned goblet, wiped it with a serviette and then stepped aside to pour the baron more wine.

Nervously, the other servant moved in to clean up the spilt wine.

'Hurry up before I give you a good whipping,' said the baron, spraying cheese into the face of the hapless man.

'Of course, sire,' said the servant, dabbing at the red stain several times and then escaping as quickly as he could.

Fletcher then stepped in and proffered the baron the newly filled goblet. The baron seized it and washed down his mouthful of food.

'I really need to do something diabolical and merciless to get my reputation back as a strong and powerful man,' said the baron, thinking aloud.

'It is not a sign of weakness to have a little accident,' said Fletcher.

With rage, the baron slammed his fist down and shouted, 'I am *not* weak! That apothecary will pay with his life for quashing any chance

I had of becoming a member of the royal household by marrying Lady Dubblenek.'

'Do you really think death is necessary for the apothecary, sire?' asked Fletcher hesitantly.

'Of course, it is!' shouted the baron, his face suddenly aflame with rage. 'Get out! All of you. Especially you, Fletcher. You have overstepped your mark.'

That night, at great risk to his own life, Fletcher had a surreptitious conversation with Bon—who had also overhead the baron's threats towards Gazba. Bon had then ridden at great speed to warn Gazba, just as he and his family were about to depart for Lord Pleasures home.

From her mountain den, Kraekhoull saw the old servant and the others cringe and bow profusely as they exited the dining room. She smirked at the baron's blustering behaviour. The man was a buffoon, and she would be easily able to manipulate him.

Suddenly, a soldier in full armour clanked into the room and stood at attention. Kraekhoull saw the crest of a boar emblazoned on the soldier's breastplate—a symbol of strength and barbarity.

'So, this is Bardozer of the boar,' said Kraekhoull thoughtfully. 'I have heard of him and surely he has the reputation of his namesake—he will be useful to me.'

'We are glad you are pleased with our choice,' said the prophetess, rubbing her hands together eagerly.

Kraekhoull's attention was brought back to the scene in the crystal ball when the baron asked impatiently of the soldier, 'What is it?'

'A message has just been delivered to the gate,' said the man passing a piece of parchment to the baron, who looked suspiciously around and then waited until the man had left the room before he opened it.

'Ah,' said the baron, perusing the message and thinking out loud. 'Just the news I wanted to hear. The king is soon to leave La Fonteyn for another pointless tournament. With him gone it will be easier to exact my revenge on his favourite, the apothecary.'

'I have seen enough,' exclaimed the witch with delight as she covered the ball with a black velvet cloth. 'Bardozer will suit my needs well. He has a belly full of bitterness—and he hates Gazba in particular.'

She cackled and grasped the hands of the prophetess and the seer and swirled them around in a crazy dance which lasted only seconds before she stopped and flopped on a chair. Then, lowering her voice, she whispered darkly:

'He is the one. *He is the one.* Bardozer of the Boar, I will be paying you a visit very soon.'

'We are so glad you have found your ally, Kraekhoull,' said the prophetess coolly. 'And, if you would excuse us, we will take our leave now?'

'Of course. Do what you will,' Kraekhoull said, waving the seer and the prophetess away. 'I have plans to make.'

Once her two advisors had left, the witch poured herself a blood-red claret and settled into an armchair, with a satisfied expression and a sneer on her lips, to both savour her plans and her drink. Then, putting down her glass, she grinned and rubbed her shapely hands together with wicked joy.

'I will soon rule this land with a rod of iron and no child-maid of Valouresse will be able to stop me,' she said with a cackle.

The demons transformed to their true appearance once outside the witch's lair.

'The child is in the forest,' hissed Bitterness, pushing back the hood of his cloak and tilting up his ugly misshapen head to sniff the air.

'Do you mean Jasmine is in the forest?' asked Jace, suddenly sitting up in bed. 'I thought she was at her grandparent's castle?'

'Oh no,' replied Nanny. 'She has done something you don't know about. She's run away to go and help her father.'

'How did she do that, and when, and why?' asked Jace, confused.

'So many questions,' said Nanny with a laugh. 'It's a writer's thing. I wanted the readers to find out all of the villain's plotting before I told them about what Jasmine's doing. Now let me get on with the story and we'll find out what she's up to shortly.'

'Okay, I understand,' said Jace. 'I'm interested in finding out how she got out of the castle, but I'll just be patient and wait.'

Suddenly the forest was illuminated as the clouds parted to reveal the moon's face, and Fear's predatory eyes quickly scanned the area for the Maid. Not finding his prey, he turned to Bitterness with his white fangs gleaming in the moonlight and asked, 'Should *we* deal with the maid instead of letting Kraekhoull do it?'

'Yes, I think so, with you at my side I think we can,' replied Bitterness, his eyes glittering maliciously through his puffy, wart-encrusted grey flesh. 'We are not going to keep exactly to *his* plan, to allow the witch to kill the child, but this is *our* chance to show the Dark Prince just how resourceful we are.'

'And maybe,' said Fear slyly, 'We could be promoted, to become like him or even … greater.'

'Let's keep that last bit to ourselves, shall we?' said Bitterness quietly. 'Now, let us go.'

They moved into the forest—two black shadows swallowed by the darkness of the forest canopy.

'How about we leave it there for the night?' asked Nanny.

'It's a bit creepy,' said Shelley with a crooked smile.

'Yes, I guess it is, but Jace would like that, wouldn't you, Jace?' Nanny said with a laugh.

'Yes, I do,' said Jace with a giggle and then he asked, 'What's a demon actually?'

'Well, to explain that I'll have to go back to the beginning when God created all the angels to worship and serve Him—they were all beautiful then, especially Lucifer.'

'Lucifer? That's another name for Satan, right?' asked Jace.

'Yep,' replied Nanny, 'but Lucifer was his name in the beginning, and it means "morning star". He was the most beautiful angel in Heaven.'

'How did he get to be bad?' asked Shelley.

'He decided that he wasn't happy being *just* an angel,' replied Nanny. 'He wanted to be the top dog and tried to dethrone God and take over Heaven. He wanted to be worshipped.'

'He couldn't do *that* though, could he?' asked Shelley.

'No, he couldn't,' replied Nanny. 'And God kicked him out of Heaven, as well as a third of the angels who had been in on the rebellion as well.'

'Are they still beautiful angels?' asked Shelley, a little confused.

'No, indeed not,' replied Nanny. 'Not beautiful at all, but twisted and ugly, inside and out. True angels are full of light, healing, and compassion—they help amplify the presence and majesty of God. Fallen angels are full of hate, wickedness, cruelty, and a desire to inflict pain, although they can—for short periods—take on a fair appearance to make an evil plot work.'

'So the fallen angels became demons, right?' said Jace.

'Right,' answered Nanny.

'So, Satan isn't so powerful then?' asked Shelley.

'No,' replied Nanny excitedly. 'Jesus lives in us, and it says in the Bible that He is our strong tower and our protector, who is the light that drives away all the darkness.'

'I've been feeling sad and angry lately, like I have darkness inside my heart,' said Shelley with eyes downcast. 'Do you think Jesus is still here—in me?'

'I am sure He is,' said Nanny. 'And the Holy Spirit, who is also called the Comforter, is in you too. He is like a soothing balm for all your hurts. We all feel down sometimes, but He will help, and it will and your sadness will pass. *And* things will look better in the morning, I promise.'

'But what can I do to make me feel better?' asked Shelley.

'You could put on some music you like,' replied Nanny. 'That often helps change people's moods—and just knowing God is with you helps too.'

'Not too loud with the music,' said Jace.

'I'll just put it on quietly,' said Shelley turning on her radio and putting it on her favourite station.

With music playing in the background, Nanny said, 'Time for sleep now, kids.'

'Love you, Nanny,' said the children, almost in unison.

She kissed them both on the forehead, put her manuscript away, and then turned off the light before quietly leaving the room.

Chapter 12

The next evening, Lillian rang Nanny to ask how the children were coping with the pets' deaths.

'It has been tough on them,' said Nanny. 'And I think I know why Shelley is being mean to you.'

'I didn't kill the pets you know,' said Lillian with a short laugh.

'Yes, I know,' said Nanny with a sigh. 'But the new baby is a big change in her life, and she's had a lot of changes happening with school. The animals were one of the main constants in her life.'

'Yes, she needs to vent, and I understand that and that I'm the one copping it,' replied Lillian sadly.

'Just be patient with her, darling,' said Nanny sympathetically.

'I do everything to make her happy,' said Lillian. 'I help her make slime and buy her those little plastic animals that she makes videos of.'

'Yes, and that's a good outlet for her,' said Nanny. 'Millions of people watch those videos on the internet, you know.'

'She's got that quirky, slightly dark, sense of humour,' said Lillian.

'Yes, I know,' said Nanny. 'I laughed all the way through the Halloween special.'

'Anyway,' said Lillian, 'have fun with my babies and make sure they clean their teeth.'

'I will,' said Nanny. 'Love you. Have a good day.'

'You too, Mum,' said Lillian.

That night in the bedroom, Nanny and the two kids were sitting on Shelley's bed, watching videos on a small computer. The videos had been filmed by their parents, Lillian and Clark.

In one video, Shelley—who was two and a half at the time—was hugging her new-born baby brother Jace and kissing him on the head, saying, 'Ah, bebbe.'

In the video, her father was watching on nervously saying, 'Careful Shelley, he's very little.'

Shelley watching the video laughed hysterically saying, 'I was so cute.'

'I was too, wasn't I Nanny?' said Jace.

'You sure were, darling,' acknowledged Nanny as they played the next video.

The next short clip showed Shelley nude, galloping around on a huge, furry toy snake, as if it were a hobby horse. Shelley loved the adoring expressions of her parents, as they watched her doing these funny little things.

'You still are a sweet thing you know,' said Nanny, putting her arm around her granddaughter's shoulders.

'I'm not as cute as I was then,' said Shelley, a little disconsolately.

'Well, I think you are,' said Nanny firmly.

'I've seen enough videos, can we read the book now Nanny?' said Jace, yawning.

'Have you had enough Shelley?' asked Nanny.

'Yes, I think so,' said Shelley, putting her small computer away under the bed and snuggling in happily to hear more of the *Apothecary's Quest*.

'Are you kids ready now?' asked Nanny.

'Yes,' said Jace excitedly. 'The demons are chasing Jasmine.'

'Well let's go after them then,' said Nanny, eagerly opening the book.

Apart from the occasional footsteps of the patrolling guards, the castle was asleep, but Jasmine was wide awake in her room and preparing to join her father on his quest. The last thing she needed to do was to write a note for her mother.

Wearing the old clothes that Ellis had given her, Jasmine sat at her desk with the lamp turned down low and, with some guilt, wrote a letter explaining what she was doing and why.

Hoping she had explained herself, she picked up the haversack that contained the things that she and Ellis had gathered together and then folded the note and put it in her pocket.

'Puppy,' she called softly as she put the haversack on.

His watchful eyes had been following her every move, and now, at the mention of his name, he came forward ready for action.

Jasmine scooped Puppy up in a cashmere bag her grandmother had made for him especially.

'Hush,' she said in a whisper as he started to whine softly and lick her face.

She looked back at her substitute sleeping figure in the bed, which was a couple of pillows covered by blankets, and then extinguished the lamp before sneaking over to the door and peeking out into the hall.

Jasmine's and her mother's bedrooms were in the solar—one of the most protected places in the castle—and at the end of the hall, Jasmine could see some of her grandfather's guards talking quietly. Jasmine slipped out of her room, carefully closed the door, and quietly tiptoed along the corridor to her mother's room.

The sound of an approaching guard sent her heart racing as she slipped into her mother's bedroom and breathed a prayer of thanks to God that her mother had not locked the door.

Moving by the light of the moon coming in through the window, she carefully placed the note under the water jug on the dressing table by her mother's bed. She gazed at her mother's sleeping face and felt quite bad about leaving her, but not bad enough to stop going on her mission. It was her big chance to prove herself, a rite of passage that might never happen if she remained cossetted by her parents or, worse, her grandparents.

Jasmine left her mother's bedside and moved towards the door where she sneaked a look along the hall in both directions. There was now a soldier standing guard some distance to the right of her mother's room—blocking her access to the stairs.

I need a distraction to get rid of that guard, thought Jasmine.

She looked around for something she could use and on a nearby hall table saw a large apple perched on top of a decorative bowl of fruit.

Silently, Jasmine crept forward and carefully picked up the apple. She then retreated back to the partly opened door where she hurled the apple down the hallway as far as she could to the left. She heard a thud as she noiselessly pulled the door closed.

With her ear to the door, she waited breathlessly to hear if her diversion had worked. Her heart raced. This wasn't the first time she had played tricks on the guards, but this time she couldn't afford to be found out.

She gave a sigh as she heard the soldier walk past the door and continue on down the corridor.

With a backward glance to see that her mother was still asleep, Jasmine quietly slid out into the hallway and tiptoed towards the stairs. Reaching the ground floor, she edged her way along the wall towards the kitchens and the servant's entrance.

Peeking from the door, Jasmine almost panicked when she saw two servants, a man, and a young boy, carrying crates of bottles from an outbuilding to a large wagon.

Oh no, what are they doing here? thought Jasmine as her hopes of escaping the castle sank.

'Come on, boy,' said the older man, who was clearly the father and a little tipsy. 'I'm tired, and we've got one more stop to do before we get home.'

'Sure, Da, would you like me to drive?' said the boy with amusement.

'No, I'm fine, you little upstart,' said the father with a laugh. 'Get the last crate and we'll be off.'

The boy disappeared to get the last crate as the driver began checking the harness of the horses.

You're so clever God—this could be my way out of the castle, thought Jasmine.

While the father of the boy inspected the bridles and before the boy returned, Jasmine crept out into the courtyard and hoisted herself up quickly into the wagon and hid behind an empty crate. Seeing a hessian bag lying on the floor of the wagon, she pulled it over the top of herself and her dog. Jasmine then placed her hand over Puppy's snout and hoped he would continue to keep quiet so they wouldn't be found.

Jasmine held her breath, terrified that she would be discovered. The wagon lurched as the older man got up onto the driver's seat. Then she heard the sound of someone approaching and almost flinched as something heavy was placed into the wagon near her foot.

'Thanks for all your hard work, boys,' a voice said from close range.

'Not a worry,' said the older man. 'I will just be glad to get back home to sleep. We'll see you next time.'

Jasmine heard the tail board being secured and then felt the wagon sway a little as the boy hopped up next to his father.

'Git along!' Jasmine heard the older man say, and the wagon lurched forward and began rumbling across the cobbled courtyard.

Jasmine began to breathe easier. Maybe her plan would work.

But then the wagon ground to a halt and she heard a male voice say, 'A late night farmer Fledge. Take care on the road, these are strange times.'

'Surely, we will, Darby. And you take care as well,' said the farmer.

Jasmine heard the portcullis scrape as it rose, and then the wagon rolled out across the drawbridge. She breathed a sigh of relief as she heard the portcullis creak and groan as it was lowered again. She had done it—slipped out of the castle under the noses of the guards.

The bright moon silvered the landscape with an eerie half-light as the wagon rattled along. Easing herself up, Jasmine peeped out from under the bag and could see the stables in the home field. She could also see the tall hedge beyond, which ran part way around the field where her pony was normally kept.

There were lots of lights on in the stables, which concerned her. Why would there be lights at this time of night? Then she remembered her grandfather saying that he would be doubling the guards and realised she would need to be especially careful not to be seen. Because of this she decided to approach the field from a side gate.

Jasmine waited until they were travelling alongside the hedge and, when clouds suddenly blotted out the light, she took her chance. Her heavy haversack and the weight of Puppy in his bag, burdened her but she managed to ease herself out from under the bag and shuffled on her backside to the end of the cart. Checking that the farmer and his son had their attention on the road ahead, she then lowered herself over the back of the slowly moving wagon and dropped to the road. The stones crunched a little as she landed, but the grinding of the wheels disguised the noise.

She ran and hid in the hedge and waited until the wagon had moved on into the distance. Then, stepping out of the foliage, she moved the short distance to the fence that also surrounded the field. The dark forms of the many horses in the field had Jasmine wondering which was her pony. Not wanting to make a noise, she nevertheless did call her pony's name softly.

Brownie gave a loud whinny when she heard her owner's voice and began trotting towards Jasmine.

'Hush Brownie, hush,' she whispered loudly.

Barking erupted from the direction of the stables.

'Oh no,' said Jasmine with a shocked gasp. 'They've heard me.'

Puppy also rose up in the bag and started to growl, but Jasmine tapped him on the nose to quiet him.

Fearing that she would be discovered at any moment, Jasmine took off her haversack and quickly tossed it through the fence, following after with Puppy held close to her chest. She then took out the tack that Ellis had secretly packed for her and arranged the bridle.

Brownie reached her and sniffed her hand in welcome. Jasmine gave the pony a pat on the nose and gently slipped the bit into her mouth. Thanking God that the dog had stopped barking, Jasmine finished tacking up Brownie and then led her quickly to the gate, unlatched it and gave a hard pull.

It wouldn't open.

She turned to look in the direction of the stable and could see lamps moving in the entrance. *If I am going to get away it has to be now*, she thought as she tried to open the gate again.

Once again, she wrenched it but the gate did not move.

'It must open. It *must*!' whispered Jasmine, now weeping with frustration.

She yanked it hard, fuelled with strength from her fear and adrenalin, when, *finally*, the gate creaked open.

Lord Pleasure's stable master, Simon, and Farrad, a sergeant of the guard, had come out from the warmth and light of the stables, where

Farrad's men were watering their horses and having a refreshing ale before riding their next circuit of the grounds.

The distant creaking of a gate made Simon suddenly look out into the darkness as his dog—who was tied up near the entrance—started barking again.

'What was that?' asked Farrad.

'It's the side gate,' replied Simon. 'The one near the hedge. Someone has just opened it.'

'That's not right, there shouldn't be anyone there,' said Farrad anxiously. 'Quickly, find out what it is.'

'Go boy!' said Simon, as he released his dog, which was lunging furiously on its leash.

The dog rushed off barking in the direction the sound had come from.

'The Marquis' granddaughter is in danger,' said Farrad, peering out into the darkness. 'We have to be very vigilant.'

'What danger?' asked Simon, curious.

'I do not know, I'm just telling you what I've been told,' replied Farrad, looking worried.

The dog's aggressive barking ceased and was replaced with yips of excitement. Jasmine was normally happy to see him, but now hissed at the tail wagging, tongue lolling guard dog.

'Benjamin, go home, go home!' she scolded in desperation.

'That's strange,' said Simon, stepping forward.

At that moment, the scudding clouds passed clear of the moon.

'Look!' shouted Simon, 'A pony and rider—a thief!'

Farrad saw the rider and heard the pounding of hooves. He immediately turned and ran into the stable to call his men to action.

'Find him!' he commanded. 'A horse thief heading for the forest.'

The soldiers mounted swiftly and thundered off, being able to see while the moon was bright.

'I need to see which horse has been stolen,' said Simon, fetching a lamp and beginning to walk toward the field. 'I have a bad feeling about this.'

'I'll go with you,' said Farrad, a crease of suspicion on his brow.

Checking the horses, they soon found it was Brownie that was missing.

Farrad shook his head and softly cursed and then, as he mounted his waiting horse, he said, 'I'll go to the castle at once and inform the captain of the guard that the lady Jasmine may have just ridden off into the darkness on her pony. If it is someone else who has stolen it, why steal a pony?'

'It doesn't seem possible,' said Simon. 'But if it *is* the young lady on that pony, she may be in grave danger, because I've seen wolves in that forest.'

'We will soon find out if it is her,' answered Farrad, walking his horse out of the stable and then breaking into a canter.

Simon looked off into the darkness and saw his dog returning, thiefless, and with its tail wagging.

'Now just what happened out there, boy? I wish you could talk,' he said as the dog looked up at him with a happy expression, panting and with its tongue lolling out of its mouth.

'Thank goodness Simon's dog went home when I told him to,' exclaimed Jasmine as she pulled Brownie to a halt at the edge of the forest. She was elated with her escape and tingling from head to toe with excitement. The sound of thundering hooves made her turn and she saw three horsemen galloping along the road towards her. Her heart sank and she felt a chill of fear.

'Where did they come from?' she exclaimed in exasperation and urged Brownie onwards.

'We'll never outrun them,' she said anxiously, as Brownie moved on at a slower pace, hindered by the darkness. '... but maybe we can hide from them.'

She turned her pony off the road and picked her way carefully through the trees towards a stream that she knew, relying on the pony's good night vision to get her there safely.

As the sound of the horses grew closer, Jasmine directed Brownie behind a large blackberry bush. She held her breath and quietened her pony as the horses passed by without her being seen.

'They will realise we are not on the road soon,' said Jasmine and then she added thoughtfully. 'And they might come back with pop's dogs, so we need to outwit them too—throw them off the scent.'

Jasmine quietly directed her pony through the trees down to the stream and urged her into the chilly current. She knew this part of the stream, having gone along it with her father collecting plants. It was free of obstacles, lined with sand and small rounded stones plus the occasional blackberry bush. She quickly urged Brownie to walk a flat figure eight, crossing and recrossing the stream before moving off.

This should fool them, she thought, as she encouraged her pony upstream, breasting the water and heading towards a small island in the middle of the steam where the waters parted around a cluster of large rocks on which was a large blackberry bush.

Jasmine turned into the left branch, which took her further away from her pursuers and then stopped because she heard the sounds of the horses returning. She held her breath and placed a hand on Puppy's muzzle to prevent him from barking, saying softly and intensely, 'Please God don't let them find me.' Her heart then froze as her pony whinnied a greeting to the other horses.

'Quiet Brownie,' she whispered hoarsely, and she sighed with relief when Brownie stopped immediately.

Jasmine listened intently and could hear the sound of hoofbeats growing fainter and fainter, so she figured that they had given up the chase and were returning to the stables. God had answered her prayer and the men had not heard her pony's whinny. She was grateful for that.

After a while, she could only hear the trickle of water over stones. The moon's light shone over the forest.

Jasmine came off the island and rode downstream, then, finding a break in the blackberry bushes, she urged Brownie out of the water. Absorbing her owner's courage, the pony stepped pluckily up the embankment, ignoring the swishing branches of the many bushes, and progressed onwards until she was on the road again.

Looking down the darkened road, Jasmine wondered how far ahead her father might be. She ruffled Puppy's head and said, 'Mummy says that the spirit of God made the stars and that He knows everything—He'll show us where Daddy is.'

Brownie's ears had flickered back and forth as she listened to her rider's voice and now she snorted, as if in reply. Her quick little hooves then carried Jasmine off through the night without needing any urging from her rider.

'That might be enough for tonight,' said Nanny, closing the book.

'No, that's not fair Nanny,' said Jace, with irritation in his voice. 'Leaving us in suspense like that. It was just getting exciting.'

'Don't worry, Jace,' said Nanny with a smile. 'Sometimes waiting for something makes it all the more enjoyable.'

'Oh, I suppose so,' said Jace, grudgingly agreeing.

'What was that other thing you were going to tell us?' asked Shelley, who didn't seem to be so disappointed about the story ending.

'I was going to tell you how God has a plan for your lives,' said Nanny. 'Are you still a bit sad, darling?'

'Yes,' replied Shelley. 'Sad, and I feel like my life has no purpose—that it wouldn't matter whether I had even been born.'

'Don't be so melodramatic, Sweety,' said Nanny, patting her affectionately on the shoulder. 'The story I was going to tell you is a true story, about how God made sure that your Uncle James lived. Do you want to hear it now? Keep in mind it's late and you have school tomorrow.'

'I want to hear it,' said Shelley. 'You said it would make me happy and I'm not really happy yet.'

'Okay,' said Nanny. 'Before I had Uncle James, I was very depressed and one day while I was in the kitchen, I pleaded with God and said, "I need to talk to you, or one of your angels, because no one knows how I feel."'

'And then what happened?' asked Shelley.

'There was a knock at the door and a friend was there, but she didn't cheer me up.'

'Why, Nanny?' asked Shelley, suddenly very interested.

'Well,' said Nanny. 'She asked me to come to an exercise class for pregnant women that she was running down at the Community Centre, but I told her that I was a little down, and that I wasn't interested. She then said that I shouldn't have become pregnant, if I knew I would be so depressed.'

'That's pretty mean,' said Jace, with a concerned little frown on his face.

'At the time, I thought it was an answer to my prayer because the knock came just as I prayed, but instead, I just felt worse. She certainly was no angel.'

'Then what happened?' asked Jace.

'That night, I woke up and I felt like a huge quilt full of love was surrounding me. I could actually feel the love, like a tangible thing. When I looked towards the doorway of my room, I saw Jesus smiling at me.'

'You mean you actually saw Him? Did He talk to you?' asked Shelley, whose eyes had grown wide with astonishment.

'Yes, I saw Him and, yes, He talked to me,' replied Nanny eagerly, prizing the lids of her eyes wide with her fingers to make her point. 'I saw Him with my own two little peepers, and I recognised Him straight away. He then spoke right into my mind, without talking out loud.'

'How cool,' said Jace. 'Telepathy.'

'Yes,' acknowledged Nanny.

'What did he say?' asked Shelley.

'He said: "I know how you feel about the little boy next door, and I don't condemn you and I will fix it". I was looking at the wardrobe at the time.'

'Fix what?' asked Shelley.

'The way I felt about the little boy. You see, he had hit Lillian on the head with a stick,' replied Nanny. 'I had been angry and smacked him, but then I had immediately felt sick with remorse because he was a brain-damaged child, and probably hadn't meant any harm.'

'I'm guessing you felt really bad after that,' said Shelley.

'I sure did,' said Nanny sorrowfully. 'I am a Christian and should have shown more compassion and tolerance—I should have known better and done better.'

'So how did Jesus fix it?' asked Shelley.

'I'll get to that a bit later,' said Nanny, her eyes shining brightly with the memory of the event.

'As He was speaking, I could clearly make out the details of the dirty linen basket near the bathroom. Jesus told me, "I love you just the way you are."'

'So,' began Jace, who was quite fascinated by this time, 'if you saw the clothes basket while He was speaking to you, your eyes must have been open. You couldn't have been asleep.'

'Exactly,' agreed Nanny. 'But I went straight back to sleep after that.'

'How could you go to sleep after that?' asked Shelley.

'I don't know, I just did.'

'That's really weird,' commented Jace.

'Is that it?' asked Shelley, a bit disappointed. 'How is that story supposed to make me happy?'

'No. There's more,' replied Nanny.

'I was due to have a scan in two weeks' time, to see if my pelvis was big enough to have Uncle James without a caesarean, because it looked like he was going to be a breech birth, meaning that he would come out bottom first. I was impatient to find out, so they booked me in for a scan the very next day.'

'I know what caesarean means,' said Jace wisely. 'They cut your stomach open and pull the baby out.'

'That's right,' said Nanny. 'They do that if the baby can't be born naturally.'

'Or if the baby is too big,' said Shelley. 'Because they can get stuck.'

'Or if it's a breech birth and comes out bottom first—they need more room to get out.'

'Why would it matter if you had a caesarean, as long as the baby was born healthy?' asked Shelley.

'You're absolutely right,' replied Nanny. 'But I was vain and didn't want a caesarean because it was unfashionable to have them in those days. That's why I wanted the scan early—to find out.'

'So, what did the scan show?' asked Shelley, whose curiosity had been aroused.

'It showed that my pelvis was big enough to have the baby naturally,' said Nanny with a croaky voice. 'But they found there was something wrong with Uncle James, and the doctor said that I would have to come straight in the next morning to give birth to him. The scan had not been due for another week and Uncle James wasn't due to be born for another two weeks.'

'What was wrong? What happened when he was born?' asked Jace. 'Was he alright?'

'James almost died. The doctors and nurses had to resuscitate him and put him in a humidicrib for a night. All the time I was crying. But I wasn't really crying for him, which I know sounds really odd and heartless.'

'Who were you crying for then?' asked Shelley, who was quite shocked.

'My heart was breaking for the little boy next door,' replied Nanny. 'I remembered his dad telling me that he'd been oxygen deprived at birth. That was how he became brain damaged. My James could have been the same.'

'Like it says in the Bible, "God took my heart of stone and gave me a heart of flesh", and all I felt for the little boy after that was pure love.'

'What about Uncle James?' asked Jace, concerned.

'The doctors induced the labour, and he got foetal distress at the end of his birth and it was touch and go as to whether he would live. The doctor told me that if he had gone his full term he would have died and, even if he had been born a day later, he would have been dead.'

'The doctor said to me, "Your baby was on a knifes edge."'

Both children were silent.

'God's timing was perfect.' said Nanny.

'So,' said Jace after a while. 'What you're saying is that Jesus got Uncle James to be born at exactly the right time, and He also made you love the other little boy.'

'That's right,' said Nanny. 'He fixed everything.'

'I don't feel so bad now,' said Shelley.

'Why?' asked Nanny, curious.

'God knew when Uncle James should be born so that he would survive, so I think I was meant to be born too. And Mum doesn't love me any less just because she is having another baby,' said Shelley, coming to a sudden realisation.

'Of course not,' said Nanny, giving her a hug. 'You and Jace are her babies too and always will be.'

'She loved me in my videos because I was so cute. Wasn't I Nanny?' asked Shelley with a little smile.

'How could she not?' replied Nanny, giving her granddaughter a tender kiss on the forehead, and then giving Jace one as well.

She stood up then and put the book on the writing bureau before going to the doorway. 'Goodnight, sweethearts,' she said, turning off the light.

'Nanny, I'm not tired now,' said Jace in the darkness.

'Me neither. I'm sort of excited,' said Shelley. 'God might have something really great planned for me.'

'That's right, and tonight, while you sleep, you might just get a glimpse of Heaven,' said Nanny.

'That would be cool,' said Shelley.

'I'm going to Heaven to fly like Superman,' said Jace, giggling.

'Have fun then,' said Nanny with a grin. 'Sweet dreams, little darlings.'

'Night, Nanny,' said the children as they snuggled into their blankets.

Nanny went off to bed as well and lay there contemplating God's goodness for quite a while. Her child had been saved and a sad relationship between herself and the little boy had been mended and now she got to tell the story of God's mysterious workings to her grandchildren to help build their hopes and dreams.

Feeling at peace, she then fell into a deep and untroubled sleep, with a smile on her lips.

Chapter 13

It was a rainy, freezing day, so the kids were absorbed in their computers and scarcely looked up as Nanny was doing housework.

'How about more *Apothecary's Quest* kids?' said Nanny, wiping her hands on her apron. 'Some exciting stuff is coming up.'

'Okay,' said Jace. 'I hope the witch and the demons are in it.'

'Oh *yes*, they *are*, don't you worry,' said Nanny with a laugh.

'I hope it's not going to be too scary,' said Shelley, turning off her computer and going to the kitchen to get some snacks.

'Jace, get yourself some snackies,' said Nanny. 'And a drink of milk.'

While the kids were in the kitchen, Nanny got the manuscript from their bedroom, and by the time they returned she was seated in her chair, waiting.

'Do you know where we were up to?' she asked them as they sat down at the family room table.

'Jasmine got into the forest just in time,' said Jace, munching a packet of chips.

'That's correct, Jace,' said Nanny, opening the book and starting to read.

Jasmine carefully followed the road through the dark, gloomy forest until she reached more grazing land. She realised it must belong to one of her grandfather's neighbours. The road here was lined on either side by old oaks and tall claret ash. The grass in the field rustled as they passed.

She smiled as she occasionally heard a cow lowing to its calf and the bawling cry of the young animal in reply. *This is not as difficult as I thought it would be,* Jasmine thought to herself. *I really don't know why father didn't want me to come.*

After a while she saw the tall form of a chateau in the distance and wondered whose it might be. Its jagged spires glinted in the moonlight, and she thought she could see guards on the parapets. She hoped that this neighbour of her grandfather didn't mind strangers travelling through their lands at night.

As she rode along, clouds once more scudded across the face of the moon, and once more she was plunged into darkness. An owl hooted as it flew low overhead, and her heart gave a little leap. She settled quickly once she realised that she was in no immediate danger.

'I was seven when I first went into the wilds with Daddy and Mummy—she used to come too,' she said sadly, speaking to Brownie and Puppy. 'We collected plants for him to use in his dispensary, and he taught me how to cook a rabbit stew and how to set up a tent and how to make fire—and he taught me archery. Of course, Brownie, he caught the rabbits, I couldn't do that cause I have pet ones at home.'

Jasmine kept up the nervous chatter to her animals because it comforted her to talk to someone, even herself. As she rode, Jasmine lifted Puppy out of the saddle bag and placed him, still in his cashmere bag, between herself and the pommel, where he would be warmer.

Soon farmland was once again replaced by thick forest—Jasmine had now passed through the baron's lands safely, just like her father.

Puppy squirmed free of his bag and leapt up to lick her face.

'I am so grateful that Daddy saved you,' said Jasmine with a laugh as she pushed the dog back down into its bag and wiped her cheek. 'You *are* a comfort to me now.'

Puppy gazed up at his mistress with adoration, his ears pricked to hear her every word.

A high, thin howl pierced the forest air and Jasmine felt like cold hands had seized her heart and her mouth became dry with terror.

'A wolf!' she gasped, clutching her reins tightly.

Puppy growled and bared his sharp little teeth.

'Come on, Brownie,' Jasmine said hurriedly. 'We had better be quick finding Daddy, or else we'll be dinner for the wolves.'

Jasmine urged Brownie into a vigorous trot. The plucky pony snorted as if in reply and barrelled on gamely into the dark night.

'Let's have a break kids,' said Nanny, putting down her manuscript and getting to her feet, 'and some lunch, if you haven't already filled yourselves up with snacks.'

'I hope we can keep going with the story,' said Jace. 'I like it even better than my computer game.'

'And that's saying something, coming from a computer fan like yourself,' said Nanny.

'Can I have a ham and cheese toastie?' asked Jace, leaping to his feet. 'It's my *favourite.*'

'Sure,' said Nanny. 'Go and get the sandwich maker out. I'll be there in a minute.'

'Can I have the same, except without ham?' asked Shelley, enthusiastically. She rose from the couch and started for the kitchen, but Nanny put her hand on her shoulder.

'How are you feeling now, darling?' asked Nanny.

'Not too bad,' replied Shelley. 'Do you think Mummy would care if I left like that, in the middle of the night like, Jasmine did?'

'She would go absolutely insane with worry,' said Nanny, putting her arm around her granddaughter and hugging her tight.

After a brief cuddle, Shelley laughingly wriggled free of her grand-mother's clutches, looked up into her face and said, 'I wouldn't want to make her that worried.'

'That's good,' said Nanny, kissing her on the forehead. 'Now let's go and make those toasties—warm food—just what we need on such a cold day.'

After their lunch, the children were keen to get on with the story and settled themselves on the couch either side of Nanny, who had opened the manuscript to read again.

'Hurry up, Nanny,' said Jace in a teasing voice. 'We want the scary stuff now.'

'It will come soon,' said Nanny. 'But can you tell me where we are up to first?'

'Jasmine is in the forest,' said Shelley. 'And she's just heard a wolf howl and she's scared.'

'That's right,' said Nanny. 'A lot will be happening all around the same time, so hold onto your seats.'

'Why do we have to do that?' asked the interested Jace.

Nanny gave a little laugh and said, 'Oh it's an expression that means to brace yourself for some big action, much the same way that they tell you to brace yourself when an aircraft is coming in for a rough landing.'

'Oh,' said Jace, nodding his head wisely while pulling a cushion onto his lap. 'Right, I'm ready.'

Nanny gave Jace a wry smile and started reading.

The exhilaration of her escape had long been forgotten and now Jasmine was simply frightened. She and her animals were now miles deep in a forest, the canopy of tall oaks blotting out some of the moon's light.

Suddenly, Jasmine heard a rustling in the undergrowth behind her. She whipped her head around but could see nothing clearly in the gloom.

'Stay on the track, Jasmine,' she told herself as she gripped the reins even tighter and inadvertently gripped Brownie's sides with her legs, causing the pony to leap forward nervously.

Puppy growled and Brownie twitched her ears, sweating even though she was now only walking.

There was more rustling, and this time Jasmine could see something as the moon's light came through a gap in the canopy. There *was* something out there—dark shapes, moving.

'Just shadows—wind in the branches, Brownie—nothing to worry about,' said Jasmine with as much reassurance as she could summon.

Then, with defiance in her voice, she gave a disdainful sniff and said loudly, 'I can beat you dark things in the night, you had better stay out of my way.'

At Jasmine's words, Brownie burst into a trot of her own volition, then into a gallop.

'Settle down, Brownie,' said Jasmine, easing her back to a walk and patting the pony's wet neck in an attempt to calm her.

The glimmer of a small fire on the side of the road ahead caught Jasmine's attention.

'Look, Brownie," she said with some relief. 'There is someone out there. We'll be safe now.'

A sudden howl came from the nearby undergrowth. The pony screamed and bucked, throwing Jasmine off her back.

Miraculously, Puppy was not squashed by the fall, but Jasmine was now on her hands and knees on the road, gasping from the shock of being unhorsed.

With growing fear, Jasmine realised that Brownie had galloped off and been swallowed by the blackness of the forest. She listened in despair as the pony's thudding hooves careered off into the distance in panic.

Instead of following the pony, the wolves turned their attention to Jasmine. There was an unnatural fury in their fierce yellow eyes, and in desperation, Jasmine got to her feet and sprinted towards the nearest tall tree.

Their hot breath was on her back as she scrambled up the tree, just out of the reach of their gnashing teeth.

Terrified, she called out, 'Help me, Lord!'

Gazba sat bolt upright as Brownie skidded to a halt near his tethered horses, whinnying shrilly in fear. In the light of his small fire, he saw his daughter's pony, wild-eyed and covered in lather, as it urgently touched noses with the other two horses, seeking safety in their presence.

'Jasmine!' he shouted fearfully, remembering the horrible vision he had seen when he'd met Chraston.

Throwing off his blanket, he climbed out of his sleeping sack. His heart was already pounding when he suddenly heard his daughter's voice screaming and wailing to the Lord for help. Then came the gurgling snarl of wolves.

Close to panic, quickly, but carefully, with trembling hands he searched his pack and pulled out a vial—a lethal concoction of his own formulation.

He grabbed a still-burning branch from the campfire, got to his feet and ran through the trees in the direction of Jasmine's voice.

'Where are you, Jasmine!' he shouted hoarsely.

The two wolves leaping for Jasmine's feet were being driven to attack her by Bitterness and Fear, who inhabited their bodies, turning them into bristling monstrosities of hate.

A sudden ethereal wind sprang up, and the wolves retreated in surprise as two angels, dressed in full armour, alighted at the base of the tree and furled their powerful wings. Jasmine, unaware of them, moved further up the tree, trusting her weight to a smaller, higher branch.

Targum in his shining armour and belt of gold stood by Keliran, whose armour and silver belt glowed powerfully.

The dark, flashing brown eyes of Targum and the ice-blue ones of Keliran glared at the wolves. The angels—invisible to Jasmine but not to the demons—stood ready with their swords that shone with a brilliant lightning-white light.

The black, thick-set wolf that was possessed by Bitterness, growled, 'Get out of our way, angels of the Lord, for we have great power.'

'Leave,' demanded Targum, with arched black eyebrows and stern ebony face framed in a glowing light.

'Now,' he added, his expression impassive.

With the hair on his back raised, the gaunt grey wolf, which was inhabited by the demon Fear, growled, 'Don't overstep your boundaries, angels of the Lord, you cannot interfere. We have claimed her for the Prince and there is no other above him.'

'The girl called for help from God,' said Keliran quietly. 'And we are that help.'

Bitterness slunk up beside Fear and said, in a low, mocking voice, 'Just how do you intend to save her. We wait for her to fall from the tree and the law of nature—the death of the weak—will be fulfilled. She will be ours.'

He revealed his fangs in what looked like a grin before continuing. 'You think you can cut short our time here on Earth, but when the child is snuffed out, the Dark Prince will raise us up and we will be more powerful than you.'

The two possessed wolves began stalking towards the tree again.

'You have been warned,' said Keliran, with his icy blue eyes flashing. His fair hair was framed by a haze of misty gold. He then raised his hand.

Suddenly, there was a loud crack and a swishing of leaves as the branch Jasmine was on, broke. But Targum was there instantly to slow her fall. His mighty purple wings folded around her as they touched the ground.

Even with angelic intervention, the girl still landed with a thump on the forest floor and all her breath rushed out of her body.

Miraculously, Puppy had been thrown free of his cashmere bag and had landed safely at the feet of the angels. He now faced the wolves and bared his teeth in a snarl and the much-larger wolves hesitated as the small puppy started to bark furiously, incessantly, piercingly.

Gazba ran on, crashing and cracking over fallen timber, drawn on by the sound of the furious high-pitched barking. He carried the burning branch in one hand and its light revealed a horrifying scene—his daughter lying on the ground being protected from two wolves only by her small puppy.

Terror gripped his soul, and he cried out instinctively and for all he was worth, 'God help her Lord!'

Puppy continued to snarl and snap like a mouse trap in the faces of the wolves, but the difference in their sizes meant he couldn't really protect his mistress.

Between Gazba and his daughter was a marshy ditch which slowed him down as he waded through it, but once again on solid ground he rushed the wolves, waving the burning branch around wildly, causing smoke, sparks, yelps of pain and the smell of singeing fur. The beasts flinched and retreated but did not run away.

They're not running away, thought Gazba with shock. *I'm going to have to use the vial.*

'Run, Jasmine—run to the ditch.'

Jasmine, having somewhat recovered from her winding, struggled to her feet, grabbed her dog, and began limping away.

Gazba, still fending off the wolves with the burning brand, backed away towards the ditch where he found Jasmine shivering with fear. He grabbed her by the shoulders and eased her down quickly, saying, 'Don't worry about the mud. Stay low.'

'I will, Daddy!' Jasmine shouted as she ducked her head.

Gazba took the vial from his pocket and started shaking it vigorously, priming its combustible contents.

He took aim at the approaching wolves, and hurled the vial with all his strength, then threw himself down over his daughter to protect her from the expected explosion.

Nothing happened.

Cold hands squeezed Gazba's heart as he realised that the vial had not exploded.

In the dim flickering light of his dropped torch, he saw the wolves, who had immediately jumped away from the vial, but were now coming forward to inspect it with noses sniffing. After that they would be coming for them in the ditch and there would be no escape.

'What's wrong, Daddy?' asked Jasmine wide-eyed and fearfully, as her dog started barking frantically again.

'Don't worry, Jasmine,' said Gazba, grabbing his now almost useless brand again. 'I want you to run. Find Brownie; she's not far away.'

Help me, Lord! he thought desperately, as he prepared to give his own life to save his daughter.

Suddenly, there was a deafening boom and a blazing white flash of light. Gazba felt a blast of searing heat pass over him.

In the sudden silence that followed the explosion, Gazba saw that there were blackened body parts of wolves littering the forest floor.

Jasmine, who was covered in mud, looked up slowly and asked tentatively, 'Are we safe now, Daddy?'

Gazba sobbed with relief. 'Yes, we are. Thanks be to God,' he said hugging her muddy body while staring soberly at the remains of the wolves.

Something made the vial explode at the right time and it wasn't me—it must have been you. Gazba looked to the sky and smiled solemnly.

While Gazba checked Jasmine for injuries, Puppy ran over to inspect the smouldering remains of the wolves.

The two angels sheathed their swords and, with satisfaction, watched the demons scurry away through the forest, whimpering.

'That will be the last we see of those two for a while,' said Keliran.

'Yes, indeed,' said Targum whose bronze face was filled with radiance. 'What a joy it is to see the peace and relief of the ones we have been given charge over.'

'Causing that branch to break was a good idea,' he said, facing Keliran, whose fair hair shone in a halo of light. 'Once Jasmine was on the ground, the dog was a brave warrior and held them off long enough for Gazba to arrive.'

'Your well-timed catch saved the child from serious injury,' replied Keliran, with appreciation in his blue eyes.

'And our flaming swords,' said Targum, 'filled with the power of the Holy Spirit, drew out the explosion just at the right moment.'

'Yes, 'replied Keliran. 'Like living lightning, it forked from our swords and struck that vial. A fine sight if I may say so.'

'The King *will* be pleased,' said Keliran, slapping his hand on the shoulder of his companion.

'Yes, a victory won,' agreed Targum. 'One of the many before the apothecary's quest is over.'

'And as for you, little friend,' said Keliran, bending down to pat the ecstatic Puppy. 'We will call you Lyon, after the lion, for the fierce brave warrior that you are. What do you think, Targum?'

Puppy, who was enjoying this attention, rolled onto his back.

'Yes, it is fitting,' agreed the dark angel, who affectionately began scratching the dog's belly.

'Farewell, little one, it is time we left,' said Keliran, giving Puppy one last pat. With that, the two angels' mighty wings unfurled and, with powerful beats, lifted them up and away.

Puppy then rolled back to his feet and trotted back to Gazba and Jasmine.

'Strange behaviour, little dog,' said Gazba perplexed. Puppy jumped up happily and began licking his face.

'You *are* a good boy, Puppy,' said Gazba, gently pushing the dog away. 'But first I must tend to my girl.'

'You've been lucky, Jasmine,' he said. 'All I can see is a nasty bruise on your cheek.'

'It's nothing,' said Jasmine bravely and a little proudly. Then she asked rather urgently, 'Have you seen Brownie?'

'Oh yes,' replied Gazba, remembering the pony arriving in a state of panic and its urgent whinnies. 'My first thoughts were of you—it is lucky she woke me.'

'God sent her to you Daddy. To wake you up and come to save me,' said Jasmine, wide-eyed with the revelation.

'Most likely he did, my dear,' said Gazba tenderly. 'But now, come back to the campsite and get warm by the fire. You have been through so much for one night.'

Jasmine faltered as she got up, so Gazba swept her up into his arms and started to carry her to his campsite. Without his torch, it was dark under the trees and so Gazba had to move carefully and slowly through the undergrowth. Suddenly, a silvery beam of moonlight came through the canopy to light his way until he could see the glow of his dying fire.

When he reached the campsite, Jasmine struggled out of his arms and ran to see to her pony, which nickered and sniffed her face affectionately. Gazba smiled and then stoked the fire to prepare her a warm herbal drink that would both calm and fortify her.

Jasmine came back to the fire and her father handed her a cup. 'Just drink this, it will make you feel better,' he said.

'That's delicious,' said Jasmine, sipping from the mug. 'It tastes like cinnamon and honey.'

'That's pretty much what it is,' said her father with a laugh. 'But with a few other good things.'

'Wow Nanny, the angels did magic didn't they!' interrupted Shelley.

'They sure did,' replied Nanny.

'Is that only in the story or can angels do stuff in real life?' asked Jace.

'I believe that angels are definitely on a mission to help us,' said Nanny with a big smile. 'Whether you ask them for help or not, because they are full of God's love.'

'Well, tell us something they have done lately,' said Jace, cheekily.

Nanny thought for a moment and then said, 'You know your mother was saved by angels, don't you?'

The children were shocked. Angels appeared in stories and the lives of other, distant people—not to members of your own family.

'No, what happened?' asked Shelley, much concerned.

'They saved her from breaking her neck,' replied Nanny.

'How?' asked Jace, who was intrigued but still worried.

'Your mum nagged and begged a leading dressage coach to give her a riding lesson and she was due to ride at about seven on a Saturday morning,' replied Nanny.

'Yes, I remember, that was a long time ago. What happened, Nanny?' asked Shelley.

'What's that got to do with angels?' asked Jace, even more intrigued.

'I woke up suddenly at about a quarter to seven,' began Nanny. 'I had a gut feeling that your mum needed protection. She is a good rider, and I don't normally worry about her safety, but this was different—God was prompting me to pray and woke me up to do it.'

'So, what's that got to do with *angels*?' asked Jace.

'Well, your mother rang me just after the lesson and told me what had happened. She was thrown by the horse, sailing through the air, and she landed very hard.'

'Why did it buck her off?' asked Shelley.

'Your mum said the side reins were probably too tight, cramping his neck and sawing at his mouth,' replied Nanny. 'And that the horse's eyes were sullen and cranky.'

'But she wasn't hurt,' said Jace. 'And what's this got to do with angels?'

'Your mother remembers the dressage instructor screaming. It was a spectacular fall—'

'You think angels saved her,' exclaimed Shelley.

'I believe so,' replied Nanny, nodding with excitement.

'So, what you're saying,' began Jace, 'is that God woke you in time to pray for help from the angels.'

'Yes,' said Nanny with a smile. 'But I have heard that they can still come and help us even if we don't pray.'

'Why is that?' asked Jace.

'Because God loves us so much—helps us even before we ask for it.'

'That's a good thing to know,' said Shelley with a contented little smile.

'It's still freezing outside, so can we do more story now?' asked Jace, eager to find out more. The fight with the wolves had whet his appetite for more action.

'Sure, why not,' said Nanny. 'Now, where was I? Ahh, here we go …'

Gazba poked at the fire and then called gently, 'Come, Puppy.'

The dog, who had been lying beside Jasmine, cocked its head, interested but perplexed, as Gazba had never shown any real affection to him before.

'That's right Puppy, come here for a pat,' said Gazba fondly. 'I want to thank you for being such a very brave boy.'

The dog whined, thrashed its tail, and slowly crawled on its belly towards Gazba, who reached out and stroked its bald head. This encouraged Puppy to bounce up and begin licking his face exuberantly.

Gazba chuckled and gently pushed the enthusiastic dog away.

'I normally don't let dogs lick my face, but tonight I'll make an exception.'

After playing with Puppy a short while, Gazba sent him back to Jasmine and started to thoughtfully stoke the fire.

'I should take you back, you know,' said Gazba, not looking up from the fire.

Jasmine shot him a look of pure desperation and said, 'I left a note for Mummy saying that I was going to help you find the unicorn. She knows where I am, so she won't be worried. Please, Daddy. Please, *please* let me come with you.'

Gazba's eyebrows had lifted at the mention of the unicorn. *Does she know more about Chraston than I have already told her?*

'Your mother will be frantic with worry,' said Gazba ruefully.

'Daddy, Chraston is my special friend and at night, when I dream, he says that I have an important part to play in the quest.'

Gazba was plunged into deep wonder. He had known that Chraston's appearance to him had charged *him* with this quest, but he had no idea that Jasmine had been seeing the unicorn in her dreams.

'Why didn't you tell me this before now?' he challenged.

'Because you would have dismissed it as a young girl inventing a story.'

Gazba looked at her face in the dancing firelight. It seemed older and wiser than her age, a little careworn and exhausted. So it was with surprise, that he realised his daughter may indeed be the *Maid*. Still awestruck, Gazba thought to himself: *this part of Chraston's prophecy has come to pass. The dark night of danger has ended well. Maybe it would be best to have her here with me now, so I can keep a better watch over her than the soldiers did at the Pleasure's castle.*

'Let me think on it,' said Gazba, taking his daughter's empty cup from her. 'Now you get some rest, it's been a very big day.'

Deep in the forest, creatures had lain low as the two wailing demons had come careering through the trees, drawn back to Kraekhoull's lair.

Although they had failed in their attempt to kill Jasmine, and had tried to do this without Kraekhoull's permission, they knew they would have to tell the witch that both father and daughter were vulnerable, alone and easy pickings.

The demons assumed their human form and entered through the doorway of the witch's cavern, and the sudden rush of air from outside caused jingling among the array of hanging, eerie green crystal chimes which festooned the cavern roof.

'So,' said Kraekhoull, turning and shooting the seer and the prophetess a withering glare. 'Where have you two been these past hours?'

Not wanting to let the witch know of their freelancing ways, the demons dissembled.

'While strolling through the woods,' began Bitterness in a casual voice, twirling the ends of her long golden hair. 'Imagine our surprise when we saw them—Gazba and the child around a campfire.'

The prophetess then nodded to Fear, who contributed his take on the "chance" meeting.

'They are alone now,' said Fear conspiratorially, 'and can easily be vanquished by your great powers.'

'My powers do *demand* to be used,' agreed the witch, and as she said this, all the wind chimes in the chamber began to tinkle gently.

The witch stared intently upwards as she thought for a moment, and then slowly and with menace in her eyes, glared at the two fallen angels.

'Do you think I don't know what you were doing out there. The child was for me to destroy *with* your help. But I know you were doing this to circumvent my authority and seek your own glory in the Dark Kingdom. And I know you failed. The Dark Prince will hear of your disobedience.'

In shock, Bitterness and Fear transformed into their normal, demonic forms then fell to the floor and began grovelling and begging the witch, 'Please no. Don't do that. Not that. We will do only *your* bidding from now on.'

The witch smiled malevolently and said, 'Good. Now assume your previous forms, for I find you far too repulsive to gaze upon as you are.'

As the two demons returned to their human forms, the witch paced her chamber, thinking.

'I know,' said Kraekhoull, 'I will conjure up a storm. A storm so powerful that they cannot possibly survive.'

'Yes, mistress, that sounds wonderful,' said the demons prostrate on the floor. 'Can we help?'

Kraekhoull threw her head back and laughed and the sound of her cackling filled the cavern.

Rising early, while the pale moon was still faintly visible in the sky and while Jasmine was still asleep, Gazba wrote to Juniper asking him to travel to Jasmine's grandparent's castle and inform them that Jasmine

was with him, and he would take care of her. He attached the tiny note to the leg of the pigeon Juniper had given him and tossed the bird gently into the air, saying a little prayer for its safety.

Gazba was preparing breakfast, having milked Bella the packhorse. Her foal was weaned, and the mare was still being used for her milk. Jasmine woke up groggily and lay rubbing her eyes, but only for a moment or two. Suddenly she sat bolt upright and pleaded urgently, 'Daddy, can I come with you? Don't send me back to my grandparents.'

'You may come,' said Gazba with a smile as he passed her a warm drink. 'Now settle down, little one, and drink this, then we will have delicious pancakes with honey.'

Jasmine's face lit up and she accepted the drink, and said, 'Daddy, we sure beat those wolves didn't we.' She then took a long sip from her steaming mug.

Gazba looked thoughtfully into the fire and said, 'Yes, we did, and it was an amazing experience … although I think we had some providential help last night.'

'What do you mean, Daddy?' asked Jasmine curiously.

'I mean, I think that God was with us,' replied Gazba, with an expression that contained remnants of the awe he had felt the night before.

'I think it also means that you are meant to be here with me, darling, for God protected us both. Perhaps this quest is for us to do together.'

'I'm so glad, Daddy. This will be a real adventure,' she exclaimed.

Gazba smiled, tousled her hair, and started dishing out the pancakes.

Jasmine suddenly looked up from her breakfast and exclaimed, 'What about Mummy? She'll be worried.'

Gazba replied calmly, 'You don't have to worry about that. I have sent word to her that you are with me and that I will look after you.'

'By pigeon?' asked Jasmine. 'The one Juniper gave you before we left?'

'By pigeon,' replied Gazba with a smile.

The two enjoyed their breakfast and the dark encounter of the previous night faded.

'Can I saddle the horses, Daddy? And take off their hobbles?' asked Jasmine, eager to be on their way. A cool breeze wafted past, and some poplars rustled and swayed.

'Of course you can,' answered Gazba, as he began to rinse the breakfast things.

Bella was dozing in the sun and hardly noticed being laden with gear. The other two horses were no longer grazing but alert and ready for travel, so Jasmine unhobbled and saddled them.

After finishing his own tasks, Gazba checked his portable barometer and gave a slight frown. It was nothing much, but the reading was a little lower than he expected, given the appearance of the fine day. He decided not to worry overly, and he and Jasmine mounted their horses to continue their journey to Epiron Rock.

Chloe had wept on and off for hours before falling into a deep sleep. She missed her husband already and was fearful that he would be swept off his feet by the incomparable Maid of Valouresse. She woke early in the morning, thirsty, and reached out for a goblet to refill from the water jug. As she did so, she noticed a piece of paper underneath the jug.

She sat up, reached for the piece of paper, and saw immediately that it was a message written in her daughter's hand.

'No!' she screamed and dropped the note.

Recovering from her immediate fright, Chloe groaned and shook her head. 'Oh Jasmine, you impulsive girl.' Reaching down, she picked up the note again. 'How could you do this?'

'Are you alright, my lady?' said someone on the other side of the door.

Chloe quickly jumped up and put on her dressing gown. Then she burst from her bedroom and ran down the hall to Jasmine's room, with the startled guards following in her wake.

Flinging open the door, she sighed with momentary relief upon seeing a huddled form in the bed. Then she remembered her daughter's strong will. Rushing over to the bed she pulled back the blankets. To her horror, two pillows fell to the floor.

She whipped around to face the guards and demanded, 'have you seen my daughter?'

The two guards looked at each other helplessly and then to Chloe, and said almost in unison, 'no, my lady.'

'We must find her!' shrieked Chloe, with tears in her eyes.

'What is it?' demanded Lord Pleasure, at the door, still tying the belt of his dressing gown. 'Where is Jasmine?'

'She has gone to find her father,' said Chloe, trembling with fear.

'No, no, no. I suspect she is just out playing with her silly dog,' said Lord Pleasure. 'Actually, I have bad news: her pony has been stolen.'

'Good morning my lord, my lady,' said Gallant as the young knight came striding down the corridor with Misk at his heels, carrying a breakfast tray.

'Is something wrong?' asked Misk nervously.

'She's left a note,' said Chloe, brandishing the paper. 'Jasmine is gone.'

'But I saw her sleeping form in the bed,' said Misk in disbelief.

'She is gone I tell you.' shouted Chloe, turning on Misk.

Misk burst into tears and whimpered, 'I am so sorry, my lady.'

Noticing her maid servant's distress, Chloe's face softened, and she put a comforting hand on Misk's shoulder saying, 'You were not to know of my daughter's intentions last night.'

Then, turning to her father, she asked, 'Why wasn't I told about the theft of the pony?'

Lord Pleasure raised his hands in an expression of powerlessness, and then Gallant spoke. 'The household was asleep, so when the captain of the guard told me of the theft, I didn't want to disturb anyone without good cause, especially you Lady Chloe. I asked Misk to check that Jasmine was in her bed, and it seemed that she was.'

Chloe's eyes glowed with determination, and she said, 'I am going after her.'

'Not on your own, you're not,' growled the Marquis.

'I will keep her safe,' said Gallant with eyes intent.

'Good man, Gallant,' said the Marquis. 'Take some men and accompany Lady Chloe. And be quick about it. We all want Jasmine back safe and sound as soon as possible.'

Gallant turned to leave but stopped when Chloe asked, 'Could I take Grunjion? He's fast and strong.'

'Are you out of your mind?' retorted the Marquis. 'That horse is as wild as a forest stag and a bolter.'

'Father, you know I can ride,' said Chloe impatiently. 'And anyway, I have ridden Grunjion many times.'

'This is news to me!' exclaimed Lord Pleasure folding his arms in a gesture of indignation. 'When did this occur?'

'Last year when I came to visit mother, while you were travelling with the king,' Chloe said. 'I rode him, and he was as quiet as a lamb.'

'It is true, my lord,' said Gallant, 'I have seen the animal become gentle at her touch.'

Lord Pleasure raised his eyebrows and then, with new respect for his daughter, said, 'I do find that hard to believe, but if it's true, I suppose you can take him. But be careful.'

Chloe gave her father a grim smile and then said, 'We must go at once. Who knows what dangers my daughter faces at this moment?'

A little while later, as Chloe entered the courtyard with her gear, she gasped and then smiled as she always did when she saw the powerful Grunjion. He was being led towards her by a nervous stable boy.

Grunjion pranced impatiently, with rippling muscles and gleaming chocolate-coloured coat. His flaxen mane shivered like a river of gold, as he neighed a welcome at the sight of Chloe.

Walking across the courtyard towards Grunjion, Chloe freed one of her hands from the riding tack load so she could pat the soft muzzle of the mighty horse.

'My friend,' said Chloe, stroking the silky neck of the regal animal. 'You must be good for me today.'

The Marquisa—hastily dressed but with her hair still a mess—approached Chloe and said, 'Please let Gallant find Jasmine. It is too dangerous to ride that wild animal.'

'No mother,' said Chloe. 'I must go. She is *my* daughter, and I will find her.'

The Marquisa saw her daughter's burning cheeks and flaming eyes and saw it was like trying to stop an oncoming storm. She turned away as tears spilled from her eyes and sought the solace of her husband.

Chloe placed her personal belongings in Grunjion's saddle bags and then swung up onto his back and landed lightly. The horse rolled its eyes and started forward, doing a few little half rears and pirouettes, spinning on the spot, and Gallant had to fight to control his mount, as it and the rest of the horses in the courtyard became infected by Grunjion's high spirits.

'Softly, my boy,' whispered Chloe in the horse's ear, while stroking its neck. 'Softly.'

The big animal's eyes lost the whites of high excitement and became dark liquid again as he stopped fidgeting and became gentle and still.

Her father looked on in disbelief as he saw the horse become so docile. But that still didn't stop him from muttering, under his breath, 'Wilful girl.'

Lady Pleasure squeezed her husband's arm and said, 'She takes after someone I know.'

'Farewell Father, Mother,' said Chloe as she turned in a small circle and directed Grunjion towards the castle gate.

Sensing his rider's urgency, Grunjion did a high rear and then plunged into a gallop and headed towards the gate at speed. In seconds, they were thundering across the drawbridge.

'God be with you,' said the Marquis to the other searchers as they began to follow. 'And take care of my daughter!'

'Thank you, my lord,' shouted Gallant as he saluted and then turned and cantered with his ten knights and their accompanying squires across the drawbridge.

I don't care if he sees my puffy eyes, thought Chloe miserably later in the day, as she rode beside the knight at a more sedate pace.

'The weather appears inclement, my lady,' commented Gallant.

'Indeed, the clouds are rolling in,' replied Chloe, watching the soldier riding in the lead looking for signs of her daughter having passed that way. 'We must pick up speed and find Jasmine before nightfall. Cannot our tracker travel a bit faster?'

'Are you all right, my lady?' asked Gallant, noticing Chloe's inflamed eyes and haunted expression.

'I am well, Gallant,' replied Chloe. 'I am just a little sad because I feel left out. I would have loved to join Gazba on his quest. But, most of all, I worry about my daughter.'

'I am sure he does love you, my lady,' said Gallant. 'But he does this for Valouresse—going on this quest that you told me about, I mean. Your husband would not wish to put you in any danger by bringing you along, and hopefully your runaway daughter is with him as we speak.'

'Yes, Gallant, hopefully they are together,' acknowledged Chloe. 'But have you heard of the Maid of Valouresse, who is a true heroine and probably very beautiful? It is Gazba's mission to find and protect her, but I do fear he may fall in love with her. She is known as a valiant heroine, and I feel inferior to her.'

The knight gazed upon his lady's pale but beautiful countenance and said, 'That is not likely, in my opinion, for I know he loves you alone. The main thing is that he will most definitely be watching over your daughter.'

Because it was not his station in life to do so, Gallant did not offer any further advice, but he yearned to comfort her. *My dear sweet lady, if you*

*were mine, I would stand by you, and defend you to the last, with everything
I had.*

'He just didn't want me to be there with him,' said Chloe, brushing
aside a few tears. She then continued speaking to herself as much as
to Gallant, 'As you well know, I ride, I can use a bow and arrow and
even a sword. You were with me when my father taught me. However,
I chose the quiet, respectable life of a noblewoman when I married Gazba.
I buried my skills and now I regret it.'

'I am sure your husband values you highly,' said Gallant encouraging
Chloe as best he could. 'For such a wife as yourself is above rubies.'

'Thank you, Gallant. I will try to believe that. I have read that in
the scriptures.'

'My lady,' said Gallant, earnestly seeking her eyes, which she turned
away from him in a gesture of modesty. 'Your father dedicated my services
to you, whenever you come to stay with him, but you must know I would
go anywhere, any time to help you.'

Chloe blushed at his ardent loyalty. She was attracted to this knight,
who she had known most of her life and who, in return, had worshipped
the ground on which she walked. It was nice to be noticed, let alone to
be listened to. Gazba was often not around, and generally just distracted
with his work.

Chapter 14

Bitterness, now in his real form, paced the empty chamber where the witch's crystal ball still flared with fire. He was afraid, and his pustulent face still quivered in reaction. His encounter with his master had been so terrifying, that he would now do anything to appease the Dark Prince.

The crystal ball suddenly became clear. Within he saw two riders, the accursed wife, and a knight, and he knew what he had to do. He was compelled to use his power to stop the woman from going to Gazba's aid. His bitter thoughts would become hers; changing her mind so that she left her husband and the Maid alone and defenceless, with no knight or soldiers to help them. Maybe the knight would become too attractive for Chloe to resist.

Bitterness drew close to the crystal ball and his substance became entwined with it and was suddenly pulled into it. For a brief moment he was gone. Then he was beside Chloe and Gallant and his greasy bat-like wings furled as he settled onto her shoulder, now diminutive, invisible, and unseen.

The demon whispered his devilish thoughts into her mind—just an insinuation of discontent.

Chloe turned her head and looked at the handsome knight riding beside her. *Gallant is more my age. He understands me and knows the things*

I can do. Maybe Gazba should leave forever—find the Maid of Valouresse and be happy with her.

She noted that the eyepatch gave the knight a swashbuckling appearance.

I have eaten dinner alone so many times—my husband missed Jasmine's toilet training celebration when she was two. And other occasions.

Chloe choked back a little sob and Gallant immediately fixed his gaze on her and asked, 'Is there something wrong my lady?'

'It is nothing Gallant, just swallowed an insect,' she lied.

Gallant looked at her intently with concern but said nothing more and turned his attention back to the road, which was potholed and rough.

Chloe shivered as she felt a cold wind whip up around her. Tears sprang into her eyes, and she made sure the knight did not see these.

Oh Lord, she prayed to herself. My heart is disloyal. I want to be strong for my daughter and my husband—please help, for I feel so terrible.

In response to Chloe's prayer, Mellion—a lovely angel who looked like an Indian princess swathed in a sparkling pink sari and ornate headdress of gold and pearls—came to her, bringing light.

She swooped low and glared at the now cringing Bitterness.

The demon snarled.

'Begone, creature of darkness,' said the angel in her sweet but stern voice. 'You have no power here, for love and faith conquer all.'

Bitterness left Chloe's shoulder and took off into the forest flapping desperately.

Mellion moved close by Chloe and closed her eyes. Then she lightly touched Chloe's forehead and breathed upon her.

'You have been heard by the King,' the angel whispered.

As if in response, Chloe smiled.

'Do you smell that?' asked Chloe. 'Something very beautiful, like a rare perfume.'

Gallant returned her smile but shrugged and shook his head.

Chloe's change of mood was immediate. Colour came back to her face, and she thought: *my husband loves us deeply and he goes on this quest to save our daughter and all of Valouresse. I will hold onto this.*

'Come, Gallant, let's hurry now,' said Chloe. 'The sky becomes darker.'

Suddenly there was a loud rumble of thunder, finishing with a loud crack.

Nanny put the manuscript down and said—with a grin and seeing by their expressions that they were hooked—'Do you want me to keep going kids?'

'Yes, please,' both children replied almost together.

'It's still too cold to go shoot some hoops,' said Jace. 'Might as well keep reading Nanny.'

'And anyway, I want to hear about the storm, so keep reading Nanny.'

'Alright then, let's go,' said Nanny, pleased to be sharing her story with her enthralled grandson.

After all the excitement of the night before, it was very pleasant to ride along a forest road that followed a sweetly singing stream nearby. Gazba stopped and let his horse drink and glanced up at the sky, where a gathering of clouds thwarted the midday sun's light.

Jasmine urged Brownie down to the stream and, while the pony drank, she looked around at the forest expectantly.

'Oh Daddy!' she suddenly exclaimed in a rapturous voice, 'I just realised we are going to find Chraston, aren't we? The unicorn. My unicorn!'

Gazba smiled, then raised his eyebrows as she mentioned the unicorn was hers but said nothing.

Jasmine dropped Puppy gently to the ground and he instantly ran to the stream and lapped up water eagerly.

'He's a good, faithful dog, unlike your pony who ran away and left you,' said Gazba, frowning as he watched the pony eating the soft green grass at the water's edge.

'Horses are often a bit more timid than dogs, and their first response to danger is to run away,' said Jasmine. 'She can't be blamed, it's just her nature.'

'You're right of course,' said Gazba, smiling at her wisdom and her wish to defend her pony's honour. He then reached down and took his barometer from the saddle bag to read.

'This forest is like I imagine Heaven to be,' continued Jasmine, changing the subject and sighing as she took in the quiet beauty of the place. 'I love the colour and the smell of the leaves at this time of year.'

'Yes Jasmine, it's very heavenly here,' answered Gazba in an unemotional manner, frowning as he finished reading the barometer, which he then buckled inside the saddle bag.

'What does it say, Daddy?' asked Jasmine with curiosity. 'Is there going to be a storm?'

Gazba glanced at the darkening clouds and saw a wave of swallows sweeping across the sky. *They know what is coming,* he thought and made his decision.

Then, turning to Jasmine, he replied, 'Yes, there will be a storm, so let's find our way to higher ground.' Urging Helga up the embankment and away from the stream, he led the way across the road and upwards into the forest, crushing bracken as they went.

'I thought there may be a storm coming,' said Jasmine, riding beside him into the silent, mossy, mysterious world of the forest. No birds sang, as if knowing that it was time to seek refuge in holes within trees to await the turbulence that was to come. Light filtered through the branches but here on the forest floor, rocks and moss were the only things it revealed apart from the violets which grew between.

'How did you know a storm was coming, darling?' asked Gazba.

'Because there are no blackbirds hopping around looking for food. They make such a mess in my garden at home, like little gardeners, turning over the earth with tiny picks and shovels but with their beaks instead,' she said with a laugh.

Gazba smiled at her comment, but he too noticed an unnatural silence and would have liked to see the industrious birds in this eerie place.

Here, deep in the forest, there was an ominous mood, something in the air. Gazba contemplated the situation, hoping that there would be no wolves to harass them now but, at the back of his mind, were the machinations of the witch—could she have been the reason that the wolves attacked them with such unrelenting ferocity?

Her black magic was an unknown quantity, but looking at his saddlebags and knowing their contents, he was confident that his alchemical skills would protect them both.

As Chloe, Gallant, the ten knights and accompanying squires—trainee knights from Lord Pleasures chateau—rode along, a strong wind suddenly whipped up.

'This has come up quickly,' shouted the knight, shielding his face from a sudden gust of wind full of leaves and twigs. 'And I think it promises to be a real storm. I think we should seek shelter.'

'Yes, I agree,' said Chloe lowering her head to avoid the brunt of the wind.

'There is an old church not far from here,' advised one of the squires, who had been this way before.

Around the next bend in the road, in the waning evening light, they perceived the outline of the church. As they got closer, they saw that the front entrance was in complete ruins, though the far walls were still stone upon stone and solid. The roof was a problem.

The squires and Gallant secured their canvas groundsheets above the worst holes in the roof just before a heavy rain started to pelt down.

The four of them then settled their horses within and prepared to wait out the storm but soon Gallant had to fix a billowing groundsheet that had come loose.

Once he had climbed down and had stripped off his soaking cloak, Chloe tapped him on the shoulder and yelled above the deafening roar of the wind, 'Gazba and Jasmine are out in this!'

As she finished speaking, there was a blinding flash of light, followed almost immediately by a loud crack of thunder.

Pale of face, and with Gallant's support, Chloe walked to the altar where she sank to her knees and started to pray fervently, her eyes fixed on the dilapidated wooden cross that still adorned the remaining wall of the church.

Gallant steadied her, then noticed, in the light from another flash of lightning, that her face was wet with tears. Then, he too, lowered his head in prayer.

Chloe wept as she prayed, repeatedly, 'Oh Lord, please keep them safe. Keep them safe.'

All the while, the storm roared around the ruins of the valiant old church.

The wind was now suddenly gaining strength. In the forest depths it was becoming harder to be heard above the storm.

'Jasmine! Quickly, tend to Brownie,' shouted Gazba, his voice barely audible. He then removed his gear from the horses, hobbled them, and also tethered them to a rope line between two strong silver birch trees close by. Then, the two of them swiftly erected a tent.

As the storm continued to build in strength, large drops of water began to filter down from the branches above, which creaked with the force of the wind.

'Just in time,' said Gazba, driving in the last tent peg.

Suddenly there was a flash of white light followed by a loud boom. The horses squealed and began milling around in terror.

'The horses will be alright, Jasmine,' said Gazba, loud enough to be heard above the sound of the wind in the canopy above. Jasmine turned and gave her father a nervous smile, continuing to put the gear into the tent.

'Good girl,' shouted Gazba, as he pushed the last of the gear into the tent and followed himself.

Despite his calming reassurances, Gazba became nervous. The wind had somehow found its way down to the little cowhide tent, the sides of which bowed in fearfully with each monstrous gust.

The roaring of the wind in the tree above and the squealing of the horses didn't let up and Gazba put on a calm face for Jasmine's benefit. However, the sound of creaking and wood cracking above the tent now made him regret his choice of campsite among the old oaks.

Gazba turned his face away from Jasmine and he began to pray fervently and quietly with fists pressed hard against his forehead. 'My Lord, protect my daughter. Do not save her from the wolves only to have her perish in this storm.'

In the unnatural fury of the storm, he pulled Jasmine close to him and started to weep softly.

The Captain of the Armies of Heaven had heard Chloe's desperate pleas—and now Gazba's. He smiled and called to his waiting angels, 'Targum, Keliran, go now.'

On powerful wings the two angels quickly flew to the small tent in the forest where Gazba, Jasmine and Puppy lay curled together, at the very heart of the storm.

Keliran and Targum saw the sagging branch above the tent and heard the ominous cracking noise coming from it. Both of them frowned and felt a cold premonition of doom.

The wind took on a high, eerie scream as it seemed to double in strength and the dark forces driving it buffeted the angels. There was malice behind the storm.

Targum's face was anguished as he struggled to stand against the swirling, evil fury. He staggered backwards and seemed to disappear into the blackness but then forced himself forward again. He drew his sword, held it high and called out loudly, 'Cease!'

Immediately, the dark forces and the wind departed, the rain stopped, and a calm descended on the area, except for the ominous creaking of the branch above the tent.

Keliran swiftly entered the tent, invisible to the humans within. Puppy, however, could see him and squirmed out of Jasmine's arms to welcome the angel.

'Puppy!' shrieked Jasmine as she broke free of Gazba's protective embrace and lunged forward to grab the dog and pull him towards her.

Gazba, surprised that the wind had dropped so suddenly, sat up.

Keliran quickly moved to his side and whispered something into his ear—a soft urgent message.

Gazba's eyes went wide.

Suddenly, there was a loud crack.

Gazba had grabbed Jasmine, curled his body around her and then rolled to one side as the tent folded in around the large branch that crashed down where she had been. It was a truly miraculous moment.

Nanny stopped reading, beamed at the two children, and asked, 'Was that exciting enough for you? The evil has been foiled for the time being, making it a fitting end to that chapter, don't you think?'

'Yeah, not bad,' conceded Jace with a little grin. 'But I'm waiting for the demons to do more stuff again.'

'All in good time,' said Nanny with a wry smile. 'And don't you mean, that you can't wait to hear about the angelic activity?'

'Yeah, that's good too, but I like scary things and seeing how the angels defeat them,' replied Jace with a cheeky smile on his face.

'I like the angels too,' said Shelley, interrupting enthusiastically.

'Will we continue then? asked Nanny. 'It's probably still too cold to go out anyway, don't you think?'

'Yes,' said Shelley. 'I want to stay in and hear more.'

'Me too,' added Jace.

'Well, then, here we go,' said Nanny as she turned the page.

'That was close,' said Keliran gravely, standing beside his fellow angel and giving him a pat on the shoulder. 'If you hadn't shifted that branch when you did, this could have been the end of them and certainly the end of the prophecy.'

Targum was very subdued. He shook his head and then faced his friend and said, 'Yes, I am aware of that. You spoke to his spirit, and I was able to move that branch in time—but it fell close to them, more closely than I would have liked.'

'That, my friend, is an understatement. However, praise be to the Lord it did not crush the Maid.'

'The Maid is still a child and does not understand her special power … which I admit I don't understand either,' said Targum with a perplexed smile on his dark, bronze face.

'The King does, and in good time I am sure He will reveal it to her. In any case, He will be pleased that she and her father have been preserved to continue the quest.'

The angels smiled at their charges and, satisfied that they were now safe, lifted off the ground, passed through the canopy unhindered, and then circled twice before disappearing upwards into the sky. Moonlight glinted off their wings like a shower of hope.

It had been barely a minute since Gazba had rolled free of the tent, fearful of what he might find waiting for them outside. Now he and Jasmine stood over the remains of the collapsed tent with water from the silent canopy above dripping on them.

A huge branch lay in the spot where Jasmine had been and Gazba's heart froze in horror at the thought of what might have happened. Gazba praised God for the sudden impulse that had made him pull Jasmine away just in time.

Then he admonished himself and thought, *I must be rational. I have always trusted science. Was it an impulse? An instinctive reflex? I don't even remember rolling us away as it came down. Or … was it the spirit of God that prompted me to move?* He shook his head in amazement as he looked at the enormous branch that could have claimed his daughter's life. *I prayed to the Good Shepherd*, he thought. *This is His doing!*

In the stillness, Gazba rested his hands on Jasmine's shoulders, looked deeply into her eyes and then gently removed a lock of clammy, wet hair from her forehead. He gave a laugh of relief, hugged and rocked her in an intense embrace, while Puppy frolicked around them happily. Gazba rigged a simple angled flysheet should it rain again and together they managed a few hours of sleep. There had been a red sky the evening before the storm, and that promised a better day.

After a while, Gazba and Jasmine took stock of their belongings, most of which seemed to be intact but wet. Gazba hung their spare clothing on a line between two trees in the sun, which had come out and now shone through a gap where the treacherous fallen branch had been.

Jasmine, who was still ferreting through their belongings, cried out with excitement. 'Look Daddy, I have found a box of flour—and I think it's dry! And a bottle of honey! We can still have pancakes for breakfast today. I have found a bit of dry wood and kindling!'

Gazba smiled at his daughter's perennial optimism, even though he knew their journey would be more difficult, now that his lantern was crushed, and a tent pole had been snapped.

After they had recovered what they could of their damaged supplies, and after the clothing was dry—and after a delicious meal of pancakes— Gazba and Jasmine loaded the remaining supplies onto Bella. They then swung aboard their horses and returned to the road, over which the canopy of old oaks met in autumnal splendour and blackberry bushes encroached from the sides.

Jasmine now drooped a little in the saddle and was unusually quiet. She did pipe up, however, after some time, saying, 'Daddy, can we pick some blackberries—they are everywhere.'

Gazba, who was preoccupied with his own thoughts, did not hear her request.

'Daddy!' shouted Jasmine, 'Can we collect some blackberries?'

'Oh … yes, of course,' he replied, looking around at the forest warily. 'But only for a short while and then we must be on our way.'

They swung down off their horses and started to pick the delicious fruit. In the gloom of the forest, the horses' ears flickered backwards and forwards, both comforted and distracted by the sound of human voices.

'Daddy let's sing!' exclaimed Jasmine, who was now also being affected by the oppressive dimness. 'Let's sing "The Rabbit and the Fox".'

'Very well,' agreed Gazba and so he started, accompanied by Jasmine.

The jolly rabbit ran, and the red fox followed.

The rabbit holed in and the foxy sorrowed.

His tail drooped low, and his hunger was strong,

But in rabbitty's hole he did not belong.

'Again, Daddy,' said Jasmine merrily. 'Let's sing it again. I like that one.'

'Very well,' said Gazba.

'Again,' said Jasmine enthusiastically after they had finished.

By the tenth time Gazba sighed and then said, 'That's enough, Darling. Enough.'

'Oh, alright Daddy,' replied Jasmine. She then started humming the song to herself as she continued picking the fruit.

They had a feast of blackberries for lunch and then mounted up and rode on.

By evening, they were still in the forest, and everything was fading from green to grey. Even though it wasn't the best place, Gazba decided to set up camp in a small clearing. The horses, once they had been hobbled, picked at the soft, thin grass, which grew up through the oak leaf litter. Meanwhile, Gazba put up the tent as best he could, while Jasmine gathered kindling.

'Daddy,' Jasmine asked, presenting him with what she had found. 'All of the leaves and this funny mossy stuff is damp. Will it still burn?'

'No Darling, it won't burn well without a little help,' replied Gazba. 'We will use the magnesium dust and flint again like I did at breakfast.'

'The wolves might get us, if we don't get a fire started,' said Jasmine in a tight, thin voice.

'Your Daddy has a trick up his sleeve,' said Gazba. 'So don't you worry.'

Gazba dug several holes around the campsite into which he had Jasmine place the kindling. Next, he shook some magnesium dust from a small pouch onto the kindling and then got out his flint. A single spark ignited the grains of magnesium, causing each fire to start with a brilliant flourish.

'I want to start a fire like that,' said Jace, his face alive with interest.

'They could show you how to do that in Cubs,' said Nanny. 'Maybe you could join?'

'I don't like the shorts,' smirked Jace.

'Wouldn't it be worth it just to learn the interesting stuff?' asked Nanny.

'Maybe,' conceded Jace.

Shelley, who had been relaxing on the couch, now propped herself up on her elbows and with wide eyes urged, 'Keep going Nanny. I just know that there will be wolves again soon. They will be in danger again, I just know it.' Her brows knitted with concern.

'You could be right. Let's find out,' said Nanny, continuing to read.

'Oh Daddy, I've never seen you do that before, you are so clever!' exclaimed Jasmine, clapping her hands and giggling with glee as each of the five fires spat into life. 'It looks like fairy land.'

'You were too young for me to show you this before, and I was afraid that you might try to start one yourself,' said Gazba fondly.

'I probably would have,' laughed Jasmine.

'I am glad you are here with me,' said Gazba, putting his arm around her shoulders.

'I like being here too,' said Jasmine.

Suddenly, an owl hooted, and Brownie reared, pulling back on her rope. The other two mares were unconcerned and continued to graze, so Brownie quietened and soon fell asleep standing between the two other horses.

Jasmine was concerned about their safety, and she blurted out, 'How will the horses protect themselves if they are hobbled?'

'There are three of them and they can still manage to get a pretty good kick in as well as biting. Don't you worry about them,' replied Gazba.

'Alright Daddy,' said Jasmine as her face relaxed into a smile.

They settled down for the night and Gazba lovingly pulled the blanket up around his daughter's neck and pecked her gently on the forehead.

She gazed up with a tired happy smile and said, 'Lucky I brought hobbles for Brownie.'

'Yes, you thought of everything,' acknowledged Gazba with a wry smile, as he realised Jasmine had indeed planned her get away with great attention to detail.

Gazba watched Jasmine's sleepy eyes close and soon she was fast asleep. He then lay back in his own bedroll and looked up through a gap in the forest canopy at the clouds, outlined in blue and silver by the white moon. They were being pushed along fast by a strong wind, and he was grateful that down here on the forest floor all was quiet.

Later, Gazba checked the fires and added more fuel to make sure they would last the night. There was something about these old, twisted trees that made him afraid. *If I look at them long enough, they start to look like hideous faces*, he thought. He looked at the cross that Friar Lucas had given him, smiled, and then put it back down the front of his shirt before settling himself down to sleep.

When Gazba woke, his first thoughts were of Baron Bardozer. *He probably has his soldiers searching for me at this very moment. At least he himself won't be looking for us because he will still be suffering the effects of the paraffin for a few more days.*

'Let's get moving, Jasmine,' Gazba said with urgency. He hoped she would not notice the tension in his voice. They had breakfast and were soon on their way again.

'Daddy,' said Jasmine as they rode off, 'I'm very brave, but I do want to get out of this creepy forest.'

Gazba smiled at his intuitive, clever little girl. He too found the forest oppressive. 'Yes,' he replied. 'I haven't seen any animals here.'

'I haven't even heard a bird for a long time,' said Jasmine.

'Some go south in the winter,' replied Gazba, trying to set her mind at ease.

Jasmine looked around furtively and pulled her cloak tighter. 'I heard something,' she said. 'But I think it was only an acorn falling, or maybe an animal foraging.'

'Don't worry, darling,' said Gazba. 'I am here with you, and we should be out of this forest soon, if we hurry along now.'

As they drew near the stream they had been following on and off as they journeyed through the forest, it suddenly made a strange gurgling sound like a cistern. This sound was nothing at all like the chatter of a stream over pebbles. The sound chilled Gazba's heart.

As if in response to his foreboding, the forest became dark, and the sun had suddenly been covered by a storm cloud. The day so far had been fair, and some of the damp had even lifted, but now it seemed like night-time, even though Gazba knew it to be only about midday.

Gazba urged his horse on and encouraged Jasmine to do the same with her pony as they sought somewhere to shelter.

Fearing another storm, they quickly set up the remains of the tent. Gazba was impressed with his daughter's embroidery skills as she had hastily patched it. Gazba started a fire using his magnesium dust again because of the dampness of the available wood.

The wind whipped up and started to scream through the woodland but there was another sound entwined within it.

'Hush,' said Gazba to Jasmine when there came a lull in the buffeting wind. 'I can hear something else.'

Then it came—a long, haunting howl.

The horses whinnied in fear.

'Be brave!' shouted Gazba and they seemed to settle, standing like sentinels, listening.

Gazba's jaw was set and, despite the cold, sweat dripped down his neck. He must protect his daughter.

'Will we be safe?' Jasmine asked uneasily.

'Just stay close to the fire,' replied Gazba.

'Yes Daddy,' said Jasmine, watching her father trying to protect the fire from blowing out. Puppy started to bark and began struggling in her arms.

Gazba peered into the darkness. He had a bad feeling about the sudden onset of yet another storm.

'Try to keep Puppy quiet,' he told Jasmine. 'I need to listen.'

Suddenly, there was lull in the wind and Gazba scanned the forest. Reflected in the light of the fire he thought he could see something shining in the undergrowth—burning, red eyes, which suddenly disappeared.

Gazba fixed a hand strongly on a newly ignited faggot. Fire had worked the last time and could work again.

Tense moments passed as he looked as deeply into the forest as he could.

Suddenly, Jasmine's eyes became wide, and her mouth was open but silent with terror. She pointed.

'Daddy!' she screamed as Puppy broke free, stood in front of Jasmine, and started barking piercingly at the wolf.

Gazba whirled around to look in the direction she was pointing as an enormous wolf burst from a bush and bounded towards them with its red mouth agape. He swung his faggot desperately and caught the wolf under the chin with as much force as he could.

The wolf was knocked sideways onto the ground and began to make gurgling, spluttering noises, coughing up a few teeth.

Keliran, invisible to Gazba and Jasmine, stood between them and the possessed wolf.

'Hateful, if you want to fight now, I am ready,' demanded the angel fiercely.

'Keliran, you pick your fight badly for I come with great power,' said the demon speaking within the growls of the wolf as it got to its feet.

Keliran, mindful that a battle might put Gazba and Jasmine in danger, decided to try to calm the wolf and send the demon on its way by singing an angelic song. He crouched by the wolf and began singing softly and soulfully in a language from Heaven. In response, the wolf dropped down onto its belly, settled its head down and calmly looked up at Jasmine and Gazba.

Puppy moved forward and started to lick the wolf's injured muzzle.

'I don't think it means to hurt us now, Daddy,' said the Maid, a little hesitantly. 'Its eyes are so kind now. I'm sure it's being forced to be ferocious and doesn't want to be bad.'

Gazba shook his head in disbelief.

Crouching down next to Puppy, Keliran continued to sing quietly and began patting the wolf, which responded by making throaty, crooning noises.

Gazba hesitantly raised the still-burning stick, preparing to bludgeon the animal.

'No, don't,' said Keliran, his sky-blue eyes suddenly filled with anxiety. He stopped his singing and got to his feet.

But Gazba couldn't hear him.

Suddenly, the wolf changed again, spluttering, and growling worse than before.

Puppy backed away and started barking furiously at the wolf as it got to its feet.

Keliran placed himself between Jasmine and the wolf. 'Hateful. Get back!'

Behind him, Keliran heard Jasmine suddenly shout, 'Daddy say "Jesus" to it, to make the bad spirits come out of it.'

The wolf had become savage again. 'You don't know the power I have been given,' growled Hateful.

Keliran took a deep breath, drew his sword, and prepared to fight. *What power does it have?* he wondered, a shadow of uncertainty coming over him.

'In the name of Jesus Christ of Nazareth, demon come out of him!' came the shouted words of Gazba from behind Keliran.

These words empowered the angel. He would and could destroy the demon.

The wolf growled and the demon within gave a screaming wail, as it burst forth from the wolf and sprang to attack Keliran.

However, the words of command from God had given Keliran speed, and the creature died as he slashed its head clean off with one lightning-fast stroke of his sword.

Keliran gave a huge sigh as the demon's body fell into ash, which also then disappeared.

He sheathed his sword. The child, who would become the Maid of Valouresse, was safe. Calling on the Lord of Hosts had saved Gazba. *This,* thought Keliran, shuddering, *had been a very powerful demon.*

Keliran smiled as he watched father and daughter embraced. He never tired of being the rescuer for his King's subjects.

Gazba rocked Jasmine side to side with joy and relief, but kept a cautious eye on the wolf, who was now licking Puppy.

He shook with emotion. They were safe again. His eyes started to smart with tears for the first time since he was a boy.

Jasmine said excitedly, 'Jesus saved us, didn't he?'

'I think he did,' replied the overwhelmed Gazba, stifling a sob.

And it came to Gazba, that God was a force for love that he couldn't understand.

Chapter 15

'That was pretty good!' exclaimed Jace.

'I like the way Puppy was licking the wolf on the chin, that was so cute,' said Shelley.

'You are cute Shelley,' said Nanny. 'And animals love you. Remember when my sisters and I visited a farm to see a foal? It wouldn't come anywhere near us adults, but it came straight up to you. Do you remember?'

'Not really,' replied Shelley.

'Anyway, I have something to tell you tomorrow. Something God did that was truly amazing.'

'Now Nanny!' exclaimed Jace.

'Okay,' said Nanny, a little reluctantly.

They had lunch of delicious, toasted ham, cheese, and tomato sandwiches then they settled down to hear about Nanny's special story, a true one.

The rain continued to pelt down outside and dribbled down the windows. They all felt cosy and protected inside. On a rainy day, that safe, warm feeling was like a hug from the house.

The two children sat on the couch either side of her as Nanny started to tell them her important tale.

'One time—a long time ago now, I went to a bible study that was being held at a friend's house just around the corner. It was a bitter, cold day like this, and my friend was as depressed as me. She was worried about her family in war-torn Croatia.'

'That's in Europe, right?' asked Jace.

'Yes, it is,' replied Nanny. 'Anyway, this day we watched a video and afterwards had a prayer time.'

'I was feeling very dry and empty both emotionally and spiritually and I was up front with God. I said to him, in my mind, *I have nothing to give,* because that's the way I felt.'

'Did he say anything back?' asked Shelley.

'Yes, he did,' replied Nanny quietly. He said, "Do what you can."'

'What did you do?' asked Shelley.

'So then,' replied Nanny, 'I held my friend's hand and stroked it while I prayed for her in a Heavenly tongue, and as I did, I felt a surge go through my spirit and I thought, *these beautiful words must surely mean something.*'

'What is a Heavenly tongue, Nanny?' asked Jace with a quizzical expression.

'It's speech that contains all your emotions, fears, hopes and dreams—everything that you have deep down,' replied Nanny. 'And God understands it, even if no-one else does.'

'So, what did it mean Nanny, when you spoke to your friend?' asked Shelley with luminous eyes.

Nanny replied solemnly but with an underlying thrill in her voice, 'my friend said that I had spoken words of comfort to her about her family, in the Croatian language. So, you see, when Gazba felt helpless, God send an angel to help him ...'

'And when you felt helpless, he gave you a special message for your friend.' added Shelley.

'Can I speak in a Heavenly Language?' asked Jace.

'Sure,' replied Nanny. 'Give it a go, and at first it may sound childish and stupid, but then it gets easier, until it flows, and you will feel the connection with God, and supernatural events can happen.'

'I like supernatural things,' said Jace, impishly.

'Let's get on with the story now and see what other wonders are to be had. But firstly, we have one very furious witch to hear from. She has just sent a very powerful demon, Hateful, to finish off Jasmine and Gazba, but it had been foiled by the angel Keliran.'

The witch paced her room and muttered fearful curses.

'My dark Prince, I am sorry to burden you, but I call on you now for special help to eradicate that girl child. She is more than I can manage. But first I have to find her.'

With that, Kraekhoull wove her thin white hands over the crystal ball, and it became at first dark and purple, then fiery within.

'Ah, she said, and then laughed with delight. 'There they are.' Gazba and Jasmine were saddling up and placing their belongings onto the pack-horse. 'I shall deal with the child, but it must be clandestine, for I don't want her father around. I can wait a bit longer.'

'My next task is to meet Baron Bardozer,' said the witch. 'He will help me conquer Valouresse.'

Gazba and Jasmine packed up their belongings, saddled their horses and were on their way several days ahead of Gallant and Chloe. Wolf left them at this point, but not before turning towards them with a soulful stare and then trotting into the woods.

'Oh, wolf is going,' said Jasmine sadly.

'Let him go darling, for he is a wild animal,' replied Gazba.

Gazba had already studied the old map from his saddle bag and said, 'We go northwest to Epiron Rock, and as fast as we can go.'

After having travelled the road from La Fonteyn and many leagues since, Gazba started to search for landmarks that would lead them to the Epiron trail.

His eyes keenly searched the sides of the road for the tree he needed to find. There were many trees of many kinds, so he kept looking, ever hopeful of seeing it and then he did—the Elderberry tree. This tree had a particular marking deep in its bark—a cross shape.

Standing under the tree, reaching up to eat the berries, was a little roe deer. It was much smaller than other deer and had a reddish coat and small pointed horns. It paused and gazed for a couple of seconds before bounding into the forest.

'Come, Jasmine, follow me,' said Gazba, dismounting and leading his horses beneath the foliage. Jasmine did the same and followed her father several leagues along a winding overgrown path, before coming to a cave.

Again, in the dimness of the thick forest near the cave entrance, was the roe deer with some rare light dappled on its coat.

Its moist nose and eyes glistened as it faced them again before it bounded away, causing a brief susurrus of turf and stones being dislodged.

Gazba and Jasmine rode on through the cave, Gazba following the directions the map had given.

He used a torch to guide their way. He noticed, on the slimy walls, mysterious carvings of winged creatures and others which he was unable to recognise as anything but deformed depictions of strange monsters.

Within were many tunnels that Gazba knew no man could navigate unless they had the map. He felt confident that Bardozer would not be able to follow. After having been silent a long time, Jasmine spoke:

'Daddy, how long will we be in here? I don't think Brownie and Puppy like it at all.'

Just as she said this, a faint light shone ahead, and they both hastened towards it.

'There we are, Jasmine,' said her father, 'we are almost out of the caves, but the hardest part of our journey begins. Are you up to it, little one?'

'Yes,' said Jasmine in a slightly tremulous voice.

As they burst into the light, both shielded their eyes and Gazba steadied Helga and his pack horse Bella. Jasmine recovered from the dazzling sunlight quickly, and gasped as she looked upwards at the steep ascent.

Both led their horses along the rocky precipitous trail.

'Just go slowly,' said Gazba. 'We will reach the high road in a couple of hours. But first let's give the horses and ourselves a drink.'

Beside them, a stream rushed down, and the horses and Puppy drank from this, whilst father and daughter drank from their gourds which they then refilled.

As they inched higher and higher, the view became more and more heart-stoppingly terrifying. One stumble and the horses could plummet to their doom. Far in the distance was La Fonteyn, and all the green woods and farmland they had passed through.

The horses pushed hard with their hind quarters and lunged with their heads and necks, coming over the rise onto the High Road. This would skirt many leagues of mountainside—but it was not a well-constructed road—not an easy route and now, because of the time of year, some was covered in snow.

They set up camp for the evening, tucked into a slight fold within the mountainside, off the road. Jasmine gathered kindling as was her usual job and she also hobbled the horses, tying them between two strong looking pines on the upper slope.

During the night came a loud flapping noise and a guttural sigh, which chilled Gazba's heart. He was glad that Jasmine was sound asleep.

In the morning it was pancakes as usual.

'How far is it, Daddy?' asked Jasmine impatiently.

'It is still far, and we must still ride our horses carefully They may be steady on their feet, but any rock could cause them to slip.'

Another week of careful riding around the flanks of the mountains went by. The trail was not level but rose up and then down and then up again—on and on, interminably. The ever present need to be careful concentrated the mind and took the edge off considering the distance or the danger.

At last, on a fine day with no clouds, they rode over a rise.

Both gasped and steadied their horses.

There stood an ornately carved ancient monastery of stone.

It was positioned on a number of strong pillars, which must have been themselves carved from Epiron Rock.

'This looks like it has been entirely carved from the rock, an impossible task,' said Gazba, flabbergasted by the remarkable building.

After tying up their horses, both climbed the stairway which led from the rock to the monastery. The door at the top opened easily despite its size and they found it to be clean and dry inside.

Every part was decorated with scenes from the gospels, including Jesus on the cross in a stained-glass window behind the pulpit. Their fears and worries eased, and they both knelt and prayed without a word.

Far away, Kraekhoull now paced the small room, sharing her fury with the two demons, Bitterness and Fear, who cringed in one corner.

'The King is away, and if I can call on help from the Dark Prince and eradicate the Delafoi family, all Valouresse could be mine.'

The witch scried through her crystal ball and exclaimed, 'but first, Bardozer is on the mountain road not far from here, and it is time to meet with him.'

'That sounds like a very good idea,' agreed Bitterness, whose expressionless face gave nothing away. 'I shall saddle your horse.'

'Yes, do that,' said Kraekhoull—thinking that her seer and prophetess had proved completely useless to her except for such tasks. She snatched up a bag with a few items and went to a copse of trees where her horse was tethered. The witch swung up into the saddle on her fiery-eyed horse and galloped off along the mountain road in a flurry, with her black cape billowing behind her. *To use my magic box for transportation may terrify the Baron and cause more harm than good.*

After several leagues she rounded a bend, and caught up to the baron, who heard her horse's hooves, and turned in the saddle to see the white-faced witch careering toward him. Kraekhoull's horse skidded to a halt and then minced nervously in circles. Bardozer's men scattered as her fierce horse then lashed out at theirs.

'My Lady?' said the surprised Bardozer, (who was now off the commode and with his men) 'Why would you be out in the forest alone?'

'I have come to see you Baron of the Boar.'

Baron Bardozer raised his eyebrows and answered, 'Yes that is I.' His velvet doublet was covered by a shaggy fur jacket much like a wild boar.

'And who are you, my lady?' inquired Bardozer. twirling his elegant moustache.

'I am Kraekhoull,' replied the witch, tilting her chin and glaring at him with her dark eyes flashing. She swirled her arms around in a graceful but sinister movement, shutting the ears of those she didn't want to hear the intrigue she was about to weave. The soldiers stood by on their horses and watched.

'That name sounds familiar,' said Bardozer. 'You tried to take the kingdom many a year ago.'

'I did,' replied the witch darkly.

'Arr, I like you already,' said Bardozer. 'We could make an alliance, you and I. The gentry and king have shamed me for far too long and I want revenge on them, not to mention gaining the kingdom.'

'I believe we have a few common enemies,' continued the witch. 'Gazba the apothecary and yes, the infernal gentry. Together, we can rule the land.'

'I'm listening,' said Bardozer. 'So how do we inflict the most damage on them?'

'Your men need to destroy Gazba's family, all of whom are on this road.'

'That suits me well,' said Bardozer gruffly. 'Only when I have dealt with Gazba will I feel vindicated. My men are enemies of the ruling class, and they hate them even more than I do.' On saying this he gave a harsh laugh.

'All of them need to be done away with, especially the child,' said the witch. 'Gazba and his daughter can stop our victory because they have a power they don't realise they have or understand,' said the witch with particular venom. 'But for now, destroy his wife and the knights she travels with first,' said Kraekhoull. 'For I have sensed they are not far from here. The child and Gazba are mine to deal with.'

'And where would the knight and the lady be?' asked Bardozer.

'I will give you a crystal ball that will give you knowledge of their whereabouts,' said the witch. She took the ball from a velvet bag and presided over it, calling out dark curses which both chilled and thrilled Bardozer. A jet-black shiny, raven settled in front of them both with a loud caw.

'Follow this bird. It knows where they are,' said Kraekhoull in a knowing sly voice.

There was an evil glint in the baron's eye as he briskly ordered his men to form a column on the road.

The raven rose from its perch on a branch of a conifer tree and slowly flapped into the forest alongside the road.

'Follow the Raven,' he ordered, to the astonishment of his men. But they obeyed.

'Anyway, shall we continue?' asked Nanny, putting the manuscript down.

'I hope that Chloe and the knights don't get caught by Bardozer,' said Shelley.

'And I sense danger,' said Jace looking quite serious.

'I think so too,' said Nanny. 'Anyway, let's keep going with the story.' She turned the next page.

Chloe, Gallant, and the other knights rode on through the silent forest on the lookout for Gazba and Jasmine who they knew would be well ahead of them. Debris lay across the road from the fierce storms that had come in quick succession.

'I hope that they are both safe,' said Chloe, anxious for her daughter and husband.

'I believe the good Lord would have been watching over them during that time,' said Gallant. 'They should be close to Epiron Rock by now. It was a two-week journey.'

'How would you know that?' asked Chloe.

'Gazba told me where he was going—and how long it would take—before he left Lord Pleasure's castle.'

'He didn't tell me!' exclaimed Chloe, wounded that he should know something about her husband that she did not.

'He didn't want to worry you my lady,' responded Gallant.

'At least we had some shelter in the old monastery, but my husband and daughter had nothing but a small tent,' said Chloe.

'Hush!' said Gallant suddenly, 'I hear something.'

They all stopped and, as they did, Bardozer and his men appeared some distance down the road behind them. There were many of them. Gallant's experience told him that their hasty approach implied battle. He made a quick decision but a painful one.

'Chloe, ride up into the forest on the side of the mountain and hide.'

'But I cannot leave you,' exclaimed Chloe.

'Please my lady,' said Gallant, 'Go and do not turn back.'

Chloe wheeled her horse around, left the road and headed up the mountain side, riding Grunjion through bracken and over fallen timber as fast as she could.

Bardozer was now close and yelling out orders to his men.

'Column B, follow the woman and kill her.'

'Column A, kill the knights.'

Bardozer's large number of soldiers swarmed the area. Many followed Chloe when—with a whiz and a thump—Chloe brought down one of her pursuers with her bow. She had turned in the saddle like she did when hunting in her youth with Gazba. She controlled Grunjion with her knees and leaning this way and that –with her weight.

Gallant initially stood his ground on the road, implacable and immoveable. Bardozer's men hesitated. *How could one knight, alone, have no fear?*

Suddenly he charged, uttering a wild and fearful cry.

Gallant managed to swipe several of Bardozer's men from their horses with his sharp sword and they didn't rise from the ground.

Gallant's Knights and squires had engaged as many of the enemy as possible to enable Chloe to get away. Being greatly outnumbered, one by one, Gallant's knights fell.

Three of Bardozer's men still pursued Chloe but only the lead rider was closing on her. Chloe gave him an arrow for his troubles. The rider peeled off his horse backwards, his foot caught in the stirrup, as his terrified horse plunged away, into the bracken.

Gallant saw that Chloe would escape. But then two of Bardozer's men surrounded him. Gallant smiled a berserker grin, and a wild fierceness lit his eyes.

'Ride, Chloe, ride!' he shouted.

The two men circled and harried Gallant until, finally, as exhaustion ensued, he was struck down from his horse. One of the men leapt down and delivered Gallant a fatal blow to the neck, causing blood to seep through his damaged chain mail.

Meanwhile, Chloe battled onward and upward, but always she could hear the crashing of the other horses coming behind her. In gasps, she urged her horse on and Grunjion, mighty animal that he was, strove to outpace the others.

Bardozer's remaining men were now so close that she felt she could almost feel their breath. One of the men swung his sword and she ducked. She gave a little cry as she almost toppled off. The man closed in on her again and again swiped at her.

Suddenly there came the sound of a fierce growl and Chloe was aware of something black between Grunjion and the other horse. It was a huge wolf.

The other horse screamed in terror, reared, and left the man stunned on the ground.

Chloe took her chance and urged Grunjion away, thinking that the wolf would seek her out next.

She glanced behind and to her astonishment saw the man who had been unhorsed, screaming and sliding down the mountain side, followed by the wolf which snapped at his heels.

The other rider that had been following Chloe retreated in panic, milling around on his horse before taking off down the mountainside as well.

Chloe kept riding, climbing higher and higher on her big, brave Grunjion, terrified that the wolf may turn back for her after it had finished with the two men below her, who let out chilling screams.

Bardozer rode his horse up the slope and met the two men who came careering down followed by rocks and clumps of dirt.

'Why are you here, have you finished off that woman?' he exclaimed angrily.

'A killer wolf chased us. We are lucky to be alive,' said the rider on his wild-eyed, panting horse.

'That's what you think,' said Bardozer with menace. 'By the time you have been given a good flogging you will learn who's lucky.'

'My Lord,' said the man who had been unhorsed. 'There is a terrible wolf up there and the woman is in its path. I am sure it will follow her and kill her.'

Bardozer twirled his moustache and looked pensive for a moment before saying, 'Mmm, I suppose you could be right.'

'At least we have finished off the knights, including this one, Gallant, I believe his name was,' said Bardozer, kicking the dead knight's shoulder. 'Take his armour.'

'Might as well go back to the camp then,' said Bardozer.

'What about our wounded?' said one of the men.

'You bring them back,' said Bardozer, 'but don't dilly dally. I have a lot to accomplish in a short time.'

'Of course, my Lord,' said the man and he started to direct the hale soldiers to place the wounded onto stretchers to be brought back to the camp. The mountain slope was littered with Bardozer's wounded or dead.

'We can leave the Lady Chloe to the wolf and have a clear conscience. She is as surely dead as if thrust by a sword. Kraekhoull will be satisfied. Come, let us go!' shouted Bardozer, signalling with his arm to go forward and his troops followed as one in a cantering mass.

Chloe slowed Grunjion and looked behind. Nothing. Maybe the wolf had tired of the chase and returned to its lair. Nothing could please Chloe more. She placed her hand on her heart and gulped as she scanned the forest. Nothing but trees and hawthorn.

She started the trek downwards again, alert for more of Bardozer's men.

Why did the wolf not attack me and Grunjion? And why did it not kill the man on foot when it easily had the chance?

Suddenly her thoughts were of Gallant. She hurried down the slope, not caring if she be eaten by the wolf or captured.

Suddenly she saw Gallant and let out an agonised wail.

'Gallant. No!' She jumped off Grunjion and then threw herself on Gallant's still body. His forehead was cold. He had no breath. Chloe then sat and cried, sobbing in unstoppable spasms. Her childhood friend gone. *I will wash his face and clean him* she thought and ripped some cloth from her dress and then went to search for water.

The whole time she wept as she stumbled along. She found a small spring and wet the cloth, then squeezed it out. She returned and started to clean the blood from Gallant's face, but she could do nothing about the gash in his neck except gently, tearfully wipe around it. Her thoughts lingered darkly on how Gallant and his knights had sacrificed their lives to save hers.

Gallant found himself in a garden unlike any he had ever seen. He remembered a mighty blow to the neck and then this, a fragrant place inhabited by birds and animals, all living peacefully together. He felt like he could stay here for the rest of eternity. He was there for hours, it seemed, and all he wanted to do was lie there and absorb the sights, smells and sounds.

However, he could hear a woman sobbing and the sound cut him to the core. *I don't want to leave this beautiful haven, but I must go back to comfort the lady who weeps.*

Appearing before him was a man who seemed familiar.

'Is it you, Lord?' asked Gallant.

'Yes, it is me, Gallant. It is your choice to stay or go back. There is no shame in either course, dear one.'

Jesus smiled beatifically and his robes seemed to glow with light. Gallant felt at home and at peace but the woman's sobbing and her hot tears falling on his face urged him to go elsewhere.

'Will I come back to the garden and see you again?' asked Gallant.

'Of course,' replied the Lord.

'In that case,' said Gallant, 'I will go back but I will always long to be in this place.'

Then, the Lord said, 'Know that I am always with you, wherever you are. Neither death nor life, angels, principalities nor powers, things present nor things to come, neither height nor depth nor any other thing can take you away from my love.'

Chloe was resting her head on Gallant's chest and her hair was wet with tears.

Suddenly Gallant's chest rose, and Chloe gave a small shriek and looked to his face.

'Gallant, you live!' she exclaimed. 'But your neck, the wound is gone. How did this happen?'

'I will tell you about it, but later, for now we have to get to safety. We must find our way to Epiron Rock where Gazba and Jasmine hopefully await us.'

'Do you know the way?' asked Chloe.

'No,' said Gallant. 'I was hoping to catch up to Gazba and Jasmine before now, but I have no fear, for during my time in the garden where I met the Lord, he told me he would always be with me—so He will find a way for us, I am sure.'

Lost and without horses, Chloe and Gallant looked at each other and shrugged.

'What now?' asked Chloe.

Just as she said this the wolf (which Gazba and Jasmine had met and that had been exorcised) leapt from the undergrowth. It stood motionless behind Chloe and the knight on the upper side of the hill. Targum (the angel with the burnished Arabian countenance) had spoken words of instruction to Wolf before the fighting began on the mountain.

'Do not hurt anyone,' he had said to Wolf, 'but drive the enemy off, and when the fighting is over, come down and accompany the knight and the woman, Chloe.'

Wolf came out of the undergrowth and calmly lay down in front of the knight and Chloe.

'This is a strange affair,' said Gallant, shaking his head but smiling at the same time. 'My time in the garden has made me think anything is possible. This wolf looks for all the world like a tame pet.'

Wolf started to whine, then got up and walked a few steps, then circled back to them and repeated this—walking away then circling back.

'I think it wants us to follow.' said Chloe.

The knight was baffled and said, 'Stranger things have happened, no doubt. Let's go then and see what fate awaits.'

As they started to follow Wolf, Grunjion and Gallant's mount stepped from the undergrowth. Grunjion whinnied to Chloe then charged forward causing Wolf to leap aside to avoid being trampled.

Chloe stepped forward and stroked the agitated horse's muzzle and patted his neck.

'It's alright Grunjion,' said Chloe softly. 'He is here to help us. See? He doesn't want to hurt us.' She then rested her palm on Wolf's head, and he was compliant as any tame dog.

Both horses extended their necks and tremulously touched noses with Wolf.

After a few tentative moments, all three animals had reached an understanding and relaxed.

Once Chloe and Gallant were mounted, they started to follow the wolf, which occasionally turned his head back as if to see that they were still coming.

As they walked along Chloe asked, 'What did you see there? I mean in the garden.'

'I saw a huge, tawny gold lion lying down with a lamb nestled into its chest between its paws and I saw a leopard nursing a young fawn alongside her cubs. Animals of all kinds that should have been natural enemies were living in peace—and the flowers! They were indescribable, in all hues, smelling so fragrant. But the most wonderful thing was seeing the Lord, who seemed like an ordinary man but for his beautiful kind eyes.'

'Which Lord was that, was it Jesus?' exclaimed Chloe.

'Yes, it was Him,' said Gallant. 'I felt his hand touch my neck and then life flowed back into me. His face was full of love as he helped me to my feet. He embraced me and I wept with joy. It was wonderful to be in His presence and to be in that place.'

'But you came back,' said Chloe.

'Your tears brought me back and I don't regret it,' replied Gallant looking at her face fondly.

'Now we follow a wolf which seems to know where it is going.'

The wolf followed Targum, the angel who hovered unseen some distance ahead.

He said, 'Come dear wolf and help these loved ones of the Lord— onward to Epiron Rock.'

Wolf padded along the road and his humans followed, now on foot. They came to an elderberry tree and followed Wolf along an overgrown, barely perceivable trail to a cave.

All followed Wolf. Chloe led Grunjion who stepped into the darkness, trusting his mistress and Gallant's horse followed, led by Gallant. Slowly they inched their way through the blackness with only the flickering light of a small torch that Gallant fashioned from supplies in his saddle bag and that he had lit with a flint and magnesium powder. It was a long time to be without the sun. They spent a night in the caves, huddled together with the horses and wolf, all lying together for warmth. Chloe had urged Grunjion to his knees and hindquarters till he sat comfortably and then she did the same with the other horse and finally wolf curled up amongst them. This created combined warmth in the cold, cold caves.

Then she and Gallant ate some supplies of dried meat and sourdough bread that were in the saddle bags, wisely packed by Chloe and the knight before leaving Lord Pleasure's chateau. Their gourds were still in the saddlebags that they had filled at a stream before entering the caves.

After sleeping the night in the cave, they all set off again through the winding labyrinth. Finally, there was a faint glimmer which grew stronger until they found themselves blinking in the bright sun. Chloe and Gallant allowed the horses to graze all morning for they had not eaten anything in the cave.

The party made their way up slowly until finally, like Jasmine and Gazba before them, they travelled the High Road traversing the sides of the mountains. Days went by as they picked their way along with any slip that could mean death. Then, one evening, the sky held the illumination of a glowing sunset which then all too briefly faded.

The stars came out and Chloe and the knight set up camp in a shallow cave in the side of the mountain. Gallant had brought a ground sheet and a sheet and set up a canvas in the front of the cave. Wolf snuggled in with them as rain slanted down on the sheet and rolled onto the narrow road and then down the slope. The horses stoically remained with tails to the wind.

One day, after a long day of walking along the rising and falling narrow rocky trail, Chloe and Gallant were ready to set up camp again but Wolf whined and paced ahead, circled, and then paced ahead again.

'He wants us to follow him even tonight, which will be treacherous to say the least.' said Chloe. 'We must keep going. The moon is full and will give us enough light, I hope. Let's keep going.'

'Very well, my lady,' said Gallant with some trepidation.

'That seems a bit unrealistic, Nanny, that Gallant would die and then come to life again.' said Jace.

Nanny smiled. She had known about the power of the Holy Spirit for a long time.

'What is so great about the Spirit, anyway?' asked Jace.

Nanny replied, 'The Spirit is awesome and wonderful. It raised Jesus from the dead and it is the same Spirit that breathed life into all creation.'

Then she remembered something else.

'I had a vision of Heaven just before my Nanna died,' said Nanny.

'Tell us, tell us!' exclaimed Shelley.

'I was in the hospital giving her my favourite teddy, but she told me it was too hot for her to have it near her skin.'

'What did you see, Nanny?' asked Shelley, pulling a cushion to herself.

'I saw something like a television screen up on the wall and saw the Mitta Hall decorated with a "WELCOME HOME GLADY" sign and streamers. There were lots of people there and Nanny walked up to Pa, and he said "Glady" in a lovely tender voice and then they danced.'

'What happened then?' asked Jace, also hugging a cushion.

'Well, in the old days, my Nanna used to be a concert pianist and also played old time dance music at the hall in Mitta. My great uncle and others used to play old time dance music too. In the vision Uncle Reg— who used to play the saxophone—said "Glady, play for us."'

'Did she play?' asked Shelley with soulful eyes.

'The thing is,' said Nanny 'my Nanna had stopped playing a long time ago because she had arthritis. But in this vision, she went straight up to the piano and played without any hesitation—it was all just so lovely.'

'That's a lovely vision to have Nanny,' said Shelley.

'Yes,' said Nanny, 'I feel very privileged to have seen that and I told my ninety-two-year-old aunty—my Nanna's daughter—about it and she found it a great comfort.'

'That wolf has helped them a lot, too, hasn't it?' said Jace. 'Wouldn't it be good if they could help you in real life, like that one did in your story?'

'Actually, said Nanny, 'during the Middle Ages when St Francis of Assisi was travelling in Germany …'

'Who was St Francis of Assisi?' asked Jace.

'He was a pious, mystic Christian who went about doing good.' said Nanny.

'So, what did he do in Germany?' asked Shelley.

'He came to a village that was being terrorised by a wolf. It would attack the villages and cause great trouble. St Francis approached it, and it sat down in front of him and held out its paw, which St Francis took in his hand and then he spoke to the wolf.'

'What did he say to it Nanny?' asked Shelley, who was very captivated with the tale.

'He said, "Brother wolf, you must not terrorise these people anymore. If you defend them and keep them safe, they will look after you and feed you."'

'Is that true Nanny?' asked Jace punching his pillow to make it more comfortable.

'Apparently it is a true story. The wolf became the defender of the village and in turn they fed him,' said Nanny, 'and there is a bronze statue in the town to commemorate it.'

'That's interesting, but keep going Nanny,' said Jace a little impatiently.

Nanny sighed and read on.

Chapter 16

Gallant and Chloe led their horses in the light of the moon. Then, with great excitement, they could make out the shining lamps and the fire that lay inside Epiron Rock monastery, just as they crested the last part of the mountain. With great joy, they ran up the last crest of the mountain leading their horses. Their approach was easy to hear in the still night.

'Mummy!' exclaimed Jasmine, running up and hugging Chloe.

Gazba held his wife close, kissed her and including Jasmine in the embrace.

Gallant gave a short bow and Gazba rested his hand on the knight's shoulder saying, 'Thank you, brave friend, for protecting my wife.'

'It is always a great pleasure,' said Gallant.

'Where are the others?' asked Gazba.

'Bardozer killed them,' said Gallant shaking his head sadly.

Gazba again placed his hand on the knight's shoulder in sympathy.

The wolf hesitated from joining his people under the monastery and cowered from the flames.

'It's alright Wolf,' said Jasmine, placing Puppy on the ground near the fire. 'See,' she said to Wolf, 'He's not afraid. Come in, it's so warm.'

After some time, the wolf did go in and lay down, but not very close to the flames.

'Our men were so brave but outnumbered by Bardozer's troops,' said Gallant gravely. 'It is a great tragedy, but it goes to show what that man is capable of doing in his desire for revenge.'

'I have sent another pigeon—which amazingly survived both storms—to my castle,' said Gazba. 'I am hoping that Brother Lucas can convince the King to send an army here to defend us and especially my daughter. I have suspected for some time that Kraekhoull is back, and it wouldn't surprise me if she and the baron are colluding. The baron is not bright enough to plan strategy alone. And goodness knows what evil the witch is concocting.'

'What makes you think she is doing this?' asked Gallant.

'I have had a few very strange experiences lately, and even cast a demon from a wolf—this very wolf that sits here so calmly now.'

Gallant raised his eyebrows after hearing about the attacks that Gazba and Jasmine had experienced and said, 'By the way, that wolf has been our guiding light. Must be the witch on the move making these creatures so vicious.'

'Yes,' said Gazba. 'I strongly suspect she's the one behind these occurrences.'

The pigeon flew strongly, as her heart dictated, to her home at Gazba's castle.

Onward into the sky, upward towards the fluffy clouds she beat her wings. But a goshawk already had his eye on her and followed her as she flitted past. He left his perch on a tall poplar and silently started to follow her.

Sensing the predator now above her, she took a sharp dive into the corridor of oaks which lined a road. This road led to home. The hawk dove again and this time clipped a feather from her tail, only missing because of the sudden proximity of branches to bar his way.

The bird panicked and dashed towards a cleft in a tree. Here she holed in.

Suddenly a strong wind pushed the hawk back, then the pigeon saw it, an angel, one sent to help her. It held its hand up and the wind became so strong that the hawk plummeted down into a maze of hawthorn and blackberry bushes.

The angel lowered her hand and the wind stopped. She gently reached into the recess of the branch and took the pigeon into her hands. The angel, Mellion, was a dusky skinned jewel of India who wore a gold and pink shimmering sari, secured with a band of peacock blue below her chest, where she clasped the bird.

Mellion flew on with powerful beats and the pigeon lay peacefully in her embrace. Soon they reached Gazba's castle where the angel placed the bird among her friends. The pigeon immediately started to strut around pecking and then taking a drink, dipping her beak into a refreshing bowl of water then tipping her head back to swallow.

Mellion's face lit up in a smile of relief on seeing Juniper coming across the courtyard carrying a small bucket of feed for the birds. She lifted through the air and was gone in an instant onto other missions.

Juniper noticed the red band on the pigeon's leg and quickly picked her up. He read it and frowned. He was to inform Brother Lucas that the King and his men would soon be needed to protect Jasmine, who he now knew was the Maid of Valouresse. He always knew she was a special girl but now it all was beginning to make sense. Her courage and resourcefulness, her pure heart all made her the perfect one.

He had already decided to replenish Gazba's resources that had been wiped out by the storm. His jaw was set as he gripped the note. He had a replica map to Epiron Rock that Gazba had drawn. He gave it to his captain so he would take supplies to the rock.

He himself would take a message to Brother Lucas to speak to the King about protecting Jasmine. Because she was the Maid, she was the one destined to save her land.

All of this would take time. King Lohnn was on the coast at a tournament and would not be able to be reached for a few days.

Juniper sent troops with the supplies to Epiron Rock and on the same tricky and difficult route that Gazba, Jasmine, Gallant and Chloe had taken.

He made sure he left a good number of men to defend the castle should anything arise. At first light the soldiers were on their way, and Juniper was on his way to La Fonteyn to visit Brother Lucas.

Juniper rode swiftly and then, after tying his horse outside, entered the rustic stone building that the Brother lived in.

Old Brother Lucas listened gravely to the message he was given, and he could see how distraught Juniper was.

He patted Juniper on the shoulder and said, 'I remember you two as children playing hide and seek. Jasmine hid in a large black cauldron over a fire in the kitchen that thankfully had not yet been lit. No one knew where she was until she emerged sooty faced and the cook nearly fainted.'

'Ah of course, strange behaviour for a future Maid of Valouresse,' said Juniper with a laugh.

'It showed her spirit,' replied Brother Lucas.

'I agree,' said Juniper and then he asked, 'So what shall we do now?'

'I will travel to the coast and meet the King,' said Brother Lucas.

'You don't want me to go with you?' asked Juniper.

'No, the king won't listen to anyone else but me for some reason and besides, you should go to be with Jasmine. I have a feeling she will need you soon.'

'Well then, I shall be going,' said Juniper. 'Farewell and Godspeed.'

'And you lad, the same,' said Brother Lucas giving Juniper another friendly pat on the back.

Juniper mounted his horse and cantered along the road from La Fonteyn back to his master's home.

Once back there, he packed quickly and shoved his copy of the map into his vest and started along the way to Epiron Rock. Juniper knew he had been entrusted with looking after the estate and he knew he should stay and do that, but one night he had a dream. In the dream, he saw a girl holding onto a branch of a small Elderberry tree at the edge of a cliff. He threw himself forward and grasped her hand just before she fell. He awoke shaking and sweating and knew then that he must flout the rules and go to Jasmine. His master Gazba would understand. Juniper made the decision to pass protection of the estate to Bon, his good and capable friend.

The others taking supplies to Epiron rock had left early in the morning. He was leaving in the afternoon, so he figured he would be spending the night on his own somewhere in the forest.

As Juniper rode on, the shadows became longer but he had a fair knowledge of where he was going. He knew that in several days' time, and travelling towards the mountains in a north-westerly direction, he would be leaving the road to go along the hidden trail that would eventually lead to Epiron Rock.

After a few hours of riding, he saw in the distance the light of fires and he heard ribald, laughing voices—Bardozer's men, and likely the man himself.

Juniper was curious and got closer to the company. Now he could hear angry shouting and could see the object of their wrath—his own cousin Jerkel—in the light of the fire, his face beaten to an almost unrecognisable pulp.

The leader of the men, who Juniper figured was Bardozer, bellowed at close range into Jerkel's battered face.

'So, you came here to tell us of Gazba's whereabouts and now you won't! I thought you hated Gazba and your cousin, but apparently, you've changed your mind—bad move. Bon, that traitor, has now told Gazba I want him dead, and you have seen your chance to betray your master. There is only one choice. Tell us where he is, or we kill you in the morning. I suggest you think it over tonight.'

With that speech out of the way, Bardozer strode away to his tent, followed by some men attending to him.

Juniper waited until all was quiet and most of the men had gone to their tents. He waited until the change of the watch came. The one taking over wanted to have an ale and a chat with the one leaving his watch.

Juniper sneaked up behind Jerkel, who was leaning against a tree, and whispered: 'Cousin, it is me, Juniper,' as he cut through the ropes on Jerkel's wrists.

'I am s-s-sorry,' the injured man started to say but Juniper hushed him.

Juniper helped him through the undergrowth and then onto his horse.

Suddenly there was a loud yell, as the watchman discovered Jerkel was gone and almost at once, men swarmed from their tents and started scouring the surrounding foliage. Some mounted their horses and went down to the road to search.

One voice bellowed louder than the rest, which Juniper recognised as Bardozer's.

'Find him!' shouted the baron in fury.

'He won't be far away,' said the captain. 'Someone has freed him, but he is in such bad shape they won't be able get far.'

The captain swung his horse down the embankment to the stream and then rode along for some distance, then back.

Juniper breathed low and prayed that his own horse would be silent.

'Maybe he has crossed and gone up the other side of the stream,' said one.

'Ride up and look around,' said the captain. 'I think we would hear them crashing about. Listen.' There was silence apart from the gurgling of the stream. The men listened for the sounds of the escapee.

Juniper wished his cousin could stifle his moans of pain. They had managed to almost reach the stream and hide in a blackberry thicket that Juniper hoped was too difficult for the searchers to navigate.

One of the men peered into the mass of thorny undergrowth. but Juniper quickly concealed himself and yanked Jerkel in among the coiling tendrils of the plant and waited. Juniper panted quietly and lowered his breath until he felt he might faint.

In the dim light, Juniper sweated in fear as he saw the soldier's face peer in. The sound of the stream covered the crackle of the ferns underfoot and the sound of Juniper's horse. 'Nothing here,' said the man.

After some time, the soldiers retreated to their camp and Juniper found his way back out of the blackberry bush, crossed the stream, and followed the part of the trail that he remembered from the map.

When he could, and he felt he was far enough away from Bardozer's men, he struck a small flint to view the map. He spotted the Elderberry tree—and thought how fortunate he had been to see it in almost darkness—and then followed the trail which led to the cave. He then headed through the cave, leading his horse with the injured man. Jerkel groaned with each step the horse made.

'They would have killed me for sure,' he said.

'Oh, I have no doubt of that,' said Juniper. 'The Baron is a cruel man. Save your strength; we have a long way to go.'

'How about we leave the story for the time being,' said Nanny. 'We have been reading nearly all day.'

'But it's been raining all day, so it's not a waste of a day,' said Shelley. 'We couldn't do anything else much anyway.'

Nanny got dinner ready and soon the children were settled in bed where they slept soundly until morning.

The next morning was fine, not a sign of a cloud and Lillian and Nanny went to the mall shopping for baby clothes. Shelley came along and met some friends. After the shopping, they all went home and picked Jace up from the basketball court, where he had been playing with friends all morning.

Evening came again and the book came out for reading.

'Tell us about the monastery on the rock Nanny,' said Shelley as she propped herself up on her many pillows.

'Very well then,' said Nanny, continuing with the book.

The next morning, on the far side of the monastery, Chloe and Jasmine discovered an old garden that still had some herbs and vegetables growing in it.

'Look Mummy,' said Jasmine, 'here are some potatoes I've just dug up. It's a shame we have no meat to make a stew.'

Just as she said this, Wolf appeared with a plump rabbit in his jaws which he dropped at the feet of his astonished mistresses.

Gallant and Gazba raised their eyebrows in surprise.

'Good boy,' said the knight enthusiastically and patted the wolf for the first time, feeling that it was now safe to do so.

Chloe looked at Jasmine with a worried expression.

'It's alright Mummy,' she said. 'It's not one of my pet rabbits and we have to have something to eat.'

'You are a wise girl,' said Chloe with a smile for she was afraid her daughter may be upset by the dead rabbit.

Chloe found a pot, put the ingredients in and cooked it over a fire. She cooked it outside, as she was wary of the fireplace in the monastery which may have needed a clean. Soon all four were enjoying a delicious rabbit stew, flavoured with oregano and sage, and bulked up with carrots, swedes, and potatoes.

'This is the best meal I can ever remember having, my dear,' said Gazba to Chloe.

'Thank you, but actually you missed many a beautiful meal that I had prepared by Mrs Beacon because you were always working so late at the dispensary, if you recall.' said Chloe not maliciously but in all honesty.

'Yes, you are right, of course, my dear,' acknowledged Gazba and then he continued to eat his meal with eyes somewhat lowered.

'I'm cold,' said Jasmine pulling the ruff of her coat up around her neck, 'and I think it will snow soon. The leaves have nearly all fallen off the trees.'

Both parents shared a concerned glance and then Gazba said, 'Don't worry my darling, we will soon have a fire burning in the monastery and you will be cosy.'

The extra troops with the supplies arrived two weeks later, five men in all, and wound their way up the hill.

'Hoy!' shouted Gallant as he saw the first rider come over the rise onto the large plateau.

'Hoy!' shouted the man back enthusiastically and behind him the others came into sight, and all let out a cheer.

Everyone helped unpack the supplies and storage places were found for some in the cellar and some in the upper part of the monastery.

'This is an amazing place,' commented the captain, Darian, a dark-haired, bearded man as he looked around the exquisitely carved stone. The pillars carved around the ground floor held the weight of the building above.

'I had no idea it was here.'

'It is a secret of ages,' said Gazba. 'I am surprised at its beauty and utility. I'm afraid there are only two stables, here underneath the mon-astery, and we have no straw to make that viable anyway. We do have plenty of places to tether the horses and from what I can see, there is plenty of grass.'

Everyone sat on carved rock seats and chatted. The soldiers relaxed with an ale and ate bread topped with salted beef and relish.

Jasmine decided that this was a bit boring, and she wanted to explore a bit more than she already had. So, she waited until everyone was talking and occupied, then sneaked off, taking a little trail which led up the mountainside above the monastery. She hadn't been here before. She was entranced by the flowers and saw a stag standing majestically on the hillside, staring straight at her before he bolted away.

I must have scared him.

Suddenly, to her right, she saw someone—a woman. She gasped with surprise and a little fear, because she did not know who this woman was, and wondered why she was so far out into the wilds.

'Do not fear child,' purred the woman, whose face was very white, and lips were red as blood.

'Who are you?' asked Jasmine suspiciously.

'I am the keeper of the woods,' said the woman. 'Come to me. I have something for you.'

'What is it?' asked Jasmine sidling away, not wanting to be close to this beautiful but strangely disturbing lady.

'Come closer child,' said the woman. 'I have the scent of the forest for you in this bottle and I think it will please you.'

Now the witch—for that's who it was—came very close to Jasmine. She took the stopper from the bottle, dabbed some on her finger and swiftly lunged forward, stroking Jasmine on the forehead with it.

Jasmine pulled away and screamed loudly, falling to the ground.

Kraekhoull got her magic box, of gold and a myriad of other colours, from her bag and opened it. There was something like a small purple whirlwind and the witch was gone.

Her dark Prince had given her the power she needed to find Jasmine. Now the witch cackled as she travelled at lightning speed through the clouds of the air back to her lair.

It was some time before anyone noticed that Jasmine was missing. Chloe started to look around the monastery calling her name, then into the garden, but she was nowhere to be found. Soon all were searching for her.

Juniper and Jerkel had arrived at Epiron Rock and were surprised to find no-one there. They were also astounded at the majesty and beauty of the place. That it existed was a complete surprise.

Carefully he helped Jerkel off his horse and into the refuge of the under part of the rock.

He had brought salve and bandages with him and now he changed the dressing on his cousin's face.

'Cousin, an ale please?' asked the rather pathetic Jerkel as he noticed several open bottles.

'Of course, cousin,' said Juniper handing him a bottle.

'The others must be somewhere close,' said Juniper.

'Yes, a mystery,' said Jerkel drinking down the ale with great enjoyment. 'You know I am so grateful to you for saving me. I was not long for this world, until you came along, and I regard my rescue as a miracle and you as almost a god.'

'I understand you were going to tell Bardozer Gazba's whereabouts,' said Juniper.

'I was,' said Jerkel. 'But I had a finer moment. Something came over me and made me a better man—I just couldn't betray those who had always treated me well. It was only my jealousy of you which had been my weakness.'

'Well, it's all forgiven and forgotten as far as I'm concerned,' said Juniper, giving Jerkel a gentle rub on the shoulder.

When the others returned without Jasmine, Juniper heard the news that she was missing he exclaimed, 'I will go seek her now!'

Juniper explained the situation with Jerkel, who was very humble and apologetic towards Gazba.

Juniper found Jasmine lying still among some flowers.

He swept her into his arms and carefully started back down the mountainside to the monastery.

When Chloe, already anguished and in tears, saw her daughter looking so pale, she started to faint and Gazba caught her.

Once at Epiron Rock, Gazba took her to one of the rooms in the monastery and laid her on a bed which had a soft quilt that Chloe had found in one of the wardrobes earlier in the day.

'Is there anything I can do, my Lord?' asked Juniper, his face white. 'Are there any herbs I can gather?'

'No Juniper, I have everything with me that can possibly help her,' said Gazba, distraught.

'Do something Gazba,' cried Chloe who had now recovered from almost fainting and was stroking Jasmine's clammy forehead.

Gazba sorted through his herbs and other apothecary medicines, trying to decide which would be the one to heal his daughter.

He tried several and in the hour that followed, nothing changed in her condition.

Chloe kept sponging Jasmine's face and limbs as she now had a raging fever and was muttering about a lady in black.

'It's the witch who has caused this!' exclaimed Gazba in rage. 'She has used a form of poison I do not know of.'

'Keep trying, you must be able to do something!' exclaimed Chloe with panic rising in her voice and eyes pleading into his.

Jasmine's breathing became laboured and both parents sobbed as they tried to help their daughter.

'Let's pray,' said Chloe in a low voice. Together they prayed. Gazba cried out, 'Please, Lord, save our little girl!'

Chloe wept and said, 'Dear Lord, save her, heal her. We need your help now.'

Then both sat by the bed, crushed in spirit, holding each other's hands.

Evening approached, and in the room long shadows crossed the floor.

Suddenly from down below came a great cry of all the men and Juniper came running into the room—he had been anguished for his Jasmine but knew to keep away while the apothecary was at work.

'My Lord, there is a unicorn below and he says to bring Jasmine down.'

'Come, quickly, this may be an answer to our prayers,' said Chloe.

Gazba carried his limp daughter down the stairs to the basement of the rock where there stood a magnificent unicorn, pure white except for its gleaming golden horn.

The unicorn shook its head, with mane rippling like waves on water and eyes like dark pools of wisdom and love.

'Chraston!' exclaimed Gazba.

'Bring the child to me and put her on my back.' said the unicorn.

'She is too ill. She will fall off!' said Gazba in despair.

'Put her on, all will be well,' said Chraston.

Gazba placed his daughter on the unicorn's back. He stood close by to catch her should she fall, which he felt was a definite possibility.

The child was still, and her arms hung down limply with no movement.

Then ever so slightly her hands moved, then her fingers slowly threaded through the unicorn's thick, wavy mane.

Gallant, who had found some armour in the monastery, now also steadied the child on the unicorn.

Chapter 17

'How can Jasmine ride the unicorn if she is so weak?' asked Shelley sceptically.

'All will be revealed in due course,' said Nanny, putting the manuscript away. 'It's now time for bed. You have a big day ahead at the Zoo.'

Nanny kissed the children goodnight but before leaving the room said, 'Frankly I don't know what's coming next in the story. You said you would help me write it, so maybe you can both think about it—but don't let it keep you awake.'

'All right Nanny, love you,' they both said as she kissed them goodnight.

The children spent most of the next day at the zoo where there was a barbeque area, and Lillian had brought a packet of meat to cook, plus salads.

Nanny came along and enjoyed the beautiful animals, especially the zebras, which amazed her with their bizarre and beautiful markings, which she saw as confirmation of the creativity of God.

In the evening, out came the book again and the children were quite keen to contribute to the story.

'Have you got any ideas?' asked Nanny.

'I think that God will have to help Jasmine,' said Jace, 'because He is the only one strong enough to stand up to the witch's power.'

'I remember a story about the Apostle Paul in the bible,' said Shelley.

'He believed in God, and he was bitten on the hand by a deadly snake while he was collecting firewood—after being in a shipwreck,' added Shelley.

'That's right.' agreed Jace. 'He just shook off the snake and the people who lived on the island thought he was a god because he survived.'

'Yes, sometimes God does do miracles like that,' agreed Nanny, who then asked, 'Shall we continue?'

'Yes!' said both children almost in unison.

Gradually the colour came back to Jasmine's face, and she opened her eyes.

'I knew you would come,' she said dreamily to the unicorn.

Chraston turned his head and snuffled Jasmine's leg with his soft nose.

'Quickly child, sit up and be prepared for the ride of your life,' said the unicorn.

'She is not well enough yet,' exclaimed Gazba.

Even as her father spoke, the girl sat upright on Chraston and gave a big smile, saying, 'I am ready to go.'

Chloe and Gazba, Gallant, in fact all present, were stunned at Jasmine's swift recovery.

'Can I go with you?' offered Juniper.

'No,' said the unicorn, 'I must go alone. You should all stay here in this place of holiness, be steadfast and pray, because a dark hour is here upon us.'

Chloe gave a sob and grasped her husband's hand and said, 'We will.'

'Hold on, little one,' said the mighty creature, starting down the mountainside. Soon he was galloping across the mountain range, as snow had just started to whiten the air. Jasmine felt secure and unafraid because, cloistered and surrounded by Chraston's power and magic, she felt warm and comfortable.

Meanwhile, in her lair, the witch was using her crystal ball and—now that she had the power of the dark lord at her bidding—she could see the unicorn rushing through the forest.

She screamed, in horror, 'What! The Maid of Valouresse is on his back!'

Her eyes became bloodshot as she immediately started muttering ancient words from the realms of the black arts.

'My dark Prince!' she shouted, shooting her arms above her head, and shaking her fists in fury. 'Send me your ghouls and demonic hosts. I will lead them all and annihilate the unicorn and her rider.'

Bitterness and Fear saddled the witch's tormented, red-eyed steed and then, in a whirl of green powdery smoke, they became their true selves—demons. The prophetess was a hideous, squat being, and Fear had a vampirish appearance.

'Come with me.' she commanded and then took out her magic box. When the purple, acrid smoke had settled, she was on her horse beside Bitterness and Fear, having travelled to the same forest as Chraston and Jasmine.

The witch then loudly ordered her demonic hordes to come. One by one they buffeted the air with their huge bat-like wings as they landed, bringing a foul stench with them.

The demons many malevolent eyes spied out the forest and their mouths slavered, revealing jagged teeth. Their limbs terminated in clawed fingers and their tails finished with an arrowhead-shaped point. Their breathing was heavy, and strings of saliva rattled in and out of their mouths with each guttural noise they made.

There were many. The witch shouted shrilly, from her circling horse, 'Kill the child and the unicorn! Follow me!'

The demons roared and surged forward, travelling in a pack, like a foaming tide of evil, just behind the witch.

Chraston went as fast as he could, nimbly leaping over fallen logs and crossing small streams. He traversed the mountain and was gradually making his way down.

Jasmine gripped the unicorn's back with her knees, and she wrapped her hands in his thick mane. Her face had a greenish tinge.

'Courage child!' Chraston said loudly, as he plunged down a deep embankment.

Now the demons were gaining and Chraston's powerful neck surged forward and back with each stride. His ears flickered as he heard the demons jeering with laughter that sounded like it was mingled with the very essence of evil. Snow was now falling through the trees.

The witch whipped her mount to greater speed, while the demons followed on its heels.

Chraston skidded to the bottom of the mountain, sending rocks and dirt flying.

In the distance was his destination, the Lake of the Moon. Mist rose from its surface, and it shone like glass.

He reached the lake and started to gallop around it. The demons followed, ever gaining momentum, filling the air with a cacophony of ghoulish sounds.

'Take them!' shrieked Kraekhoull in a fit of impatience. Her horse was tiring so she signalled for the demons to overtake her and make the kill.

Chraston sweated and although he was an angelic being, his stamina was waning.

His legs were becoming heavy, and he was blowing hard.

Jasmine turned her head back and exclaimed with a sob, 'Chraston, they are right upon us!'

Sure enough, one of the monstrous bat creatures—the one in the lead—strained to reach Chraston, almost clawing his hind quarters.

As Chraston careered around to the other side of the lake, with this black tide inching ever closer, there appeared to be no way out, no place to hide, just a huge oak tree which was directly in their path.

The same demon dipped in mid-flight, snatching furiously for Jasmine. She felt its hot breath and pressed closely down onto the unicorn's back, almost fainting with terror.

Chraston thundered on, and flecks of saliva came from his mouth.

The evil beast swooped and grasped.

It missed.

It swooped down again.

Its hands reached out.

It grasped again.

Jasmine pressed into Chraston's back.

The demon's hands came together, but on empty air.

Jasmine's heart chilled as she heard it say, 'You are mine, child!'

At that moment, a magnificent door opened in the oak tree and glorious, heavenly light flooded out.

The demon fell back and screamed, covering its eyes.

Chraston soared through, his neat hind hooves outlined in gold as they disappeared.

Then the door slammed shut, leaving no sign as to where it had been.

The demon which was following so closely behind, slammed into the oak and fell, dazed and uttered profane language.

The other demons arrived and paced around the tree, scratching and biting it, trying to find the way in, all the while uttering foul demonic words.

Then Kraekhoull arrived like a black swirling whirlwind.

Her vitriol was as acid as a boiling pit of lava. The demons shrank back from her relentless fury. She passed her hands over the bark of the tree, looking for the entrance to wherever Chraston and the Maid had gone.

'This is magic, certainly, but of a type I have never encountered before,' she said, exasperated.

'Wow, Nanny,' said Jace, 'I like this part of the story. Where did they go?'

'We'll find out next time, but I do have a story about my life that is a bit magical.'

'Tell us Nanny,' said Shelley hugging her favourite toy, a unicorn cat.

'Well, when I was about your age,' said Nanny, 'my friend told me about a magical land she had read about where animals talked and there were other wonderful beings.'

'What other beings Nanny?' asked Shelley dreamily.

'Oh, water sprites, tree sprites and fauns—which had a top half that was human and two goat legs on the lower half of their body.'

'We were so in love with this mystical place that we decided we would try to go there.'

'So did you?' asked Jace with interest.

'Yes and no,' replied Nanny. 'We walked up a hill where there stood a dead tree and a big rock. It was a magical place that felt like the portal to another world. Then we prayed to the god of that world—which was a mighty lion, to take us there.'

'What happened then?' asked Jace.

'Nothing happened,' replied Nanny, 'but I heard the lion say, "You will come to my world, but you have many important things to do in your world first." Jesus and the lion seemed like the same person to me, strange as that may seem.'

'But you could have been imagining him saying that to you,' said Jace a little sceptically.

'Well, I've come to listen to the mysteries in my soul and believe them,' replied Nanny, with a smile.

'So, you're still hoping to go there, right Nanny?' said Shelley. 'Can I come with you when you go.'

'I can't pick the timing,' replied Nanny, 'but we will meet there some day, I'm sure.'

'And me too,' said Jace with enthusiasm.

'You too,' said Nanny with a laugh.

She kissed and tucked them in. She put the manuscript, which was on Shelley's bed, back up on top of the bureau and left the room.

The next day, the children played on their portable devices as the rain teemed down outside.

'Would you like to hear more of the story, kids?' Asked Nanny. It had become a wet-weather staple.

'Yes, why not,' said Jace putting down his device. 'You know it's a good story to make me want to give up this video game.'

Shelley was keen. 'Tell us where they went Nanny,' she said.

'Alright, let's get going then,' said Nanny, opening to the bookmarked page they were up to the night before.

'Chop it down,' demanded the witch. The demons obeyed and hacked away at the old tree—with axes supplied by the magic of the witch. It groaned and fell with a loud crash.

Kraekhoull, mystified, studied a handful of oak chips as they ran through her fingers, growled in fury, then threw them on the ground.

She then spoke ancient words from the dark arts and waved her hands over her crystal ball which she took from its velvet bag.

'Dark Prince, show me where that door, the portal is?' she asked.

Just before the witch got out her crystal ball, angels Keliran and Targum took up their place in the portal and spread out their wings. Kraekhoull could not see them nor what lay within, and she spat with fury.

The ball cleared of its purple smoke within and showed nothing but the surrounding forest trees. No door, no portal. Only a faint sound like the rustling of leaves, which she didn't recognise as the sound of her enemy's feathers.

Kraekhoull muttered in a low voice, 'Something is stopping me from seeing within the portal.'

She swirled her cape around and, as she did, she commanded the demons to return to the Dark Prince. They left on their greasy black wings, stirring leaves and dust as they lifted off. They flew up briefly and then dove down into a dark abyss that opened to swallow them.

Chraston was exhausted and landed, skidding slightly, on the soft green grass of a hillock and then slowly, gently knelt.

'Chraston, are we safe?' murmured Jasmine weakly.

'Yes, my child,' answered the unicorn, who was still blowing from the gallop.

'Good,' she said with a yawn and stretched her arms at the same time. She fell asleep and slowly slipped off Chraston's back onto the soft turf.

Chraston stood up again, sleeping on his feet, but his ears flickered backwards—on guard. He was woken by a voice he knew well saying, 'Chraston, beloved,' and a familiar hand stroking his neck.

The unicorn leant his cheek against the Lord's, who smiled and said, 'Well done, good and faithful servant.'

'Thank you, my King,' said Chraston.

'Go and have a roll in the grass,' said the Lord 'you are covered in dry sweat. I will watch the Maid. She will be able to heal now that she is here in Heaven.'

'It was a desperate chase, my Lord, but she is safe, and we escaped those hell hounds,' said Chraston.

'I am so proud of your courage,' said the Lord. 'Rest here now and be replenished by what you see and hear and smell. It is all good.'

Chraston had his roll, shook, then lifted his head high to view the mountains and to sniff the fresh tantalising air.

'I feel so invigorated,' he said with a whinny. 'I don't feel tired anymore, in fact I feel like I could gallop to those misty mountains this very moment.'

'Do it,' said the Lord. 'Heaven has that effect on us all. You can mount up like wings of an eagle, run, and not grow weary.'

As he said this, an eagle's high piercing scream could be heard overhead, calling the unicorn on.

'Come brother,' it sang. 'Come to the mountains and renew your strength. The waterfalls and streams speak life and joy. Come.'

Its feathers were bronzed in the light as it hovered above the unicorn, circling, and waiting.

'The child will rest in the shelter of my wings,' said the Lord. 'I will make sure of that.'

Chraston rested his muzzle in the Lord's palm then lifted his head and said, 'Very well, I will go but I will be back soon.'

'Farewell, dear one,' said the Lord giving him one last rub on the neck.

'Farewell my King,' replied the unicorn tossing his beautiful, expressive head. Facing the Lord, he reared up, then gracefully spun around, and galloped off, whinnying to the eagle as he went.

Looking down, the Lord smiled as he watched Cassiopia, a female leopard and her cubs, entwining around the body of the sleeping Jasmine.

'You are a good girl,' he said to the leopard as she pushed her head up onto his palm to be stroked.

'Keep the child comforted and let her sleep as long as she likes,' said the Lord.

'The vibrations of Heaven will heal her of the witch's poison.'

Cassiopia licked Jasmine's forehead and then the Lord's hand.

'You really have a scratchy tongue Cassiopia, but I like it,' he said with a laugh.

As she slept, angels came to view this very special little girl and among them were Keliran and Targum and Mellion, who had been put in charge over her. They all longed to be seen by Jasmine and here in this spirit world, this would be possible.

Time went by, how long one will never know, because time in Heaven was where minutes there could be years on earth, or the other way round.

One day, Jasmine did awake and felt something wet and warm on her nose. As she opened her eyes, she saw a fawn—covered in white spots— looking into her eyes with its big liquid black ones.

Cassiopia gently grabbed the young deer by the neck and hugged it. *This is not the way animals normally behave—this must be a special place,* thought Jasmine. The deer didn't pull away and now the leopard cubs jumped on it in play.

Jasmine gave a little gasp of joy as the cubs then leapt onto her with their soft, squirmy bodies.

Now that the effects of Kraekhoull's poison had worn off, the angels visited Jasmine. Keliran, and Targum furled their wings and walked across to where Jasmine was playing with some baby rabbits.

'Who are you?' she asked, carefully placing the rabbit on the ground, and staring at the astoundingly garbed visitors.

'I am Targum,' said Targum. 'And this is Keliran,' he said gesturing to his companion in glowing white with sky blue eyes and gold hair, who nodded and smiled at the girl in greeting. Targum, whose eagle like demeanour with bronze complexion and garbed in purple continued, 'We have been rescuing you night and day, but we never tire of it.'

With that, Targum unfurled his huge, purple feathered wings and then Keliran did the same revealing his snow-white ones.

'You are angels!' she said with a gasp of joy. Jasmine looked up to see an angel dressed like an Indian princess lower herself to the ground with mighty downward wing beats. She then approached Jasmine.

'Yes, we are,' said the angel with a merry laughing voice. 'I see you have met Cassiopia.'

The leopard rubbed her head against Jasmine's hand.

'Y-y-es she is my friend,' she stammered, in awe, still stroking the animal distractedly.

Jasmine's eyes were wide with wonder at the angel's pink sari, laden with gold embroidery and her stunningly beautiful face.

'I am Mellion, dear one,' said the angel, gently placing her hands on Jasmine's shoulders and kissing her cheek.

'Come,' she said, 'I have something to show you. Keliran and Targum, you come too.'

Mellion took Jasmine's hand, and they walked through a field of intoxicatingly fragrant flowers. The colours dazzled Jasmine's senses.

'Some of these colours I have never seen,' she said.

The angels smiled.

'These flowers, the smell and the colours make me so happy that I can hardly stand it!' she exclaimed to the angels.

The angels laughed to see her innocent bliss.

Then Mellion asked Jasmine. 'Would you like to come to the waterfall that comes from the River of Life?'

'I sure would,' said Jasmine eagerly.

'Enough for the moment. What do you think?' asked Nanny, putting the book down.

'We'll make our own sandwiches, Nanny,' said Shelley, leaping up to go to the kitchen. 'Do you want one Nanny?' she asked.

'Thanks darling—a peanut butter one would be nice.'

'It's a bit hard to believe that a leopard would play with a fawn and not hurt it,' said Jace, joining Shelley.

'Well, actually,' said Nanny, 'I heard a true story about a leopard in Africa that found a little antelope and adopted it.'

'It is a sad story because the mother leopard tried to defend the little antelope from the other leopards, and in the end, they killed it.'

'That's a horrible story, Nanny,' said Shelley glowering.

'Yes, it is sad, but it shows how amazing things can happen here on earth, just the same as in Heaven, where there is no death. I have a true funny story to cheer you up. A cat in Ireland adopted some little ducklings that had lost their mother. The cat had already had her own kittens, but she rounded up the ducklings and even fed them milk.'

'That's *really* weird Nanny,' said Jace with a laugh. 'How do you know that is true?'

'It was filmed in England and on a news program,' said Nanny. 'That's how Eden was in the beginning—all the animals getting along. And it says in Genesis in the Bible, that they all ate green plants and seeds.'

'So, they didn't eat each other?' said Shelley who was munching into her sandwich while Nanny was telling her story.

'All the different species lived in harmony and didn't kill each other,' said Nanny.

Shelley spoke up.

'I've seen your painting in the shed, of a leopard with an antelope on its back and a hippo with a crocodile resting on top of it while the hippo is sleeping,' said Shelley. 'So, that's what you think it was like then?'

'Yes,' said Nanny, 'that's how I imagine it to be, and I think that we get glimpses of it—Eden—even today.'

'With the ducks and the cat?' said Jace as he munched his toastie and then exclaimed with enthusiasm, 'Come on Nanny, more book please!'

'Yes, it's still raining, and I want to know what happens next,' said Shelley.

Holding Mellion's hand and with the other two angels walking beside her, Jasmine came to the side of a crashing waterfall hundreds of feet high. She giggled with delight as she watched the crystal-clear water plummet down and create vapour that rose so high that she could feel its atmosphere.

'Would you like to fly over it?' asked Targum, his dark eyes deep and filled with expectation.

'If you think I can, I would love to,' said Jasmine eagerly. 'Will you help me fly, Mellion, and hold my hand?'

'Of course, my dear, and Targum will hold your other hand,' she replied.

'And I,' said Keliran with a laugh and a cheeky smile, 'will fly below you both should anything go awry.'

'Don't worry, child,' said Mellion. 'Both these two angels are always teasing.'

'Are you ready,' asked Mellion, as the waters thundered below.

'Yes, yes, I feel brave now,' shouted Jasmine, but with her eyes shut.

'Very well, let's fly!' exclaimed Mellion as down over the grassy cliff all four dove, down, down and into the rising mist of the waterfall.

Jasmine squealed with joy and exhilaration at the sight of the rising mist as she opened her eyes. Mellion exchanged glances with the other two angels. who smiled broadly at the little girl who was experiencing the wonder of flight.

'You can fly on your own if you like,' said Mellion. 'We are right here with you. Do you want to try?'

'Oh yes I do,' replied Jasmine, who was filled with anticipation and excitement.

Mellion and Targum released their grip on Jasmine's hands, and she was buffeted up by a wave of rising air, mixed with mist.

'Come with us, little one,' said Mellion with joy. 'Come and see the wonders of Heaven.'

The three angels changed direction and turned across from the waterfall and upwards into the sky with Jasmine flying between them.

They flew across valleys of green, with rocky snow-covered mountains either side. The valleys were occupied by all kinds of animals. One valley held giant lizards grazing on trees and grass—some walked four footed and others on two legs.

They swooped down to get a closer look at some animals in a valley by a stream.

'See the young ones playing together?' asked Mellion. 'The lion cubs and the lambs, the bears and the calves in the fields below?'

'Yes, I see,' said Jasmine. 'A bear cub has the kid's head is in its mouth, but the kid doesn't seem to mind.'

'All of Heaven is like this,' said Mellion.

'Nothing hurts anything,' said Targum. 'All is at peace. But now we have someone for you to meet, someone who loves you very much.'

'Is it Mummy or Daddy?' asked Jasmine eagerly.

'No,' answered Targum. 'But it is someone who has known you from the beginning of time.'

'Since I was a baby?' asked Jasmine.

'Even before then,' answered Targum as he flew around, leading the way back to where Cassiopia had played with her cubs, on the hillock where Jasmine had rested—a special place.

They landed lightly.

'We will leave now,' said Targum. The gold belt encircling his purple tunic gleamed as did Keliran's silver one.

'But we will be back,' said Keliran in his white, glowing tunic and belt of silver which shone brightly. The angels spread their wings and, with several powerful beats, disappeared up and out of the forest.

'No, don't go!' said Jasmine anxiously watching them leave, then looking behind her said, 'Cassiopia is not here, or her cubs.'

She sat on the grass and gave a sob, burying her face in her hands and suddenly feeling very alone.

'Why the tears little one?' came a kindly voice.

She looked up. It was a bearded man whom she felt she recognised.

'Is that you Lord?' she asked through her tears.

'It is, my child. Come sit here and don't cry. All is well.'

Jasmine sat on the grass next to the Lord and shyly gazed up. The Lord smiled and held out his hand, which she took.

'Do you like it here Jasmine?' he asked.

'Oh yes,' she replied, 'I love it.'

'Do you know why you are here,' the Lord asked.

'No,' she replied.

'Here,' said the Lord, 'You can build up your strength and courage to go and do a mighty deed.'

'I am but a child,' said Jasmine. 'And I don't know whether I can do anything great or brave.'

'I will be with you always,' he said. 'You can overcome evil, and you will be given valour—to save Valouresse.'

'Oh, that sounds the same, valour and Valouresse,' said Jasmine with a laugh.

'Yes, named after you, my child,' said the Lord. 'A long time ago when the legend of the Maid of Valouresse was first born.'

'Oh, my King,' pleaded Jasmine. 'Can I stay here longer because I really love it here? I will miss my angel friends and the animals when I go back—mind you, I do want to see my parents.'

'You may stay here as long as you like,' said the Lord. 'When the moment is right, the unicorn will take you to your parents.'

'What about the angels,' she asked. 'Will I ever see them again?'

'Of course, you will,' said the Lord. 'In your world, they are not often seen, but you can be sure that they are still there watching over you.'

'Oh good,' said Jasmine, 'That is a comfort.'

She paused.

'Jesus?' asked Jasmine timidly. 'Are you still angry with the people who hurt you?'

'No, not at all—and do you know why?' he asked. 'Because all is well, all will be well, and all manner of things will be well.'

'What does that mean?' asked Jasmine.

'It means,' said the Lord, 'that all will be restored to perfection, just as it is in Heaven, so it will be on earth. And love conquers all.'

'I asked my Father to forgive them because they didn't know what they were doing.'

'I don't love everyone,' said Jasmine bluntly. 'I hate the witch who poisoned me.'

'That is a tricky one,' said Jesus with a laugh. 'Loving your enemies is hard to do, but love is the only way forward my child. It changes things in miraculous ways.'

Then He asked, 'Would you like to take a walk in my garden?'

'Yes please!' said Jasmine eagerly. Hand in hand they made their way along an overgrown path through the woods.

The path wound on for maybe a league, but it didn't seem far to walk. On either side, leafy green plants encroached onto it. It was untamed, but strangely comforting in its wildness because she held her Lord's hand.

The trees and bushes parted into a spacious and fragrant garden. Jasmine's eyes were wide and when her eyes met her Lord's he was smiling broadly.

'Come my child,' he said. 'Judah wants to meet you.'

From behind one of the huge rose bushes stepped a great tawny-coloured lion.

It shook its head and sauntered up to Jasmine, who gave a little scream and hid behind Jesus, clinging to his robe.

'Judah is harmless, except towards creatures of darkness. He won't hurt you. In fact, he loves you dearly and just wants to be near you.'

'Really, he loves me?' said Jasmine with delight.

The lion allowed her to run her fingers through his thick, gold-coloured mane and then he licked her on the arm. Jasmine cried out, 'He is beautiful!'

Judah then walked around her, leaning into her while she stroked his powerful back.

'Come, Judah, Jasmine,' said Jesus. 'Let's walk in my garden.'

All three took a tour of the garden.

A flock of swallows swept overhead, and Jesus sighed and said, 'My heart sails with them.'

'Are you sad, Jesus?' asked Jasmine.

'No, my child, I am happy, and the swallows remind me that all will be well in the end, that freedom and love will prevail.'

They came to an arched bridge over a stream. Jasmine threw in a leaf and watched it float through to the other side.

Hours passed and Jesus introduced Jasmine to the many animals living in the garden. They eagerly ran to Him to enjoy His affection. He rubbed behind the large mobile ears of the antelope and after that a bear lumbered over and had his head scratched.

By this time Jasmine was completely at ease with these large, and what to her would normally be frightening, animals. She found herself sitting on a bear's back. He moved sideways and she fell into his paws. He licked her on the face, and she giggled.

So it went with Jasmine in Heaven. It was one glorious day after the next and she quickly forgot about her mission to save Valouresse. She saw the King every day, and they talked about many things. She flew with the angels and explored lands within Heaven. Every day was an adventure.

'Nanny, I think I want to go to Heaven right now,' said Shelley in an enraptured voice.

'But not before your time,' said Nanny, turning the page of the book.

'We want more story, Nanny,' demanded Jace impatiently.

'Alright but say please, please,' replied Nanny with a laugh, as she continued with her reading.

'Please,' said Jace.

Since Juniper had spoken with him, Father Lucas was on his way to speak to King Lohnn and travelled as fast as he could in a carriage with fine, strong black horses. Juniper had gone on to Epiron Rock—a place that Brother Lucas knew well, but the location of which he knew must never be known to the witch.

He stopped at an inn for the night and was settling down to sleep after a hearty stew, some mead, and a bath.

He knelt by his bed and prayed as was his usual ritual.

'Dear Jesus,' he said quietly. 'Please watch over those in the forest and especially the little girl. Keep the angels vigilant. They hid her from Kraekhoull—I saw that in a dream after Chraston dove into that oak tree. She is safe now but will need to be protected when she returns to earth. Please let me get to the king in time and make his heart amenable to returning to protect Valouresse and the Maid.'

After this, Brother Lucas plumped up his pillow, snuggled into the blankets and went to sleep.

Kraekhoull was still in a foul mood because she had not been able to see Chraston and Jasmine within the portal and had no way of getting through herself.

She roamed restlessly around her lair thinking out loud. Bitterness and Fear kept away from her because they had failed her when they were in the form of wolves some time before.

'Who would know of the Maid and where she would go?' she asked.

'There must be someone.'

Her brow creased and her eyes became dark with thought.

'A holy person might know.'

Suddenly she gave a shriek, and she smiled devilishly.

'Of course, it is Brother Lucas!' she exclaimed. 'It is him. He would have such knowledge, and I will get it from him! I must terrify the old man, and he will give in.'

Kraekhoull started her incantations and wove her hands over her crystal ball. It became purple, then fiery within and then she saw what she wanted to see—an old man helpless and asleep in his bed.

'Come dark ones,' she said. 'With the power of the dark Prince—show Brother Lucas the true horror of your faces and get him to open the portal to where the Maid is.'

Outside Brother Lucas' room a storm had risen, and the window of his room banged open furiously.

The evil ones were on their way.

'Dratted weather,' said Brother Lucas as he secured the window. 'I hope we don't get bogged tomorrow.'

He went back to bed and listened to the wail of the wind, screaming like voices. He snuggled a little deeper into his blankets.

The window rattled again and flew open, but as he went to shut it, strong hands gripped the side of the window, and the demons pushed themselves in.

Brother Lucas fell backwards in horror. These demons were showing themselves for what they really were, as he had never seen them before.

The sharp teeth of the tallest creature glinted, and its foul sneer was revealed in a flash of lightning. Its long tail, with arrow-shaped pointed end, waved restlessly, like a whip.

The other demons behind it laughed hideously and came closer to the old man, breathing their foul stench on him.

'Show us the portal that the unicorn and the Maid entered,' said the biggest demon, reaching for Brother Lucas, who was in a state of terror.

The demon grimaced as it played with him like a cat with a mouse—the old man whimpered, paralysed with fear.

Suddenly Brother Lucas sat up on the bed and held his cross and said, 'Not by might, nor by power but by my spirit says the Lord.' The large demon screamed as if it were being burnt.

'Jesus, Holy Spirit, come!' shouted Brother Lucas, with bravery and command in his voice.

There was a blinding flash then a mighty boom of thunder. The creatures screamed and vanished. The old man sat shaking on the bed.

'I would never show them the portal. Thank you, Lord, for increasing my faith and my strength.'

Brother Lucas was keen to get moving the next morning and was up early, watching the ostler harness the horses. He offered a handful of grass to the lead horse and whispered, 'Take us swiftly and safely to King Lohnn, my beauty.'

The big mare snuffled up the grass and enjoyed having her nose gently rubbed.

The carriage travelled well and fast, until it encountered murky ground. Stones and logs were placed under the wheels to give it traction and then the able-bodied men pushed it through the tacky mud.

Brother Lucas prayed under his breath and the carriage rolled free onto solid ground.

Kraekhoull once again raged around her den, throwing and knocking things over. She screamed at Bitterness and Fear in frustration and anger, 'How could one feeble old man resist the powers of darkness? I don't understand?!'

'The demons are the ones to find the Maid and destroy her,' said Bitterness, seeming very calm and beautiful, 'but Bardozer's men are the ones to take Valouresse. The city of La Fonteyn will be yours, Kraekhoull.'

'The demons have failed more than once, as you two know. It seems that I will be the one to end that child. How yet, I don't really know—but it will happen!' she exclaimed, slamming her fist on a table, and causing everything on it to teeter precariously.

The carriage made good time and within a few days it had reached the coast.

As it bounced and rolled along the coast road, Brother Lucas gazed out of the window at the blue sea and fluffy clouds. It was perfect weather with a slight breeze.

Brother Lucas was smiling but then he frowned. *How will I address the king to make him realise the gravity of the situation? His courtship with the princess must wait, as well as his further tournaments. The legend of the Maid of Valouresse is no legend. He must protect her for all of Valouresse is at stake.*

The old man went over and over in his head how he would persuade King Lohnn to listen to him.

Then he remembered the Victors Ball and how the king had given him high praise in front of hundreds of people.

He also remembered giving Chloe the cross and the words that Gazba would need on his quest. Juniper had told him of Jasmine's flight from the castle to join her father and, ever since then, he had prayed for them both and that they would be reunited.

The carriage lurched to a halt in front of King Ranown's castle. The horses snorted, and steam rose from their bodies.

King Ranown was the father of Melissa, the princess that King Lohnn was courting.

Brother Lucas was escorted by servants through to the Great Hall of the castle, where he met both kings seated at a long table, having wine and an assortment of cheeses.

'This is my friend, Brother Lucas,' said King Lohnn, gesturing to the old man.

'Please be at ease, seat yourself.' said King Ranown, as one of the servants pulled out a chair for Brother Lucas.

'Have some wine and cheese, Brother. By the looks of you, it has been a long trip.'

'Yes, my lord it has,' said Brother Lucas, 'and eventful.'

Then he said to King Lohnn: 'There is a grave threat to the Maid of Valouresse and as you know, she is the one destined to save the land.'

'Oh!' scoffed King Lohnn leaning back in his chair and planting his wine glass heavily on the table. 'She is a myth, no more. The whole story is a myth, and I wouldn't worry about it, Brother.'

Brother Lucas' face held exasperation as he struggled to convince his king.

'But my lord, I believe it is true and that the danger to Valouresse is very real. The witch has returned and is on the move, and Baron Bardozer covets your land, and has killed some of your knights.'

'I would not have travelled here, if I wasn't sure Valouresse was in danger and your people at risk.'

'I will be back in La Fonteyn in a couple of weeks, and we can continue this discussion then,' said King Lohnn.

'I have important business here with the King and his daughter.' He winked at King Ranown.

He continued: 'The story about the witch being on the move has been circulating for years and nothing has come of it. And as for Bardozer, a buffoon like that surely can't be taken seriously.'

'Brother Lucas,' said King Ranown, 'rest and eat and you will regain your strength.'

'Thank you, my lord,' said Brother Lucas in a defeated voice. 'I will retire now.'

'Show Brother Lucas to his room and attend to his needs,' said King Ranown to his servants.

'Brother Lucas, enjoy your rest and we shall see you later no doubt,' said King Ranown.

'I think I will stay in for the night now,' said Brother Lucas with a gentle smile. 'I have had enough cheese to satisfy my hunger. I just need to rest now, thank you my lords.'

'Very well,' said King Ranown smiling at the old man.

'Rest well old friend,' added King Lohnn. 'And don't worry about things that may never happen.'

Brother Lucas turned his head away, raising his hand in a helpless parting gesture.

Chapter 18

'The king wouldn't listen to brother Lucas? said Jace. 'What now?'

'We will find out soon,' said Nanny with a laugh. 'You are always one page ahead of the situation, aren't you?'

'Why wouldn't the king listen to him?' asked Shelley, disappointed.

'He was occupied with other things, such as courting a princess. We can all be like that at times.' said Nanny.

'What, courting princesses?' asked Jace cheekily.

'You know what I mean,' said Nanny. 'Taking your eyes off the important, big picture.'

'Do you want more book?' she asked.

'Sure,' answered both children.

That night in King Ranown's castle, Brother Lucas slept soundly with no fear. He said his prayers as usual and felt such a peace afterwards, that no demon from hell could penetrate it.

King Lohnn, on the other hand, tossed and turned in his bed, unable to sleep.

The words of the priest had gone deep into his mind, and he could not shake them.

He kept going over and over in his thoughts the facts that he believed he knew.

The witch hasn't been seen for a decade, and Bardozer is too much a fool to plan an attack on La Fonteyn. But then again, what if they were working together. What if the Maid is real, what if …?

And so it went, all through the night. Over and over.

Early in the morning, long before the sun had come up, when all was still and dark, King Lohnn suddenly sat up.

'Listen to the brother!' came a loud voice. King Lohnn scanned the room. His heart pounded.

'Who is there, show yourself!' he shouted reaching for a knife on the bedside table.

'It is I, the Captain of the Heavenly Host,' said a deep resonating voice.

And once again the voice said, 'Listen to the brother!'

'I will,' said King Lohnn shaking.

King Lohnn went to Brother Lucas' room and hammered on the door.

Brother Lucas came to the door and opened it to see his king trembling and white.

'I heard a voice,' said King Lohnn, 'It was the Lord's voice, and he told me to listen to you.'

'Well, praise God for that,' said Brother Lucas, overjoyed. Then he put his arm around the King's shoulders and sat with him on the bed.

'We must rally men to battle Bardozer,' said Brother Lucas, 'because from what I've heard, he has recruited many to fight with him. The Maid must be protected, for she plays a vital part in saving Valouresse from both the witch and the baron.'

'What part does she play?' asked King Lohnn.

'That I don't know yet,' said Brother Lucas, 'but I think we both understand greater forces than ourselves are at play here. The Captain of the Heavenly Hosts and his angels are on our side, although we may not see them with our mortal eyes. And in the same way, this girl will have a powerful and mystical effect on the outcome of this conflict.'

'I will leave for La Fonteyn tomorrow,' said King Lohnn. 'But first I will tell King Ranown what the Captain of the Heavenly Host said to me.'

'I shall accompany you home, my lord,' said Brother Lucas, grasping King Lohnn's hand.

'So be it.' said King Lohnn.

Later that morning the two kings spoke in the Great Hall, over breakfast.

'So, you heard the voice of God himself?' said King Ranown in wonder.

'Yes, I did. It was an awesome experience,' said King Lohnn, 'and I feel bound to obey the one behind such a commanding voice.'

'I will pledge an army to defend Valouresse and La Fonteyn,' said King Ranown.

'I will keep you posted as to our battle plans,' said King Lohnn.

'We shall be ready when the call comes,' answered King Ranown.

Brother Lucas and King Lohnn farewelled King Ranown in the square of the castle and the carriage lurched forward, pulled by prancing, snorting horses.

The witch was frustrated and furious that the demons did not find out the whereabouts of the portal from the old priest.

'The Maid's parents must still be in the forest. They would know where she is and I will find her,' she shouted.

Then, whirling around to face Bitterness and Fear she said, 'You two have been a huge disappointment, but here is one task for you to complete. Help me find the child's whereabouts from her parents, otherwise I will send you to the Dark Prince for punishment.'

'We obey, your ladyship,' said Bitterness and Fear backing out of the lair, shaking.

'Come,' said Kraekhoull, casting her cloak around the two frightened demons then, taking out her magic box. All three vanished leaving a purple smoke wafting behind.

Once back in the forest, the demons took on a bat-like flying form and started looking around for Epiron Rock.

'Go, go,' said the witch, shooing them on their way.

The witch retraced her steps to where she last confronted and poisoned Jasmine. She walked down the path which led to Epiron Rock. Suddenly the path came to nothing but thick foliage. The witch cursed and forced her way through the bushes.

Jasmine had squeezed through here when she went exploring the day of her encounter with Kraekhoull. The witch was bending down through the heavy foliage. Just as she went to look up, a battalion of angels landed and unfurled their wings, hiding the monastery from view.

The witch took out her crystal ball and saw nothing. She hissed and spat like a cat and, after being scratched by the blackberry talons, she gave up the search. She got out her magic box, opened it and disappeared, taking the two demons with her and leaving scorched leaves floating in her wake.

The angels ascended, having accomplished their deed of obscuring the monastery and the location of Gazba and Chloe, for Jasmine was gone for the time being. Kraekhoull had missed capturing the Maid.

One day when Jasmine was walking with the Lord he said: 'Do you want to meet my father and the winged creatures that fly around his throne?'

'Oh yes, Lord!' exclaimed Jasmine.

Just then, from North, South, East, and West came a loud rushing noise and four winged beasts arrived. They hovered above the Lord and cried out to him in greeting.

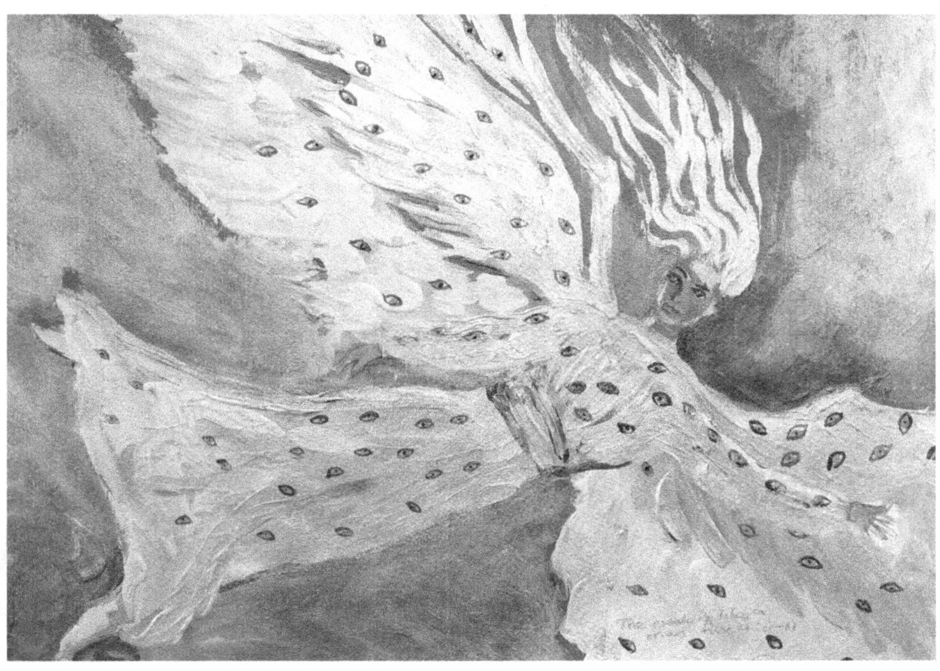

They had eyes all over their bodies and each had six wings. One was an eagle, which landed and allowed Jesus to ruffle the feathers of its head. Another was a bull which stood before the Lord, and one was a lion, both of which he patted affectionately. Then an angel like a man laid his hand on the Lord's shoulder and embraced him.

Now they whirled up into the air higher and higher, above the waterfall with is rainbow mist and upwards towards billowing clouds of darkness.

'Lord,' said Jasmine 'I'm afraid. Stay with me.'

The four creatures all gathered close around her and she felt the warmth and comfort of their bodies and the Lord held her hand.

'I won't leave you, little one,' he said.

Suddenly all of them burst through the clouds and were dazzled by myriad rainbows and fire, which all seemed to blend somehow.

The creatures left her and started to fly around a green jasper throne. On the throne was a powerful man whose eyes and face shone with a beautiful radiance. He smiled at Jasmine and Jesus and beckoned them to Him. He rose from his throne and embraced them both and looked deeply into their eyes.

'Little one,' he said, 'Always know that the power of Heaven is within you and that I will watch over you.'

'As will I and the Holy Spirit,' added Jesus, still holding her hand.

The creatures cried out ecstatically, 'Holy, holy, holy is the Lord God almighty, who was and is and is to come, Holy, Holy, Holy!'

With that, Jasmine found herself flying downward from the rainbow and fire clouds, back down to the waterfall, then up from it and over to the soft turfed ground.

'My child, do you feel ready to go back yet?' asked the Lord. 'My father, I and the Holy Spirit as well as the angels, will strengthen you.'

'I'm a little bit scared.' answered Jasmine, firmly holding the Lord's hand.

'Just as you feel my hand now,' said the Lord. 'It will be in yours, even if you cannot feel it back on the earth.'

'Are you ready, my child?' the Lord asked again.

Jasmine gazed up into his eyes and nodded, saying, 'Yes. I am.'

The Lord picked up a shofar—the large ram's horn—and put it to his lips.

He raised it and blew. The deep resonant herald was calling.

In the distance of mauves and greens, of mountains and streams, fields and valleys, Jasmine could hear a thundering.

The noise became louder, and she could see in the distance—something white.

As he swung through a copse of maple trees, Jasmine recognised her dear friend.

As he got closer, she cried out with joy, 'Chraston!'

The huge beast skidded to a halt in front of Jesus and Jasmine, and then touched

Jasmine's head with his soft quivering muzzle, snorting from his gallop.

'So, the time is here?' said Chraston. 'Climb aboard, little one.'

Jesus helped Jasmine mount the great snowy coloured beast.

'Farewell,' Jesus cried out. 'To the pool of the moon, go and then return to Epiron Rock.'

He held out his hands and the same shimmering, glittering lake appeared, where they had gone through the oak tree door.

Now there was no oak tree to come back through and Chraston landed lightly on the ground.

'Stay here, dear one, behind a tree,' he said. 'I will check the surrounding area.'

The unicorn lifted his head high and sniffed the air, while Jasmine admired his beauty from behind an oak.

He came back over to her and said, 'Hop on, little one. We must be swift, for the witch is gaining power.'

Through the forest Chraston galloped, weaving in and out of trees, leaping over logs and splashing through streams.

The forest was still, but Jasmine was nervous, and said—loud enough to be heard over the unicorn's thundering hooves—'Are we nearly there yet?'

'Nearly,' said Chraston, breathing hard.

Suddenly they burst through some thick bushes—the ones the witch had tried to come through but was hindered by the angels. But, for the unicorn, the bushes seemed to fall away.

'There it is,' exclaimed Chraston through his laboured breath.

'Are you alright?' asked Jasmine, stroking his sweaty neck.

'I am well, only a bit puffed,' said Chraston turning his ears back to hear her voice.

'Isn't the monastery beautiful? said Jasmine in awe. 'It looks like it was made by angels.'

'It certainly is beautiful and does have the hand of the divine upon it,' agreed the unicorn.

The soldiers bowed to the unicorn as it stepped into the mighty rock cave that lay under the monastery.

Juniper was there in a moment to help Jasmine off the unicorn's back, but she sprang off on her own.

Chloe and Gazba, on hearing of her return, rushed down the staircase to see her.

'Jasmine!' exclaimed Chloe, embracing her daughter and crying tears of joy. 'Where have you been?'

'I'm sorry, Mummy and Daddy.' said Jasmine.

'What for, my love?' answered Chloe, still hugging her child.

'For being gone so long,' replied Jasmine.

'You were only gone one day, darling,' said Chloe, 'But it was the longest day!'

She sobbed.

'Oh,' said Jasmine. 'I'm sorry.'

'Where did you go?' asked Gazba, 'We waited for you? We know you were with Chraston.'

'Chraston took me to Heaven through a door in an oak tree,' replied Jasmine.

'Heaven?' said Gazba and his eyes lit up.

'Oh Daddy,' replied Jasmine, 'It was more beautiful than anything I have ever seen here on earth—and I met Jesus!'

'Jasmine,' said Chraston. 'There will be time to talk about that later. But first, you must go to the upper stronghold of the monastery.'

'Why?' she asked.

'It is secure,' he replied. 'Go at once child.'

Jasmine took her mother's hand and ran up the stairs with her.

Gazba and Chraston spoke in the huge, open cavern that underlay the monastery. The men sat on wooden benches and listened intently.

'Gazba,' said Chraston. 'Prepare for battle. I don't know how close Kraekhoull is or how ready for war or even if she knows how to get here, but we must protect the Maid at all costs.'

'What is her part in all this?' asked Gazba with concern.

'I do not know,' replied Chraston.

'She is my daughter, and I worry for her, desperately,' said Gazba.

'Fear not, for in the Lord's time all will unfold. He cares for Jasmine. She may be only a child, but remember it is "not by might, nor by power, but by my spirit" says the Lord. He will imbue her with the strength she needs.'

'So, He will give her the strength she needs to accomplish this?' asked Gazba.

'He will give her the power of Heaven to draw on,' replied Chraston, adding, 'And she will have us.'

Chapter 19

'That's pretty exciting Nanny,' said Jace, thinking back to the earlier part of the chapter. 'When King Lohnn heard the voice of the Lord—can that really happen?'

On the couch, Jace lay on his back with his hands behind his head and looked contemplative.

'Have you ever heard the voice of God, Nanny?' he asked.

'Well, I have heard Him say things, yes, but not out loud,' said Nanny. 'But when I was about four, I woke up to see a giant hand hovering over me. It was the most comforting feeling.'

'Was it trying to smother you Nanny?' asked Jace.

'No,' laughed Nanny. 'It was hovering above in an attitude of protection.'

'So, what you're saying is, that it was God doing that, right?' asked Jace.

'Yes,' replied Nanny. 'It was God's hand, and I have never felt so loved as in that moment.'

'That's nice,' said Shelley with a smile. 'I hope those sorts of things will happen to me,'

'If you seek you will find,' said Nanny. 'Jesus is right here right now,' she said, putting her hand on her heart. 'He is never far away.'

'So, he's in my heart, is that what you mean?' asked Shelley.

'Yes, there and all around.' replied Nanny.

'Okay then, that's good,' said Shelley. 'Let's keep going with the book Nanny.'

'Sure,' said Nanny and she started to read.

'Nanny?' interjected Jace with excitement.

'Yes, darling,' replied Nanny.

'You know how Jasmine is only a child, and she is going to be a warrior?'

'Yes,' replied Nanny.

'Well, don't you think she should have armour?'

'Yes,' agreed Nanny. 'That is a good suggestion. I'll keep it in mind.'

Once up in the high part of the monastery, the stronghold, Jasmine started to explore. She hadn't had a good chance to look around before, but now she could.

There were many beautifully crafted glass vases and other objects of art on the skilfully carved old mahogany dresser.

She found a small room off the main dining area which had a closet. In it was a large oak trunk.

While her mother was in another room preparing dinner, Jasmine went over to the box and opened its lid.

She gasped with surprise as the setting sun came through a window, causing the armour inside within to gleam.

'Mummy, look!' she exclaimed. holding up a breastplate.

'Goodness me!' said Chloe. 'Tiny armour, maybe made for a dwarf.'

The sky became mauve with sooty clouds. In the cavern it was almost dark.

The unicorn spoke to the men, few that there were.

'I think,' he said, 'when the time comes, Gallant, Juniper, and you, Gazba, should take up a position close to the stronghold, in front of me, and have the rest of the men stationed around the entrance to the cavern. I shall stay just below the stairs, closest to the Maid.'

'That sounds like a good plan,' said Gallant. 'But we will be very out-numbered—with little hope of success. Our reinforcements who came with the supplies are not nearly enough.'

Juniper spoke gravely: 'Also, God willing, Brother Lucas has convinced King Lohnn to return to La Fonteyn and rally his forces.'

Kraekhoull was again striding around her lair, thinking of a strategy.

Her eyes lit up, as she decided to consult her crystal ball once more, and the Dark Prince.

She wove her hands over the ball and her words were chilling—filled with ancient hate and murderous intent.

'My Prince,' she cried in a fierce ecstasy and raised hands. 'If you give me your inner form and power, I will know where to find the child.'

In the ball, she saw a great, black dragon hissing and spitting flames, curling and writhing, Laughing, at first, her face changed to an expression of horror as she fell to the ground, twisting and screaming.

Suddenly she was still. 'I feel you in my being, my Prince,' she said, with eyes closed in rapture. 'I see the place. The place where they have hidden the child.'

Now locked into her mind was Epiron Rock, the location given to her by the evil one.

Kraekhoull pulled herself up onto a chair and sat, panting and perspiring.

Her eyes roved around the room, thinking about what her next actions would be.

'To Bardozer!' she cried as she grabbed her bag containing her crystal ball. She found her horse saddled in the glade by the demons Bitterness and Fear—who had become to her more like domestic servants, than powerful entities of darkness.

She used her magic to transport her and her horse onto the road to Bardozer's camp. She then barrelled along with her cape flowing behind her like a giant, black bat in the half light.

The camp was in a clearing on the side of the road above the stream, in the same place it had been for several days. Tents were dotted all around, and she could see men coming and going about their duties in the flickering light of the fires.

'Hey!' shouted a guard, raising his sword to Kraekhoull as she barged into him with her almost uncontrollable horse.

'Silence!' she yelled. 'I have come to see the baron.'

The guard fell to the ground, gagging and holding his throat.

'That is for your insolence,' she cried.

The whole camp had now been disturbed. Bardozer lifted the flap of his tent and stepped out.

Seeing the man choking, Bardozer shouted in rage, 'Kraekhoull, cease your magic on my soldier.'

The witch raised her hand, and the man gasped as air rushed back into his lungs. He collapsed against a tree, still rubbing his throat.

'You and your men must respect me,' said Kraekhoull imperiously.

'As you must respect me,' growled the baron.

'Very well, so be it,' said the witch.

'You have come here to talk of war against Gazba?' said the baron.

'And the destruction of the Maid of Valouresse.' replied Kraekhoull.

'She is only a child,' said Bardozer, 'And surely not a threat.'

'The prophecy says that she will save Valouresse.'

'Well, if you believe in prophecies hundreds of years old …' said the baron.

'I cannot take the chance,' said the witch. 'Valouresse must be ours and I want to take down the cossetted gentry.'

'You have no argument with me on that point,' said Bardozer with a sardonic laugh.

'We need to move quickly, while Gazba's company are at Epiron Rock. They are only a tiny band and will be quickly annihilated by your forces—and mine,' she said slyly.

'Yours?' asked the baron. 'I wasn't aware you had your own forces.'

'Well, I do,' said the witch, secretively. 'Not for you to know about at this stage.'

'How do I know where Epiron Rock is?' asked the Baron, perplexed. 'Will the raven take us there?'

As she took the black velvet cover from the crystal ball, she glanced at the baron and saw his glittering, eager eyes.

Kraekhoull used her incantations, and as he stared into the raven's yellow eyes, Bardozer's face registered recognition.

'Ah,' he said with satisfaction, 'I see and know.'

'Very well,' said the witch, 'It is time to assemble your men and make the attack. But one thing …'

'Yes,' replied the baron through narrowed eyes.

'The child is mine to deal with,' said the witch, 'So no one else is to harm her.'

'Very well, all is understood,' said the baron, leering and curling his moustache.

'I will take my leave,' said Kraekhoull. 'And join you in the morning as the sun rises.'

'How far is Epiron Rock?' asked the baron.

'Oh, many leagues, two weeks travel away,' replied the witch.

'Gazba may be expecting us,' said the baron.

'He will not be expecting us because we don't know the way, do we?' answered Kraekhoull with a snickering laugh, knowing full well that now she indeed knew the way.

In the cavern under the monastery, the men prepared for war—a pitiful array.

'Realistically we haven't a chance,' the knight whispered to Gazba. 'But I do believe in Heaven, and the Lord can do great things. He gave us Wolf to guide our way here, and he has been catching us food.'

Gallant patted Wolf on the head and it gave a little crooning noise.

Puppy curled up with Wolf by the fire, a comforting sight for the men, who smiled at the odd friendship as they ate their evening meal.

King Lohnn gathered a strong force of soldiers together and started on his way to Epiron Rock, using the directions from Brother Lucas on a small vellum parchment. This scroll was in a watertight metal canister.

He was a week behind Bardozer's troops.

He chose the swiftest and most powerful horses for the journey, able to climb the rugged twisting path and able to endure.

The knights had assembled in the early morning in front of King Lohnn's castle.

They were armed with swords and were in full armour. The herald carried the pennant displaying the Red Lion and Unicorn against the gold background. His tabard also displayed King Lohnn's coat of arms. The horses fought the bit and rocked on the spot, keen to be off.

King Lohnn sat proudly on his powerful white horse, Florian, which cantered around and around in a pirouette, as he shouted encouragement to his men.

'My knights, it is courage and faith that shall win the day—trust the Lord.'

The citizens had risen with the morning light to watch King Lohnn lead his men at a gallop across the drawbridge. A mighty cheer rose as the knights disappeared swiftly along the road westward leading from the city.

King Lohnn kept up the pace. His horses had been trained hard and it was several leagues before he gave the signal for the riders to steady their horses to a trot.

Under his breath, King Lohnn said, 'Mighty one, you who spoke to me in the night, help us endure and reach Epiron Rock in time.'

After a while, the horses needed a rest. They had now entered the forest, and each man led his horse to water at the stream below the road. The sun stood at noon height.

'Don't give them too much to drink,' said King Lohnn, 'or they may get colic.'

The men got out their rations and ate warily, looking into the forest.

After their meal, the knights were on their way again at a steady trot.

As leagues went by, King Lohnn kept his eyes and ears open for any sign of Bardozer's men—for he feared there would be many—although he suspected they would be far ahead.

The forest had become darker and thicker on either side of the road. It was cold and the horses were steaming. The afternoon had now arrived, and it was time to find a place to camp.

King Lohnn ordered his men to walk the horses for several leagues, until their sweat had dried off. He found a sheltered area of well turfed ground, surrounded by wiry silver birches that would be suitable to tether the horses and there was a stream nearby.

The squires removed their knight's armour and gathered kindling to make several fires and set up bedrolls. There would be no tents this night, as the men would be rising early and there would be no time to take them down.

As they ate their evening meal, King Lohnn said: 'It has been a long ride today, men, and an even harder one tomorrow, so sleep well.'

King Lohnn lay on his bed roll and gazed up at the winking stars. He then tossed and turned for several hours trying to sleep.

How are we going to rout Bardozer's men if we can't catch up to them? We are the only force that can stand against him. Gazba and his band are so few in number.

But, like any mortal, he had forgotten to reckon on the Army of Heaven.

'So,' said Nanny. 'How are you liking the book?'

'I don't like their chances,' said Shelley mournfully. Gazing up at Nanny from her big armchair with the footrest up, she gazed out of window at the pelting rain and the general greyness of the day.

'What do you mean,' asked Nanny.

'Well,' said Shelley, 'It's just that the baddies are so close now, and there's hardly anyone to defend Jasmine. And King Lohnn won't be able to reach Bardozer in time to stop him from killing everyone in the monastery.'

'Yes, it does looks grim,' said Nanny, 'but if you have faith, things can change.'

'I was in the car with your grandfather years ago heading for the coast when a caravan started rocking on the back of a car in front of us. It was tilting and swaying all over the road and getting worse by the second. I was terrified that everyone would be killed if it tipped over and crashed.'

'I know what you're going to say Nanny!' said Shelley with a little smirk.

'Yes, I know you know,' said Nanny with a laugh. 'That's right, I prayed, and in front of your grandfather, out loud—and I didn't care what he thought.'

'And the caravan went back to normal,' said Shelley.

'Yes, it did,' said Nanny. 'So don't worry, we have to have courage—even when listening to a fairy story.'

'All right, keep going Nanny,' said Shelley, 'And read fast.'

As the first pale light came to the dark sky, King Lohnn and his men were already on the road at a canter.

The herald was riding just behind the king and as the morning light hit his pennant the red lion and unicorn stood out against the gold background of the pennant. It filled the knights with courage and pride.

They had long before passed through farmland, even the rough heather-filled fields and now were once again in the forest.

King Lohnn pushed men and horses on through the dark forest. Then, after several hours of riding, he saw the remnants of the campsite of an army—he reasoned it to be Bardozer's.

There was no warmth in the deepest ashes of the dead fires, as he felt them pass through his fingers.

They must be at least two days ahead of us, ten leagues, maybe more.

After leaving the campsite, King Lohnn and his men soon encountered a scene of horror. Dead knights lay scattered on a hillside. This must be where Bardozer's men had killed the knights assigned to protect Chloe. King Lohnn was filled with sorrow. News had reached him of her valiant bid to find her daughter, with Gallant and the knights at her side.

King Lohnn and his men crossed themselves as they passed the dead. They passed under the elderberry tree, and along the overgrown trail and then navigated the caves. Silently they started to lead their mounts up the narrow and perilous trail that would lead to the High Road. Once there, it would be a long and dangerous ride, winding for leagues in and out around the side of steep mountains.

Suddenly a horse scrambled for its footing and a knight battled to calm the beast and lead it back onto the steep trail.

King Lohnn quickly turned back and grabbed the reins of the struggling horse. With the encouragement of his own fine animal, the other horse found its way back on to the path.

'Good fellow Florian,' he said, patting his charger on its snowy white neck.

They reached the High Road but progress was slow as the trail was narrow convoluted. There was not much foliage, just some heather and tall, sparse pines, made precariously crooked from erosion on the mountain. Small rivulets supplied Lohnn and his men with water. King Lohnn could see fear in the eyes of his bravest men.

'Take courage men,' he said. 'And trust your horses as they trust you.'

Time was not on their side. Bardozer's men would be about ten leagues ahead of them at least. King Lohnn had seen, from the dead knights, that there would be few to defend Epiron Rock.

I should have taken heed of Gazba's warning the day before he left and not gone to the coast jousting.

King Lohnn shook his head. 'Lord!' he shouted in rage (mainly at himself), shaking his fist. 'Get us to the rock in time.'

The knights saw their exasperated, desperate king and urged their horses on even faster than was probably safe.

Now they led the horses down a particularly slippery slope and the horses struggled for a footing. Some hawthorn bushes whipped against them, causing them to baulk. The knights spoke calming words to them.

'Bardozer is far ahead of us,' said King Lohnn to his companion knight. 'We have no hope of catching them now. All will be lost and the Maid as well.'

'We will make the best of it, sire,' said the knight.

They continued to ride in silence, carefully watching their horses' footing, but still pushing them along the path as fast as was possible.

Suddenly, King Lohnn gasped with shock and surprise and his horse reared slightly.

He and his men had ridden right into the tail end of Bardozer's troops.

'It cannot be!' exclaimed King Lohnn, mystified, but he wasted no time.

'Charge!' he shouted, wielding his sword, and urging his charger forward up the last steep slope to where the path widened.

His men followed him with a loud battle cry.

Bardozer looked behind incredulously, mouth agape and with a hideous frown.

He roared, 'Re-form, forward!' and his soldiers and their horses scrambled up to the level ground of Epiron Rock with its large plateau.

Once there, Bardozer bellowed 'Turn and attack!' His men wheeled around and charged King Lohnn's force.

King Lohnn's horses clambered up the last rise and met the enemy head on. To his surprise, he saw a large army of knights emerge from a tunnel hidden by heather. Fearing the worst and that he had been out-flanked, King Lohnn looked anxiously at the force. It was led by King Ranown, accompanied by his standard bearer, who held the sky-blue guidon with its red-orange seahorse emblem.

'You have come as you promised!' King Lohnn yelled.

'What are friends and future brothers-in-law for,' King Ranown joked, deploying his companies.

The entrance to the cavern of the monastery stood a mere forty feet away.

Five soldiers guarded the outer perimeter of the cavern below the monastery, with Darian, Juniper, Gallant and Gazba interspersed between them, to bolster their confidence.

The battle was close and furious around them, but the small group at Epiron Rock didn't advance or take part in the fighting, but just kept their guard of the Maid.

Inside the cavern, close to the sanctuary, Chraston pawed the dust and tossed his head. His mane shivered like a waterfall.

'Stand fast,' he cried. 'King Lohnn and King Ranown do battle for us.'

It was mayhem as the opposing forces battled on, while at the same time they struggled to maintain a footing on the slippery ground, as light snow had started to fall.

There were shouts and grunts as the men hacked at each other. Horses skidded and fell, leaving men to fight from the ground.

All was going well for the forces of the two kings, despite the truly large numbers that Bardozer had managed to recruit.

One by one Bardozer's men fell.

Now most of the fighting was on foot.

In her cave back near La Fonteyn, the witch watched the battle through her crystal ball. She scowled and cursed as she watched Bardozer's men falling, like the snow that now filled the air. In her room the glass chimes were all tinkling, powered by her rage.

She grasped her magic box in her hands and closed her eyes. and in a puff of purple smoke was suddenly transported to the scene of the battle.

'Now it is my time,' she said loudly.

Her hands were like claws as she raised her arms and called on the power of darkness—to her Prince.

'Come, Dark Lord,' she cried, as wind and snow sent her hair whipping across her face. 'And bring creatures from your kingdom!'

A darkness came down and sat upon the mountain—and it was thick with terror.

King Lohnn stopped momentarily and looked up at the swirling grey mass that sent horror through his soul.

He flinched and gasped as he saw the face of his new opponent, a monstrous creature.

It was not human, and its eye held a ghoulish gleam as it grimaced like a madman and fought like one too.

As King Lohnn battled the creature, he saw his own knights, and those of King Ranown, fighting the same kind of demonic foe, as well as fighting Bardozer's troops.

Bardozer's soldiers were swarming across the plateau and were now steadily making their way towards the cavern underneath Epiron Rock.

'Forward men, protect the cavern,' shouted King Lohnn, as he hacked and pierced his way through his adversaries.

Many of the King's men fell as they cut a swathe through Bardozer's forces.

Some of the witch's demons had reached the stalwart few guarding the fortress.

Juniper slew man after man and monster after monster with deft jabs of his sword as did Gallant, Darian, Gazba and their handful of soldiers.

Juniper said with a gasp, 'the demons keep coming.' He pulled his sword free ready for the next thrust.

'They are driven by an ungodly strength,' replied Gazba again plunging in his sword.

The demon gave a terrible scream and fell frothing at the mouth.

But it got up and kept fighting.

Gazba gave Juniper an exhausted glance.

Both looked at the enemy approaching.

Then they glanced at Chraston guarding the stairs of the monastery keep.

He whinnied, rolled his eyes, and pawed the ground. Sweat made his coat dark.

Back and forth he paced, never venturing away from the stairs.

Jasmine could hear the battle cries and horrible screams from below.

She cringed and wrung her hands.

'Mummy,' she said. 'The enemy come for me; I know it. Daddy and the others are in danger because they fight for me. I cannot let it go on, I cannot!'

Suddenly her mother fell in a swoon to the ground.

'Mummy!' screamed Jasmine, going to her mother and then running to the top of the stairs and calling to her father.

Gazba heard his daughter's scream and rushed up the stairs to see Jasmine propping her mother's head up on a pillow and then covering her with a blanket.

'What is wrong with Mummy?' asked Jasmine in distress, as her mother lay still with a greenish tinge to her face.

Gazba got to work and used all of his alchemical skills to bring his wife to consciousness, but nothing worked in the slightest.

Under his breath he muttered darkly: 'The witch.'

While he had been working to help Chloe, Jasmine had gone to the little room and dressed herself in the armour of the dwarf.

She stood in front of her father and, having overheard his comment, exclaimed, 'It's the witch, isn't it? I will stop her and make Mummy well, whatever it takes.'

Chapter 20

‘I would be so upset if that was our mummy that was sick like that!’ said Shelley.

‘Your mummy is having her baby very soon, so you must be very kind to her, okay?’ said Nanny, looking deeply into her granddaughter's eyes.

‘Yes,’ said Shelley. ‘I have decided I will love the baby, and I don't care what my friends at school think. She is my mummy and I love her!’ said Shelley emphatically.

‘That's great,’ said Nanny.

‘I feel the same way,’ said Jace.

‘Shall we get on with the story then?’ asked Nanny.

‘Sure!’ exclaimed both children.

‘No, Jasmine!’ shouted Gazba as his daughter disappeared down the stairs. He sighed in exasperation and said a prayer that the unicorn would protect her because he could not leave his wife, who seemed to be on the brink of death.

Jasmine leapt from the staircase onto Chraston's back. He reared and gave a roaring neigh as he galloped to the entrance of the cave.

Jasmine gave her own battle cry and held her sword high.

The throng defending the entrance suddenly parted as the unicorn galloped on through.

Demons fell screaming by the wayside—as did Bardozer's men—as if struck by some unseeable force—a wave of power.

At the end of the corridor of fallen men and demons, was the one Jasmine sought—the witch.

Kraekhoull laughed and suddenly grew very tall and sinuous. Her face became long and within her hateful eye was a dark thin slit for a pupil.

Her jaw elongated and opened revealing long, sharp teeth which faced backwards like hooks. She was changing in size, shape, and power.

Combined with the dark Prince, she had become a dragon.

Her black coils soon towered above Chraston and with one swipe of her clawed arm, she dislodged Jasmine from the unicorn.

Jasmine gave a cry as she was winded and tried to struggle to her feet. Juniper, Darian, and Gallant rushed forward to try to help her. They slashed down many evil men and demons in their wake.

Demons surrounded Jasmine, laughing and leering, while Chraston ran among them, impaling them with his horn. He was surrounded and fighting valiantly to defend his girl.

Wolf tussled with—and was hard pressed by—a group of demons. He struggled underneath their feculent bodies, lunging and snapping.

Kraekhoull now pressed down close to the child and breathed on her with her rank breath and hissed, 'You have failed, Maid of Valouresse, failed to save your land and your mother.' Then the witch cackled, which then turned into a deafening roar from the throat of the witch-dragon.

Jasmine crawled on her belly, whimpering and weeping.

Again Kraekhoull, the dragon, lowered her head until her chin almost touched the child.

Jasmine whispered angrily, 'You will not take my mother, witch.'

'Oh, and how will you stop me?' hissed the dragon gleefully. She was drunk on the growing power of her transmutation.

Jasmine crawled on further and started to pull herself up.

Again, the witch breathed on her—a suffocating stench of coal and sulphur—and Jasmine fell flat on her face in the dirt.

She still had her sword and she slowly held it up and started to speak.

'What is it you want to say?' asked the witch goading Jasmine as again she pressed her clawed hand down on the Maid, almost crushing her.

Darian was fighting a demon with a reptilian face which held a knife to his throat and his arms trembled with the force of pushing it back, despite using all the strength he could muster. His breath came in short, sharp gasps.

Juniper and Gallant struck the dragon on its head and arms, but their swords bounced back. The two men were close to exhaustion and sweat ran down their faces, almost blinding their vison. The dragon swiped them away and they flew through the air and landed, bruised and winded.

Jasmine now struggled to stand, but the cruel, clawed hand of the witch-dragon pushing on her back crushed her face into the dirt.

Then she remembered something, something she knew in her heart from long ago. She made an utterance, weak and barely audible, a breathless and constricted whisper from her soul.

'Not by might, nor by power ...' she sobbed.

The witch screamed and flung the child across the ground.

Again, the Maid spoke, but this time with resolve, as she lifted herself up onto her elbows and started to raise her sword.

Jasmine staggered to her feet, weeping, and then shouted weakly and hoarsely: 'Not by might, nor by power, but by my spirit, says the Lord!'

With her call, the angels Keliran and Targum arrived with swords drawn and looked on intently.

The witch fell back with a scream and dropped her knife, but the Dark Prince flung her towards Jasmine and roared, 'Pick up the knife. Do it!'

'I cannot!' screamed Kraekhoull, 'I have no power!' Her witch-dragon self was flickering on and off, as she began to resume human shape and stature.

'Get up!' came a cold voice from the pit of hell, 'and finish the child.'

The demons closed in on Jasmine with their leering faces and sharp brown teeth, pushing her towards the witch. There was no mercy in their eyes.

Given fresh mettle—from being in great fear of the Dark Prince—and by being goaded onwards by the demons, the witch sprang towards Jasmine with the knife.

Jasmine, who was struggling to stay upright, once more tried to raise her sword, and shouted this time, 'Not by might, nor by power, but by my spirit, says the Lord!'

There was a horrible, gut-wrenching scream.

'No! Not the sword of the spirit!' came the witch's voice from within the Dark Prince. The other demons screamed and fell away like fluttering bats.

Jasmine's weapon now shone like white lightning and a strong hand supported her wrist—it was the Lord of Hosts, Jesus, King of the angels who stood beside her. His angels were slashing and destroying the evil ones.

No evil could stand against their swords. Chraston also leapt forward, driving his horn deep into the evil one. The earth shook and a black, swirling cloud descended upon everything. The Dark Prince gave an agonised roar, knotting himself in his own coils, then screamed and cursed. Jasmine was half-fainting in terror in the surrounding darkness.

The dragon gave another agonised scream as blackness took the light of the Maid's sword the instant it pieced its scaly hide, using the last of Jasmine's strength.

Then the Lord spoke.

'Silence!' and the beast that was the Dark Prince said nothing more.

All was quiet.

The witch somehow leapt away from the clutches of the Dark Prince who she feared would take her to oblivion as well and ran for her life. In that instant of silence, The demon attackers that were harassing wolf fell to ash and he grabbed Kraekhoull by the arm. She struggled and cursed but was unable to escape his strong grasp.

Darian's throat was a hair's breadth from being slashed by a demon's knife.

He grasped its wrist and tried to push the knife back.

Darian thought of his family and how he would miss them. *So, this is it—death.*

But at the moment the Lord spoke, the demon gave a hideous grimace and dissolved into ash.

Darian was astonished, quickly glancing around for the demon, but it was gone. He then immediately ran to Jasmine.

Keliran gave a grim but satisfied smile and—with sword still gleaming and having dispatched that demon—moved swiftly to help Gallant and Juniper who were surrounded by ghouls in the same moment.

The points of demonic pikes clanged against their breast plates. Juniper and Gallant gasped, waiting for this vile band to piece their armour and drive their pikes into their hearts.

But also, as with Darian at the moment of the words of the Lord their enemies fell into ash, from which hatred and sorcery had animated them.

Keliran had cut the enemy that threatened Darian down with one swift lunge of his sword, at the command of 'Cease!' uttered by Lord.

Juniper and Gallant stood panting for a moment, looking at each other, perplexed, as does anyone who has been delivered by a miracle. They then rushed to Jasmine, who was being carried in the arms of Jesus. Light beamed down upon them, and the men also stood covered in the glorious, heavenly rays of light.

'Please come up and save my Mummy, Jesus,' pleaded Jasmine weakly, looking up at him and having now regained consciousness. 'My Mummy is so sick. Come and heal her, please!'

'You are weak, child, but you have been so brave,' said Jesus, carrying her towards the Monastery.

Chraston and Wolf, as well as the others, followed. Wolf still had a firm grip of the witch. 'Let go of her now,' said Jesus and she tumbled to the ground, on her hands and knees, gasping like someone who has been drowning. She averted her eyes, as she could not bear to see His radiant magnificence.

'There was a time when your soul was not perverted by evil,' Jesus said gently and with infinite compassion. Like a worm on a fishhook, Kraek-houll's body was wracked by tremors.

'If you are taken to Valouresse to account and atone for your crimes, many will hear what evil you perpetrated over the years, especially when in league with the Dark Prince. So, we must deal with you here and now, either by the laws of earth, or the laws of Heaven.'

'We have two earthly lords present, King Lohnn and King Ranown and the Lord of Heaven. Who do you choose to judge your crimes?'

Kraekhoull knew she faced execution or a life of prison in La Fonteyn. But how much worse would be the judgment of the Lord of Creation himself? Her body spasmed again and again as she laboured to choose.

'Look into my eyes, child,' said Jesus.

The witch gazed up and could only see love and the promise of forgiveness in the face of the Lord of the Heavenly Hosts.

'I want you, Lord!' she finally gasped, as if it hurt for the words to escape her lips.

The witch swallowed heavily.

'Forgive me, Lord,' she said, but it came out like a squeak and sent her body into spasm.

'I am so sorry,' she cried in anguish, black bile dripping from her lips.

'FORGIVE ME LORD!' she cried in despair, bursting into tears and then collapsing.

They all gasped as the witch transformed into a thirteen-year-old girl in a soft blue dress. Jesus stooped over her inert form and lightly touched her forehead. She woke with a start, her eyes wide in rapture to see the love in his face.

'My beloved April,' he said, 'welcome back into the light, after the dark dream you have had. Continue your life and service as hand Maiden to the Maid of Valouresse and devote yourself to kindness and enjoy the beauty and wonder of the world I have given you.'

Jesus then turned his attention to Jasmine.

'We will go to see your mother,' said the Lord. 'Have faith, and know I love your mother beyond words.'

'I will have faith my King,' said Jasmine with determination and resolve in her voice.

Chraston snuffled his little Maid's tear-covered face, and she reached out and held his nose.

All the remaining soldiers of King Lohnn and King Ranown, who had arrived at the last part of the battle, were very sad to hear of Lady Chloe's grave illness.

The battle victory could not make them feel happier. Too many brave souls had died.

They all waited outside the monastery and bowed their heads in prayer for Lady Chloe.

'Nanny?' asked Jace. 'I don't want to interrupt but how did the corridor happen so that Chraston could gallop through with Jasmine, and not get killed because there were so many men and monsters crowding in front of them?'

'I can explain that in the story if you are patient,' replied Nanny.

'Okay,' said Jace, settling back into his chair and watching the rain dribble down the window.

'But now,' said Jesus, 'to the monastery.'

The angels created an archway for the Lord with their swords and remained below in the cave, while he ascended the stairs holding Jasmine's hand, for she had now recovered enough to walk.

Darian, Gallant, and Juniper remained downstairs, also praying fervently.

Chloe had a ghastly grey pallor and lay still. Puppy lay with his head on her waist and whined softly. He had not been part of the battle but had been here the whole time with her.

Gazba looked up at the Lord and Jasmine as they entered the room.

'She lives!' he exclaimed. 'My beautiful wife lives!' He wept as he held Chloe in his arms, and she smiled and even gave a little laugh. Her skin was once more, pink, and full of life.

'What is all the fuss?' she said, giggling.

'My child,' said Chloe stroking Jasmine's face, with tears of joy bursting from her eyes.

Now, in front of Jesus and everyone present, the angels appeared in all their glory. The Rock was incandescent with many colours and many shining faces.

Jesus addressed them. 'Thank you for cutting the swathe through the enemy and fighting for us. Many of you have been hurt and will need my healing touch, which I freely give.'

Jesus went among his angels, laying his hands on them and their severe wounds disappeared. He came to one young angel with a greenish tinge to his face, wan and clammy and on the point of death. Jesus knelt beside him and kissed him on the cheek. Almost at once, the boy's eyes opened, and colour came back into his face.

'My Lord!' he cried as he threw his arms around Jesus's neck and embraced him.

'My brave young boy,' said Jesus.

All who had survived the battle were watching the healing of the angels and were filled with wonder.

While the angels were being healed, the Lord's presence was so powerful and filled with love, that it radiated through the dead in the field and they revived, including Bardozer's men. They got new limbs to replace the severed ones, and gaping wounds closed. Slowly, totally healed, they rose to their feet, staring at their bodies in amazement.

'Thank you, my Heavenly Hosts. I honour you,' said Jesus, with love in his voice towards his angels.

'*We* are honoured, Lord,' said Keliran, bowing low and speaking for the rest of the angels who all knelt and lowered their heads.

'After all, you are our Captain, Captain of the Armies of Heaven.'

'We are here to protect your loved ones,' said Targum, smiling at Keliran and then at Gazba stroking his wife's cheek.

'Thank you,' said Gazba, gazing up at the glorious ones who he had not seen until now, but had long suspected that they existed.

'It is our pleasure,' said bronze-skinned Targum, smiling. His purple wings spread out, almost reaching the roof of the room.

'My darling!' said Gazba, gently stroking his wife's forehead with a look of ecstatic joy in his eyes. He turned and fervently started to say, 'Thank you my Lord …' but Jesus was gone.

Then Chraston spoke: 'The dark ones are gone, and a new age is born in Valouresse. It will be on earth, as it is in Heaven.'

'We will go to the Captain of the Heavenly Host and wait for the Spring and the celebration by the Betrothal Tree,' said Keliran in a joyful triumphant voice.

Then the angels saluted those present and rose up through the air with mighty downward beats of their wings and disappeared into the sky.

Chraston disappeared in a cloud of swirling gold dust, back to Heaven and back to his beloved King.

After a little while, Chloe was on her feet and preparing some food for the men—Juniper, Darian, Gallant, her daughter and her husband. Gazba insisted that she didn't, but she insisted otherwise. Jasmine joyfully helped her mother chop vegetables for a huge, steaming stew, combined with several rabbits that Wolf had captured the day before.

King Lohnn and King Ranown's men captured the remainder of Bardozer's men. Strangely they showed no fight, gave themselves up and talked of a new life that they would live. King Lohnn felt some leniency for them, especially after their resurrections. They most certainly were changed men.

Before they left, Gazba thanked the two kings and invited them and their knights to stay for a meal. The king's men went out and shot a deer which fed everyone and would be of great use to them on the trip home, however it was surprising just how much stew could be made from a few rabbits and plenty of vegetables.

To the kings he said, 'I thank you for saving my daughter and for coming to our aid. I am forever in your debt.'

'No!' exclaimed King Lohnn to King Ranown. 'Thank you for coming to our aid, but how did you get here for you had no map?'

King Ranown replied, 'Brother Lucus gave me a copy he had made and discovered a secret route through the centre of the mountain which opened out where you saw us emerge. It was most fortuitous—a miracle that he found this. He is a marvel, a man tuned into the vibration and knowledge of the Lord.'

Both kings thanked Lady Chloe for the meal, as did their men, but then they had to leave before the road became impassable.

'Farewell and Godspeed,' said Gazba to King Lohnn of La Fonteyn and King Renown from the coast. 'I will see you both in La Fonteyn in the Spring, for a great celebration.'

Gazba embraced both kings, who then mounted their horses and led their soldiers on down the incline from Epiron Rock.

Bardozer, as belligerent as ever, was also taken in chains back to La Fonteyn.

He sat on a horse grumbling and every so often, one of King Lohnn's soldiers—the one assigned to mind the whining baron—would give him a whack with the flat of his sword to shut him up.

The small group, including the soldiers who had brought the supplies to the monastery, settled in for the winter, as the snow now came thick and fast and Gazba did not want to risk the lives of his soldiers, his friends, and his wife and child, by attempting to return to the city.

There would be no getting back to La Fonteyn until the Spring.

Many tales were told as meals were had around the campfire. Wolf seemed to be able to find game, even in the snow, no doubt aided by his skilled nose.

Chloe gained her strength back completely.

Chapter 21

'But the Dark Prince, what happened to him?' asked Jace.

'He was turned to ash, as you know,' said Nanny, 'but the Lord and the angels would be judging him on his evil deeds, evil deeds done for many ages, and to many innocent people. I don't know what became of him, but God is the one who delivers justice.'

'So, what you're saying,' said Jace, 'is that he may be still punished, even though he was turned to ash.'

'Possibly,' replied Nanny.

'Look, the sun is coming out,' exclaimed Shelley, looking to the hills where a brilliant white gold light edged the grey clouds.

The rain had stopped, and the children went out to feed the rabbits their dry food and give them some more straw bedding.

Shelley picked up one, a female with seal point markings, a real beauty.

'Isn't she cute Nanny?' she said, while Nanny stroked the soft gentle creature.

'She is like you,' said Nanny with a smile.

'My nose doesn't twitch like that,' laughed Shelley. 'Can we hear more story at bedtime? It's nearly finished, isn't it?'

'It's a race to the finish line to see whether your mum has her baby before we finish the tale. Your mum is overdue to have your little brother.'

'Oh,' said Shelley, 'that sounds weird. My little brother. Do you think I'll love him, Nanny?'

'Oh yes,' replied Nanny with a fond smile and while stroking her granddaughter's forehead.

Nanny started the story again, which the children were eager to hear.

'One moment Nanny,' said Jace, interrupting.

'Yes Jace?' asked Nanny putting the manuscript down on her lap.

'Well,' began Jace, 'why didn't the angels show themselves when they made a way for Chraston and Jasmine to get through the crowd of enemies?'

'Maybe it was to provide a surprise for the wicked ones, so that they would not know where to fight, where to turn and where to strike.'

'That's a clever idea,' said Jace, 'But Jasmine saw Targum and Keliran in Heaven. So why don't we see them—angels that is?'

Nanny's voice became low and mysterious, and she said, 'I have seen them and Jesus in the spirit.'

'Tell us Nanny,' said Shelley, who was now intrigued.

'I was with my Mystic Christian Group, and we were singing beautiful harmonies from Heaven, when I saw Jesus, walking around, kneeling and washing our feet.'

'What do you mean Nanny?' asked Jace. 'Do you mean like when you saw him before Uncle James was born—like for real?'

'This was real, but in a different way,' replied Nanny. 'This particular time, I could see him with my inner sight—but he was still there, very much so, and he was so very close.'

'Did he wash *your* feet?' asked Jace with interest.

'Yes,' replied Nanny, 'but when he got to me, I was so shy because I didn't feel worthy and I looked away from him and said, "Thank you."'

'I looked up and saw him give me a cheeky smile and a quick toss of his head indicating the others who were singing. He said, "Don't thank me—thank them."'

'Why did he say that, Nanny?' asked Shelley with large luminous eyes.

'He was grateful for the others, praying and singing—bringing the Kingdom of Heaven to Earth with all its wonder and beauty. That's just like him. Always thinking of others.'

'So, you saw him,' said Jace, 'but what about angels? Have you seen any Nanny?'

'Another time,' began Nanny, 'while at the same place, we were worshipping, singing Heavenly harmonies .and seeking whatever God may have for us—a scripture, a vision of something, things like that. Seeing what God was saying to us.'

'What then Nanny?' asked Jace, curious.

'Well, as we were all doing our thing, I saw a tall angel dressed in white, going around passing out to each of us the bread—a wafer—or what in the Catholic church, is called the emblem.'

'At the end of this, I saw the angel throw out a gossamer thin piece of fabric that settled over all of us.'

'After everyone opened their eyes, we told of what the Lord had given us—a vision or a scripture and someone wrote them up on a white board, so we could figure out what God might be telling us.'

'So, what was God telling you, Nanny?' asked Shelley who was very engaged with the story of Nanny's vision.

'I was quite embarrassed to tell everyone about the emblems the angel was passing out, having been taught anti-Catholic dogma from my childhood.'

'I'm not Catholic,' I said, 'but I think the angel was passing out strength and power and the ability to fulfil our mandate for God on this earth—to make earth as it is in Heaven.'

'What did the others say Nanny?' asked Shelley.

'Nothing,' replied Nanny, 'they just listened and then I got a brain wave and said: 'I know what the gossamer fabric was, it is the garment of peace, which we are to dwell in when we are doing our mission for the Lord. We are to be at perfect peace and at rest, the whole time as it rests on us.'

'In ordinary English, Nanny,' said Jace.

'The angel was imparting—giving—strength to us, to use our gifts for God and people—to bring the wonders of Heaven to earth.'

'So, did you actually see the angels and Jesus those times?' asked Shelley.

'Yes, I did in the spirit,' said Nanny. 'It was different to the time I saw my Nanna going into Heaven in the Mitta Hall, because that was sort of in the distance, and I was watching from a distance. This was different because Jesus and on the other occasion the angel were very close to myself and the others in my group.'

'But now how about we get on with the story?'

In the Spring, the company left Epiron Rock and the winter haven of the Monastery, to return to La Fonteyn.

The treacherous trail from the mountains took more than a week to descend, especially with the wet ground, from the melted snow.

They reached the main road to La Fonteyn and travelled along its final hundred and fifty leagues to the city. It took them another two weeks, but their spirits were high, and they sang almost the whole way.

'They are coming!' shouted the sentries on the battlements of the city, above the Gatehouse of the curtain wall.

The king and his knights assembled inside the marketplace to greet the pilgrims.

Gazba trotted through the gates on Helga, the great white mare who lifted her legs high and arched her thick neck.

Chloe came next on the prancing, snorting Grunjion, followed by Jasmine barrelling along on her fat pony, Brownie with Puppy squeaking happily from his cashmere bag.

Gallant and Darian and Juniper trotted over the drawbridge and Wolf led Bella the pack horse by a rope, to everyone's astonishment.

King Lohnn threw his arms affectionately around Gazba when he had dismounted his horse, and both men laughed.

Then Gazba embraced Joachim and asked: 'How did my patients behave?'

'Oh, as well as could be expected,' answered his faithful assistant with a laugh.

'My lovely lady,' said the king, kissing Chloe's hand. 'It is so good to see you recovered.'

'Thank you, my king,' said Chloe curtsying.

'And you, Jasmine!' exclaimed the King kissing her hand. 'You, the Maid of Valouresse, who saved our pleasant land from a bleak and terrifying future. Brave girl!'

'Sire,' said Jasmine, 'My Puppy saved my life when Daddy and I were travelling to Epiron Rock, against Wolves.'

'A brave dog indeed,' agreed the King patting the dog's bald head, as it licked him profusely.

Now was time for celebration and rest.

The day was fine and bright. Butterflies flitted around like falling leaves, except that this was Spring not Autumn. They lifted and floated along with the petals of the fruit trees.

The heady blossoms floated by as Chloe and Gazba walked together, hand in hand, down the path to the Betrothal Tree. Chloe was dressed in a silk dress of milk-white, and her daughter followed behind carrying the train.

King Lohnn pointed and cried out, 'Look, He comes, the Great King!' He then bowed low as did every other person there.

Riding up the green rise towards the Betrothal Tree, was the Lord of Heaven on his big white horse.

He dismounted and joined Gazba and Chloe. With a joyful smile he placed one hand beneath and one hand on the top of both theirs in a loving bond and said: 'Bless you my dear children'.

Chloe curtsied and Gazba bowed low, and both said, 'Bless You, my Lord.'

Gazba tilted Chloe's chin up until she shyly met his gaze, and then he kissed her gently on her soft pink lips.

After he had blessed her parents, Jesus turned his attention to Jasmine.

'Little one,' he said to her, as she still held her mother's train. Her face beamed as Jesus gently stroked her cheek.

Suddenly the sky became radiant with the light of many angels. They filled the air with the sound of glorious heavenly harmonies.

Many angels—including Mellion, Targum and Keliran—held their swords high in salute over their Captain of the Armies of Heaven and over Chloe, Gazba and Jasmine.

After the ceremony, which was a marriage renewal, there was the celebration. A huge table laden with food out in the open.

There was enough food for all, including every subject of La Fonteyn. Many came from Heaven, those who had hidden from the Dark Prince, and now were free to show their faces.

It was a strange sight for the people of La Fonteyn to see Cassiopeia the leopard with her cubs, and a young deer join them at the table. The Maidens of the forest danced in their leafy, gossamer, green garments with fauns. A Centaur pranced up to the Lord and gave him a hearty slap on the back.

'Steady on old chap,' said Jesus with a laugh as he almost toppled over from the sheer strength of the centaurs greeting.

'So, my king,' said the centaur joyfully. 'It really is on earth as it is in Heaven, for we mystical creatures are now welcome here.'

'That you are,' said the Lord, looking up at the powerful centaur.

'What shall be done with Bardozer and his men?' asked King Lohnn, entering the conversation, as he was quite worried about the old enemy.

'Bardozer and his men shall go to an island off the mainland, where dear Brother Lucas will kill them with kindness,' replied Jesus, 'with the help of my angels.'

'Oh,' said King Lohnn. 'If it were up to me, I would have their heads.'

'The way of kindness is the true way,' said the Lord.

'And by the way, Lord?' asked King Lohnn, 'Do you have any idea how my knights and I managed to catch up to Bardozer on that treacherous High Road?'

'That would have been my Father, who holds all time in His hands.'

'Can you pass on my thanks to Him?' said King Lohnn.

'You can thank Him yourself, my friend, for He is always listening,' replied the Lord.

Then the centaur spoke again, 'We have hidden in the Heavenly Realm all these many years, unbelieved in and unable to come to this earth. But now we come from the unseen realm, and it is pure joy to be included in this celebration.'

'That it is my friend,' said the Lord amiably, then added enthusiastically, 'Let's eat!'

Jasmine found her friend Ellis, who was at the feast and April (the former witch, who had now become Handmaiden for Jasmine).

'April, I introduce you to Ellis,' said Jasmine happily.

April hung her head a little shyly and sadly, for she still had some distant memory of evil self as a witch.

Jasmine put an arm around both girls and said, 'I know we are all going to be great friends.'

April gave a little smile and said, 'I would like that very much.'

A little later, when April was meeting some others for the first time, Ellis came over to Jasmine.

'I missed you,' said Ellis as she threw her arms around her good friend. 'And I didn't know whether you were alive or dead!' A couple of tears burst from her eyes.

'After all, it was me who helped you escape from the castle and smuggled your supplies out.'

Juniper, who had just overheard the conversation, said with a laugh, 'I wouldn't worry about Lady Jasmine, she is an unstoppable force of nature.'

'Well thank you, Juniper,' said Jasmine with a coy smile. 'I believe you and several of the others, Darian included, are going to be knighted—is that right?'

'Yes, that's right,' he replied, then quietly and a little shyly added. 'Maybe I could ask for your hand in a few years' time, my lady?' he said looking very intently into her eyes with ill-disguised tenderness.

'One day I will be a great Lady and you may then court me—maybe.'

She continued, 'I see myself with my unicorn seated in the Autumn leaves, wearing a wreath of flowers and with gold brocade on my garments.'

'Did you know, Juniper and Ellis,' said Jasmine joyfully, 'that my Jesus, God and my Holy Spirit made the universe, the heavens and all the creatures?'

'I know Jesus and God,' said Juniper—'although I've not seen God, but who is the Holy Spirit? Have *you* seen him?'

Just then Chraston walked up and put his head over Jasmine's shoulder.

'This is he,' she said as she stroked the Unicorn's soft quivering nose.

'But he is a unicorn! exclaimed Juniper, 'surely he should be a man.'

'He is my Holy Spirit, and it is not important to me what he looks like. This is just what he looks like to me.'

'You had better not argue with her,' said Chraston, with a laughing whinny.

Ellis also stroked the unicorn's nose and found a bit of green grass to feed him, which he quickly munched down.

'Look!' exclaimed Jasmine pointing up, 'the bird of Valouresse!'

Sure, enough there was the beautiful rainbow-coloured bird, with its streamer-like tail flying overhead.

Chapter 22

‘That's a lot to take in Nanny,’ said Jace, from his bed.

‘Yes, I agree,’ said Nanny. ‘Let's get to bed and rest. The story is over, except for two more things I want to add—to do with two paintings I have in my house. It's an indulgence really. I just want to add them, although they probably don't have much relevance to the novel.’

‘That's alright Nanny, just do it,’ said Shelley.

The next day was like an arctic storm—freezing cold and windy, and there was some snow. The children both wanted to hear about Nanny's addendum.

They both sat in the lounge room, as cosy as can be with the heater blasting away.

‘Well,’ said Nanny. ‘You know the painting I did that's in my bedroom—the one of the fairy, the mouse and the frog?’

‘And the rabbit and the fish,’ added Shelley.

‘Yes,’ replied Nanny. ‘The story goes like this.’ Then Nanny started to make up the story as she went along, because there was nothing written down to read.

‘Once upon a time,’ said Nanny, ‘there was a dragonfly nymph called Flight, a very beautiful name for an ugly and ferocious beast that crept around the bottom of the lake, attacking anything smaller than himself.’

'One day he had a yearning for the sunlight, so he wiggled and swam to the surface.'

'He crawled out onto a warm stone and sat there in the sun for quite a while until he started to dry out. Along the top of his back, he felt a crackling.'

'It was a good feeling, and soon he had a set of glistening wings. He gave them a try and they buzzed beautifully.'

'He tested them out and flew around the lake and even found a mate, but towards evening he became tired.'

'I have had such a lovely day, but now I need to go somewhere safe. I can't go under the water anymore. I have been such a wicked, cruel creature. There will be nowhere for me to rest.'

He wept as he drooped and dipped, feeling very lost and alone.

Then he heard a soft voice and a light touch on his tired wing.

'Come,' said the angelic creature—who looked very much like a fairy. 'Come Flight, a place has been prepared for you, and all has been forgiven.'

'Where did he go Nanny?' asked Shelley with tears brimming in her eyes.

'He went to dragonfly Heaven silly,' said Jace knowledgably.

'Yes, and even though he had been a wicked creature, he was sorry, and he entered his rest.'

'That's the end of that one,' said Nanny. 'I have a poem that I would like to read you. It belongs with the painting in the lounge room, the one of Queen Hatshepsut, the Egyptian Queen, floating down the Nile in a boat.'

'Go on Nanny, read it please,' said Shelley enthusiastically.

Nanny began.

QUEEN HATSHEPSUT

While Jasmine petals fell slowly down.
Upon the crystal rose
I saw three eye lined sages wander slowly by,
In gleaming golden robes.

The scent of Egypt's legacy the tombs long hidden now seen
A Sarcophagus inlaid with jade of deepest green.

The crystal rose, a thing of recent cheaper days shone clear.
Yet in its eye,
The falcon god Horus flew by.

The jackal-headed god sat poised to leap,
To defend his queen in her deep sleep.

How was it made, the pyramid? A mystery yet,
Pharoah sipping his wine, gazing from his palace,
Saw it was made with great toil and sweat.

Hatshepsut reclines on a boat of reeds and asks her servant girl,
'What is your creed?'
The girl turns her face and stammers, 'I am of the Hebrew race.'
Hatshepsut softly says, 'I know you have been made to be afraid in this place.'

Tenderly she strokes the girl's cheek, then gently throws her pet dove up
and bids it farewell, watches it fly away.

For Hatshepsut must go to her tomb on an appointed day.

Does she suspect that her fine temple will be shattered by a jealous pharaoh?
After her death, her last breath?

All she knows is that the river will glide for millennia.
Till the stars fall from the sky, one by one
Till the King of Kings returns and His will be done.

The sand of a thousand years
Hides huge sandstone body parts, broken and too dry for tears,
Which now cry out and beg, not wishing to be alone,
But wanting to be turned to living bone.

The Queen will take the dust of Egypt and make it live once more.
Will blow it from her palm and call upon the rains to fall.

Glittering palaces will ring with laughter,
As the most high's children
Rejoice for ever after.
The overseer's whip will lie curled in the sand,
A proclamation of peace throughout the land.

Jasmine flowers softly brushed the prism sides of the crystal rose,
Releasing life's fragrant woes.
Hatshepsut will blend the now and then,
Until the rose becomes dewy
Velvet in her trembling hand.

The young lions will awaken in their dens,
And come out to join her and rule the land.

'So, Nanny,' asked Jace, 'what is that one about?'

'It is about peace in the Middle East between all the peoples there, a beautiful dream I see happening.'

'I have one more real story that I would like to tell you, about my horse and me,' said Nanny.

'Sure, Nanny, go ahead,' said Jace munching on a carrot—which was unusual for him, since it was a healthy alternative food.

'A few years ago,' began Nanny, 'I was heading off to a Combined Training Day at my local horse-riding club. We were to have some training and then a competition at the end of the day—with ribbons!'

'I so longed to get a ribbon in the dressage test and I had practiced it many times and memorised the test.'

'While I was trotting down to the arena, my mare was already pulling and being nervous. The Lord spoke to me and said, "If you want your horse to have a nice day, it is up to you to keep her happy and calm."'

'Okay,' I said to the Lord in my mind, 'I will forget about ribbons and make sure she is happy.'

When it came time to canter the left circle in the dressage test, I had a slight moment of panic. I wanted her to stride out leading to the left with her left front leg. Horses can feel the slightest change in your balance and will act accordingly, and I thought she could lead out on the wrong leg.

Then I remember the Lord's words and I shut my eyes briefly and sat deeply in the saddle and leaned in the direction I wanted her to go. My mare floated around in a beautifully relaxed canter, leading on the correct left front leg.

'That was a great test,' my friend shouted to me, as I walked out of the arena with my mare at a swinging walk on a loose rein—still relaxed.

'I know,' I replied happily.

'The point of this story is to show you that being relaxed and happy is important, and that God will grant you the desires of your heart, if you listen to Him.'

'So that means I'll do better at basketball if I trust God?' asked Jace.

'Yes,' replied Nanny giving him a cuddle, as he ate his carrot like a rabbit to make her laugh.

'Oh,' said Nanny, 'I have three more short stories for you—one about your mother and another two about my grandfather and my mum's mum. They are very special.'

'Go on then Nanny,' said both children.

'A few years ago, now,' began Nanny, 'Our minister at the church died. It was very sad because he was only a young man.'

'And Mummy knew him?' asked Shelley.

'Yes, she did,' replied Nanny. 'One night, she dreamt a very vivid dream about him.'

'She was in Heaven, and it was really beautiful with green grass, trees and flowers with the Holy City in the distance.'

'And she saw her pastor?' asked Jace.

'Yes,' replied Nanny, 'and she said he looked really handsome—better than he did when he was alive on earth. She asked him if he ever regretted anything that had happened on earth. He held out his arms indicating all the beauty and wonder of Heaven and said, "You can't when you're here with all of this around you?"'

'Then what?' asked Jace.

'Then he showed her a seat and said, "This is your seat in Heavenly Places".'

'We are told in the Bible that we have seats in Heaven where we rule with God, even though we are on earth—isn't that awesome!?'

'Tell us the other two stories please Nanny,' said Shelley.

'Well,' began Nanny, 'My dad's dad, the one in the vision I had of them in the Mitta Hall in Heaven, had died long before Nanna. It was very sad to see him suffering. I used to dream that he had died, long before he actually did.'

'One night sometime after he had actually died, I had a beautiful dream that was very vivid. I visited my Pa (because that is what we called him) and he was in an old country hospital. The hospital was a wooden structure with a quadrangle in the middle of it, and on the first floor sat my Pa in the beautiful fresh air and sun.'

'He was recovering from his illness, and he was alive and well. I remember thinking, with great excitement, he's alive! It was as though he had gone to a hospital in Heaven that made him better.'

'Cool Nanny!' exclaimed Jace.

'Tell us the other one Nanny,' said Shelley enthusiastically.

'Okay,' said Nanny. 'These stories finish off the novel in the same way that a ribbon decorates and completes a gift.'

'Go on Nanny,' encouraged Shelley.

Nanny began. 'In a dream, I was with my Nanna, my mum's mum, in the lounge room of the old farmhouse in front of a blazing fire. It was so real, and my Nanna was teaching me lace making, which was really comforting.'

'That's lovely Nanny,' said Shelley, then Nanny spoke again.

'I just thought of something else that happened in that room. One night I had terrible asthma and could hardly breathe. My mother stayed up with me to keep me calm and comforted. She took away my fear. I will always remember that.'

Suddenly the phone rang, and Nanny's face lit up as she answered it.

'Yes, yes!' exclaimed Nanny. 'Tell Lillian I am so excited. Please keep me posted, Clark. Okay, so you want me to mind the kids and bring them in later. Sure.'

'What is it, Nanny?' asked both children.

'Your little brother is on the way!' said Nanny with a thrill in her voice.

'Can we pray for him Nanny?' asked Shelley.

'Of course,' said Nanny.

All three held hands and each prayed. 'Keep our little brother safe, Lord,' said Shelley. Then Jace prayed, 'Yes, and look after Mummy.'

Then Nanny prayed, 'Bless the whole family and let this be a wonderful time, and please let Lillian get plenty of rest afterwards.' Nanny remembered well how exhausting babies could be.

After several hours little Seth was born, and the children went in with Nanny to the hospital, to visit him for the first time.

'He is very small,' said Shelley, as the baby clasped her little finger tightly in his tiny fist.

'He is much smaller than our two little cousins ever were when they were babies,' said Jace.

'They were this size, but you probably don't remember,' said Lillian, fondly ruffling Jace's hair.

'Nanny read us a really long story over the holidays,' said Jace. 'Most of the time it was too cold to go out anyway.'

'Did you like it?' asked Lillian, who now cradled baby Seth in her arms.

'They sure did,' said Clark with a laugh. 'They preferred it to talking to me every night.'

A few months later, Uncle James and his two little girls were visiting Lillian and Clark. They laughed and played with Seth, bouncing in his jolly jumper, which was suspended from the door architrave. He giggled as his cousins and siblings pulled the bouncer and released it, sending him hurtling up and down and around. His fat little legs pushed and he sprang back, with each dip of the jolly jumper.

In the evening, Nanny settled down in her favourite chair. The children had gone home as the holidays were over and, as she thought about the story, she was glad it had a happy ending. She was glad her family were happy. She still wanted to go to that place where the Great Lion ruled, the magical land, but would bide her time on this earth. She knew in her heart who the great lion was and was content.

Then she started fixing Judah again, the Lion toy that had featured in the manuscript. There were many loose ends, and it would take a while to sort all of that out, but overall, she was pleased with the novel and more than pleased at having been able to share some of her life with her grandchildren.

She thought of Julian of Norwich, the fourteenth century Mystic Christian nun, who had often been visited by Jesus. He spoke to her and one of the things he said to her was: 'All is well. All will be well, and all manner of things will be well.'

Nanny smiled and thought to herself, 'and so it will be in the end.'

THE END

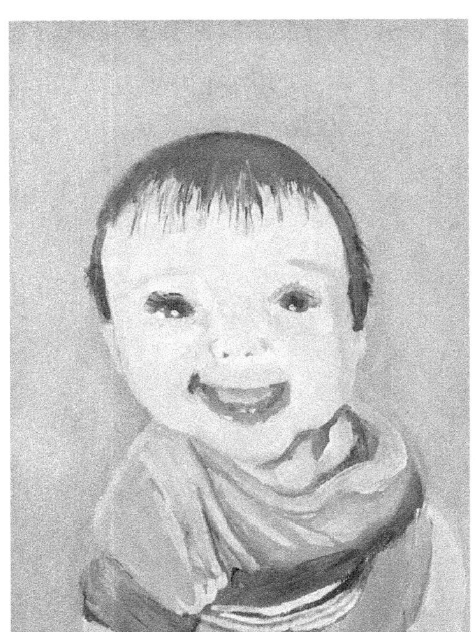

9 781764 004343